THE PURGING OF KADILLUS

FACED WITH AN ork invasion of Piscina IV, the 3rd Company of the Dark Angels believes the threat to be minimal. As enemy numbers continue to increase, their commander, Captain Belial, insists that his company are strong enough to resist. But Scout-Sergeant Naaman knows just how dangerous this foe can be, and when a renewed greenskin offensive takes the Dark Angels by surprise, the orks swarm towards Kadillus Harbour. Little do the Dark Angels know of the technological power available to the xenos, and the true scale of the threat they face. Belial, Naaman and their fellow Astartes fight a desperate siege at Kadillus, knowing that they must hold out until Imperial reinforcements arrive or the planet will be lost.

In the same series

RYNN'S WORLD
Steve Parker

HELSREACH
Aaron Dembski-Bowden

HUNT FOR VOLDORIUS
Andy Hoare

More Space Marine fiction from the Black Library

SALAMANDER
Nick Kyme

SOUL HUNTER
Aaron Dembski-Bowden

· SPACE MARINE ANTHOLOGIES ·

HEROES OF THE SPACE MARINES
Edited by Nick Kyme and Lindsey Priestley

LEGENDS OF THE SPACE MARINES
Edited by Christian Dunn

· OMNIBUSES ·

THE ULTRAMARINES OMNIBUS
Graham McNeill
(Omnibus containing books 1-3 of the series:
NIGHTBRINGER, WARRIORS OF ULTRAMAR and
DEAD SKY, BLACK SUN)

THE BLOOD ANGELS OMNIBUS
James Swallow
(Omnibus containing books 1-2 of the series:
DEUS ENCARMINE and DEUS SANGUINIUS)

A WARHAMMER 40,000 NOVEL

THE PURGING OF KADILLUS

GAV THORPE

BLACK LIBRARY

A Black Library Publication

First published in Great Britain in 2011 by
The Black Library,
Games Workshop Ltd.,
The Black Library,
Nottingham, NG7 2WS, UK.

10 9 8 7 6 5 4 3 2 1

Cover illustration by Jon Sullivan.

Map and illustration of Captain Belial by Adrian Wood.

A CIP record for this book is available from the British Library.

UK ISBN 13: 978 1 84416 896 5
US ISBN 13: 978 1 84416 897 2

See the Black Library on the Internet at
www.blacklibrary.com

Find out more about Games Workshop
and the world of Warhammer 40,000 at
www.games-workshop.com

Printed and bound in the UK.

IT IS THE 41st millennium. For more than a hundred centuries
the Emperor has sat immobile on the Golden Throne of Earth.
He is the master of mankind by the will of the gods, and master
of a million worlds by the might of his inexhaustible armies. He
is a rotting carcass writhing invisibly with power from the Dark
Age of Technology. He is the Carrion Lord of the Imperium for
whom a thousand souls are sacrificed every day, so that he may
never truly die.

YET EVEN IN his deathless state, the Emperor continues his
eternal vigilance. Mighty battlefleets cross the daemon-infested
miasma of the warp, the only route between distant stars, their way
lit by the Astronomican, the psychic manifestation of the
Emperor's will. Vast armies give battle in his name on uncounted
worlds. Greatest amongst His soldiers are the Adeptus Astartes,
the Space Marines, bio-engineered super-warriors. Their
comrades in arms are legion: the Imperial Guard and countless
planetary defence forces, the ever-vigilant Inquisition and the tech-
priests of the Adeptus Mechanicus to name only a few. But for all
their multitudes, they are barely enough to hold off the ever-
present threat from aliens, heretics, mutants - and worse.

TO BE A man in such times is to be one amongst untold
billions. It is to live in the cruellest and most bloody regime
imaginable. These are the tales of those times. Forget the power of
technology and science, for so much has been forgotten, never to
be re-learned. Forget the promise of progress and understanding,
for in the grim dark future there is only war. There is no peace
amongst the stars, only an eternity of carnage and slaughter, and the
laughter of thirsting gods.

PROLOGUE

A FUEL TANK exploded, showering squat bodies and shards of metal across the refinery. Guttural laughter rang around the bare rock walls of the asteroid-ship, against a backdrop of chattering guns and flames. A handful of stocky figures stumbled from the fire, airsuits tattered, thick beards and bushy sideburns smoking. They carried high-velocity riveters and fired them at the mob of green-skinned attackers thundering down the tunnel. A few orks fell to the fusillade; others returned fire with their crude weapons, filling the tunnel with muzzle flare and bullets.

'Give 'em anuvver!' Ghazghkull barked at an ork to his left.

The greenskin loaded another improbably sized rocket into its launcher and stood with legs splayed, aiming at the survivors through an array of cracked lenses. The rocket hissed wildly for a moment before the propellant erupted into flames, blowing apart the launcher, tearing off the ork's arm. The ork's pained cursing was drowned out by Ghazghkull's deep laugh.

'Wun fer da doks,' said the warlord, waving roaring warriors forwards with a claw-sheathed hand. Ghazghkull's laughter stopped as a slew of rivets pattered across the thick plates of armour protecting the warlord's gut. The massive greenskin turned his red scowl upon the scattered demiurgs sheltering in the ruins of the refinery. 'Time to finish 'em off. Get stuck in, boyz!'

Following their warlord, the orks charged into the burning debris, hacking and chopping with serrated cleavers and whirring-toothed blades. Ghazghkull levered aside a twisted sheet of metal to reveal a demiurg hiding behind it. The warlord roared along with his multi-barrelled gun as he blazed away, shredding the miner into bloody lumps.

'Dakka dakka dakka! Dat's 'ow ya do it!'

Ghazghkull's gaze fell upon another victim scurrying into the collapsed doorway of an outbuilding. The massive ork shouldered his way through the wall after the fleeing miner, erupting amidst a cloud of tangled reinforcing rods and shattered stone. The demiurg swung a rock-drill at Ghazghkull, aiming for the chest. The diamond-edged bit skittered and shrieked across the warlord's armour and bounced away, the impact almost wrenching the drill from the miner's hands.

'Nice try,' growled Ghazghkull, looking at the scoring across his chestplate. The ork lifted up an armoured, energy-wreathed fist. 'My turn, stunty!'

The claw crackled with arcs of power as Ghazghkull

smashed in the demiurg's craggy face, the force of the blow thudding the miner's head into the far wall. Smoke billowed from the exhausts of the warlord's armour as Ghazghkull lifted up an armoured boot and crushed the headless body beneath its deep tread. It was always worth making sure.

Thundering out through another wall, Ghazghkull looked around. Scattered pockets of orks were running here and there looking for more targets, but it appeared the refinery was empty of enemies. The warlord spied a tiny figure scrambling through the rubble, dragging a huge pole and banner behind him.

'Oi, Makari!' Ghazghkull bellowed at his standard bearer. The gretchin flinched and turned wide eyes to his master.

'Yes, boss?' Makari squeaked. 'What can I do fer ya?'

'Where's da meks? Dey needs to be gettin' da ore and worky-bitz back to da ship.'

'I'll go find 'em, boss,' said Makari. He planted the flag in a pile of debris before gratefully scurrying back down the tunnel.

Ghazghkull strode to the top of a slag heap and looked around. The stunties hadn't provided much sport, but the warlord didn't mind. The orks were here for loot and gubbinz. The meks could make some really good stuff with stunty gear.

Another explosion rocked the artificial cavern, a blossom of fire engulfing a mob of orks investigating one of the mine entrances. Ghazghkull thought it was a secondary explosion, but it was soon followed by three more, each heralded by the telltale smoke trails of rockets.

'Dat's odd.'

'What's dat, boss?' asked Fangrutz, clanking up the slag heap, the joints of his armoured suit wheezing and whining.

'Look at dat,' said Ghazghkull, pointing a serrated claw towards the explosions. 'Dose is rokkits. Oo's firin' rokkits at us?'

'Da stunties?' suggested Fangrutz.

'Stunty rokkits don't smoke and whirl about like dat.' Ghazghkull smacked Fangrutz on the head again for making such a stupid suggestion. 'Dey iz orky rokkits!'

In confirmation of Ghazghkull's suspicion, a horde of green-skinned warriors poured out of the mine entrance, guns blazing in all directions. They wore yellow-and-black body armour and jackets, the back banners of their nobz decorated with stylised grinning half-moons.

'Dey ain't our boyz!' Fangrutz declared. Ghazghkull's gun clanged loudly across the back of Fangrutz's head again. The nob's eyes crossed momentarily and he stumbled.

'Course dey ain't, ya zoggin' squig-brain. Get down dere and give 'em some dakka. Dey're after our loot!'

Ghazghkull set after the boys as they poured into the firefight, which in some places became a vicious scrum of blades and fangs. Smoke churning behind him, Ghazghkull lumbered into a run, bellowing orders.

'Stop 'em gettin' up on dat roof! More dakka dat way! Give 'em some boot levver!'

The warlord watched a blur of red and black come

sailing out of the mine; it quickly resolved into one of his boyz, a ragged hole in the chest. The body splattered and bounced noisily across a rock just in front of Ghazghkull. The ork heard a rapid-fire din above the creaks and puttering of his armour's engine, a drawn-out rattle accompanied by a flare of orange in the mouth of the mine entrance. A swathe of orks fell to the ground, bloodied holes punched across their bodies. Through the gap, Ghazghkull saw another huge ork advancing from the mine, chain gun hurling bullets in all directions.

The rival warlord was wearing mega-armour as well, painted a garish yellow and decorated with black flames. Compared to the rusty joints and oil-spattered pipes of Ghazghkull's suit, the newcomer's armour was spotless, haphazardly inlaid with chunks of gold and – Ghazghkull sneered at the ostentation – dozens of ork teeth.

'Wot a show-off,' the warlord muttered as he levelled his gun at the newcomer.

Ghazghkull opened fire, spraying the remaining contents of the magazine at the enemy warlord. Bullets skipped off the floor and walls of the mine tunnel, and a few found their mark, rattling over the plates of his foe's mega-armour. The Bad Moon warlord – such gaudy displays of wealth were unmistakeable – turned his own weapon on Ghazghkull as a series of empty clicks from his gun echoed around the chamber.

'Oh zog!' grunted Ghazghkull.

He was engulfed in a firestorm of flashing projectiles. A particularly vicious burst caught him in the right shoulder, sending slivers of metal spinning in all directions. The armour's engine gave an alarming cough but continued working, although with a new rattle.

The two warlords closed in on each other, the boyz parting to allow their leaders to get to grips, the ground trembling under the combined thudding of metal-shod boots.

Ghazghkull struck first, swiping his power claw across his foe's chest, shredding metal. He winced as the Bad Moon smashed his own long claw onto the top of Ghazghkull's armoured head. A boot found Ghazghkull's knee plate, which clattered off to the right. Ghazghkull brought down an elbow spike onto his opponent's left shoulder, driving it hard between the armoured plates, but was thrown back a moment later by a knee-trembling blow to his gut.

Parted for a moment, the two warlords locked glares. Around them the fighting between the rest of the orks died away to some desultory shooting and the occasional punch or kick. Dozens of red eyes were turned towards the pair, expectantly awaiting the combat to recommence.

'Zog off!' roared Ghazghkull. 'Dis is my loot!'

'I woz 'ere furst!' the other warlord bellowed. 'You zog off!'

"Ow?' asked Ghazghkull. 'I ain't seen no uvver ship. 'Ow did yoose get 'ere?'

The Bad Moon rippled back his thick lips in a grin.

'Dat's fer me ta know, innit?'

'Don't you knows 'oo I am? I'm Ghazghkull Mag Uruk Thraka, da proffet of Gork an' Mork. I'm da biggest, baddest warlord dere is. Ya got ta tell me!'

'I 'eard of you,' said the other, stepping back another pace. 'You gave da humies a good kickin', I 'eard. You might be da proffet of Gork an' Mork, but nobody makes betta proffet dan me.'

Something in Ghazghkull's memory tinkled into place: Bad Moon warlord, stupidly rich, plenty of dakka.

'Nazdreg?' he snarled.

'Dat's da wun!' beamed his opponent. Nazdreg's eyes narrowed slyly. 'I 'eard yoose a bit special, bit of a finker.'

'Dat's right,' said Ghazghkull. 'I 'ear da wordz of Gork, or mebbe itz Mork, itz 'ard ta say. Dey tell me clever stuff, and dat's why I'm da baddest warlord dere is.'

'I got an idea fer ya, Ghazghkull Mag Uruk Thraka.'

'Yeah?'

'We can fight dis out until wun of us iz dead, in good orky fashion…'

'Sounds good ta me!'

'…or we can come ta some kind of deal.'

Ghazghkull looked hard at Nazdreg and his boyz. There were quite a lot of them. He was sure he could probably beat them, but… It'd taken him ages to get enough boyz together after being chased around by that Mork-cursed humie boss, Yarrick, and it did seem a bit of a waste to be killing other orks when he could be killing the hated humies.

'What you offerin'?' he asked cautiously.

'I'll tell ya 'ow I got on dis rock wivout a ship, if you and yer boyz come wiv me on a li'l job I got planned.'

Ghazghkull suddenly became aware that he was the

centre of attention from both sides. He waited for a while to see if Gork or Mork had anything to say on the matter. There were no voices in his head, so he guessed that they didn't care either way. He took a deep breath and lowered his power claw.

'I'm lissenin'…'

BLUE-FEATHERED GULLS CIRCLED screeching above the wall.

Tauno followed them against the dismal grey sky, humming quietly to himself. As one of the birds dipped past, Tauno looked back across Kadillus Harbour. Surrounded by the high curtain wall, the city squatted on the steep coast of the volcanic isle, a mess of grey and silver against the dark rock. The raised landing platforms of Northport jutted out from the wall a few kilometres away; an orbital craft the size of a city block rose from the starship dock, smoke and plasma wreathing protective blast ramps, while atmospheric craft buzzed and growled to and fro, borne aloft by jets and rotors.

From the gatehouses, highways of cracked ferrocrete cut through sprawling tenements and smoke-wreathed processing plants, converging at the central plaza. Next to the square loomed the spire of the Dark Angels basilica, a towering edifice of buttresses and gargoyles broken by stained-glass windows and ornate balconies. The buildings around the basilica seemed cowed by its presence, none reaching higher than three storeys, as if to be higher would be an affront to the spectacle of the Space Marines' temple-keep.

Past the basilica, Kadillus dropped steeply towards

the harbourside. The sea was little more than a glint-
ing blur on the horizon, obscured by a tangle of cranes
and gantries that stooped over the high warehouses. A
dozen wharfs stretched into the ocean, where super-
trawlers three kilometres long unloaded their harvests.

Tauno heard a grunt of confusion from Meggal next
to him in the watchpost.

'Have a look at this,' said the other sentry, handing
Tauno the magnoculars. 'Looks like a dust storm or
something.'

Tauno looked through the magnoculars and could
see a thick wall of dusty cloud coming towards Kadillus Harbour, still at least half a dozen kilometres away.

'Anything from the comm?' he asked, not looking
away.

'Nope,' replied Meggal. 'Come to think of it, aren't
Kendil and his lot meant to check in from Outpost
Theta?'

Tauno flicked his blond hair from his face, increased
the magnification and tried to hold the magnoculars
as steady as he could, peering into the dust storm. He
could see nothing save the cloud billowing up from
beyond a rise in the ground. He caught movement, a
darker shape within the dust. Resting his arms on the
parapet he concentrated, trying to focus the magnoculars.

Suddenly in pin-sharp clarity he saw figures
emerging from the dust. Steadying himself again, he
gently thumbed the focus rune a little more. More and
more shapes emerged from the haze, churning up the
dirt in their wake, a great crowd of figures on foot:
stooped, green-skinned, waving weapons in the air. As

the seconds passed, Tauno could see the columns advancing steadily in a seemingly endless procession. There were thousands of them.

'Emperor's balls…' gasped Tauno, the magnoculars dropping from his cold fingers.

THE TALE OF BOREAS
Dark Cathedral

A ONE-EYED LION stared down at Boreas from the shattered stained-glass window. His black armour was dappled with red and blue and yellow by flames flickering inside the window. Detonations continually rocked the rubble-strewn street; one shell exploded atop a buttress above him, showering chunks of plascrete from the basilica onto the Chaplain and his squad. Fanged green faces leered from windows in the upper storeys. The orks spat down at the Dark Angels and occasionally rattled off bursts of fire with equal effect.

A growl welled up from deep within Boreas as he waited for the other squad to assemble on the opposite side of the ruined basilica. He looked through the remnants of the main doors into the central nave. The open space was filled with piles of rubble and green-skinned bodies. Banners hundreds of years old lay smouldering in the ruin.

'In position at the east entrance, Brother-Chaplain,' Sergeant Peliel reported over the comm. 'Awaiting your command.'

'Squad Heman ready for overwatch,' crackled the next report in Boreas's ear. The Chaplain glanced over his shoulder and saw the Devastators aiming their heavy weapons from a rooftop on the opposite side of the street.

'The Lion's shade revolts at the presence of this filth in his shrine,' Boreas rasped to his battle-brothers. 'Bring peace to his soul and honour to his memory with bolt and blade. Commence the attack!'

For the third time since arriving at the shrine, the Chaplain stormed up the steps and plunged through the shattered doorway, bolt pistol in his right hand, crozius arcanum in the left. The eagle-headed maul blazed with blue light that threw sharp shadows across the central hall of the basilica. The walls and windows of the upper floors exploded inwards as missiles and lascannon blasts from Squad Heman pounded the ork positions. Green bodies flopped over the gallery railing above the hall, tumbling to the rubble trailing thick blood.

Plascrete crunching underfoot, the Chaplain turned sharply to his right and headed for an iron spiral staircase next to the crumbled remains of a minor altar. On the other side of the nave, Peliel and his Dark Angels headed for the steps descending into the catacomb.

The orks opened fire as Boreas reached the bottom of the stairs, bullets and blasts of energy sending up dust and shards around him. Sparks surrounded the Chaplain as he pounded up the steps, bullets shrieking from the metal, the whole staircase shaking under the weight of his tread. Behind him, the other Space Marines returned fire. The whole nave echoed with the roar of bolters. Fiery trails cut the gloom, each ending in a small explosion that rocked the upper gallery.

Boreas reached the gallery at a run. It was even darker here; with a vocal command Boreas switched his autosenses to thermal. Several orks were sprawled lifeless along the marble-inlaid floor, blood cooling in greasy pools. He spied the yellow heat-outlines of living foes at the far end of the gallery, their guns blazing harsh white, bullets zipping down into the squad below.

The Chaplain levelled his pistol. A targeting reticule sprang into view as his finger touched the trigger. His first shot took the top off an ork's head, blood spraying against the wall in a red chromatic display. Two bolts took his next target in the chest, exploding the ribcage and breastbone, ripping apart organs. To his heightened senses it seemed as if the orks turned on him in slow motion, drawing up their guns towards this new threat. A fourth round ripped through the shoulder of the next foe, sending the ork spinning through a doorway.

The first bullets zipped around Boreas as he subconsciously registered the thunder of more Space Marines coming up the stairs behind him. Sending another bolt into the gut of an ork, Boreas spared a millisecond glance to his right, across the nave where more orks had gathered.

He saw a blossom of fire and flung himself against the wall as a rocket spiralled towards him, the warhead smashing into the plascrete just behind him. The rosarius hanging on a thick chain around Boreas's neck blazed with power as shrapnel engulfed the Chaplain; the rosarius's energy field converted the mass of the shards into flares of bright light. Boreas heaved himself away from the cracked wall as more bullets skipped and screamed along the gallery. He headed straight for the orks, bolts from his battle-brothers whipping past either side of him, detonations cracking along a crude barricade the orks had built out of splintered furniture and bundled wall-hangings.

The Chaplain emptied the rest of his bolt pistol into the greenskins as he charged the barrier, sending them reeling back. He leapt as he reached the barricade, one foot atop the broken remnants of a cabinet, driving his other into the face of an ork swinging at him with a snarling chainsword. The alien's head snapped back as Boreas's momentum carried him into the thick of the orks, his crozius crashing under the upraised arm of another foe to liquidate flesh and bone.

Boreas landed and rolled, sweeping the legs from another enemy with his right arm as he regained his feet. Something hammered into his backpack and he turned on his heel, driving an elbow into the face of an ork, fangs splintering, jaw breaking. A heavy blade slashed out of the throng and caught him on the right side of his helmet, its serrated edge scraping through paint and chipping ceramite.

The ork backed away, just out of reach. Boreas hurled his empty pistol into the beast's face, this distraction giving the Chaplain a moment to follow up with a bone-crunching kick to the knee that brought down the alien. The rosarius flared into life again as more blows rained down on the Chaplain, blinding the orks. Boreas smashed one across the face with his crozius, the wing of the eagle-head burying itself deep in a red eye. He chopped with the edge of his hand into the throat of another, lifting the beast from its feet, wind-pipe smashed.

Bolt-round detonations sprayed the Chaplain with gore as the following Dark Angels joined the melee. Bursting through the barricade, the Space Marines fell upon the orks with chainblade bayonets and monomolecular-edged combat knives.

The dozen or so remaining orks were not about to give up the fight, and hurled themselves at the squad roaring throaty war cries and obscenities. Four of them bore Brother Zepheus to the floor, stabbing at his face and chest, levering their blades into the joints of his armour, blasting away with heavy pistols, the ricocheting bullets as much a danger to themselves as the Dark Angels.

Boreas's crozius smashed into the skull of an ork pinning down Zepheus, splitting it wide open. The ork reared up, still alive, dragging its serrated blade from a crack in Zepheus's armour. It swung the weapon at Boreas and missed, spattering the Chaplain's skull-helm with droplets of his battle-brother's blood. Incensed, Boreas shoulder-charged the greenskin, tackling it at chest height to drive it into the wall with a snap of bones, plascrete exploding into dust around them. Boreas snapped the ork's neck in the crook of his arm to be certain and cast the limp body to the floor. He turned to see Sergeant Lemael burying his chainaxe into the armpit of the last greenskin, the whirring blades spraying gobbets of flesh and shards of bone over the gallery rail.

Boreas pressed on to the archway at the end of the gallery, past which were found the inner chambers of the basilica. Lemael split his Space Marines into two combat squads, joining the Chaplain with Brothers Sarion, Dannael, Aspherus and Zamiel. The remainder of the Dark Angels took up overwatch positions along the gallery while they waited for an Apothecary to attend to the badly wounded Zepheus.

'You might want this, Brother-Chaplain,' said Aspherus, proffering Boreas's bolt pistol, which he had evidently retrieved from the pile of ork bodies. The Chaplain took it with a murmur of thanks, slammed home a fresh magazine from his belt and darted a look through the archway, looking for foes. A corridor ran to the northern end of the basilica, shattered windows on the right-hand side, half a dozen doors leading into the scriptoriums on the left. There was no sign of the orks. Boreas switched off his crozius to conserve its power cell and nodded the Dark Angels forwards.

'Check and clear every room,' Lemael told his warriors. 'Be vigilant for booby-traps. There is no telling what these filthy greenskins have been up to.'

Sarion went up on point, kicking in the remnants of the first door while Dannael kept watch along the corridor. The Space Marines hurried into the room, bolters ready. Within, all had been upturned. Illuminating desks and low stools were broken, and tattered and soiled manuscripts were scattered across the floor. Digiquills and styluses lay in a snapped heap beneath the broken door of a storage cabinet and crude ork glyphs were daubed on the walls in black and red ink. Blossoms of green and yellow and purple and blue showed where pots of other colours had been dashed against the walls, floor and ceiling for amusement.

'Scum,' muttered Boreas.

He had expected such desecration, hardened his anticipation of it, but it was still something of a shock to see it wrought in rooms where only a few days before he had walked amongst the company serfs as they copied out the great texts of the Dark Angels Chapter. It had been an ordered, serene enclave in the midst of the bustling port-city, dedicated to reflection on the Lion's teachings, the wisdom of the Emperor and the doctrine of battle.

His eye was caught by a scrap of plasti-parchment, edges wrinkled and melted from an attempt to set it alight. He hung his crozius from his belt and picked it up, recognising the partially obscured illustration in the margin. He gave an ironic laugh.

'Page fourteen of the *Contemplations of Castigation*,' he told his battle-brothers. He read the first lines out loud. 'Blessed be the warrior that punishes the unclean. In his purgation of the Heretic, the Mutant and the Alien, the blessed Astartes proves his purity. Only he that is free of taint can uphold the role of Executioner of the Imperial Will.'

The rest was unreadable, but Boreas knew it by heart. His voice turned to a snarl as he continued from memory.

'With the honour of that duty there comes the responsibility to prosecute such punishment to the

23

utter lengths of possibility. No Heretic, no Mutant, no *Alien* is above the reproach of the cleansing fire of battle. If the Imperial Will is to extend to all corners and reaches of the galaxy, there can be no respite from the eternal pursuit for justice and the perpetuation of vengeance against the immoral.'

Boreas crumpled the sheet in his fist and dropped it to the ground. Pulling free his crozius, he thumbed the weapon into life, bathing the room with its blue glow.

'The vilest of offences has been committed against us, my brothers,' growled Boreas. 'The orks do not simply attack a world of the Imperium, they attack a world under *our* protection. This building is not simply a strategic asset to be held against an enemy. This is a basilica of the Dark Angels, an extension of the Tower of Angels, a spiritual part of lost Caliban. An attack here is an attack against the Dark Angels Chapter. It is an affront to the Lion! It is not only our duty to bring righteous persecution against those who have sinned against us; it is our *right*!'

Sergeant Lemael answered, echoed by the rest of the Space Marines.

'Kill the alien!'

THE NEXT TWO rooms were equally ransacked and equally empty of foes to punish for the act. As the Dark Angels left the third chamber, Lemael commanded them to stop. Boreas listened, his autosenses picking up what the sergeant had first detected: grunts and scrapes from the adjoining room.

'An interesting development,' remarked the sergeant. 'Orks attempting an ambush?'

'The strange subtlety of thought is not matched by their subtlety of action,' replied Brother Sarion as the clatter of something dropped on the wooden floors sounded from the next room.

'Teach them the lesson of their error,' rasped Boreas, holstering his bolt pistol to pull a fragmentation grenade from a belt-pack.

'Zamiel, do your duty,' ordered Lemael.

The Space Marine lifted his flamer in acknowledgement, the harsh blue of its igniter reflected from his dark green armour.

'Purge the alien!' shouted Boreas, kicking open the next door.

He caught a glimpse of fanged mouths snarling at him as the orks rose from their hiding positions behind overturned lecterns and tables. The Chaplain tossed a grenade into the back of the room while four more arced past him, bouncing off the walls and ceiling. Boreas ducked back as simultaneous detonations filled the chamber with shrapnel, smoke and metal spilling from the doorway.

A moment later Zamiel stood at the door, flamer spraying white-hot promethium into the scriptorium, the crackle of flames blanketing the harsh yells and panicked bellows of the orks within. He panned left and right, coating everything with the sticky fuel, setting light to wood and flesh and parchment. Only when every surface was burning did he release the trigger and pull up his weapon, stepping back to allow the others to enter the inferno.

Surrounded by flames, the Space Marines burst into the room, firing their bolters into the twitching, charring bodies of the orks. Boreas could feel the heat of the flames, but a glance at his power armour's integrity display showed that the guttering blaze was well within tolerable limits. As the promethium burnt out, the Chaplain found himself standing inside a blackened shell, a few licks of fire flickering here and there. The bones of the orks lay in contorted heaps, stuck with chunks of burnt flesh, steam hissing from boiling marrow and blood, while pools of fat sizzled beneath them.

'We must move on to secure the spire and dominate the city square,' announced Lemael. 'Haste is required before the enemy send reinforcements.'

'Righteous is our cause,' said Boreas. 'We shall not fail the Chapter.'

Leaving the burned-out room, the squad moved on, continuing their sweep towards the apex of the basilica, where the main spire reached one hundred metres into the sky above Kadillus. This was their goal: the highest point in the city centre, from which the Dark Angels would be able to pour fire into the surrounding buildings and, more importantly, accurately direct the artillery fire of their allies against the ork army that had seized the harbour over the previous two days.

The ork attack had taken the people of Kadillus unawares, and with that surprise the greenskins had driven through the heart of the city, directly for the docks and wharfs. Nobody yet knew where the enemy had come from; there had been no warning from orbital arrays, nor the Dark Angels ship circling high above Piscina IV.

It was fortunate that the Dark Angels were here at all. The Chapter had arrived four weeks ago as part of a much-delayed visit to take recruits from the neighbouring world of Piscina V. The bulk of the Chapter had left six days ago, leaving the 3rd Company and a few auxiliary squads from other companies to oversee the last stages of recruitment. Had it not been for the swift reaction of Master Belial and his warriors, the whole city might have fallen within hours. The company commander had faced the ork warlord once already, and from what Boreas had heard, Belial had been fortunate to survive the encounter.

As it was, the orks were holed up in the waterfront district and along a line of buildings that stretched to the central square. In the close confines of the city and without a clear idea of enemy numbers or their purpose, even the Dark Angels were wary of facing the brutal orks head-on. Master Belial's plan was to contain the aliens at the docks, whilst breaking the link with those in the city centre. The two forces could then be purged separately once the planet's defence force, the Free Militia, had been fully mobilised.

The first stage was to secure the basilica, but that had proven easier ordered than accomplished. This was Boreas's fourth attempt, and was showing the greatest success so far.

As the Dark Angels forged further into the press of rooms, resistance was sporadic and scattered; the orks had evidently split their numbers to avoid sharing the spoils, and so were easily overcome by the Space Marines. However, their progress through the three storeys of administrative chambers between the central nave and the spire did not go unnoticed by their green-skinned adversaries.

The orks counter-attacked as the squad gained the first landing at the base of the stairwells leading up into the spire. Lemael had his foot upon the first step when something clattered around the landing above, bouncing down to spin gently at his feet. It was a stick grenade.

As Boreas and the others turned away, the grenade went off, filling the enclosed space with a storm of metal shards. Everything went silent for a moment as the Chaplain's autosenses cut in to block the concussive effect of the detonation. His rosarius blazed, engulfing him with its protective shield, but still he felt dozens of impacts on his armour as shrapnel swallowed the squad. When Boreas's hearing was restored, the hallway was still ringing. Lemael lay slumped against the wall, his right leg armour cracked by the blast, his knee twisted at an unnatural angle.

'Cover the stairs!' snapped Boreas. 'Protect your sergeant!'

Dannael and Sarion advanced a few steps up the stair as Zamiel and Aspherus slung their weapons and dragged Lemael down the hall, leaving a trail of dark blood.

More grenades clanged down from above. Most exploded harmlessly before reaching the Space Marines; Dannael threw two back up the stairs before they detonated, much to the surprise, and apparently some amusement, of the orks. Another buzzed and smoked just out of reach but failed to go off.

The thudding of boots on the bare plascrete warned

of the descending ork mob. Sarion opened fire first, cutting down the first greenskins to come around the corner of the landing. Some of the following orks tripped on the bodies of the first, but others leapt over the corpses, ploughing down the steps with reckless disregard for balance. As Sarion stopped to reload, Dannael took up the fusillade, firing steadily into the press of green bodies rushing him, each shot blowing a fist-sized hole in flesh and bone.

Undeterred, the orks leapt to the attack, smashing mauls and blades into the Space Marines' armour, the stairwell resounding with wordless yells and the crack of fracturing ceramite. Within moments Dannael and Sarion were swept off the stairway and back into the hall, battering at their foes with bolters, fists and feet.

Boreas joined the defence, bolt pistol spitting rounds, crozius leaving a trail of burning energy as he swept the power weapon into the orks. The hall was barely wide enough for the three Space Marines to stand abreast, Sarion to the Chaplain's right, Dannael to the left. The orks were similarly hampered and could not bring their greater numbers to bear down the stairwell. A violent stalemate ensued: Boreas, Dannael and Sarion battered down any greenskin that reached them, but were unable to press further forwards.

'Brother Boreas!' Sergeant Peliel barked urgently through the Chaplain's comm. 'The orks have breached the catacombs from the sewers. Encountering extreme resistance. Three brothers lost. We are falling back to the central nave. Advise that your current position will become untenable.'

'The Astartes do not retreat!' Boreas snarled back. For two days possession of the basilica had constantly changed hands. The Chaplain was determined it would not fall to the orks again. 'Fight to the death, sergeant!'

The comm crackled for a moment before Peliel replied. Boreas parried a saw-edged cleaver swung at his gut and fired a bolt-round into the gaping mouth of the ork wielding it, the back of the greenskin's head spattering across those behind.

'Sacrifice at this point offers no tactical benefit, Brother-Chaplain,' the sergeant said calmly. 'Enemy armed with portable heavy arms and powered weapons capable of penetrating Astartes armour. Last-stand scenario would not provide sufficient delay to their advance. We are executing a fighting withdrawal to the main basilica. Urgently suggest you perform same.'

Boreas suppressed a snarl of frustration. Distracted, he did not see a gun muzzle thrust through the press of orks. Once again his rosarius saved him from the worst, enveloping him with light as bullets sprayed against his chest. He smashed aside the gun with the tip of his crozius.

'Acknowledged, Sergeant Peliel. Will rendezvous in the nave in three minutes.' Boreas heard the click of the intersquad channel closing and addressed the Space Marines with him. 'Take Sergeant Lemael and reform your squad on the gallery. Brothers Dannael, Sarion and I will guard the withdrawal.'

Boreas concentrated on fending off another wave of orks as affirmatives sounded in his ear. He fired the

last bolt from his pistol into the back of an ork cling-
ing to Sarion's left arm, the projectile shattering the
creature's spine.

Side-by-side, the three Space Marines back-stepped
along the hallway. Sarion had discarded his mangled
bolter and fought with his combat knife; Dannael
fired his weapon in a long burst, cutting down half a
dozen foes until the bolter was empty, opening a gap
of a few metres between the Space Marines and their
adversaries. They came level with a doorway that led
into a narrow room at the front of the basilica, the
outer wall dominated by a huge rose window.

'Cover,' Boreas told the other two, stepping back
behind them. They closed shoulder to shoulder. He
ejected his bolt pistol magazine and slammed in
another: his last one. 'Fall back to the gallery.'

Even as he issued the order, a larger ork shouldered
its way through the mass, taller even than the Dark
Angels. It swung a huge axe two-handed, blade
crackling with forks of energy. The blow connected
with Sarion's neck, shearing off the battle-brother's
head in one sweep.

Boreas fired his pistol, the salvo of miniature missiles exploding across the breastplate of the gigantic
alien. The ork was thrown back, dropping to one knee.

'Full retreat, brother!' the Chaplain told Dannael. 'I
shall protect you.'

One of the orks leapt in front of its leader, blazing
away with a pistol. Boreas swayed, taking the brunt of
the salvo on his left shoulder pad, ceramite cracking
and showering to the floor. The Chaplain glanced
down at his rosarius and saw the power crystal

glowing fitfully. Another fifteen or more orks crowded down the stairs behind their leader, jeering as Boreas backed into the doorway leading to the rose window. He ripped another frag grenade from his belt. He held it above his head for the orks to see and thumbed the activation switch.

'Kill the alien!' he snarled, the words roaring from the external speakers of his helmet. He tossed the grenade into the orks as they scrambled and shoved each other back up the stairs; all except the leader, who launched itself at the Chaplain with its axe held overhead.

Boreas met the ork with a step, crashing his armoured fist into its broad chin as the grenade exploded on the stair. The blow barely slowed the creature's charge, but was enough to make the axe blow swing harmlessly past Boreas's left shoulder. The ork's momentum carried it forwards, crashing into Boreas, sending both sprawling to the floor.

As the Chaplain pushed himself to his feet in the doorway, the surviving orks thundered down the steps, leaping and tripping over the mounds of their dead, firing their guns. The wall and doorframe splintered with bullet impacts. The ork leader hauled itself upright and took a fresh grip on its weapon. It grunted something Boreas could not understand and heaved its blade at the Chaplain's head. Boreas ducked back as the crackling axe head sliced into the doorway, ripping through wood and plascrete before becoming stuck. The Chaplain brought up his crozius under the beast's straightened arm, smashing into the ork's elbow. Bone shattered and the arm bent strangely. The ork gave a howl of rage and pain, let go of the axe and smashed a fist into Boreas's face, cracking an eye lens, the blow tearing away a breathing pipe.

Forced back by the punch, Boreas found himself trapped in the window room. Crowding around their wounded leader, the orks pressed through the door; Boreas could hear pounding feet as others chased after Dannael. The Chaplain's crozius opened up the face of the first to lunge at him, smashing teeth and bone.

With his free hand, Boreas pulled the last grenade from his belt.

'I am Astartes, warrior of the Emperor!' he barked, tossing the frag grenade into the centre of the room. As it left his hand, the ork leader surged through the press, clamping an iron-strong arm around Boreas's neck.

The grenade detonated. The blast combined with the ork's impetus to send Boreas and his foe crashing through the rose window. They tumbled head-over-heels through the air, locked together in a violent embrace. The ork tried to bite Boreas's face through the wreckage of his helmet, breaking a tooth, while the Chaplain battered at its back with his crozius.

Spinning and fighting, the two fell thirty metres to the open square below, crashing into the ferromac ground. The ork took most of the impact, chest crushed by Boreas's weight, head smashed to a bloody pulp on the hard surface. The Chaplain's right shoulder pad disintegrated into flying shards and he felt something snap in his arm just above the elbow. His neck wrenched from side to side as he bounced heavily, backpack carving a furrow through the reinforced bitumen. Red indicators flashed across his vision, warning of widespread damage to the power armour's systems.

Even before he could focus again, Boreas felt adrenal fluids pushed through his veins as his twin hearts pounded and blood raced through reinforced arteries and veins. He felt the pain as a distant sensation, something witnessed rather than experienced, and lay still for a moment, analysing the situation.

Only a few seconds had passed since he had fallen, but he realised the danger he was in. The city square was contested ground, held by the orks to the east and the Imperial forces to the west. As if on cue, the buildings to his right were illuminated by firing; the orks had moved some of their field guns into a half-ruined Administratum tithe house and now shells erupted just to Boreas's left. He gave silent thanks that the orks were notoriously poor shots.

Gritting his teeth, the Chaplain pushed to his feet and broke into a limping run, explosions tearing up fresh craters in the ferromac around him. He reached sanctuary behind one of the basilica's buttresses as counterfire screamed and screeched from the other side of the square. Las-fire rippled through the air; the Piscina Free Militia must have taken up the guard duties from the hard-pressed Dark Angels.

'The Emperor protects,' he muttered, heaving out of cover and dashing for the corner of the basilica, dust and plascrete raining down on him from impacts on the wall above.

He rounded the corner to see Sergeant Peliel and the survivors of his squad firing at some foe inside the main nave, their bolts flashing through the open side doors and ruined stained-glass windows. Knowing that he was in no position to fight for the moment,

Boreas sought the cover of the buildings on the opposite side of the street and found the remnants of Squad Lemael waiting for him. They stood guard at the windows, bolters ready for any orks that dared to leave the sanctuary of the basilica. There was no sign of Dannael.

Straightening proudly, Boreas walked calmly to one of the windows and looked at the ravaged cathedral. Smoke was billowing from an upper floor, no doubt a flare-up from Zamiel's flamer. He turned to the other Space Marines.

'Never fear, brothers. We are not yet ready to surrender our shrine to the orks. We will give them no respite. We will return!'

TRACER FIRE AND explosions illuminated the streets and rooftops of Kadillus Harbour, except where thick banks of smoke choked the twisting roads and drifted slowly up from the docks. Next to Sergeant Peliel, Boreas looked at the silhouette of the basilica from the roof terrace of a worker tenement two streets away, one of the higher vantage points in the city still in the hands of Dark Angels and the Piscina forces. The neat flower beds had been churned up by a procession of armoured boots, the balustrade rail pocked by stray bullet holes from long-range ork shooting.

With a sub-vocal command, Boreas increased the magnification of his autosenses, zooming in on the spire of the basilica. He linked his view through the short-range command channel so that it displayed in Peliel's helm.

'It is not just a matter of our Chapter heritage,

brother, though that is reason enough to retake the shrine,' the Chaplain said quietly. 'The view provided by the basilica is of strategic importance. When we regain the position, local forces will be able to deploy their artillery observers and bring down heavy fire on the ork positions around the docks.'

The thud of boots heralded the arrival of Techmarine Hephaestus, followed by two robed and cowled Chapter serfs. They carried replacement parts for Boreas's broken armour. He flexed his arm without thought, testing the re-set bone and subdermal bracing performed by Apothecary Nestor a little earlier. The joint was stiff, but he felt no discomfort.

'I have had to retro-fit some Mark VI parts for your armour,' said the Techmarine. One of the four servo-arms extending from his backpack whined forwards, a tubular section of arm plate in its grip. 'I will do my best, but you should be wary of taking too many blows to your right side.'

'I understand, brother,' replied Boreas. 'I am sure that your best will be more than sufficient.'

The Techmarine and his attendants set to work restoring Boreas's armour, arc torches sparking, ceramite-welders hissing. The Chaplain pushed the activity from his thoughts and addressed Peliel.

'You are reluctant, brother-sergeant.'

'I am,' replied Peliel. 'Four times we have occupied the basilica and four times we have suffered assault and been expelled. I do not believe it is prudent to expend further energy on a direct assault. We should drive the orks from the main square and surround the basilica from all sides.'

'We lack the numbers for such a cordon,' said Boreas. 'Shock assault – that is what we do best, brother. Once we have total possession of the basilica, the orks will not be able to retake it.'

'The Planetary Defence Forces have plenty of soldiers for an encirclement, Brother-Chaplain.' Peliel waved a hand to the east. 'More forces arrive from the outlying fortifications.'

'Delay, delay, delay!' spat Boreas. 'I find your lack of fervour for this battle unsettling, brother-sergeant. I will not have it recorded in the Chapter history that I allowed the basilica of Piscina to fall into ork hands and then required the Planetary Defence Force to retake it! Would you have your name put beside such an entry?'

'No, Brother-Chaplain, I would not.' Peliel bowed his head in apology. 'I do not wish to be judged reluctant for battle. I hope only to aid you in assessing your strategy. Forgive any impudence on my part.'

'When Kadillus is retaken, we shall discuss your penitence in the basilica,' said Boreas.

'Perhaps it would be wise to consult with Master Belial on the best course of action?' suggested Peliel.

Boreas stepped back – to a muttered complaint from Hephaestus labouring on his armour – and scowled at the sergeant.

'The company master is in command of all the forces in the docks. He has entrusted the battle for the centre of the city to me, and needs no further distraction.'

'I understand, Brother-Chaplain. But if–'

'Enough!' roared Boreas. 'It is my command that we retake the basilica. You will restrict your comments to those that will improve the chances of success with that objective in mind. You have not been sergeant for long, Brother Peliel. Honour Master Belial by proving that his faith in you is well placed.'

'Of course, Brother-Chaplain,' said a chagrined Peliel. His next words were spoken with a growled conviction. 'My squad will lead the next assault. I will deliver the basilica to you, Brother-Chaplain!'

'That is good, brother-sergeant. Prove your courage and dedication not by your words, but by your deeds in battle. It is the orks that try to shame us; it is the orks that will suffer the punishment.'

Peliel looked long at the basilica. Nothing could be seen of his expression inside his helmet but his voice was edged with fervour.

'No ork will live to rue the day they chose to test the might of the Dark Angels.' Peliel placed a hand on the Chaplain's chest. 'Thank you for your guidance and patience, Brother Boreas. Your wisdom and integrity are examples to us all.'

'Make your preparations well, brother-sergeant,' said Boreas. 'There will be hard fighting this night.'

'None will fight harder than I,' Peliel declared. He turned on his heel and strode down the steps leading into the tenement.

'How much longer will this take?' Belial asked Hephaestus.

'Only one more thing, Brother-Chaplain,' the Tech-marine replied, his servo-arms recoiling behind his back. Hephaestus gestured to one of his serfs, who came forwards carrying Boreas's skull-shaped helm. The cracks had been sealed and the broken lens replaced; fresh white paint glistened in the flickering light of the burning basilica.

Boreas put on the helmet and tightened the seals. He ran through a rapid series of autosenses checks and confirmed that all systems were working. Satisfied, the Chaplain tried out the replacement fibre bundles and armour on his right arm. His fist smashed through the stone of the balustrade without effort.

'Good work, brother,' Boreas said, smiling. 'Now, if I could press upon you to find me a replacement pistol, I will cite you for the benedictions of the Chapter...'

THE NAVE WAS strangely quiet. The footfalls of the Space Marines echoed coldly in the empty hall. Thermal vision could not detect any ork presence in the main chamber, and a sweep with his suit's terrorsight confirmed to Boreas that the orks seemed content to hold the upper rooms.

'Let us narrow the battlefield, brother-sergeant,' Boreas said to Peliel.

The sergeant signalled to two of his squad, who carried between them a large demolition charge. Covered by two more of their battle-brothers, the Space Marines descended into the catacombs. The rest of the fifteen Space Marines took up overwatch positions around the stairwell, guns trained on the galleries overhead and the main door at the end of the nave.

'Charge in place, Brother-Chaplain,' came the report. 'Timer set.'

'Confirmed,' replied Boreas. 'Regroup with main force.'

The Space Marines pounded back up to the nave and

the whole group took shelter at the far end, away from the catacomb entrance. A countdown timer running down in the right of Boreas's view reached zero and the basilica shook with the detonation, a dense cloud of smoke and dust sweeping up from below, filling the hall. With a drawn-out rumbling, part of the floor gave way, burying the steps and barring any egress into the main hall.

The Chaplain detached five Space Marines to watch the remaining entrances and signalled to the others to follow him to the upper floors. This time the orks would not push the Dark Angels back.

THE FIGHT THROUGH the upper rooms was every bit as fierce as the previous encounters. The orks had received reinforcements through the breached vaults beneath the nave and defended every stairwell and doorway with a storm of bullets and a forest of blades. Hour by bloody hour the Dark Angels battled their way through the maze of rooms and tunnels, with bolter and grenade, missile launcher and flamer. In many places walls collapsed from the exchange of fire, opening up new avenues for the Space Marines to press forwards and the orks to counter-attack.

The under-strength Dark Angels squads broke and reformed as the flow of battle dictated, sometimes a solitary Space Marine holding up a mob of aliens, other times Boreas's warriors coming together to break through particularly strong resistance. At times the fighting became so chaotic that even Boreas was not sure whether an adjacent room contained friends or foe; a constant stream of reports across the comm gave only half the picture as the fortunes of the Space Marines and their enemies ebbed and flowed.

Boreas fought for the most part with his thermal vision, falling upon the orks through the night-shrouded, smoke-filled corridors like the mythical angel of vengeance that featured on so many of the Chapter's banners and murals. Any other warrior would have described the dark rooms and flickering of flames as hell; to the Space Marines they were simply the perfect environment for their style of warfare. Though the orks were not to be underestimated at close quarters – they were savage fighters who relished hand-to-hand combat – the experience, coordination and armour of the Space Marines proved decisive. One room at a time, one floor at a time, the Dark Angels drove back the orks until only a knot of resistance remained at the top of the spire.

Boreas gathered his Space Marines for a final attack. Peliel was amongst those eight that joined the Chaplain at the foot of the final flight of stairs.

'One last push for victory, Brother-Chaplain,' said the sergeant. 'Let us be at the foe and finish this!'

'Your zeal is noted, brother-sergeant,' replied Boreas. 'You may have the honour of leading the attack.'

Peliel raised a fist in thanks. The sergeant turned to the five members of his squad that were present. Boreas listened intently to Peliel's words, searching for any hint of reluctance. There was none.

'The enemy have nowhere left to run, brothers. *Executium non capitula.* We will strike like the sword of the Lion, swift and deadly. No mercy!'

'No mercy!' chorused the Space Marines.

Peliel and his warriors headed up the stairs at a run, feet crashing on the stone steps. Boreas followed at a steadier pace, reaching the foot of the stairs as the first flashes and roars of bolter fire sprang into life above. The remaining three Space Marines followed him with their weapons levelled, ready to spring into action if needed. Judging by the remarks over the comm, Peliel had the situation well in hand, his orders echoed by the rattle of fire and *crump* of grenades in the spire chamber.

For several minutes the firefight continued. Boreas gripped his crozius tightly, resisting the urge to bound up the steps and join Peliel. It was the sergeant's resolve that had caused him concern, not his ability, and it was important he was given the chance to prove himself. The ragtag orks that had survived the Space Marines' onslaught would be little threat. As the echoes of the last shots died down and silence descended, Boreas addressed his companions through the external vocalisers.

'Move back to the nave and join with your brothers there. We will rendezvous with you shortly and prepare the defences.'

He ascended the steps quickly as the three Dark Angels set off back the way they had come. The stairs emerged in the centre of the upper spire room. Green-skinned bodies were piled all around, at least two dozen; more than Boreas had expected. The gouges in Peliel's armour and that of his squad told their own testament to the fury of the trapped orks. The sergeant prowled the dark room with his power sword in hand, decapitating every corpse that still had a head. It was standard doctrine when facing orks, who had a distinct ability to recover from seemingly fatal wounds, sometimes rising up from mounds of their fallen to strike when unexpected.

A thick-runged ladder led to an open trapdoor in the ceiling, through which gleamed the first ruddy hue of dawn. Boreas glanced at the opening with suspicion. Peliel must have noticed his look.

'The roof is clear of foes, Brother-Chaplain,' said the sergeant. 'None have escaped.'

'That is good. Send your squad to the others and follow me.'

Boreas climbed through the trapdoor and pulled himself up to the roof atop the spire. From this vantage point he could see far across Kadillus Harbour, all the way to the curtain wall in the east and the docks in the west. It was possible to trace the path of the ork attack by the ruined buildings and smouldering fires. It told of a strange, single-minded purpose. Rather than spreading out through the city in all directions, as Boreas would have expected looting orks to do, a line of devastation arrowed almost directly from one of the outer gates to the power plant at the heart of the dock workings.

Why the orks had been so determined to seize the harbour was beyond Boreas. Not knowing the orks' motivation was an aberration that niggled at him, as had their behaviour during some of the fighting in the basilica.

His thoughts were disturbed by the clang of Peliel's boots on the ladder behind the Chaplain. Boreas walked to the edge of the roof tower, which was surrounded by a thick wall that reached to his waist. Small, cowled figures with angels' wings stood as silent stone guardians, each gripping a sword in its gauntleted fists.

'The basilica is ours, Brother-Chaplain,' announced Peliel, joining Boreas as he looked over the main square. He could see movement on both sides, but for the moment the firing had ceased.

'Your actions have proven your dedication, brother-sergeant,' Boreas said, turning his head to look at Peliel. 'This would make a fine firepoint for Sergeant Heman and his Devastators.'

'Indeed it would. Or perhaps Sergeant Naaman and some of his Scout snipers.'

'Naaman? Naaman can be skittish, far too prone to acting on his own whims. Maybe that is a desirable trait for one who operates on his own for so long, but it is not a good example for those he is training. No, I will contact Heman and tell him the basilica is ready for his squad.'

'Do you think the orks will attempt another attack here?'

Boreas considered this. In the growing light, he could see movement through the alleys and buildings to the west. The enemy were already gathering their numbers.

'It is certain. I do not think the orks desire the basilica other than because we also wish to possess it. It is beyond them to comprehend its spiritual significance to us, and I doubt that they can understand the strategic importance of its location.'

'It was one of their first targets of attack when they

entered the city, Brother-Chaplain,' countered Peliel.

'Coincidence, brother-sergeant.' Boreas pointed out the line of the orks' first advance. 'The basilica is situated on the main route through the city. We chose to defend this place, so it was inevitable that they would attack it. The ork mind is not complex, brother-sergeant. They fight where the enemy are, for the love of the fighting itself. Had we defended a market hall or the fish exchange, they would have attacked with equal vigour.'

'What is your plan for the defence, Brother-Chaplain?' asked Peliel, stepping away from the wall to survey the other approaches to the basilica.

'With the catacombs sealed, it will be a simple matter to protect the other routes of entry into the main hall. If we can hold them at the main shrine and prevent them entering the upper storeys again, the task should be within the capabilities of a single squad. We must build such barricades and defences as we can and then it is merely a matter of waiting.'

'The orks have displayed some cunning in their tactics so far. Breaking into the catacombs from the sewers was unexpected. Should we not expect them to try by some means to gain direct access to the upper levels? Jump-pack troops, perhaps? Or some other means of circumventing our defences on the ground.'

'You make a good point. A combat squad positioned on the roofs, with a spotter here, should be sufficient to deter such a move.'

The two of them crossed over the tower to look at the sloping tiles atop the rest of the basilica. A single roof more than a hundred metres long dominated, broken by several small towers along each side. At the far end, the rear of the cathedral, garrets and sub-structures nestled together. Here and there smoking holes had been torn in the slate by explosions within the shrine. There was a gap of some thirty metres between the roof and where they stood atop the rectangular main spire.

'As you say, Brother-Chaplain,' said Peliel. 'A combat squad can move freely enough to counter an attack from any direction.'

Boreas glanced again to the west. He wondered how the rest of the company was faring in the docks, where they were fighting to contain the main force of the orks. It was only that containment that prevented the enemy bringing overwhelming numbers to the centre of the city. In their race to secure the docks and its power plant, the orks had allowed themselves to be cut into two: one in the harbour, the other in the commercial and residential districts west and north of the basilica. It was vital that the two forces were not allowed to join. The basilica was only the first part of a plan that would see Boreas and his Space Marines lead the Free Militia against the smaller concentration.

It was a sound strategy, but relied on Master Belial keeping the orks at the docks from breaking out. A strange localised atmospheric interference – possibly some unknown contrivance of the orks – was making long-range communications all but impossible. Boreas simply trusted Belial to succeed in his part of the plan.

'We should return to the others, Brother-Chaplain,'

said Peliel. The sergeant walked to the ladder. 'There is still much to be done.'

'Be proud of your actions today,' said Boreas as Peliel swung himself onto the top rung.

'I am, Brother-Chaplain. Thank you for keeping faith in me.'

Boreas lingered for a short while longer. It was doubtful the orks would know yet that the basilica was again in the hands of the Space Marines. He unfastened the seals on his helmet and took it off, filling his lungs with the Piscina air. The salt of the sea, the smoke of explosions, the soot of chimneys, the tang of blood from the ork bodies below, all combined into a melange of sensation.

His eye fell upon one of the stone guardian angels atop the wall. Its left wing had been broken at some point in the fighting, alone amongst all of them. The missing piece lay on the roof behind the wall, its intricately carved feathers chipped. He hung his crozius from his belt and picked up the broken wing, turning it over in his fingers. He reached to the belt pouch below his backpack and brought out a slab of two-part resin that was used to make rapid battle repairs to armour. He kneaded the putty into a blob and delicately fixed the broken wing back in place, discarding the surplus resin over the parapet. It was a poor fix, but it would do. When the orks were driven from Piscina, he would have one of the Chapter serfs effect a cleaner, permanent repair.

It didn't matter that fires raged in Kadillus Harbour and the rest of basilica was half in ruins. Here, where he stood, everything was as it should be – or as close as he could get it. What was the point of being a Chaplain if one let the small things go unnoticed?

Pleased with his efforts, he turned and headed back to the others.

NOT A SINGLE window pane remained unbroken, and every inch of the floor was covered with dust and debris. The basilica's wall hangings had all been torn down, many of them burnt beyond recognition. The altar tables had been smashed, their remnants of stone and wood used as barricades. The screens between the main nave and the sanctifying area beneath the gallery had been toppled to block access to the upper levels. Grotesques and statues lay in pieces across the floor.

At the head of the main hall, a single statue stood, four times the height of a man, eyelessly glowering over the scene. It was a figure robed and cowled, face hidden, a bastard sword held between its gauntleted hands, its tip upon the plinth. The folds of the robes were much chipped by gunfire, the white marble stained with soot and blood. At some point during one of the many ork occupations, a greenskin had decided the statue had been lacking and had daubed a line of glyphs down one side in vivid red paint.

Boreas spared no thought for the lone survivor of the battle. For five days since the orks had first stormed the basilica he had battled for control of the shrine. Having had no time for food or drink or sleep, he was sustained wholly by the systems of his armour, and even they were showing signs of fatigue. Battle damage had impaired several of the muscle-like fibre bundles in the suit's limbs, and in particular the right arm jury-rigged by Hephaestus had developed the annoying tendency to seize up if he extended his elbow too swiftly. The air in his helmet had a bitter tang to it, evidence that the filtration systems needed to be cleaned. The Chaplain's veins were constantly abuzz with the stimulants pumping through him, from his own altered organs and the power armour. There was a dull ache inside his gut caused by his implanted organs working so hard to clear out the impurities in the fluids pumped through his blood vessels.

Despite these inconveniences, Boreas was as sharp as ever. He scanned the ruined doorways and windows, eyes searching the buildings on the western side of the basilica for warning of the next ork attack. For the last day the Space Marines had decided against clearing out the corpses, hoping that they would serve as a deterrent to further ork assaults. Flies hovered in a thick swarm over the bloated, bloodied bodies.

Ammunition had been dangerously low for the last two days. That was no longer a problem: Squad Exacta had arrived from the docks, despatched by Master Belial with supplies and information. The company master had confined the orks to the south-eastern arc of the dockyards, an area around the geothermal power station that provided Kadillus Harbour with energy; the master would be sending further reinforcements to Boreas as soon as possible. The Chaplain knew he had only to keep the basilica safe for a few more hours – and the ork lines broken – before the Dark Angels 3rd Company would be united again.

'Do you think that the orks understand their predicament, Brother-Chaplain?' asked Sergeant

Andrael. His ad-hoc squad, drawn from across the 3rd Company, were positioned behind a line of upturned desks and lecterns brought down from the upper floors before the gallery had been cut off.

'It is possible, but not likely, brother-sergeant,' Boreas replied. 'I do not think their tactical observation skills would recognise the threat to their position.'

The telltale rattle of debris drew the attention of all the Space Marines, weapons swinging to point at the western doors and windows. The noises stopped for a second and then a throaty roar engulfed the basilica as green-skinned warriors poured into the building, charging across the street and through the splintered doors, more of them clambering over the sills of the demolished windows.

The war-cry of the orks was met by a thunderous salvo of fire from the Dark Angels. Boreas fired his bolt pistol into the mass of aliens plunging through a window to his left. Torrents of flame erupted from his right, engulfing a mob surging through the doorway. The feeling of repetition was startling. This scene had been played out a dozen times already: sometimes the orks forced the Space Marines to withdraw; other times they were beaten back before they could establish a foothold. With victory so close, the Chaplain was determined that it would be the latter this time around.

As more greenskins poured into the hall, Boreas fired without pause, every bolt finding a target, emptying the magazine of his pistol. He reloaded quickly and wondered for a moment if the greenskins had, against his expectation, recognised the plight of their position and were making one last push towards their leaders in the harbour. It seemed inconceivable that this many orks did not make up their remaining forces in the centre of the city.

Despite the heavy toll taken by the flamer and bolters of the Dark Angels, the greenskins reached the barricades. Alien and Space Marine traded blows across the splintered wood and piles of rubble. Boreas parried a buzzing chainaxe aimed at his head and smashed the brow of his helmet into the wielder's face, splitting the skin with a deep gash. A rivulet of blood trickled from the wound. The ork stepped back, licked the thick fluid from its lips and launched itself at the Chaplain with a snarl. Boreas fired his bolt pistol into its gut as he caught the whirring blade on the haft of his crozius. Blood and intestines erupted over the broken plascrete and the ork fell back. The Chaplain stepped up into the space the ork had occupied and swung his crozius at the back of another's head, caving in the creature's skull.

A sputtering rocket caught the Chaplain in the chest, knocking him sideways. As he extended his leg to keep balance, the rubble shifted under his weight, falling in a small rockslide that sent him toppling backwards. Twisting to right himself as he fell, Boreas stuck out his right arm. He cursed the instinctive move as the elbow joint whined and locked in position, jarring his whole arm as he crashed onto the floor. Ork boots and blades rained down on him as he struggled to roll to his back, encumbered by the useless arm. His vision blurred as something crashed into his head.

He kicked out as best he could, sending three orks toppling down, their leg bones shattered. With a grunt, he heaved himself onto his right side, fending off the orks with the crozius in his left hand. A heavy blade connected with his left wrist, shearing through the armoured seal into the bone within. Boreas's hand spasmed and he let go of his crozius, the gleaming eagle-headed weapon clattering out of view beneath stamping ork feet.

Peliel arrived at that moment, a blue-bladed power sword in his fist. The sergeant carved through neck and limb, cutting down half a dozen orks as he fought his way through the press to stand protectively over the fallen Chaplain. With a few seconds' respite, Boreas was able to heave himself half-upright. He grabbed onto Peliel's backpack to pull himself the rest of the way up. The Chaplain's right arm jutted uselessly out to one side, pistol still in hand. He swung his whole body to direct the weapon at the orks and fired the three bolts remaining in the weapon.

Two more of Peliel's squad waded in with bolters and knives, pushing the orks back to the doorway. Boreas powered down the energy to his right arm and let the limb flop uselessly. His eyes scoured the floor for his crozius, but he could see no sign of it amongst the debris.

Boreas and his companions were slowly forced along the hall towards the statue. Another storm of gunfire engulfed them. Peliel went down, a lucky hit exploding through the exposed seal around his neck. Boreas stooped to pick up the fallen sergeant's sword just as a grenade landed at his feet. The detonation threw the

Space Marine back against the statue plinth and sent the weapon flying in the opposite direction. In the smoke and confusion, Boreas found himself cut off from the others, one arm useless and without a weapon.

A burst of plasma fire from Squad Exacta at the far end of the hall cut through the orks, vaporising their bodies with white-hot balls of energy. In the moment of distraction this provided, Boreas slipped behind the plinth and analysed the situation.

Andrael and Squad Exacta were penned in beneath the gallery. No more orks were coming in from the street; those within appeared to be the last. Several dozen of them exchanged fire with the Space Marines from behind the columns and piles of rubble. To his right, Boreas spotted a small group sneaking through the gloom, trying to outflank Exacta's position. He recognised the telltale glitter of power weapons in their hands – these must have been the same orks that had pushed Peliel from the catacombs days before.

The Chaplain took an instinctive step towards the orks but stopped himself. Even with both hands he would be unlikely to overcome them unarmed. He cast about for a discarded knife or bolter or anything he could use as a weapon. Seeing nothing, his gaze was drawn up to the massive statue. There was only a small gap between the stone Dark Angel and the wall. Boreas pushed himself into the space and pulled himself up a few metres with his good arm, pushing with his legs.

Bracing his shoulder against the plascrete of the wall, Boreas bent his knees and drew his feet up, placing them against the back of the statue. Diverting what power he could spare to the leg servos, the Chaplain thrust out with all of his considerable strength. Thick, waxy sweat beaded on his brow as he strained every muscle. Orange warning lights flickered to red as the power armour fibre bundles fought against the weight of the statue.

A loud crack resounded across the hall as the statue broke from its plinth. It tottered forwards and then settled back again.

'For the Lion!' Boreas roared, pushing with every ounce of his strength.

Slowly at first but gathering speed, the statue fell. With ponderous grace, it crashed down onto the orks, smashing them into the rubble, shattering into shards that cut down those that had survived the impact. With nothing to brace against, Boreas plummeted to the floor, head bouncing off the wall before slamming into the plinth.

Ears thudding, half-blinded, Boreas dragged himself to his feet. Supporting himself on the edge of the plinth, he limped through the rubble to see the results of his handiwork. There were mashed body parts beneath the broken remains of the statue, and several orks crawled away trailing blood through the dust. Zamiel's flamer crackled, engulfing the surviving orks with a sheet of burning promethium. The racket of bolters died down and silence descended.

'All enemies purged, Brother-Chaplain.' Andrael's voice was quiet and hissed with static over the comm.

Boreas looked across the nave of the basilica. There were greenskin dead heaped amongst the rubble; the head of the shattered statue leant against the crushed remains of an ork. In his mind he did not see the smashed windows, the charred and ripped tapestries, the hacked and burnt wood. He saw the basilica as it would be again, filled with the light of lanterns and thousands of candles, echoing to the solemn recitals of the Dark Angels and their serfs. At the lecterns and illuminating desks on the ravaged floors above, the scribes would again copy out the great texts of the Chapter, recording and refreshing the wisdom of the Emperor and the Lion.

Sometimes you had to bring a thing to the brink of destruction to preserve it, so that it could be built anew from the ruins; just as had happened with the Dark Angels themselves.

'Praise the Lion for his enduring will,' Boreas said.

FROM THE WALL tower, Boreas could see the smoke and dust of the forces to the east moving into position along Koth Ridge. To the west and south, there was still vicious fighting around the harbour, where the orks were holed up around the power plant.

'It's only a matter of time, Brother Boreas.'

The Chaplain turned and saw Master Belial striding into the tower from the curtain wall. He was wearing full armour, his personal standard hanging from a back banner, the white robes of the Deathwing over his green armour. Beneath the robe was evidence of the master's fight with the ork warlord, and Boreas could only guess at the injuries Belial had sustained.

'This will be a great victory for the Dark Angels,' the company commander said. 'Intelligence suggests that our foe is the warlord Ghazghkull, the infamous Beast of Armageddon. Many will be the honours from the Chapter for destroying this monster.'

'Indeed, brother-captain,' said Boreas. 'I have drawn up a list of battle-brothers suitable for extraordinary mention to Grand Master Azrael when we join up with the Chapter, both living and posthumous.'

'I expect there will be more names to add to the roll before we are done here,' replied Belial. 'The orks' landing site is somewhere to the east. Our forces occupy Koth Ridge to prevent any further reinforcements reaching the city, but that is just a precaution. I cannot imagine that the remaining ork strength outside Kadillus Harbour is any threat.'

'Will we be attacking the landing site, brother-captain?'

Belial directed a long look at Boreas and there was a hint of humour in his tone when he spoke.

'You wish to be involved in the assault? While the will might remain as strong as ever, I fear your armour and body must first be healed, as must mine. I will think on it. As yet, the landing site has not been located. We will see what sort of enemy awaits us. It may be that our foes are few enough in number to finish with orbital bombardment. Before that, we must drive the orks out of the defence-laser silo they have occupied in the docks. Though it is unlikely the orks understand how to operate the weapon, I am not willing to risk the *Unrelenting Fury* in low orbit while it is still in enemy hands.'

'Do you think it was the defence laser Ghazghkull wanted when he took the city, brother-captain?'

'It is a distinct possibility. Possession of the defence laser negates the orbital supremacy handed to us when the orks landed their ship. I am certain the ork ship is still on the surface: no launch has been detected. When we retake the defence laser, the *Unrelenting Fury* will add orbital firepower to the arsenal at my command.'

'When do you expect to signal the Chapter with news of our victory here?'

Belial turned to the window and gazed east out of the armoured glass.

'Very soon. With the combined might of the Third Company and the Piscina Free Militia, the ork resistance in the city will be crushed. I have Scouts and Ravenwing squadrons searching for the remnants of the orks outside the city. *Xenos temperitus acta mortis.* It will not take long to eradicate the last of this filth.'

THE TALE OF NAAMAN
Cut and Run

'UNDERSTOOD, BROTHER-CAPTAIN,' SAID Sergeant Aquila. 'We will continue to sweep for enemy activity.'

Scout-Sergeant Naaman waited expectantly as the Ravenwing sergeant switched off the comm-unit mounted on his heavily armoured motorbike. The black-armoured Aquila walked slowly across the road to where the Scout-sergeant was waiting with his squad.

'We have new orders?' asked Naaman.

'Negative,' replied Aquila. 'We are to continue patrolling the Koth–Indola highway. Master Belial believes there may be some dawdling ork forces still moving towards Kadillus Harbour from the landing site.'

'Which landing site would that be, Brother Aquila?' asked Naaman. He spoke quietly and moved away from the Scout squad lying in the grass along the side of the road, their attention fixed to the east; there was no need for them to overhear two sergeants arguing.

'I do not understand your question, Brother Naaman. The ork landing site, of course.'

'The landing site that we have not yet located?'

'Yes,' replied Aquila. Evidently he did not understand the implications of Naaman's question or was choosing to ignore them. The Scout-sergeant suppressed his irritation and kept his voice even.

'That would be the same site where the orks landed without being detected, would it?'

'No sensor is one hundred per cent reliable, Sergeant Naaman. You know as well as I do that even the most dense security screen might fail to detect a single ship entering orbit.'

'I agree, Brother Aquila. It does surprise me that the ship that happens to have eluded detection on this occasion is large enough to disgorge many thousands of orks directly to the surface of the planet. If one ship has been capable of this, it stands to reason that there may be others, or that the ship still contains forces that present a viable threat to our position.'

'Master Belial's orders are quite specific, Naaman.' The omission of the sergeant's honorific was an indication that Aquila was losing patience with the conversation. 'If such forces do exist, the squads spread across the eastern approaches to Koth Ridge will detect them. That is precisely why we are here and why we will be following Master Belial's command.'

'It is my belief that we should scout further eastwards, beyond Indola and into the East Barrens. If there are further forces, it would be wise to detect them as early as possible in order that Master Belial can consider the most appropriate response.'

Aquila shook his head and strode back to his bike. Naaman followed a step behind, unwilling to let his battle-brother simply end the conversation by walking away. Aquila swung his leg over the seat of the bike and looked at Naaman.

'Why do you persist with this fear that the orks continue to pose a credible threat?'

Naaman shrugged. He enjoyed the gesture, only possible because his armour was much lighter than that of the regular battle-brothers. For him the greater ease of movement allowed by his wargear was symbolic of his role as a sergeant in the 10th Company. Like his armour, that role also had a significant downside: it offered less protection.

'It is not a fear, it is a concern. I am cautious by inclination, and I would rather not have the future battle-brothers of the Dark Angels under my command encounter an enemy that they cannot overcome. It is our purpose to ascertain this sort of information for the company master and the reason why my squad and others were attached to Belial's command. It is a waste of our abilities to restrain us to this sort of front-line patrolling.'

'Do you not think it is good experience for your charges? When they become full battle-brothers they must have the discipline to carry out these tedious but necessary duties. Perhaps you would have preferred secondment to some other, more glorious command?'

Naaman laughed.

'It is Master Belial's right to choose how and when he deploys his Scouts. That he chose to keep us from the fighting in Kadillus, as he put it "for our own protection", is entirely within his right. I am suggesting that we interpret his orders in such a way that we gather as much intelligence as possible regarding the situation to the east.'

Aquila thumbed the bike into life and his next words were barked over the throbbing engine.

'Orders are not interpreted, Naaman; they are followed. Remember that.'

The Ravenwing sergeant gunned the bike and set off in a slew of grit and dust. As he leaned the bike over onto the highway, the other four members of his squad roared into formation behind him. Soon they were lost behind the brow of a hill, heading in the direction of the Indola Mines.

Naaman returned to his Scouts, who were still patiently laying up along the roadside.

'On your feet,' he told them. 'Form up for a march.'

'Yes, brother-sergeant,' the Scouts chorused as they straightened in the long grass.

Kudin, the eldest of the squad and unofficial corporal, saluted Naaman with a fist to his eagle-blazoned chestplate. He was the most advanced of all the Scouts under Naaman's command, fully a head taller than his brethren – almost as tall as Naaman. It was likely that Naaman would recommend him as suitable for graduation from the 10th Company when this business on Piscina was settled. Then he would undergo the last transformative operations that would turn him into a full Space Marine. It was also then that he would be fully inculcated into the Chapter's creed and given his new name. Scout Kudin would cease to exist, all trace of his past life forgotten, and a battle-brother of the Dark Angels would be born. Kudin's presence was a source of pride to the others in the squad, none of whom had been in the 10th Company for more than two years.

Naaman saw the unspoken question written in Kudin's features.

'You have something you wish to ask, Scout Kudin?'

The Scout wiped a gloved hand through his close-cropped black hair, and glanced at the others before he spoke.

'We have noticed that there is an unusual tension between you and Sergeant Aquila, sergeant.'

'Have you?' Naaman's glare passed over the line of Scouts. Each of them bowed his head in submission rather than meet his gaze, even Kudin. 'As you know, when two battle-brothers of equal rank fight together, the seniority of command is determined by length of service. I have been a Dark Angel for several years longer than Sergeant Aquila. However, Scout assignments are secondary to seniority, for we are not part of the Third Company's standard command. In those circumstances, preference of ranks goes to those brothers and officers of the company. What does that mean, Scout Teldis?'

Teldis looked up, surprised by the question.

'That both you and Sergeant Aquila have equal authority?'

'No, Scout Teldis,' Naaman replied with a shake of his head. He looked at Keliphon.

'Sergeant Aquila has seniority?' suggested the Scout.

Naaman sighed with disappointment. He threw a

hopeful look at Kudin, who rounded angrily on the other Scouts.

'Sergeant Aquila is from the Ravenwing! He is also on secondment to the Third Company and that means neither he nor Sergeant Naaman have explicit authority. Pay attention and learn to fill in the gaps of the information you have to hand.'

'Does that not mean that your seniority becomes relevant, sergeant?' asked Keliphon. 'Don't you have authority?'

'Yes it does,' said Naaman quietly. 'However, Sergeant Aquila has related orders from the company commander, so it doesn't matter which of us has the final say. Master Belial instructs us to patrol to the east, and that is what we are going to do. Contrary to any suspicions I may have, Master Belial has laid out the course of action we will follow.'

The Scouts acknowledged this information with nods. In silence they fell into line behind Naaman as he headed down the road with bolter in hand. He was content to leave the more rigid Chapter teachings to the Chaplains; he considered it his duty to introduce an element of flexible thinking to the recruits under his command. Intransigence and unthinking dogma did not encourage suitably fluid tactical thinking. Doctrine was the beginning of tactical awareness, not the end. For all that, he would be the last brother to suggest to the Scouts that the chain of command could be ignored – quite literally if the Chaplains ever heard that he had done such a thing.

They had covered about a mile when the sergeant spoke again.

'Of course, when we reach Indola, I will have the conversation with Sergeant Aquila again.'

'Do you think he will change his mind?' asked Kudin.

'Probably not. But remember the teachings of the Chaplains: stubbornness is a virtue. I may yet wear him down...'

KOTH RIDGE DROPPED down to the East Barrens, the rocky highland giving way to a gentler slope at the base of the main dormant volcano that formed the island of Kadillus. The Scouts continued along the highway as it stretched towards the horizon, cutting directly east through the fields of long grass. Low cloud smeared across the mountainside, blanketing everything with the hue of slate. Naaman heard the chatter of birds and the rustling of foraging animals. Insects buzzed across the tips of the grass stalks. The ever-present westerly wind rustled through patches of short, thorny bushes that sprouted haphazardly in the lee of rocks. Now and then he caught the scent of something decaying out of sight: the mouldering remains of those that had lost the tooth-and-claw fight for survival.

The edges of the road were littered with detritus from the main ork advance: piles of dung; discarded bones and food scraps; expended ammunition cases; oil cans; broken gears; bent nails; pieces of tattered clothing; sheared bolts; and various other pieces of rubbish whose origins and purpose could not be identified.

The road itself bore scars of the orkish progress.

Weathered and cracked with age, the rockcrete was mark by skid marks of tyre rubber and the welts of heavy tracks. Potholes marked its surface where the tramp of ork feet and the ploughing of ork vehicles had caused parts of the road to subside.

And all about was the ever-present odour of the greenskins: a mustiness in the air that lingered in the nostrils and clung to clothes.

He ignored these background distractions, senses tuned for the abnormal, the irregular: signs of danger. The growl of the Ravenwing bikes had receded from hearing more than an hour ago, but the oil of their exhausts still hung in the air. He caught the distant stench of something fouler and waved the Scouts to leave the road and head northwards, following the source of the smell. A few hundred metres from the wide stripe of rockcrete, Keliphon signalled that he had found something. While Ras and Teldis stood watch with their sniper rifles, Naaman and the others investigated a swathe of flattened grass.

It had been trampled by many booted feet – undoubtedly a gang of orks had passed from the road on some unknown purpose. After following its course for a few minutes, Naaman came across an ork corpse. It was lying face down in the flattened grass, flies buzzing around it. The body had been stripped except for a few scraps of clothing. The exposed skin showed dozens of bloody wounds in the arms and back, as if the ork had been set upon by a number of foes. With his boot, Naaman turned the alien to its back. Gasses wheezed from the slashes to its chest and gut, causing the Scouts to turn away in disgust.

'Look at it!' snapped Naaman. The Scouts reluctantly obeyed, covering their mouths and noses with their hands. 'What do you see?'

The Scouts crowded hesitantly around the body.

'It's dead,' ventured Kudin.

'Are you sure?' asked Naaman.

'Yes,' the Scout replied. 'Orks are rank when living, but this is decomposition. Experience says that ork wounds do not get infected. There is something in the blood which stops gangrene and other blood poisons. It is one of the things that makes them such dangerous foes.'

'Good, Kudin.' Naaman looked at the others. 'Anything else?'

'Its teeth are missing,' said Gethan. The Scout bent closer to the creature's face and pulled back its lips, exposing bare gums. 'They even took its teeth.'

'Who took its teeth?' asked Naaman.

'Whoever robbed it,' replied Gethan. 'The body's been stripped of all armour and weapons, even the boots and teeth are gone. It looks like this one was set upon by others and killed, rather than falling dead and then being looted.'

'There's a strange substance in the wounds,' said Keliphon. He pulled out his knife and scraped it over a gash in the ork's chest. Strands of white fibrous mould clung to the blade.

'Spores,' said Naaman. 'You'll find them on all orkish dead. Ork bodies have to be burnt to ensure the spores do not spread. When this present threat is dealt with, the Free Militia will have to cleanse the whole area where the orks have been. I expect the docks in the city will have to be torched and rebuilt.'

'What do the spores do?' asked Ras.

Naaman looked at the crushed grass and saw its route bending back towards the road. It seemed likely that the ork, or a group of orks, had wandered away from the others and had been attacked. The robbery completed, the survivors had headed back to join the main body. There was nothing of significance here.

'Form up to continue the patrol eastwards. We'll stay off the road until nightfall.'

'What do the spores do, sergeant?' Ras asked again as the squad spread into an uneven line and set off through the waist-high grass.

'I don't know,' Naaman replied. 'Better to be sure with this sort of thing. All sorts of xenos breed in all sorts of ways. It is never a waste to eradicate all evidence of their presence after victory: their bodies, their constructions, their weapons. Utter annihilation ensures no regrets.'

With a last distasteful look at the deceased ork, Naaman set off after the squad as the cloud-shrouded sun sank beneath the shoulder of Koth Ridge.

DARKNESS HAD ENVELOPED the Scouts for more than two hours by the time they reached the tatty chainlink fence that marked the boundary of the disused Indola Mines. Poorly fastened, rusting sheet metal roofs rattled and creaked in the wind. The great lift tower over the mine shaft stood out against the semicircle of one of Piscina's three moons, the girders and gears a skeletal remnant of the industry that had once taken place here before the mine had been exhausted.

A yellow glow dominated the open space between the

worker shacks and the remains of the ore storage houses. From the open doorway of a large building that had once housed the ore transporters, the light of lamps shone. Large shadows moved across the yellow glare, tall and bulky: Aquila's Ravenwing.

'Sergeant Naaman and squad moving to your position from the west,' Naaman broadcast over the comm. 'No enemy detected.'

'Outpost established in the vehicle maintenance hangar,' came Aquila's reply. 'No enemy detected by our sweep, either. No further patrols necessary until dawn. Rest your squad with us, Naaman.'

'Will join you shortly, Aquila,' Naaman finished. He cut the link and ghosted through the darkness, the Scouts behind him.

The bikes of the Ravenwing squadron were formed into a small laager inside the cavernous maintenance garage, arranged so that their lights – and forward-mounted twin bolters – were pointing towards the entrances. Aquila and his Space Marines had made a rough camp from the remains of parts crates and ore containers. Three of them sat hunched on these improvised seats while two of them did the rounds of the perimeter. Brother Aramis raised a hand in greeting as the Scouts emerged from the shadows. Naaman answered with a nod of his head and directed his squad to rest up.

Aquila looked across the hangar as Naaman entered the circle of light. The Ravenwing sergeant had taken off his helmet, revealing a narrow-cheeked face and sunken eyes. His shoulder-length hair was swept back by a silver band, decorated with a single black pearl at his brow. His right cheek was tattooed with a red rendition of the Dark Angels' winged blade insignia – the symbol of the Ravenwing. Anybody other than a Space Marine might have described him as darkly handsome. Such considerations never occurred to the Astartes.

'No unexpected second ork wave?' asked Aquila. The corner of his lips lifted in a slight smile. 'No green-skinned ambushers waiting for us?'

Naaman sat down opposite Aquila and smiled back.

'Not today, at least,' said the Scout-sergeant. 'There is always tomorrow, of course.'

'Of course,' echoed Aquila. 'Perhaps your missing orks were delayed by an important engagement. A society event, maybe?'

Naaman laughed at the image conjured in his mind. He had no idea about Aquila's background before becoming a Dark Angel – the Scout-sergeant could little remember his own childhood – but he guessed from the sardonic wit that it had been very different from Naaman's upbringing in the deserts of Kalabria. There had been no 'society events' that Naaman could recall, only a daily grind for survival.

'Perhaps they protect their landing zone, expecting their army to return in victory,' suggested Naaman.

'Unlikely,' replied Aquila. 'Orks don't strike me as the type to give up the chance to loot a city so that they can stand around guarding a ship.'

'You're right,' sighed Naaman, conceding that his suspicions were entirely unfounded. 'It seems that Master Belial will soon be able to send word to the Chapter of a notable victory over the orks.'

'Ghazghkull, no less,' added Brother Demael from

Naaman's right. The Scout-sergeant's eyes widened with surprise. 'We received word today that the ork forces are led by the Beast of Armageddon.'

'That would be a prize for the Third Company, a grand prize indeed,' said Naaman. He glanced at his companions before adding, 'And the Ravenwing, of course.'

'The Tenth shall share in the glory also,' Aquila said generously, raising a fist in salute to Naaman. 'The Beast of Armageddon, who escaped the Blood Angels, Salamanders and Ultramarines, now to be crushed by the might of the Dark Angels!'

'All the more reason to ensure Ghazghkull has no means of escape,' said Naaman. 'He has proved elusive and cunning for an ork warlord. Let us not repeat the mistakes of other Chapters...'

'The Beast is trapped in Kadillus Harbour, with the Third Company and almost the entirety of the defence force to keep him caged,' said Brother Analeus, the Ravenwing squadron's plasma gunner. 'Ghazghkull's an ork, not some wretched eldar! He won't be getting off Piscina.'

'I agree with you, brother, I really do,' said Naaman, turning to face the Ravenwing Space Marine. 'But to ensure that absolutely, would it not be better to secure the means by which he reached the planet in the first place?'

'If he were to try to escape by ship, it would have to land at Northport on the outskirts of Kadillus Harbour,' said Aquila. 'That would be impossible.'

'I am sure Commander Dante and the other noble leaders on Armageddon believed escape was impossible,' said Naaman. 'It is highly improbable; taking that ship would make it impossible.'

'Why are you so determined to head east, Naaman?' asked Analeus. 'This could be interpreted as an unhealthy obsession.'

Naaman laughed again.

'You are probably correct, brother,' he said. The Scout-sergeant grew serious and glanced to his squad who were sat beside the rusting hulk of an old ore hauler. 'Being in the Tenth Company engenders a certain obsession with obtaining all of the facts, no matter how inconsequential they turn out to be. We find it ensures the continued survival of our future battle-brothers.'

'It is time to perform our evening dedications,' announced Aquila, standing up. He looked at Naaman. 'You and your squad are welcome to join us.'

'That would be good, brother,' said Naaman, also standing. He called to his squad to join them. 'It would be wise not to leave ourselves without sentry, though. I will stand guard while you perform your dedications.'

'You do not wish to join us, Naaman?' The feeling of offence was clear in Aquila's tone.

'I will make my own dedications while I keep my watch,' Naaman replied. 'Tomorrow, one of your brothers can take the duty and I will make my dedications with you.'

Aquila seemed mollified by this reply and nodded. The two Space Marines walking sentry came into the hangar and Naaman left them kneeling in a circle as Aquila began to chant.

'Today we served again under the watchful eye of the

Emperor and the Lion. Today we lived again under the protection of the Emperor and the Lion. Today we fought again...'

Naaman allowed the words to drift from his attention as he stepped out into the night. He made his way to the rusting tower of the mine-workings and climbed a ladder to the first platform. From here he could see the whole of the Indola Mines. Unslinging his bolter, he began to pace around the platform, eyes scanning the darkness for any movement, ears tuning out the rasp of the wind and the creaking of the ramshackle buildings.

In his thoughts he gave praise to the Lion for the teachings he had passed on to the Dark Angels, the same teachings Naaman now passed on to future generations of Space Marines. One in particular kept coming back to him: 'Knowledge is power, guard it well.' Knowledge. It was knowledge Naaman sought. Knowledge of how the orks had come to Piscina undetected; knowledge of how many of them were left outside the city; knowledge of what threat still remained. He paused in his slow circling and stared to the east.

Hundreds of square kilometres of wilderness stretched out in that direction; enough space to hide an army, certainly enough to hide a starship large enough to carry an army. The news that the foe they faced was Ghazghkull perturbed him. Ghazghkull was no ordinary warlord. News regarding his invasion of the world of Armageddon had been spread by the Ultramarines, Blood Angels and Salamanders, sent to every Chapter that would listen. That an ork warlord could cause so much havoc, inflict so much destruction and escape retribution was remarkable enough.

That he had continued to elude the Imperial forces sent in pursuit was almost unheard of. Such warmongering fiends only rarely disappeared, and always made some fatal mistake, either of overconfidence or out of sheer brutality. Ghazghkull had not only escaped the carnage of Armageddon, he had been able to rebuild his strength and stay ahead of the forces sent to destroy him. To appear here, hundreds of light years from where he was last seen, did not bode well.

Ghazghkull's presence explained many things that had seemed incredible earlier, most particularly the single-minded nature of the orks' attack on the city and their drive for control of the harbour. Master Belial believed he had Ghazghkull trapped, encircled by forces around the Kadillus Harbour power plant. Belial was not so sure Ghazghkull wasn't exactly where he wanted to be. And if that was the case, it begged an answerable question: what did Ghazghkull want with a power plant?

Naaman took up his circuit again, troubled by his thoughts. Knowledge. Knowledge would see the Beast truly trapped, and that did not lie in Kadillus Harbour, but in the East Barrens, where the orks had come from.

The Scout-sergeant reached a decision. Come first light, no matter the arguments of Sergeant Aquila, Naaman and his Scouts would not be heading back to Koth Ridge. They would continue eastwards to find out what was there.

* * *

'ENEMY DETECTED.'

At those two words buzzing in his ear from the comm-bead, Naaman was instantly awake. He scrambled to his feet, bolter in hand. A look around brought the pleasing sight of his squad alert and armed as well.

'Movement to the north-east, three hundred metres.'

'Will investigate,' replied Naaman. 'Stand by for report and orders.'

The sergeant nodded to his Scouts and the squad set off at a jog, out the doors of the hangar to cut through the buildings to the north. With a glance over his shoulder Naaman saw Brother Barakiel climbing down from his vantage point atop the maintenance shed. Picking up speed he led the Scouts to a long, low outbuilding close to the north-eastern part of the broken fence.

'Confirm enemy and report,' he said to Kudin.

Gethan slung his bolter and cupped his hands, acting as a step for Kudin as he pulled himself onto the flat roof of the shed. The senior Scout crossed with quiet footsteps and hunkered down, bringing the scope of his sniper rifle up to his eye. Naaman took position at the corner of the building and looked eastwards through the ragged links of the fence. The first fringes of dawn were touching the horizon and he could see the faint darker shapes in the gloom that had alerted Brother Barakiel.

'Ten orks, advancing directly towards us,' hissed Kudin. 'Two hundred and fifty metres beyond the perimeter. No discernible formation or precaution. No other forces within sight.'

Naaman nodded to himself with satisfaction. By

Kudin's assessment, the orks were unaware of the Space Marines and were probably heading to the mine for some other reason. He activated the comm-bead.

'Sergeant Naaman to Sergeant Aquila,' he said.

The comm buzzed for a second.

'This is Aquila,' replied the Ravenwing sergeant. 'What do you see?'

'Small ork unit, ten-strong,' said Naaman. 'Threat minimal. We will engage from here with standard weapons. Suggest you engage when we begin firing.'

'Affirm, Naaman,' said Aquila. 'We will use your fire to mask our engines and loop around from the south.'

'Confirmed, Aquila.'

As Naaman cut the link, he ejected the magazine from his bolter and swapped the gas-propellant silent rounds with a cartridge of standard ammunition from his belt. He gestured for Keliphon to join Kudin on the roof with his sniper rifle, and for the three remaining squad members to take up positions within the shed; the metal sheets of the walls provided enough gaps to use as impromptu loopholes. The sergeant stayed where he was, resting his bolter against the corner of the building to steady his first shots.

They waited while the shapes in the darkness resolved into something more discernible.

'One hundred and fifty metres,' reported Kudin.

In the pre-dawn still, Naaman could hear grunts and growls from the orks. He watched as they continued closer, utterly at ease, arms swinging, strutting through the grass on bowed legs.

'One hundred metres,' said Kudin.

'Engage,' Naaman calmly ordered his squad.

A *chuff-chuff* from the sniper rifles preceded the collapse of two of the greenskins; the orks thrashed in the grass as toxins coursed through their bloodstreams. Naaman pulled the trigger of his bolter, directing his fire at the closest ork, putting three rounds squarely into its chest. The flicker of other bolts broke the gloom. Some scored hits, others missed their mark and whined into the darkness.

The orks were thrown into disarray by the ambush. They brought up their crude automatic rifles and fired randomly, unsure of their attackers' location. Another one fell to sniper fire, his gun blazing in his dying grasp, spitting bullets in all directions. Naaman fired again, the hail of explosive bolts ripping the legs out from an ork as it turned on him.

The orks turned and ran, still firing at unseen foes, the bolts of the Scouts rasping after them. Above the cough of bolters, Naaman could hear the bass timbre of the Ravenwing's bikes. He saw them to his right, in a single line abreast, a moment before the riders switched on their lamps, bathing the orks with harsh white light. The orks continued to run, firing over their shoulders at the swiftly approaching bikers. Muzzle flare erupted from bike-mounted bolters, the hail scything through the few survivors of the Scouts' ambuscade.

The orks collapsed into the grass out of view. Aquila and his Ravenwing pulled out their pistols and continued to fire into the downed greenskins as they sped past, ably steering their bikes one-handed as they bounced and rocked over the uneven ground. At their head, Aquila slewed his bike around, churning up a cloud of dirt from the back wheel of his bike. He fired twice more as the Ravenwing circled and reformed into an arrowhead behind him.

The firing stopped and the only sound to cut the stillness was the noise of the bikes' engines. The Ravenwing followed their sergeant as his course curved towards the northern gate, his honour pennant streaming from a pole behind his saddle.

'Enemy destroyed,' Aquila reported.

'Confirm report,' Naaman said to Kudin. The Scout rose to one knee on the roof and swept to the north and east with his scope.

'No enemy sighted. Confirm report,' he said.

'Stand down,' Naaman told his squad, bringing his bolter up across his chest. 'Return to camp.'

The hangar was hazy with the bikes' exhaust fumes, the *tick-tick-tick* of their cooling engines amplified by the metal walls. Aquila was still astride his bike, a cable from the long-range comm plugged into an opened armour panel on his left forearm. The others had dismounted and were performing post-battle rites on their machines: checking ammunition feeds, cleaning the gun barrels and applying Techmarine-blessed lubricants to the engines. Seeing that the Ravenwing were occupied, Naaman posted Ras and Kudin to stand guard outside.

Naaman sat on one of the crates and stripped out his bolter while he waited for Aquila to finish his report. He cleaned and reassembled the gun without thought, keeping one eye on the Ravenwing sergeant: for such a small engagement Aquila was spending a long time on the comm. Aquila was nodding occasionally and

Naaman could see that his bike display was set to the digimap of the Koth Ridge region. Naaman had finished cleaning his bolter and was clicking replacement bolts into the magazine he had used by the time the Ravenwing sergeant pulled out the comm-cable and swung off his machine.

'Bad news, brother-sergeant?' asked Naaman as Aquila sat down next to him. The metal box sagged under the power-armoured Space Marine.

'A mix, brother-sergeant,' replied Aquila. He still wore his helm so Naaman could see nothing of his expression, but Aquila's slow speech suggested he was picking his words with care. 'Ours is the fifth report of such an encounter in the past three hours. There is a confirmed ork presence in the area east of Koth Ridge, but it is scattered and weak. No Dark Angels casualties suffered. It is Master Belial's assessment that we are encountering stragglers behind the main ork advance. We are to continue to sweep the region for other such survivors and exterminate them immediately.'

'I understand, brother-sergeant,' said Naaman, digesting this news. 'May I use your comm-unit, brother-sergeant?'

'For what purpose?'

'I wish to request a change to our orders so that we might continue further east in an attempt to locate the site of the ork landing zone. If we are able to do so, we can coordinate our coverage against further incursions more effectively.'

'Of course, brother-sergeant,' said Aquila, waving a hand towards his bike. 'Be advised that the brother-captain is occupied with the reduction of the ork position in Kadillus Harbour. He may not think kindly of your wilder suspicions.'

'Thank you for the advice,' replied Naaman, crossing the hangar. 'It is not the brother-captain's kind thoughts I am after, merely his permission.'

Naaman hooked himself into the bike's comm-link and punched in the command frequency codes. He listened to static for a few seconds before Master Belial's curt tone cut through the interference.

'Company captain, identify,' said Belial.

'Veteran Sergeant Naaman of the Tenth Company, brother-captain,' said Naaman.

'You have something to add to Sergeant Aquila's report, brother-sergeant?'

'No, brother-captain. I am requesting to expand our patrol grid fifty kilometres to the east. It is my belief that we should locate the ork landing site as a priority.'

'I concur, Sergeant Naaman,' said Belial, to Naaman's slight surprise. 'Ork forces encountered may be guarding the landing site. If that is true, it suggests to me that the enemy ship is closer to Koth Ridge than I currently believe. A fifty-kilometre extension stretches our cordon too thinly. You may extend your patrol by twenty kilometres. If you have not discovered the landing zone within that distance, it is far enough from Koth Ridge to pose no immediate threat and can be dealt with once we have destroyed the orks in Kadillus Harbour. Confirm orders.'

'Extend patrol grid by twenty kilometres to the east, brother-captain,' said Naaman.

'Good. I want you to find out where these orks are coming from, Naaman. I will also extend patrol sweeps north of your position. Dedicate your duty to the Lion and the Emperor!'

'For the Lion I live, for the Emperor I die!' replied Naaman. The link buzzed in his ear. He cut the connection and unplugged his headset. Naaman directed a smile at Aquila. 'Updated orders, brother-sergeant. We head east!'

THREE HOURS AFTER dawn, Naaman and his squad were occupying a hillock that rose over two hundred metres above the plains beyond Indola. From here he could see the East Barrens all the way to the horizon, the seemingly endless grassland devoid of road or settlement. It was broken by scattered upthrusts of rock like the one on which he stood: the remnants of millennia-dormant volcanic eruptions that had once wracked the whole of Kadillus in the pre-history of Piscina IV.

Bringing his monocular up to his eye, he swept to the left and right, seeking any sign of the ork ship. He found no landing site, but he did detect a haze of smoke a few kilometres to the south. He adjusted the monocular's display and took a range reading: two-point-five kilometres. Too far to be Aquila's squad. He activated his comm-set.

'Sergeant Aquila, are you receiving my signal?'

The Ravenwing sergeant's reply was faint, almost drowned out by the hiss of distance interference. He was obviously at the limit of Naaman's comm range.

'Please confirm your location, brother-sergeant.'

There was a pause while Aquila checked his position.

'We're one-four kilometres from Indola, vector nine-two-zero-eight. Have you found something, Naaman?'

The veteran sergeant checked the monocular again. Two ork buggies plunged through the grass, bouncing wildly over the uneven ground, their thick tyres gouging furrows in the dirt. He could not yet make out the details, but there was some kind of heavy weapon mounted on each buggy. He rechecked the range and heading in the monocular display.

'Confirm visual contact. Two enemy light vehicles. Wheeled. Heavy weapon-armed. Location one-six kilometres from Indola, vector eight-three-five-five. Enemy heading almost directly westwards. They will pass us about three kilometres to the south. Too far for us to intercept.'

'Confirm report, brother-sergeant.' The dry words of the communications protocols did not mask Aquila's apparent delight. 'Have calculated intercept route. No assistance required. Proceed to the twenty-kilometre patrol limit. Will inform you of engagement outcome. Good eyes, Naaman.'

'Confirm, brother-sergeant. *Raptorum est, fraternis eternitas*. Good hunting.'

Naaman switched off the transmission and clipped the monocular back into its pouch at his waist. He waved the squad to their feet.

'Continue to patrol eastwards,' he told them, setting off from the brow of the hill.

'Are we not going to engage the orks, brother-sergeant?' asked Teldis.

'That is not our duty, *Scout* Teldis,' Naaman replied. 'This is the reason we have been paired with Sergeant Aquila's squad. We provide the reconnaissance and he provides the mobility and firepower. Would you like to try running after those buggies? I do not think they will wait for you to catch up.'

As they walked down the slope at brisk pace, Naaman felt another 'teaching' coming on. Eyes still scanning the landscape for signs of the orks, he took a deep breath.

'The Astartes are the culmination of the application of precise force,' he quoted from the *Book of Caliban*, written by the Dark Angels' primarch ten thousand years before. Naaman had heard it so many times, and repeated it almost as often, he entered an almost trance-like state of recollection. 'Through careful consideration of the enemy and the strategic situation, the Astartes commander must conclude the most effective targets for the application of that precise force. It is with offensive, pre-emptive action that the Astartes achieve victory. Central to this assessment must be the gathering of all relevant intelligence pertaining to the enemy's abilities, resources and disposition. There are many means which can be employed in the gathering of these data.

'From orbit, starship-based augurs can detect large population centres; the movement of sizeable bodies of troops; energy networks; vehicle columns; and static defences. On the ground, scanning devices can detect thermal, radioactive, laser, microwave and other energy-based signatures. They can detect sound and vibration, even changes in aquatic temperature and air currents. A number of such devices used in concert may triangulate their findings to determine the enemy position. Even the humble tripwire is a detector that can be employed in this information-gathering.

'But for all the capabilities of these technological marvels, there is a singular truth that all Astartes commanders must accept. This truth is that there is no intelligence greater or more accurate than the testimony of an Astartes looking upon the enemy with his own eyes.'

His verbatim recital concluded, Naaman looked at his Scouts and saw the understanding in their expressions.

'You, my young brothers,' he said, 'are the greatest and most accurate means for detecting the enemy. The Lion said that. When you become battle-brothers and are eager to engage the enemy, remember these words and pay attention to the reports of the Scouts.'

As SUNSET APPROACHED, Naaman and his squad moved northwards along the twenty-kilometre limit of their patrol. They had directed the ferocity of the Ravenwing against the orks twice more that afternoon, spotting two bands of greenskins moving westwards on foot. With the light failing, Naaman signalled a rendezvous point to Aquila and the Scouts set up an observation post on an outcropping of rock. With the thermal scopes of their rifles, Kudin and Keliphon kept watch as night descended. Naaman shared the squad's ration of protein bars and they took cover from the strengthening wind in the lee of the rocks.

The growl of the Ravenwing's engines broke the quiet dark just before midnight. With lights off, the bikers steered through the night using the enhanced vision of their autosenses. Kudin spotted the exhaust plumes of the squad as they approached from the south.

'Squad Aquila, this is Sergeant Naaman. Confirm your approach on our position.'

'Sergeant Naaman, this is Aquila. Confirm approach on your position from the south. One kilometre distant. Have received updated intelligence on enemy activity. Be ready to receive a briefing on my arrival.'

'Confirm, Aquila,' replied Naaman, curious to know what new information had come to light. Perhaps another of the Scout or Ravenwing squads searching the East Barrens had found the ork ship.

It was with some impatience that Naaman waited for Aquila and his bikers. They drove into the shelter of the rocks without comment, and attended to the maintenance of their machines before Aquila gestured for Naaman to join him a short distance away.

'Greetings, brother-sergeant,' said Naaman. 'You do honour to your company and the Chapter with your deeds today.'

'Master Belial contacted me an hour ago, with some grim news,' said Aquila, dispensing with the customary preamble. 'He has lost contact with three patrols on duty east of Koth Ridge. Two Scout squads and one Ravenwing land speeder have failed to report their positions. All three had sporadic enemy contacts throughout the day, increasing in frequency towards nightfall.'

'Failure to report does not mean our brothers are dead,' said Naaman, absorbing this sombre information. 'There is communication interference in Kadillus Harbour, perhaps the orks have some similar device on their ship.'

'That is a possibility,' said Aquila. The Ravenwing

sergeant turned his gaze to the north. 'It is the brother-captain's assessment that these patrols have discovered the location of the ork landing site. Whether due to range, interference or enemy activity, the patrols have been unable to pass on this information. Master Belial has analysed the patrol patterns and believes the ork ship to be located roughly thirty kilometres north-east of where we are. Our orders are to investigate this potential site, attempt to make contact with the Dark Angels forces in the area, and confirm the presence and strength of the enemy.'

'We will set out straight away,' said Naaman, stepping towards the others. Aquila halted him with a hand on the Scout-sergeant's arm.

'There is something else I wish to bring to your attention, Naaman,' said Aquila. 'A matter has been puzzling me these last few hours.'

'Speak freely, Aquila. I will do what I can to make any matter clearer.'

'Seeing you and your charges brought back to me memories of my own time in the Tenth Company. In particular, it reminded of something my sergeant told us: notice not that which is the same, but that which is different.'

'A good lesson, no doubt. It is the breaking of patterns, the irregularities observed, which convey the most information. Have you seen something?'

'I do not know if it is important or not. The orks I have killed today appear different in dress and armament in comparison to those at Kadillus Harbour. Amongst their usual garb, the orks fighting under Ghazghkull display a preference for bold patterns of black, white and red. The ork corpses I have examined after today's encounters wear yellow and orange. I do not understand the significance of this.'

Naaman paced for a moment, pondering the importance of this discovery.

'I have no clear answers for you, but I can add my own speculation if you wish.'

'Please do.'

'I am no expert on ork markings, but from what I understand, colours and symbols are often used to denote allegiance. I would take this to mean that Ghazghkull's force has assimilated several smaller factions under his command. Perhaps these yellow-clad orks are somehow out of favour with their chieftain, hence why they were left behind to guard the ork ship? An alternative theory could be that having been abandoned by their commander, the orks left at the landing site have chosen to form their own faction and split from the main command of Ghazghkull. Ork influence is enforced purely by proximity and physical action. These orks may well have grown bored protecting their ship and are now heading west in search of loot and battle.'

Aquila tapped his fingers against the back of his other hand as he considered this.

'I can see no argument why either of these theories directly impacts on our orders. Observations confirm that the remaining orks outside of Kadillus Harbour have been steadily moving westwards. It may be the case that the landing site is no longer contested. It would be reasonable to assume that this movement would quickly peak as those left behind realise they have been abandoned and set off after the rest of their forces. Perhaps it is this peak in activity that our patrols encountered?'

'That is a distinct possibility. However, we should still proceed with some caution. Orks are unpredictable even in normal circumstances. Given that these orks appear to have no solid leadership, they could be roaming the wilderness at random and the movement westwards only a general trend rather than an absolute.'

'I agree. My squad will provide a roving support while your Scouts move on the objective. *Corvus vigilus*. Separation to be no greater than one kilométre, standard high-risk theatre contact procedures.'

'Confirm. "Alert Raven" formation with one-kilometre separation. We'll watch each other's backs.'

Aquila nodded and held up his fist in salute.

'For the Lion!' he barked.

'For the Lion!' echoed Naaman.

The Scout-sergeant called Kudin to form up the squad while Aquila moved back to the Ravenwing and passed on the plan. The bikers mounted up a few seconds later and were already roaring northwards as Naaman rejoined his Scouts.

'We have a new objective,' he told them as they performed their weapons checks. 'No rest for us. We are heading north-east, night march. From this moment on, the East Barrens are to be considered extremely hostile territory. If you see anything – anything – that looks out of the ordinary, you signal the squad. You will all halt and take cover until I have assessed the threat.'

Naaman walked up and down the line, emphasising his instructions with chopping motions.

'We keep silent. Watch your sector and trust the rest of the squad to watch theirs. No one is to open fire without my order. We will be moving at pace without lights, so equip nightsight goggles and watch your footing.'

He stopped and addressed his next words to Kudin in particular.

'If I fall, you are to immediately withdraw from any engagement when it is safe to do so. You will then head directly back and report to our Chapter forces on Koth Ridge. It may be that some squads have already been lost. There is no asset to protect, no objective that needs to be taken and no civilians to watch over. This is a reconnaissance mission, not a search-and-destroy. Should we encounter stiff resistance, we will withdraw with whatever intelligence we have gained. It is vital, and I mean vital, that Master Belial has as much information as possible regarding ork activity in this area. The only way he can receive that information is if you are alive to deliver it.'

Kudin, Ras and Keliphon nodded their understanding. Gethan and Teldis looked worried. Naaman laid his hands on the shoulders of the squad's youngest members.

'These orders are precautionary,' he told them. 'I have been a Dark Angels Space Marine for one hundred and seventy-four years, the last twenty-six years of which I have spent with the Tenth Company. I have not achieved the rank of veteran sergeant by letting myself get killed.'

The Scouts chuckled at the poor joke but they became serious again when Naaman waved them to begin the march. He fell in at the back of the squad as they set off at a trot, breath puffing mist in the cold air. The sergeant activated the comm-link to Aquila.

'Aquila, this is Naaman. We are on the move towards the objective. Any contact?'

'Negative contact, brother-sergeant,' replied Aquila. 'You are clear for the next kilometre.'

NAAMAN CALLED THE squad to a halt just after dawn. They had reached the intended objective without further encounters with the orks, which vexed the Scout-sergeant. Ahead, the ground heaped up in a series of increasingly steep creases caused by some great seismic shift in a past age. The slopes appeared clear of enemy and a brief look with the monocular revealed no telltale smoke clouds or other evidence of ork activity.

'Aquila, this is Naaman. Do you think we have passed through the ork line in the dark? I see nothing here.'

'Naaman, this is Aquila. We are north of your position, detect no enemy. The landing site is not here. We will withdraw in the direction of Koth Ridge and report our lack of success. There is no secondary ork force.'

'Negative, brother-sergeant. We will continue east. Better to return with solid intelligence than an absence of it.'

'Those are not our orders, Naaman! Master Belial commanded us to investigate this gridpoint. We have done so and it is our duty to return and report the lack of significant ork forces. We will receive fresh orders from the company captain. If he agrees with your assessment, we will return and continue further east.'

'I cannot comply with that assessment, brother-sergeant,' said Naaman, walking away from his squad, voice terse. 'It is a day on foot back to Koth Ridge. To return for fresh orders will delay our search by two days. That is too great a window of uncertainty. As the senior sergeant in action, I am exercising my authority to continue the patrol.'

'Your decision is in error, Naaman. We have already lost forces without report in this region. Master Belial is depending upon us to return with our reports as soon as possible. If further investigation is needed, the company commander will issue those orders. You should make your representations to Master Belial and allow him to decide the best course of action.'

'We have found no evidence of the enemy, nor any evidence that sheds light on the fate of our missing battle-brothers. To withdraw now is premature, Aquila. Let me make my position clear. I *will* lead my squad further east. I am requesting your continued fire support in this move, but if you choose to withdraw it will not affect my decision and we will proceed without support. We are the Tenth Company, we are prepared for such operations.'

There came a growl in reply. Naaman did not wish to put Aquila in this difficult position, but he was intent on discovering what had happened to the other Dark Angels patrols. If that meant the Scouts would go on alone, he was comfortable with the consequences.

'As you say, Naaman. *Persona obstinatum*! I will delay withdrawal and continue in support. It will not be said that Squad Aquila abandoned their brethren of the Tenth Company. I must insist that you agree to an extension of no more than six hours. If we find nothing in that time, you must concede that there is nothing to find.'

'You have my agreement, brother-sergeant. Thank you for indulging my curiosity and caution. The Lion's spirit lives on within.'

'I will raise this matter with Master Belial when we return. I do not think your behaviour befits the position you hold.'

'I understand, Aquila, and I appreciate your candour. I will accept full responsibility for my decision.'

'Good. Now that we have settled this, let us make sure nothing untoward happens.'

'I agree. I hope that you are right and I am wrong, brother-sergeant.'

Naaman killed the link and walked back to his squad.

'We will head for that first ridgeline. I want to have an observation post there by noon. Ready for march.'

Naaman glared at the rising ground ahead, as if his stare alone could force it to yield its secrets. There was more happening on Piscina than he or anybody else could guess; of that he was certain. There were more orks here, of that he was equally certain. He just had to find them.

TWO HOURS ON, Naaman and his squad were halfway to the line of hills breaking up the East Barrens. Other than the routine check-in comms, he had not conducted any further exchanges with Aquila, so it came as a surprise when the comm buzzed in his ear.

'Naaman, this is Aquila. Direct your attention southeast of your current position. What do you see on the ridgeline?'

Naaman took out his monocular and looked along the line of hills from left to right. With the first sweep he saw nothing. Knowing that Aquila would not have contacted him for confirmation without being sure there was something to see, Naaman swept the hill again.

He stopped, adjusting the focus. There was a dark haze rising from behind the hills in the direction Aquila had suggested. It was being quickly dispersed by the strong wind pushing over the ridge, but it was definitely there.

'Aquila, this is Naaman. It looks like heat haze and possible exhaust pollution. Is that what you are seeing?'

'Confirm, brother-sergeant. The location appears to correlate roughly to the position of the East Barrens geothermal site.'

'Another energy plant? What would the orks want with that?'

'I would not hazard an opinion on the subject, brother-sergeant. It is a confirmed ork presence. We should withdraw and report.'

'It could just be smouldering buildings, burnt while the orks advanced. We haven't confirmed anything yet, Aquila. It is only a few kilometres away.'

'Is there any point in debating this, Naaman?'

'None, brother-sergeant. Let us go and have a look.'

The comm crackled loudly as Aquila sighed.

'All right, Naaman. We'll take the lead, follow us up the ridge.'

'Confirm, brother-sergeant. We are heading off now.'

The Scouts crossed the broken ground at speed, dispersed in a wide formation, weapons ready. Naaman kept glancing in the direction of the mysterious haze to confirm its location. After they had covered a little more than a kilometre, he called the squad to an abrupt halt. There was something strange about the scattered smoke. He used the monocular again to fix on the drifting cloud. It was darker, heavier. The wind did not seem to have altered, so the greater concentration of fumes meant one of two things. Either the source was growing stronger, or the source was coming closer…

Naaman swung the monocular sight across the ridgeline, looking for Aquila's squad. He found them on the third attempt, riding slowly up a rocky ravine about half a kilometre from the crest, two kilometres ahead of the Scouts. Naaman urgently activated the comm, still staring through the monocular.

'Pull back, Aquila!'

There was a frustrating delay before Aquila answered. The Ravenwing squadron were disappearing behind a lip of rock.

'Naaman, this is Aquila. Repeat your last communication.'

Naaman took a deep breath, aware that his squad were watching him closely. His hearts were already beating rapidly, blood and hormones surging through his system, readying him for battle. He had to keep calm and clear.

'Aquila, this is Naaman. The cloud is exhaust fume. I believe a sizeable ork force, including motorised elements, is beyond the ridge and moving in our direction.'

'Confirm, brother-sergeant. What is your estimate of enemy force size?'

'Inconclusive. Prevailing wind speed is dispersing the cloud. Accounting for the general pollution level of ork engines, I think there are several vehicles in close proximity to each other.'

'Sergeant Naaman!' The call came from Kudin, who was looking through his sniper scope at a point on the ridgeline almost directly east of the Scouts. 'Enemy sighted!'

'Withdraw from your position, brother-sergeant,' Naaman snapped over the comm even as he redirected his monocular towards the area where Kudin was keeping watch. 'Enemy approaching from north of your position.'

Coming over the ridge were several dozen orks on foot. Naaman's attention was wrenched back to the right by the crack of a large detonation. A plume of fire and smoke issued from the gorge where the Raven-wing were advancing.

'Enemy ambush!' Aquila snarled over the comm. Gunfire rattled along the hillside, quickly drowned out by the thudding thrum of bolters echoing along the cleft. 'They were waiting at the head of the gulley with tripmines and grenades. Brother Carminael is dead, bike destroyed. No assistance required.'

Another explosion rocked the ridgeline. Naaman snapped his attention back to the orks advancing over the hills. There were at least fifty of them now, some of them heavily armoured and armed. The orks continued down the ridge, a spreading blot of green and yellow.

'Enemy attackers destroyed, withdrawing to your position,' reported Aquila.

'Negative, Aquila. The orks have not seen us yet. Do not draw attention to our position. We will withdraw undetected. Rendezvous two kilometres west of our position.'

'Confirm, Naaman. Two kilometres west.'

'Squad, listen,' said Naaman, quiet but insistent. 'You will withdraw immediately and directly to the west. Join up with Squad Aquila at two kilometres.'

'What are you going to do, sergeant?' asked Teldis.

'I will continue to make observations of the enemy,' said Naaman. 'I will rejoin you shortly. Move out!'

The Scout-sergeant hadn't moved his eye from the monocular throughout the exchanges. As he heard the Scouts moving away across the rocky ground, he switched back to the smoke cloud. It was certainly denser and a few individual plumes could be seen. The vehicles were almost at the ridgeline. He just needed to hold on for a minute or two to get an idea of the orks' strength.

The foremost gangs of orks on foot were now less than half a kilometre away.

Naaman unrolled his cameleoline cloak and fastened it to his shoulder guards. Drawing up the hood, he pulled the cloak over his arm and settled behind a rock, monocular in one hand, bolter in the other.

He checked on the progress of the vehicles. Three bikes had broken over the ridge, smoke dribbling from their twin exhausts. Behind them trundled two flat-bed transports, their open backs filled with green-skinned warriors. There was more smoke behind them, coming from other vehicles that were still out of sight.

The orks on foot were four hundred metres away.

The greenskins glared warily along the ridge, guns in their clawed hands, alerted by the attack on Aquila's squadron. Naaman lowered himself to his stomach and looked back at the crest. The column of ork infantry seemed to be all in view, a few less than one hundred of them. There was no way of knowing if more were following unless he stayed here and waited for them.

The rumble of engines reverberated along the rocky ridge from the south. A motor with a deeper timbre grew in volume. Naaman glanced to his right as he slithered back from his observation position. A larger vehicle crested the hill, its front bedecked with pintle- and turret-mounted guns. Half a dozen orks stood in its back, wearing brightly painted, heavy armour plates. Through the monocular Naaman could see wisps of smoke trailing from exhausts on their backs, the armour powered by spluttering engines.

Naaman was about to lower the monocular and move away when he noticed one of the armoured orks was much larger than the rest. It was a gigantic beast, yellow armour decorated with black flames, a long banner stitched with ork glyphs hanging from a banner pole on its back. It was another warlord!

With his other eye, he saw the nearest orks were now only two hundred metres away. It was time to leave.

Slipping away through the rough bushes, Naaman shook his head at what he had seen. There was no mistaking it. Another warlord could only mean one thing – there were two ork armies on Piscina. Though there was no way of telling how strong this second force was or what their connection was to the army in Kadillus Harbour, Master Belial had to be told this news. The orks were clearly marching on Koth Ridge; the earlier encounters must have been advance parties, rather than stragglers. Koth Ridge was held mostly by the Piscina Free Militia, with only a couple of Dark Angels squads in support. It was vital that the defensive line was reinforced.

Wrapped in his camouflaging cloak, Naaman broke into a crouched run, heading down the slope as fast as he dared. The bikes to the south were already level with his position, the trucks and battlewagon not far behind. Ahead, a cluster of boulders broke the thin soil. Naaman took cover between two of the upthrusting rocks and turned to face the orks. They were coming at him at some speed, though he was sure he had not been seen.

It was time to slow them down.

He levelled his bolter on top of one of the boulders and took aim at a cluster of three orks near the centre of the group. The bolter coughed in his hand, the gas-propelled bolts zipping soundlessly through the air. Their standard warheads replaced with a heavy mercury core, the stalker bolts punched silently through the padded armour and flesh of the orks. Two of them dropped immediately, the third fell to one knee, blood spurting from a wound in its shoulder.

The sudden attack sent the orks into confusion. Many of them dropped down and began firing at random patches of cover. Others flung themselves onto the rocks, their panicked warning shouts carrying as far as Naaman, who smiled grimly to himself. A few of the leaders began bellowing orders, pointing this way and that, sending their underlings scurrying behind bushes and boulders with little sense of order or discipline.

'Dumb brutes,' Naaman muttered, slinging the bolter strap over his shoulder.

Satisfied the orks would be sufficiently delayed, Naaman backed out of his place of cover and continued down the slope at a brisk march, breaking into a run as he reached the level plain.

'WHY MUST YOU continually disagree with me, Naaman?' snarled Aquila. 'Your contrariness would stretch the patience of the Lion.'

It was mid-afternoon and the orks were pouring westwards in increasing numbers. The greenskins did not appear to be advancing with any particular cohesion. For two hours, Naaman and Aquila had led their squads in careful retreat towards Koth Ridge. As the sun sank into dusk, it was clear to Naaman that his Scouts could not outpace the ork vehicles following them. Naaman had requested the conference with his fellow sergeant and told Aquila to leave the Scouts behind.

'The information we have gained is too vital to risk, brother-sergeant,' Naaman said. 'You must get within transmission range of Koth Ridge and give them warning of the ork attack.'

'It goes against my honour to leave you without protection,' argued Aquila. 'We are only ten kilometres from communication range. You can keep ahead of the orks until that point is reached.'

'And would give those on Koth Ridge less time to prepare their defences,' Naaman said, pacing impatiently. The lead ork squadrons were only a kilometre or two behind and catching up swiftly. 'Aquila, my brother, your duty is clear. If nothing else, we will be able to elude the orks better without the presence of your bikes to attract attention. If you really wish to help, strike against the orks and lead their pursuit northwards. At the moment we are being forced too far south and will be cut off from Koth Ridge if we continue in this direction.'

'I see the merit in your suggestion, brother-sergeant,' Aquila said slowly, mulling over the idea. 'We will perform a diversionary attack and withdraw to communications range. Once I have relayed our intelligence to Master Belial, we will return and cover the rest of your withdrawal.'

'That won't be necessary, brother. Your energy would be better spent defending Koth Ridge against the orks. If the line fails, it would reverse all of our victories so far.'

Aquila's head swayed left and right for a moment, the sergeant conflicted between the possible courses of action. Aquila said nothing as he strode back to his bike and signalled for his squad to move west. The bike's engine growled into life and the comm crackled.

'The Lion will protect,' said Aquila.

'May the Dark Angel speed you upon his wings,' replied Naaman as he watched the Ravenwing ride off into the growing gloom.

With the distraction of the Ravenwing squadron removed, Naaman set about analysing the situation. The orks would not reach Koth Ridge before daybreak. The coming night would be the best cover his squad could ask for, and it was likely the orks would make camp during the hours of darkness. Twice already he had seen warbikes and ork buggies in the distance, roaming freely across the plains. They did not appear to be searching for Naaman's squad in particular, but they clearly knew that there were Space Marine forces in the area. With dozens of vehicles following behind, it was crucial that the ork patrols did not raise the alarm. If that happened, it would only be a matter of time before the pursuing greenskins caught up with the Scouts.

Naaman wanted to move directly west, straight to Koth Ridge, but the ground was far too open; the rock of Kadillus pushed through the grasslands like a bald patch, offering no vegetation or other cover. The Scouts would have to circle the rocky flats to the south, until nightfall at least, when Naaman would reconsider the plan.

Reaching his decision, Naaman passed on his orders to the squad and they set out a fast pace, eager to put as much distance as possible between themselves and the orks while the sun was still in the sky.

* * *

THE MARCH TOOK on a watchful monotony: run, stop, scan the surrounds, run again. For minutes into hours, for kilometre after kilometre, the Scouts ran.

They ran without great pause for three hours, hugging the shallow folds in the plains to avoid being seen. Now and then they took cover, hunkering down in the long grass as one or other of the squad spied ork vehicles coming closer. So often had Naaman heard the distant growl of engines, he hardly paid it any mind any more. Only when he detected a change in volume that indicated vehicles approaching did he truly become aware of the noise.

As the afternoon turned to ruddy evening, the distant heights of Koth Ridge were silhouetted against the setting sun. The craggy spur rose up against the red sky like a wall, still too distant to make out anything of the defence force and Space Marines standing guard there. Naaman offered a prayer to the Lion, hoping that Aquila and his squad had evaded the orks and spread the warning of the massive greenskin advance.

Searchlights and lamps broke the gloom of nightfall, giving Naaman a clear idea of exactly where the ork forces were in relation to his position. Some distance behind, other lights, including the flickering orange of fires, sprang into life across the East Barrens. Looking at the glow that lit the early night sky, he realised just how many orks there were: thousands of them. The bulk of movement was to the north, but the flash of headlights and the sporadic chatter of exuberant weapons fire betrayed a group of several vehicles almost directly behind Naaman's line of advance.

He was still cautious about turning north; that

would put him and his squad squarely in front of the main ork thrust. Heading south was not much of a better option: too far in that direction and the Scouts would come up against the kilometre-deep, near-vertical Koth Gorge. Even if they negotiated that obstacle, the route would take them to the coast rather than Koth Ridge. For better or worse, the only option seemed to be to keep heading west in the hope that orks following behind would stop or change course. Naaman resolved to himself that if the orks came within half a kilometre, they would dig slit trenches and take cover; the orks might miss them in the darkness and if they didn't, at least the Scouts would have a rough position to defend.

Two hours after the sun had settled behind Koth Ridge and was nothing more than the slightest glow in the west, Naaman was feeling slightly vindicated. The orks coming up from the rear had gradually bent their course northwards to join the rest of their force, passing the Scouts more than a kilometre away. Though there was light and exhaust smoke far ahead of the Scouts, it seemed to Naaman that they now had a clear run to Koth Ridge. If they kept up their current pace – and there was no reason they could not – they would be amongst the rocks and gulleys before dawn.

THE GRASSLANDS OF the plains were thinning. Patches of heather and stubby bushes broke the swaying sea of long stems. The ground had started to slope gently upwards and Naaman judged it to be no more than another three kilometres to Koth Ridge proper. It was still dark; Piscina's moons had set and it would be another two hours until dawn coloured the eastern sky. The air was chill but Naaman barely noticed, the cold registering as an abstract environmental factor rather than something he actually *felt*. It was the same with the fatigue from the constant running. His arms and legs pumped methodically, his limbs a separate entity from his conscious mind. There was no pain, no shortness of breath, no cramp or dizziness that a normal man might have suffered.

The Scouts were not so physically blessed, each feeling the strain depending upon his implants and development. Kudin ran as effortlessly as Naaman; Ras and Keliphon were breathing heavily but were keeping pace; Teldis and Gethan showed the worst signs of their exertions. Their faces were red, their strides short, perspiration soaking their uniforms. For all the hardship, neither had offered any complaint or asked for a rest. That was good, because the will to continue was every bit as important as the body's ability to carry on.

Nobody spoke. Each watched his sector with gun ready, but there was nothing to report. It seemed that they had left the orks a kilometre or two behind. Naaman was unsettled by the quiet, particularly the silence of the comm. Although he was not within transmission range, he had expected to be able to receive command signals at this range from Koth Ridge, but he heard nothing. It occurred to him that Aquila might have done something foolhardy and allowed his squad to be cornered by the orks before sending the warning of the ork advance.

'Sergeant!' Keliphon's hushed voice cut through Naaman's thoughts. The Scout was at the rear of the squad and had stopped, sniper rifle raised to his shoulder.

'Squad, halt here,' snapped Naaman. 'Keep watch. Make your report, Scout Keliphon.'

'I thought I heard an engine, sergeant.'

Naaman walked back and stopped next to the crouching Scout.

'You heard an engine, or you did not hear an engine?' he asked.

'I heard an engine, sergeant,' Keliphon said with more confidence. 'Behind us.'

'Distance? Size?'

'I do not know, sergeant. I can see a thermal haze in that direction.' The Scout pointed towards a dip in the plains the Scouts had passed a few minutes previously. Naaman was pulling his monocular from his belt when the Scout continued, voice tense. 'I see them! Three ork vehicles. Two flatbed transports. Single armoured battlewagon. No bikes or infantry. They are coming directly at us!'

Naaman could see nothing with his naked eye, even though the sight of a Space Marine was as good in low light as a normal man's at noon. The orks were driving without lights. Were they deliberately hunting the Scouts? He looked through the monocular and confirmed what Keliphon had reported: three ork vehicles catching up with them, crammed full of ork warriors.

Naaman looked around for the best defensive position. There was a stand of low trees a few hundred metres to his right, and a narrow stream cut down from the ridge thirty metres to his left. The trees would take them further from the orks' probable route of advance, and provide some visual cover, but the wiry, twisted trunks and branches offered little physical protection. The stream cut at least a metre deep and bushes lined the side, but it went directly across the orks' projected course. Naaman made a last sweep with the monocular and assured himself that there were no other ork forces close at hand. If the Scouts were discovered, they would only face the three vehicles and their belligerent cargo.

Collapsing the monocular and stowing it away, he made his decision.

'Into the stream bed, four-metre dispersal, snipers front and back!'

They covered the ground at a sprint and splashed into the brook, which was about three metres wide but barely covered the tops of their boots. Naaman led the squad a little further upstream, where the water curved around a boulder and cut to the south for a short distance, almost perpendicular to the ork advance.

'We cannot allow the enemy to get between us and Koth Ridge,' Naaman told his Scouts. 'We will wait for the enemy to pass us and engage them from the rear. If the Free Militia on the ridge are paying attention, they may even see the fight and send assistance.'

The Scouts nodded, wide-eyed and filled with adrenaline. They took up their positions, using clumps of grass and bushes to conceal their weapons, crouched against the waist-high mud bank. Peering between the fronds of a plant, Naaman watched the orks, his bolter resting on the bank in front of him. The enemy were three hundred metres away and approaching at a reasonable speed. This was no reckless dash for Koth Ridge, this was a considered advance. The idea of orks showing this kind of circumspection unsettled the Scout-sergeant. Orks were dangerous enough without them actually thinking.

Naaman could feel the ground trembling as the vehicles came closer and closer. The heaviest was a slab-sided half-track with a driver's cabin on the right-hand side, an open turret sporting a long-barrelled cannon on the left. There was a rickety gantry behind on which stood two orks holding guns strapped to a rail. Behind them, above the tracks, over a dozen more orks hunched behind the metal sides of the troop compartment, peering over the side, guns in hand. Smoke billowed from a cluster of exhausts along the far side, dirt sprayed from the tracks in the transport's wake.

The other two vehicles were about half the size, with four balloon-tyre wheels that churned through the mud and grass. He could see the drivers hunched in a wide compartment at the front of each, a gunner beside them standing behind a pintle-mounted weapon. Ammunition belts trailed onto the open deck behind, where more orks squatted close together, their helmeted heads turning this way and that as they kept a lookout for enemies. As they came nearer he could hear the guttural chatter of the greenskins among the noise of engines.

The battlewagon crossed the stream bed about fifty metres upriver, crashing across the gap without halting. The trucks found it harder going. One driver revved the engine in a huge cloud of black smoke and tried to jump the gap. This met with mixed success: the truck surged into the river and smashed into the far bank, tyres ripping through dirt and plants, dragging the vehicle free as half the orks on board tumbled out of the back. The second truck approached more cautiously and bellied into the water with a loud shriek of tearing metal. It stayed there, smoke dribbling from the exhausts. Naaman guessed an axle had snapped.

There followed an argument punctuated by shouts, punches and kicks, which culminated in the orks deciding to abandon the vehicle and continue on foot. Naaman gave the order to open fire as the last of them were scrambling up the opposite bank.

Bolts screeched into the orks' exposed backs, blowing out chunks of flesh, shattering spines and ripping off limbs. Naaman directed his fire onto the abandoned truck, stitching a line of explosions across its flank until something ignited. Flames crackled, and with an explosion that sent a ball of fire dozens of metres into the air, a fuel tank exploded. Pieces of armour and chassis scythed through the nearby orks. The waters of the stream swirled with thick blood.

It was difficult to see what had happened to the battlewagon: it was lost behind the pall of smoke streaming from the exploded transport. The other truck turned around and drove straight at the Scouts, skidding across the grass, the gunner spraying a hail of bullets at the bank.

Teldis gave a shout and flew back into the water, his right cheek and eye missing. He looked around desperately with his other eye, one hand flapping at the water, the other still holding tight to his bolter. Naaman blocked the Scout's pained grunts and snorts from his mind and swung his weapon towards the fast-approaching truck. Heavy-calibre bullets ripped through the dirt and sang over the Scout-sergeant's head. Naaman sighted on the driver through the cracked glass of the truck's windshield.

He loosed off two rounds in quick succession, the first punching through the glass to explode in the ork's chest, the second missing by the smallest margin to tear into the troop compartment behind. The ork wrestled for control of the vehicle despite the gaping hole in its ribcage, head lowered protectively.

Naaman heard a dull thud. Less than a second later a shell exploded on the stream bank behind the squad, showering the Scouts with dirt and water. He realised that Teldis had stopped making any noise, but did not break his gaze from the truck. More fire from the pintle gun sprayed along the bank and Ras ducked back with a cry.

'Emperor's hairy arse!' the Scout yelled, waggling his hand fiercely, blood spraying from where a finger had been shot away.

'Cease your blasphemy!' snapped Naaman, firing another burst of shots, this time aiming for the gunner. The ork fell away from its weapon, head split apart by a detonation within. 'Do not speak of the Emperor in vain!'

'My apologies, sergeant,' answered Ras, taking up his firing position again, altered blood already clotting his wounded hand. 'I shall report to the Chaplains for penance when we reach our brothers.'

The ork slewed the truck to a halt a dozen metres away. The greenskin pulled a pistol from within the cab and started firing as its passengers spilled over the side. Naaman ignored the driver and directed his fire at those disembarking. Two orks were dead before they hit the ground, their bodies mangled by multiple bolt-round explosions. Four more dashed straight at the Scouts, cleavers in hand, pistols spitting bullets. A lucky hit caught Naaman across the right side of his head, smashing his comm-link and taking off the top of his ear. Out of the corner of his eye, Naaman saw the driver slump backwards, a neat hole in its forehead from a sniper round.

'Good marksmanship, Scout Kudin,' Naaman said, swapping his empty bolter magazine for a fresh one.

There was no reply. Naaman glanced to his right and saw Kudin doubled up in the stream, blood pouring from a vicious gash across the side of his neck. Gethan was using the wounded Scout's rifle.

Naaman rose up to his full height and pulled out his combat knife as the orks lunged towards the stream. A greenskin tried to vault over him, but he slashed at its groin as it went past, opening up a cut along its thigh from pelvis to knee, slicing through muscle and tendons. The greenskin floundered to one side as it landed, unable to keep its balance on the ruined leg. Naaman turned and fired a bolt-round into its face.

The battlewagon opened fire again. This time the shell exploded in the stream, shredding what was left of Teldis and ripping apart two orks as they dropped down into the water. Gethan fired past Naaman as the last greenskin splashed along the waterway, the shot taking out its throat.

There came a brief pause. The orks from the first

truck were all dead, those from the other were running along the bank to close with the Scouts. The battlewagon ground forwards slowly, smoke drifting from the muzzle of its cannon as the ork gunner clumsily reloaded.

'One thing at a time,' Naaman said to nobody in particular. He reached down to his belt and pulled free a perfect sphere of dull metal. There was a rune etched into it. The activation sigil glowed red as he rubbed his thumb across it. Pulling himself up the bank, Naaman took aim on the battlewagon, bullets zipping around him, and hurled the grenade. Upturned ork faces watched the globe arcing through the air until it sailed into the back of the battlewagon.

There was no explosion. Instead of fire and shrapnel, the stasis grenade erupted with a shimmering globe of energy, engulfing the battlewagon and everything within ten metres of it. Inside that hazy bubble, time slowed almost to a stop. Naaman could see the gunner with a hand on the breech lever of the cannon. He saw the scowling face of the driver, flecks of saliva flying from between its fangs. Bullets fired by the two pintle gunners on the gantry hung in the air, moving so slowly they had appeared to have stopped. Orks were frozen in mid-leap as they bundled out of the troop compartment, flecks of rust and sprays of dirt colouring the air around them.

He had only bought a little more time. The stasis field was already weakening, the sphere of energy slowly but perceptibly shrinking. Naaman felt Gethan come up beside him as the sergeant took aim at the mob of orks running towards them.

'It's just us, sergeant,' whispered Gethan.

'No it isn't,' Naaman replied, firing a volley into the orks, cutting the legs from beneath a greenskin.

The rumble of engines Naaman had first heard a few seconds earlier became a roar of throttles as the Raven-wing bikes leapt across the stream just behind the sergeant. Their bolters chattering, Aquila's squadron drove straight at the orks, ripping a swathe through the unruly mob. Return fire rang from their armour and their bikes as they ploughed into the midst of the enemy, chainswords in hand, hacking and slashing.

With an audible pop of air pressure, the stasis field imploded. Bullets fired almost half a minute earlier suddenly screamed over Naaman's head. The throb of an engine being gunned brought Naaman's attention back to the functioning truck; gunner and passengers dead, the driver accelerated straight at the sergeant.

'Down!' he rasped, hurling himself into the stream, one hand dragging Gethan with him.

The truck hurtled over the bank and tilted to one side, front wheel catching on a rock, sending the whole machine cart-wheeling over Naaman and Gethan. It crashed in a plume of water and smoke, the driver hurled through the remnants of the windshield in a shower of glass shards. Amazingly, the ork was still alive. It dragged itself through the mud in Naaman's direction, pistol clicking empty in its grip.

'Kill it!' Naaman told Gethan. The Scout raised the sniper rifle and put a crystal-tipped round through the wounded ork's left eye. It shuddered for a few seconds as the sniper bullet shattered on the inside of its skull, releasing toxins through the alien's bloodstream.

The distinctive *crump* of the battlewagon cannon echoed along the stream. A moment later, a shell exploded in the middle of Aquila's squadron. Naaman saw two bikes and their riders flung high into the air, armour plates spinning, engine parts flying in all directions. The twisted remains of Space Marines and machines crashed to the ground trailing smoke as debris rained down into the burning grass.

'Time to move on,' Naaman said, pushing Gethan onto the bank. Scrambling up afterwards, Naaman saw the two pintle gunners on the battlewagon sighting in their direction. Even as a warning left Naaman's lips, Gethan was shredded by the hail of bullets, holes punched through his armour and body.

The Scout fell backwards, red froth bubbling from his lips. Naaman spared a second to see if there was any chance of saving the Scout. There was none. Had Gethan received some of the later implants, his wounds might not have been fatal, but he was simply too young, his body too normal, to survive such punishment. Naaman put a bolter round into the youth's skull to spare him any more pain and rounded on the orks with a fierce cry.

'Death to the xenos!'

Though his body was filled with the fire of fury, Naaman directed his rage, siphoned it from a wild, uncontrollable flame into a white-hot focus. The orks that had spilled from the back of the battlewagon became the object of his wrath as he advanced with bolter levelled, every burst of fire hitting its mark, every salvo of rounds ending the life of an enemy.

Aquila and the surviving member of his squadron

circled around the battlewagon, raking it with fire, but its armour was too thick for the explosive bolts to penetrate. Hunkered in its turret, the gunner was almost impossible to hit as the cannon fired again, this time missing the speeding Ravenwing by a considerable distance.

Aquila's course brought him swinging around the battlewagon and up to Naaman from behind. The sergeant throttled down and came to a stop beside Naaman, and addressed him through his external speakers.

'Head for Koth Ridge, brother,' said Aquila. 'I have sent warning to Master Belial, but what you have seen is far more valuable than my report.'

'You have nothing to take on that battlewagon, brother,' replied Naaman. 'You should withdraw while you can. My life is not worth the sacrifice of yours.'

'It is, Brother Naaman,' said Aquila. He slapped a fist to his chest in salute. 'Not just for what your head contains, but also for what is in your heart. You make the Tenth Company proud, Naaman. *Exulta nominus Imperialis*. I can think of no other to serve as the best example to those who would be the battle-brothers of the future.'

Before Naaman could reply, Aquila opened up the throttle and sped away, the Scout-sergeant's parting words lost in the bike's roar. The two riders lanced through the ork mob with mounted bolters and flashing chainswords. In the thick of the fighting, Aquila's companion was wrenched from his bike when his chainblade caught in an ork's chest. Surrounded by greenskins, he battled on, cutting down two more foes;

his defiance was cut short by another shell from the battlewagon, which tore apart the Dark Angel and orks without distinction.

All that remained was Naaman, Aquila and the battlewagon. The Ravenwing sergeant lifted his chainsword to the charge position and drove straight at the flank of the armoured vehicle. The prow of his bike smashed into the battlewagon's right track, shredding links and buckling wheels. The impact hurled Aquila forwards, the sergeant bouncing against the slab side of the armoured transport; as he tumbled Aquila grabbed the top of the troop compartment. The bike exploded as Aquila dragged himself over the side of the truck. Flames crackled from the battlewagon's engine as ruptured fuel lines sprayed their contents across the grass. Through the smoke and fire, Naaman saw the black-armoured figure smash his way through the back of the driver's cab. A moment later, a severed ork head sailed from the window and bounced through the burning grass.

'For the Lion!' Naaman shouted, believing that Aquila would make it out alive. All he had to do was kill the gunner.

With a blast that hurled Naaman to his back and sent debris hundreds of metres into the air, the battlewagon exploded. Track links and pieces of engine showered down on the flattened grass and fell into the burning crater where the battlewagon had been. As ragged shards of metal continued to thud into the dirt around him, Naaman headed into the devastation to look for Aquila. There was a slim chance that the sergeant had avoided the worst of the detonation and his power armour had protected him.

He found a black-armoured leg, sheared bone jutting from the cracked and stained ceramite. After that Naaman gave up. He didn't want to find anything else.

Returning to the stream, Naaman piled the bodies of his dead Scouts under the lip of the bank and covered them roughly with branches and ripped-up clods of earth and grass, hoping that the orks would not find and mutilate the corpses. When the Dark Angels had destroyed the orks, Naaman would come back and ensure the remains were returned to the Chapter for the proper funeral rites.

He took one of the sniper rifles and refilled his ammunition pouches. Buggies with searchlights and the headlamps of half-tracks were panning left and right in the distance, scouring the pre-dawn gloom. The fight had obviously attracted attention from the orks. He had to get moving.

Veteran Sergeant Naaman once more broke into a loping run, heading for Koth Ridge.

THE TALE OF NESTOR
Hold the Line

THE CREST OF Koth Ridge was a mess of activity. Like ants building a nest, hundreds of Piscina troopers were using spades and trenching tools to dig what defences they could. Empty ammunition crates were filled with the dirt from these foxholes and used to make barricades, while clearing teams worked further down the eastward slope, using saw and flamer to hack and burn away the cover provided by scattered trees and thick mats of waist-high thorny bushes. Other squads laboured at digging up the boulders that dotted the hillside, but only the smallest could be moved and rolled up the slope to improve the defences.

Amongst the grey-and-green fatigues of the defence troopers stood the green-armoured figures of the Dark Angels, both directing the labour and keeping watch for the approaching orks. Apothecary Nestor walked through the throng, his white armour standing out amongst his brethren. He was looking for the field commander, Sarpedon. Nestor spied the Interrogator-Chaplain's black armour and bone-coloured robe amongst a squad of Devastators standing guard from a sandbagged position to the north.

The troopers stayed clear of Nestor's path as he strode along the line. A few bobbed their heads and touched a finger to the peaks of their caps in deference; most turned away and busied themselves with their work. Nestor could sense their fear even though they tried to keep their nervous expressions hidden. The tang of the sweaty air was tinged with adrenaline. The back-breaking work was as much to keep their minds occupied as it was to erect a defensive line against the orks. Anticipation – foreboding – was just as much a threat to the Koth Ridge defenders as ork guns and knives.

Sarpedon finished his conversation with the Devastators as Nestor approached. The Interrogator-Chaplain walked away from the squad as the Apothecary waited respectfully for his superior to join him.

'Brother-Chaplain, I wish to speak with you,' Nestor called out when Sarpedon was a few paces away. The Chaplain's skull-faced helm was hung from his belt, revealing Sarpedon's square-jawed face, his broad cheeks each etched with a scar in the shape of the Dark Angels' winged sword symbol.

'Brother Nestor, how can I be of assistance?' asked the Chaplain, stopping in front of Nestor.

'I am concerned by the lack of medical supplies possessed by the Free Militia,' said the Apothecary. 'It seems that they have brought only the most basic medikits from Kadillus Harbour. Could you request that Master Belial sends more of the Apothecarion's supplies from the city?'

'Do you have sufficient supplies and equipment to attend to our battle-brothers?' asked Sarpedon, his expression impassive.

'I foresee no shortages if the estimates concerning the coming engagement are correct,' replied Nestor. 'You have told me that we should not suffer any significant casualties. Is that estimate to be revised?'

'Negative, Brother-Apothecary. Master Belial has passed on the report of Ravenwing Sergeant Aquila, which estimates enemy numbers to be in the low hundreds. We have good fields of fire, an elevated position and our defensive posture is highly advantageous. There are no reports of heavy enemy vehicles or war machines, and little if any support weapons or artillery. We dominate the field. Additional forces are en route to our position from Kadillus Harbour.'

Nestor glanced west towards the city and then looked east where dust clouds and smoke could be seen at the foot of the ridge. Dawn was slowly spreading across the plain, revealing the vehicles and mobs of the orks a few kilometres away.

'It is unlikely that reinforcements will arrive before the orks, Brother-Apothecary,' said Sarpedon, guessing Nestor's thoughts. 'Master Belial is extricating such squads as are available from the fighting in the docks. Withdrawing troops from such a position is time-consuming if they are to arrive here intact. It is imperative that the orks do not gain any foothold on Koth Ridge. If they do so, they will be able to attack our reinforcements as they arrive.'

'I will keep the brothers fighting whatever the orks bring against us, brother,' said Nestor. 'While a Dark Angel still breathes, no ork will set foot on this ridge. I am still concerned for the wellbeing of our allies. Casualties amongst the defence troopers will be much higher. We are relying upon their continued survival to add weight to our position. I believe that we should provide their medical officers with whatever assistance we can to ensure that happens.'

'The Piscina force is suffering heavily in the city; we cannot divert supplies from that battlezone. It would be self-defeating to shore up the defence here only by allowing the orks to break free of the city. The Piscina officers will have to do what they can with the resources at hand, Brother Nestor.'

'I understand,' said the Apothecary. 'Where do you wish me to take my place in the defence?'

Sarpedon's grey eyes scanned up and down the ridge. A thin smile twisted his lips as his gaze fell upon Squad Vigilus at the heart of the defensive line. The Terminators from the Deathwing Company wore huge suits of bone-white multilayered armour, capable of shrugging off fire from anti-tank weapons and heavy artillery.

'I think that Sergeant Scalprum and his Devastators would benefit the most from your presence,' said the Chaplain.

Nestor nodded in agreement. It was unlikely the Deathwing would require Nestor's attention given the apparent lack of heavy weapons possessed by the orks.

'The blessing of the Lion upon you,' said Sarpedon, patting a hand on Nestor's shoulder pad.

'May you stand tall in his eternal gaze, Brother-Chaplain,' Nestor replied.

The two parted and Nestor continued towards Sergeant Scalprum. The Devastators' leader had split his warriors between two crate-lined emplacements, one covering the broken-down ruins of an old hunting lodge half a kilometre down the slope, the other with a wide arc of fire overlooking the approach to the line of troopers to the south. Each combat squad of five Space Marines included a heavy bolter and a plasma cannon, the first for cutting through the massed ork infantry, the second for destroying their light vehicles.

'Hail, Brother-Apothecary,' Scalprum greeted Nestor. 'I think you will be using your bolt pistol more than your narthecium in this battle.'

'I share your confidence, brother-sergeant,' replied Nestor. Flexing his left fingers, Nestor activated the narthecium gauntlet, a whirring bonesaw spinning into life beneath his fist. 'Of course, the narthecium can be used to wound as well as heal, brother. I am glad that Master Belial saw fit to despatch me to your side with such speed.'

Scalprum laughed.

'It did give me a moment's pause for thought when I saw that Thunderhawk landing and only you walking down the ramp,' said the sergeant. 'I wondered if perhaps there was something Master Belial was not telling us!'

'Rest assured that my hasty entrance was only made possible because I had been tending to our wounded behind the front line in the city. Those who are more involved are proving difficult to extricate without unnecessary risk.'

'I heard the same from Brother Sarpedon,' said Scalprum. 'With the strength of the Lion to protect us, I think that our battle-brothers will arrive to find the battle already won.'

'Let us hope that is the case,' replied Nestor. 'Has there been any update from Sergeant Aquila?'

Scalprum's armour whined as he shook his head.

'No, there has been nothing more from Aquila since we received his last transmission early this morning,' said the sergeant. 'There was some sporadic fighting about two hours ago, at the foot of the ridge. If we had not sent the Rhinos back to Kadillus to pick up the reinforcements, we might have intervened. As it was, there was nothing we could do from here. Though I hope I am wrong, I believe our brothers in the Ravenwing and Tenth Company have made the ultimate sacrifice bringing us warning of the ork advance.'

Nestor looked out across the brightening slope and wondered what had become of Aquila and the others. Two of the Ravenwing squadron had not yet had their progenoid glands removed for the Chapter stores. Containing the gene-seed of the Dark Angels, these implants were vital to the creation of future generations of Astartes.

'When we have pushed back the greenskins, we will conduct a search and ensure the bodies of our fallen brethren are attended to by the proper rites,' said the Apothecary.

The thought brought something else to Nestor's mind and he turned back to Scalprum. He opened the data panel in the side of the bulky narthecium enclosing his left forearm and hand. Tapping in a sequence of digits, he brought up a list of names.

'If my records are correct, Brothers Anduriel, Mephael, Saboath and Zarael still have progenoid glands intact,' said the Apothecary.

'That is correct,' replied Scalprum. He stabbed a finger to three of the Devastators in the emplacement with them. 'Mephael, Saboath and Zarael are here, you'll find Anduriel in the other combat squad.'

'I am sure they will continue to guard the Chapter's due for some time to come, until we may relieve them of their burden in more peaceful circumstances,' said Nestor, retracting the blade of the narthecium. 'Your squad was involved in the fighting in Kadillus Harbour. Is there anything else I should be aware of?'

Scalprum looked at his squad, one hand resting on the holstered bolt pistol at his waist.

'There is nothing acute that needs tending to. Saboath has a crack in his left femur, Hasmal has a laceration to his right side and Anahel has a torn preomnor that has been causing him some discomfort.'

Nestor nodded as he committed these facts to his memory. As rugged as Space Marine physiology was, the intrusive treatments and surgery of battlefield medicine were always a short-term measure. Being unaware of an existing injury or condition greatly increased the risks of any intervention. Sometimes it came down to preserving the life of a battle-brother for a few hours whilst knowing that the treatment itself would kill him later. Such were the hard lessons of the

Apothecarion, and Nestor's tutor, Brother Mennion, had talked at length regarding the difficult decisions every Apothecary would face.

It was these minutes and hours before battle that always tested Nestor's resolve, more than the blood and shouts of the wounded. When battle was in motion, training and experience ensured that Nestor acted without hesitation, and could make such harsh decisions without a moment's remorse or reflection. In the cold, quiet time before and after battle, it was far harder to be so dispassionate.

Nestor excused himself from the Devastators and found a patch of shade behind a jutting pillar of rock. He looked south, where the Koth Ridge dropped dramatically down to end in cliffs, beneath which the Piscina Ocean crashed against jagged rocks. Further out, the sheet of blue seemed still, untouched by the conflict that had engulfed this small upthrust of land.

He took a deep breath and absorbed the calm radiating from the sea. He pushed away the bleak thoughts of what injuries might befall the brothers behind him – painful fates that he knew with microscopic precision – and quietly recited the Litanies of Diagnosis, Salvation and Mercy.

While he strengthened his will with these words, part of Nestor detected the approaching growl of engines and the stronger presence of hydrocarbons carried on the wind from the east. The comm chimed in his ear and Sarpedon's calm tones cut through Nestor's recital of the Prayers of Battle.

'Enemy in sight. Zero-three-fifty. Devastator range in one minute. Our faith is our shield.'

Nestor unholstered his bolt pistol and headed back to his place in the line.

His autosenses darkening to filter out the bright morning sun, Nestor watched the Devastators performing their duty. The ork army was approaching in two waves: a swift-moving body of vehicles followed some distance behind by their infantry.

Nestor could see that the greenskin approach was fatally flawed. Carried away by their enthusiasm for battle, the bike riders and buggy crews raced ahead of the main force. It was probable that the ork commander wished to use the faster elements of the force to occupy the Koth Ridge defenders while the foot-slogging ork warriors moved up the slope. In theory that was not such a bad decision, but Nestor could tell at a glance that the plan would not work; the ork light vehicles were not numerous enough nor carried enough firepower to face the Space Marines and Free Militia force on their own.

Though dozens of ork vehicles streamed up the slope leaving plumes of smoke and dust in their wake, the defenders had every advantage of position and elevation. The lascannons of the Free Militia opened fire first, streaks of blue energy lancing down the ridge at the oncoming vehicles. The firing was premature and somewhat inaccurate but several half-tracked bikes were turned into smouldering piles of slag by the blasts. The *brak-brak-brak* of autocannons joined the rip of laser energy splitting the air. Grass and mud and stone and metal and flesh were sent flying along the slope in almost equal measure as the guns stitched their mark across the rock-strewn ridge.

With a deep thrumming, Brother Saboath charged up his plasma cannon. Coils glowed bluish-white with the build-up of energy and sparks danced from the vented muzzle of his weapon. Without haste, he altered his aim a little to the right. Nestor followed the muzzle of the gun and saw a squadron of war buggies racing recklessly up the slope, bouncing across rocks and narrow fissures.

With an explosive wave of compressing air, Saboath fired. A miniature star erupted from the plasma cannon, casting harsh shadows as it flew down the slope to crash into the foremost buggy. The vehicle's engine block disintegrated in a shower of molten metal and super-heated fuel, the vapour of which ignited, engulfing the vehicle in a sheet of blue fire, incinerating the driver and gunner, melting the tyres and warping the chassis. The wreck smashed to pieces on a boulder, hurling burning oil and red-hot bolts across the thin grass. Patches of smoking plastic and cooling metal dotted the mud and rocks amongst the spreading patches of fire.

'Good hit, brother,' said Nestor.

'The first shot is always the easiest,' replied Saboath.

Another ball of ravening energy seared down the slope from the other combat squad, punching clean through the side of another buggy to erupt from the other side in a spray of molten steel and liquefied flesh. The whine of the plasma cannons' generators grew in pitch as the weapons recharged.

'Mark target at fifty-three-five, seven hundred metres,' announced Sergeant Scalprum. Nestor realised the Devastator sergeant was using the broad-address frequency, talking to the Free Militia as well as the Dark Angels.

He looked in the direction described by Scalprum and saw a few dozen smaller greenskin slaves – the gretchin – manoeuvring crude artillery pieces into position behind a cluster of low rocks. Two of the war machines were large-bore cannons mounted on wheeled platforms. Another appeared to be some kind of engine-powered catapult. There were two other war machines: large rail-mounted missiles, each twice the size of a Space Marine. The gretchin crews, whipped into action by burly ork overseers in heavy masks, jostled and struggled to point their artillery up the slope.

Nestor heard the multiple pops of mortars firing from the sandbagged enclaves behind him, in response to Scalprum's instructions. Craning his neck, he followed the blur of the bombs sailing into the overcast sky and watched them fall on the ork war machine position. Half the bombardment fell short, exploding harmlessly against the rocks, but four or five bombs landed in and around the big guns, shredding the crews with shrapnel, dismounting one of the crude rockets.

All along the ridge to the left and right, the Dark Angels and Free Militia poured fire into the attacking orks. Smoking wrecks and charred green corpses littered the slope, where fires were growing in strength, crawling up the ridge towards the defenders, hurried on by the prevailing wind. The smoke was as much a hindrance to the orks as the defence troops as bikes crashed onto unseen rocks and buggies tipped into hidden gorges; the Devastators had no problems seeing their targets, the thermal vision of their autosenses cutting through the thickening bank of smoke as easily as their plasma cannons cut through the armour of the ork vehicles.

To the north, Nestor's left, the crack of ork guns intensified. Half a dozen buggies raced along the ridge parallel to the defenders' line, machine guns and cannons ripping into sandbags and punching holes into the dirt-filled crates and boxes protecting the defence force. Here and there an incautious trooper fell back bloodied, but for the most part the soldiers kept their heads down and the furious fusillade passed over them or was stopped by the makeshift barricades.

A strange whistle cut through the hammer and clamour of fighting, attracting Nestor's attention. Corkscrewing wildly, the remaining ork rocket flew up through the cloud trailing flames and sparks. The defence troopers turned tripod-mounted heavy stubbers to the sky, tracer bullets leaping up to meet the arcing missile. This fire missed its mark and the rocket completed its rising course and dipped sharply towards the ridgeline.

The steady roar of heavy bolters erupted close to Nestor as the Devastators opened up on a squadron of bikes that had come within range. The Apothecary ignored the ork vehicles racing closer to the Devastators' position and kept fixed on the trajectory of the missile. Beneath it, troopers hurled themselves to the ground, throwing themselves into foxholes and slit trenches.

The rocket landed behind the front line of defenders, crashing to the rocks in the middle of a mortar battery.

The impact threw up a huge plume of mud and rock shards but there was no explosion. At first Nestor thought the warhead had failed to detonate, but as shaken men popped up their heads, looking around in disbelief, the ground began to vibrate. A pulse of green energy erupted from the crater where the rocket had landed, rippling through the air and ground.

Where the green wave touched something, it tossed the man or object into the air, shaking apart guns and hurling troopers tens of metres into the sky, bones snapping, limbs contorting unnaturally. Nestor could feel the weak edges of the vibration through his feet and the particles of dirt on the crate barricade danced with the reverberations. The pulse disappeared and the unfortunate troops that had been picked up dropped to the ground like stones, their falls breaking necks, cracking open skulls and crushing organs.

Nestor could see a dozen soldiers not moving, twice that number rolling around or trying to crawl to safety. Secondary detonations from the cache of bombs popped inside the mortar pit, scattering metal fragments through the survivors.

A glance to his right confirmed to Nestor that the Devastators' position was still secure: the tangled wreckage of five bikes smoked and sparked further down the slope, the closest at least three hundred metres away. He was about to set off towards the injured troopers to see if he could assist when the rocket pulsed again. The shockwave was slower this time but more violent; the ground rippled like a pool when a stone has been tossed into it. Dirt and rocks exploded in a growing circle, hurling more troopers from their feet; the barricades they had laboured so hard to erect were cast down by the pulse, shallow trenches collapsing, burying those inside with stones and dirt.

Into this devastation roared buggies and warbikes, guns blazing. Nestor saw a young officer pull himself to his feet, straighten his cap and then collapse again as a hail of bullets ripped into his chest and gut. The handful of mortar crew that had luckily survived the rocket impact dragged themselves across the ground, bullets tearing trails around them. A youthful trooper leapt bravely over a wall of sandbags, a grenade in hand. His face disappeared into a bloody mush and the primed grenade flew from his fingers, exploding amongst his squad mates.

Their drivers cackling, buggies veered and swerved through the emplacements, bouncing over the dead and wounded, crunching bones beneath their wheels, guns hammering a staccato beat of death. A small ork half-track roared through the chaos, a fuel tank trailer bouncing madly behind it. Flames licked from its barrel-shaped turret, indiscriminately setting fire to ammunition stores and troopers. Burning men flailed through their fellow troopers, spreading the panic.

Nestor set off at a run, bolt pistol ready. Behind him he heard Scalprum barking orders at the split combat squad, directing their fire along the ridgeline. Just ahead of the Apothecary, Sergeant Vigilus and his Terminators advanced through the breach in the line, storm bolters roaring, the flickering of rounds blurred against the dancing flames. Reinforcements poured in from further up the line, great-coated officers bellowing at their men to take up the empty positions. Having wreaked considerable carnage, the ork vehicles screeched away back down the slope, evading the vengeance of the Dark Angels and Piscina troopers arriving at the break in the defences.

Nestor arrived as the Deathwing took up a firing position within one of the half-ruined emplacements. The Apothecary saw nothing but charred bodies within and moved on, heading for the mortar pit. A choking sob to his right drew Nestor's attention and he slowed to search through mangled bodies sprawled between the rocks and boxes. A trooper surged from a pile of corpses, one leg trailing uselessly after him, his face masked with drying blood.

'Help me,' he begged, falling down just in front of Nestor.

'What is your name, trooper?'

The Apothecary rolled the Free Militiaman to his back, ignoring his cries of pain. His left thigh was a gory mess, broken bone jutting through the flesh. As Nestor's fingers twitched at the controls of the narthecium, a scalpel blade snicked from his index finger. Holding the struggling man down with his other hand, Nestor sliced open the wound on the trooper's inner leg. Magnifying his autosenses, the Apothecary examined the blood flow and concluded that the soldier's femoral artery was intact. He was suffering from an oblique fracture in the distal zone of his femur. He could be saved.

'Your name?' Nestor asked again.

'Lemmit, sir,' the man said between haggard gasps.

'Do not be afraid, Trooper Lemmit,' Nestor said

calmly. 'What I am about to do will hurt a lot, but it will save your leg. Do you understand?'

Lemmit nodded, eyes wide with fear.

None of the painkillers in the narthecium could be used; they would put any non-Astartes into a coma if they didn't kill Lemmit outright. With his free hand, Nestor ripped Lemmit's belt from his waist and thrust it between the trooper's teeth.

'Bite on this if you need to,' said Nestor.

The Apothecary fixed the bone first, pulling apart the fracture and resetting it while Lemmit howled in agony. Nestor cut the audio-feed on his helmet to blank out the distraction. Selecting the medical riveter, he worked the narthecium along the broken bone, fixing the two pieces in place. It only took a few seconds, but when Nestor glanced at Lemmit he saw the man had passed out. As with the painkillers, the stimulants in Nestor's possession were too strong for a normal human.

Quickly checking that Lemmit's breathing and pulse were still within tolerable limits, Nestor decided to let him stay unconscious. Using a quick-sealing resin, the Apothecary bonded the riveted pieces of thigh bone. Switching attachments, he sprayed a fine mist of biological adhesive on the wound and pulled together the sides of the incision he had made, holding them together for a few more seconds until the adhesive had dried. Retracting the adhesive dispenser, he made double-sure by stitching along the wound with the auto-suture.

Checking that the man had no other acute surface injuries or internal damage, Nestor picked up Lemmit and carried him to a wall of dirt-filled boxes and leant him against the crates, propping up the damaged leg with a rock.

'Wake him up and give him some water,' the Apothecary instructed a passing sergeant, who accepted the Space Marine's order without question and knelt beside Lemmit, uncapping his canteen.

Nestor moved on, the experience of the procedure filed away in his memory for future reference. He came across a badly burned trooper who stared at the Apothecary with one eye from a blackened, twisted face. Lowering to one knee, Nestor could see that the man's chest was burnt through to the sternum and showed the line of ribs down his left-hand side. Subdermal burns extended over a third of his torso, a purplish fluid leaking from the open wounds. Death was a certainty. He placed his left hand across the trooper's face, obscuring his view. With his right hand, Nestor pulled his combat knife from his belt and punched it quickly but smoothly through the exposed ribs, puncturing the heart. The unfortunate trooper trembled for a moment and fell still.

The Apothecary wiped his knife clean on the man's tunic and sheathed it. He stood up and looked around for someone else needing his aid. He saw a cluster of men gathered around another lying on the ground, one of them thumping the trooper's chest to get his heart started. Nestor took a step towards this group when the comm chime sounded.

'Brother Nestor, infantry assault imminent. Return to combat position,' instructed Brother Sarpedon.

'Confirm, Brother-Chaplain,' replied Nestor. He gave

the dead and the wounded one last look and turned away, heading back to the Devastators.

As he strode along the ridge, he could see that the orks had paid heavily for their tactical naiveté. Dozens of vehicles smoked along the ridgeside, the bodies of those orks that had tried to escape lying next to their wrecked bikes and buggies. Other than the breakthrough at the site of the rocket strike, the orks had not managed to get closer than a couple of hundred metres from the defence line.

Now the mass of the orks poured forwards, hundreds if not thousands of green-skinned warriors hurrying up the slope as their cannons boomed behind and the catapult launched bombs that exploded in the air above the defenders, raining down red-hot metal shards.

Something clanged from Nestor's shoulder just before he reached Squad Scalprum. He glanced to his left and saw the white paint on his pad scraped away, revealing the grey ceramite beneath. Something hissed at his feet. He bent down and picked it up, examining the fragment between thumb and forefinger. It appeared to be a piece of bolt, the thread melted, head warped by the explosion that had thrown it against the Apothecary.

Nestor tossed the piece of shrapnel away. If that was the worst threat the orks had to offer, it would only be the lightly armoured troopers that would need his attention.

As THE ORKS died in their hundreds, Nestor did not think of it as a massacre. It was simply a cleansing, as one might purge a wound of infection. The Free Militia and Dark Angels purged Koth Ridge of the ork infection with lascannon and autocannon, mortar and heavy bolter, plasma cannon and heavy stubber. The Apothecary had not even fired his weapon yet: no ork had survived to come within range.

'This is Interrogator-Chaplain Sarpedon to all defence forces. Those without eye protection should avert their gaze from the east. Incoming bombardment from orbit. I repeat, incoming orbital bombardment includes plasma attack. Do not look at the attack site with unprotected eyes. Attack to commence in one hundred and eighty seconds.'

'This should be worth seeing,' said Scalprum.

Nestor nodded and increased his autosense visual filtration to maximum. Koth Ridge darkened in his eyes, the swarm of aliens clambering over gulleys and running through clusters of rocks becoming a darker shadow in the gloom.

'This is Brother Sarpedon,' the Chaplain said over the Dark Angels' ciphered comm channel. 'The *Unrelenting Fury* is cleared for a short pass only. Orks are still in control of the defence laser site at Kadillus Harbour. If the bombardment does not break the ork attack, we cannot expect further orbital support. Ready your weapons and your souls and believe in the purity of our cause.'

'Confirm, Brother-Chaplain,' Nestor heard Sergeant Vigilus reply. 'Any further information on the arrival of reinforcements from the city?'

'Transports and armoured vehicles have left Kadillus Harbour. Time of relief estimated at four hours. Expect to hold until dusk.'

'Understood, Brother-Chaplain,' said Vigilus. 'We shall be the shield of Kadillus.'

Nestor looked up into the grey sky. Even without the cloud, he would have been able to see nothing of the Dark Angels battle-barge manoeuvring into firing position hundreds of kilometres above. The *Unrelenting Fury* would be dipping down towards Piscina's atmosphere, rotating about its axis to bring the dorsal bombardment cannons to the correct angle. Shells the size of buildings were being loaded into massive breeches – much of the size and weight was ablative shielding that would melt away during entry into the planet's atmosphere – while armoured turrets like small city blocks turned slowly into position.

The first salvo appeared as two blurs barely visible through Nestor's darkened autosenses. They streaked groundwards, punching out of the cloud at ultrasonic speed. The warheads had been set to airburst, exploding five hundred metres above the orks, two kilometres from the defenders of Koth Ridge. Two stars burst into life against the darkened vista. Even through the filter of his autosenses the blossoms of plasma were bright enough to make Nestor's surgically improved eyes water. The explosions scorched the sky, raining down fire, a shockwave advancing ahead of a sheet of flame, obliterating everything in its path. Molten destruction rained down on the orks, consuming a swathe of the advancing greenskins in a bright conflagration. Nestor heard the strangely high-pitched shrieks of the orks; the cries of blinded troopers too stupid to have heeded Sarpedon's warning; an ear-splitting crack of air and water molecules being ripped apart.

An area half a kilometre across was devastated in three seconds, shattered rocks turned to glass, orks reduced to a haze of ash and dust, patches of grass and stands of bushes no more. Two overlapping smooth-sided craters were all that remained of the hundreds of orks that had been beneath the twin detonations.

Rocked by the suddenness of the attack, the ork advance stopped in its tracks. There were fearful shouts, while a few of the greenskins fired their guns vainly at the clouds, yelling defiance. Some of the orks were evidently clever enough to realise the bombardment could not strike too close to the ridgeline without hitting the defenders. This orkish wisdom spread through the lines and the army broke into a charge, striking up the slope in their hundreds. Ranting and panting, the orks closed on the Dark Angels and the Piscina troopers, but it was not to their benefit. Although safe from death from above, the orks now plunged into range of the bolters and lasguns of the Koth Ridge defenders.

A storm of red las-beams streaked down the hillside while bolters and storm bolters coughed death at the oncoming wave of greenskins. As the most headstrong orks were cut down by the volleys of fire, two more shells plunged down from orbit, this time set for a ground burst. The whole of Koth Ridge jolted under-foot as the pair of shells exploded inside the rock of the slope. Thousands of tons of debris erupted into the air with all the violence of one of Kadillus's many volcanoes. Bloodied and battered ork bodies fell like rain. A long stretch of the slope sheared away and tumbled down into the East Barrens as a massive landslide of rocks and corpses.

A beam as blindingly bright as the plasma detonations lanced into the sky from many kilometres behind Nestor. The power of the shot boiled a hole through the clouds and a few seconds later there came a sharp rumbling like a compressed crack of thunder.

The orks had worked out how to fire the defence laser.

'Did they hit?' barked Nestor.

The comm stayed silent for several seconds, during which the Apothecary and the other Dark Angels nearby looked at each other.

'Negative,' replied Sarpedon. 'Close miss. The shields took the brunt of the residual radiation. Master Belial is withdrawing the *Unrelenting Fury*. He does not wish to gamble on the orks improving their aim. It is just us now. Give the enemy no respite! Pour our wrath upon this foul horde and remember that we defend one of the Emperor's worlds!'

THE CHAOS AND confusion of close battle engulfed Koth Ridge. To the north, Piscina troopers unleashed disciplined volleys of lasgun fire into the charging orks while their heavy weapons continued to pound away with las-bolt and shell and bomb. Scalprum's Devastators added their bolter fire to that of the plasma cannons and heavy bolters, reaping a harvest of death through the packed mobs of the greenskins. With bullets whipping past over the barricade, Nestor added his own fire to the fusillade, picking off those few orks that managed to struggle through the storm of plasma blasts and bolts.

Despite the heavy casualties, the greenskins pushed

up the slope into the teeth of the onslaught, using what patches of cover remained to close with their enemies. Barely a hundred metres from the Free Militia were the clustered remains of a building compound, abandoned for centuries, partly swallowed up by grass and bushes. Within the tumbled walls and half-destroyed outhouses, several dozen orks found shelter. They fired over the tumbled-down bricks at the Piscina troopers with little accuracy but a considerable weight of fire. As soldiers were forced behind their barricades, more orks streamed forwards into the lessened fire, scrambling up the steep slope to take cover behind rocks and in gulleys and hollows.

Nestor heard Sarpedon barking orders over the comm, demanding that the Free Militia draw more troops into the fight from further north to ensure the line held. While ork rockets and bombs fell amongst them, the troopers were reluctant to leave their slit trenches and emplacements. Exasperated, Sarpedon ran from the Dark Angels' position, his robes fluttering behind him, a glowing power sword in his hand.

'Squad Vigilus, Brother Acutus, with me!' bellowed the Interrogator-Chaplain. 'Into the enemy! Drive them back!'

The Deathwing Terminators of Squad Vigilus stomped down the slope, storm-bolter fire exploding across the rocks and walls protecting the orks. From the midst of the squad emerged Brother-Lexicanium Acutus, wearing the distinctive blue robes of the Librarium. In one hand he carried an ornate carved staff, topped with a marble carving shaped as the winged sword of the Chapter. With the Terminators

gathered close to shield him against the bullets and
blasts of energy flying from the guns of the orks, Acutus raised the staff above his head, grasping it in both
hands. Psychic energy flared along the length of the
staff, crackling from crystal symbols embedded into
the haft. Dirt and stones circled the Librarian in a psychic gale. Sparks erupted from the ornate structure of
crystalline wires around his head.

Acutus swept the staff down in front of him. A short
distance in front of the Terminators, molecules tore
apart with a shrill screech. The Librarian cleaved a rent
in the fabric of reality, opening up a gash between the
material and immaterial. Colours and sounds swirled
from the breach, scintillating and blinding. Following
the Librarian, the Deathwing stepped into the vortex
and disappeared.

A few seconds later, Nestor glimpsed a second tear
appear beside the walls of the ruined compound. The
Deathwing advanced out of the void, the flare of storm
bolters lighting the inside of the moss-covered walls.
Brother Amediel let loose the fury of his heavy flamer,
a burst of white fire roaring through the ruins, exploding from shattered doors and windows, roasting alive
everything inside.

The orks poured from their hiding holes, some with
patches of flamer fuel still burning their flesh, club-
bing and chopping at the Terminators. The Deathwing
attacked back with glowing power fists and whirring
chainfists, smashing bone, pulping organs and slashing through flesh. Acutus emerged from his
warp-walk, staff tipped by a glowing scythe of psychic
energy. A wide arcing blow sliced the heads from three

orks; another cut the legs from beneath two more.

The orks had seen enough and fled the ruins, the bolts of the Deathwing roaring after them. Nestor had no time to see what happened next as a warning shout from Scalprum heralded another ork push against the Devastators.

The renewed attack began with the explosion of several shells around Nestor. Crates exploded into splinters that skittered from the Space Marines' armour, scratching the paint of their dark green livery but doing little else. Spreading out to limit casualties from the devastating blasts of the plasma cannons, the orks snarled and yelled as they pounded up the slope, trusting to speed rather than cover.

'Two reloads remaining,' reported Brother Hasmal as he slammed another magazine into his heavy bolter.

Beside Nestor, a plasma cannon blazed again, the blast erupting amongst the orks, charring flesh and burning bone. Still the orks came on, and past the green wave Nestor could see a bulkier shape advancing – some kind of walker twice the height of the orks, with claw-handed arms and heavy guns.

'Enemy Dreadnought,' warned Nestor.

'I see it,' replied Scalprum.

The orks were less than fifty metres away, many of them passing into a dip in the ground that hid them from view.

'Prepare for close quarters combat,' said Scalprum, lifting up his power fist. A shimmering blue field wreathed the heavy gauntlet, crackling along reinforced knuckles.

Nestor refreshed the magazine in his bolt pistol and

slipped out the bone saw from his narthecium. There was a final hail of bolts as the orks rushed across the last few dozen metres of open ground, but it was not enough to stop their momentum.

The Apothecary stayed behind the barricade and picked off orks with his bolt pistol as they came charging straight at the squad, fanged mouths baying for blood, red eyes wild with alien ferocity. He fired into the face of an ork just a few metres away, the bolt shattering the creature's skull. The Apothecary had time for one more shot – through the gut of another foe – before the orks were at the barricade, firing their pistols at point-blank range and swinging with their cleavers and mauls.

Standing against the shock of the orks' first rush, Nestor parried the first blows with the blade of his narthecium, keeping the greenskins from clambering over the battered wall of crates and sandbags. He fired into the press of green bodies until his pistol was empty. He dropped the empty weapon to the ground and punched his fist into the chin of a greenskin trying to climb over the barricade, hurling it back.

Another ork swung an axe at Nestor. The Apothecary swayed back, avoiding the blow. The ork stumbled forwards as Nestor caught the creature's wrist in his empty hand, bones cracking in the Space Marine's superhuman grip. With a turn of the body, Nestor dragged the ork halfway across the crates and brought the whirring blade of the narthecium down onto its arm, shearing through just above the elbow. The ork barely noticed the injury, lifting its pistol to blaze a hail of bullets into Nestor's chest. The Apothecary replied with a straight-arm jab that plunged the narthecium blade into the creature's left eye, the spinning teeth chewing into its brain.

As Nestor ripped the narthecium back, Scalprum appeared next to him, dark orkish blood steaming from his power fist and staining the golden eagle blazoned on his chest plastron.

'Saboath is down,' said the sergeant. 'I'll hold here.'

Nestor pulled back out of the melee at the barricade and turned to see the plasma cannon-wielding Devastator on his side, his weapon lying in the grass a short distance away, still connected to Saboath by its power feed. The Dark Angel's face plate and left arm were heavily cracked and blood leaked from a long gouge down the right side of his chest.

'What happened?' asked Nestor, kneeling down beside the wounded Space Marine.

'Some kind of power blade,' Saboath replied, his voice quiet. 'I think my secondary heart was punctured.'

'Any damage elsewhere? How is your arm?'

'Painful. Possible dislocation.' The Devastator reported his injuries as dispassionately as he would explain a fault with his armour or a weapon malfunction.

Nestor removed Saboath's helmet and examined the dilation of the blood vessels in the Space Marine's eyes. It was less than expected, the pulse sluggish. It was likely that Saboath had been right and he was operating with only one heart. The Apothecary withdrew the bone saw and selected an adrenal booster from the narthecium.

'This will cause some tightness in your chest. Tell me if you have difficulty breathing,' said Nestor as he pushed the long needle into Saboath's carotid. The Space Marine spasmed for a second as the injection mixed with his body's boosted hormonal system.

'That burns like the fires of Gehenna,' Saboath spat between gritted teeth.

'Good,' replied Nestor. 'That means your biscopea is still functioning.'

The Apothecary pulled open the crack in Saboath's armour to better examine the wound. The ork power blade had cut clean through the Space Marine's fused ribcage leaving an incision across the bone and cartilage. Investigating further, Nestor found that the tip of the weapon had grazed one of the veins leading into the secondary heart, filling the chest cavity with blood.

'I am going to close off your secondary heart function,' Nestor explained. 'That will stop the internal bleeding. Damage is not critical, so I should be able to operate once I have some more time. Your blood pressure will drop. You'll feel some loss of strength and perhaps a little light-headedness. You may find it difficult to swallow and your breathing may be affected, though I'm going to give your third lung a boost to make sure blood perfusion is maintained.'

'Just repair me so that I can get back to the fight, brother,' said Saboath.

Nestor nodded and set to work, injecting the secondary heart with a localised sedative and applying micro-clamps to the blood vessels to redirect the bloodstream through the Space Marine's regular heart. He pumped out the blood already in the chest cavity and sprayed fixative foam into the wound. The foam hardened into a spongy mass within seconds, sealing the gash and hardening around the severed ribs. It was not as good as a proper reconstruction but it was quick and provided a temporary seal for the armour. Saboath would soon be back on his feet.

With the chest injury dealt with, Nestor looked at Saboath's shoulder. After a short inspection he concurred with the Space Marine's assessment. Dislocation was easy to fix. Rolling Saboath further onto his side, Nestor opened up a panel in the side of the Space Marine's backpack. He entered his diagnostic cipher to access the traction and compression controls of the suit's fibre bundles.

'Lift your arm and straighten it as much as possible,' Nestor instructed his patient. With a grunt, Saboath complied as best he could.

'Get ready,' Nestor warned. He punched in the automated sequence required and activated the suit's internal muscle system. With a crack and a further grunt from Saboath, the armour extended the Space Marine's arm and pushed the ball joint back into place with a twist. Pleased, Nestor deactivated the system and locked down the panel.

'Watch out!' bellowed Saboath.

Nestor looked round to see the ork Dreadnought looming above the barricade, flames billowing from one of its arms, its claws closing in on Sergeant Scalprum. Heavy bolter rounds pinged off its armoured hull.

Nestor leapt across Saboath and heaved up the plasma cannon. Rolling to his back, the Apothecary fired high, aiming for the ork machine's hull. The plasma bolt smashed into the Dreadnought with a blinding explosion, knocking the machine backwards, metal droplets streaming from the molten casing. Sergeant Scalprum leapt over the barricade, swinging his power fist. Fingers splayed, the sergeant smashed his hand through the buckled metal and wrenched out a spume of wires, cables and half-crushed gears, sparks showering from the machine.

Saboath clambered to his feet, stepping over the power conduit attaching the plasma cannon to his backpack.

'I think it best if I let you have this,' said Nestor, holding out the plasma cannon. 'Try not to get involved in any hand-to-hand fighting – I don't want you losing your other heart!'

Saboath grinned and put his helmet on, giving it a twist to make the seal. He took the plasma cannon from Nestor, hefting the weapon in one hand to check its readouts.

'Thank you, Brother-Apothecary,' said Saboath. 'I will find you after the battle is won and you can finish the treatment.'

Nestor nodded and turned back to the fighting. The ork rush had been turned back with the loss of their Dreadnought. The greenskins were retreating to cover further down the slope. To the south, where more Piscina troopers were waiting, the flank of the ork army surged again. Nestor checked his chronometer.

It was less than two hours until the reinforcements' ETA.

* * *

FOR AN HOUR the orks held off, bombarding the Imperial line with the catapult and cannons. Though many of the barricades had been thrown down by the ork attacks and foxholes had caved in, this bombardment had little effect on the Free Militia and none at all on the Dark Angels. In the relative calm of air-bursting shells, Nestor had checked again on Brother Saboath's condition, refilling his suit's stimulant system from the narthecium. Normally the Apothecary wouldn't have used so much of his supply in this way, but he was beginning to agree with the predictions of Sarpedon and Scalprum: the orks simply did not have the kind of weapons that would be a threat to Space Marines, at least not in any numbers. Saboath's injury had been the worst, though several other Dark Angels had suffered minor inconveniences – a couple of broken bones and a few cuts and bullet wounds through the weaker joints of their armour.

Even the Free Militia were coping, their own medics better equipped than Nestor to treat the burns and cuts suffered by the troopers. Nestor was almost bored as desultory fire echoed back and forth between the two armies, an exchange that was not in the orks' favour.

'Are they massing for another attack?' asked Nestor.

'Possibly, brother,' replied Scalprum. 'Perhaps they await the arrival of heavier weaponry and vehicles to test us. It is an oddity that we have seen only the one Dreadnought, and nothing of their battlewagons and larger guns.'

'Such was also the case in Kadillus Harbour,' observed Nestor. 'Masses of infantry and little else. It seems our foes are poorly equipped.'

'I doubt they expected to face the wrath of the Dark Angels,' said the sergeant. There was a hint in his tone that he shared Nestor's disappointment at the lack of challenge presented by the enemy. 'If they were expecting anything at all, that is. I cannot imagine this simple scum put much planning into their campaigns. Once we regain control of the defence laser, the *Unrelenting Fury* will rain down death from the heavens and the orks will have nowhere else to hide.'

'We will still have to chase them down and eradicate them on the ground, brothers. Complacency is a foe as deadly as any other.' This was from Sarpedon, who entered the Devastators' emplacement, his robe tattered, stiff with the gore of the orks.

'As you say, Brother-Chaplain,' said Scalprum.

'I feel the reinforcements may find their journey from the city has been wasted, brother,' said Nestor.

'Do not be so sure,' replied Sarpedon. 'Lexicanium Acutus senses something is stirring within the ork army. They are gathering their numbers and he detects some new force focussing their will. Be ready for another attack.'

'Always, brother,' said Scalprum.

'Conserve ammunition and maximise your fire. I feel this battle may yet have more twists, brothers. Let us not celebrate victory before it is won.'

Nestor and Scalprum bowed their heads in deference as Sarpedon left, heading towards the Deathwing squad.

'A new force arriving?' said Nestor, looking at the sergeant. 'The orks seem spent to me.'

'The ways of the psyker are strange, brother,' said

Scalprum. 'It is best not to delve too deeply into their mysteries.'

'A truth I share, brother,' replied Nestor. 'I am more comfortable with artery and nerve than the twisting powers of the warp. Let us hope that Acutus's suspicions are nothing more than a hunch.'

The two of them turned back to face the slope. The orks were certainly gathering from where they had been scattered by their unsuccessful attacks. A few hundred remained, a kilometre or so down the ridge. Plumes of smoke betrayed the arrival of several more vehicles. Nestor increased the magnification of his autosenses and saw three battlewagons crawling through the mobs of orks. One of the transports carried heavily armoured orks with colourful banners and a swarm of small gretchin attendees.

'Curious,' said Nestor. He opened the comm-channel. 'Brother Sarpedon, direct your attention to these reinforcements. It appears that the enemy have been joined by another warlord.'

There was a pause while Sarpedon investigated Nestor's report.

'I concur with your observation, brother,' the Chaplain eventually replied. '*Vigilus est fortis maximus.* Remain alert. Doubtless a fresh enemy attack is imminent. Let our weapons be the instruments of the Emperor's ire.'

A few more minutes passed before the orks poured up the slopes again. Behind the defenders, the sun was almost at the horizon, an orange orb burning through the low cloud. The long shadows of the orks streamed behind them as they advanced with purpose through blood-slicked grass and across blackened dirt. The smoke from the battlewagons hung low to the ground as they followed behind the infantry, keeping pace. The few remaining bikes and buggies darted to the north, arcing around the right flank of the ork army. It seemed that the enemy had realised the weakness of its earlier tactic and would now attack with its infantry and vehicles together.

The Piscina troopers opened fire at extreme range with their mortars, lascannons and autocannons, eager to stave off this fresh offensive. Most of their shots fell short or were wide of their targets. Around Nestor, the Devastators needed no command to hold their fire.

Oblivious to the bombs of the mortars, the orks closed together, forming three large groups each shadowed by a battlewagon. One group angled north to accompany the light vehicles, the other two came straight on, heading directly for the Dark Angels' position. The warlord seemed determined to overcome the Space Marines head-on, perhaps – correctly – perceiving them to be the biggest threat despite their small number. Amongst the green-skinned warriors, Nestor saw another of the clanking Dreadnoughts, waddling forwards on mechanical legs, oily smoke pouring from its engine.

The grumble of the vehicles' engines rumbled up the slope. Nestor listened for a moment and realised that similar noises were coming from behind him. He turned and strode the hundred metres or so to the western slope of Koth Ridge. A couple of kilometres away, he spied a column of vehicles, in the colours of the Dark Angels and Piscina Free Militia. Dark green Rhino transports advanced along the road behind the guns of a Predator tank, while further down the column came the Chimeras of the defence troopers. Two heavy Leman Russ tanks followed behind, while Assault Space Marines bounded alongside the convoy with great leaps powered by their jump packs.

The firing had intensified at the front line and Nestor hurried back, certain that Sarpedon was already in contact with the reinforcements. He arrived back in the emplacement just as the Devastators opened fire again, raining heavy bolt and plasma blasts down upon the orks.

The battlewagons returned fire, tracer bullets whipping past the Devastators' position. A blossom of fire and smoke from a turret presaged the impact of a shell, giving the Space Marines enough warning to duck back as the impromptu barricade exploded in a cloud of splinters and dirt. Falling stones rattled against Nestor as he glanced around, checking for any injuries.

Another shell exploded close to the other Devastator emplacement. As more rounds fell screaming onto the ridge it became apparent that the first strike had been a lucky hit. Explosions erupted all around the Space Marines but none were close enough to be anything more than a distraction.

While the heavy weapons of the squad continued to fire, Nestor helped Scalprum and the other brothers rebuild the barricade as best they could out of the broken remnants of the ammunition boxes and storage crates. It provided little protection against the bullets converging on them with increasing fury, but it would hamper the orks if they tried to storm the position.

More shells from the battlewagons engulfed the line, hurling shards of rock into the air. Out of instinct Nestor glanced across to the other combat squad and was taken aback by the sight. Two of the Space Marines lay draped over the barricade, one of them missing an arm, the other with his backpack ripped away, armour rent open.

Nestor sprinted across the divide as more detonations rocked the ridge. The shockwave from a nearby impact sent him off balance. He stumbled and crashed shoulder first into a jutting boulder. Righting himself in an instant, the Apothecary continued his run as the hoarse ork shouts and zing of bullets sounded ever closer.

'Who has fallen, brothers?' Nestor demanded as he leapt over the spilled dirt and broken wood from the ruptured barricade.

'It is Hasrien and Anduriel, brother,' came the reply.

Nestor attended to Hasrien first, the Space Marine who had lost his right arm and seemed most likely to survive. The shell detonation had ripped away the whole limb, leaving a ragged hole in Hasrien's shoulder. Blood leaked slowly from shredded blood vessels despite the Space Marine's quickly clotting blood. The Apothecary blotted out the sound of bolters adding to the din and concentrated on the task at hand. It was important to preserve as much of the existing skeletal, nerve and blood vessel structure as possible if a prosthetic replacement was to be viable.

Hasrien's system was pumping Larraman cells

through his bloodstream, which would harden into a protective layer on contact with the air. The downside of this rapid healing with major wounds was the possibility of air bubbles being trapped in the blood vessels, leading to necrosis and cell death if the Space Marine did not receive proper treatment swiftly. Nestor applied a thinning agent to slow the process and then used the cauteriser to seal the broken vessel more completely. After injecting a cocktail of anti-inflammatory and cell-growth drugs, the Apothecary doused the open wound with a compound that would boost the scabbing effect of the Larraman cells coursing through the Space Marine's system. Within seconds the whole area was encrusted by a quickly hardening scar.

Nestor realised Hasrien was talking, an incomprehensible stream of words spilling quietly from his lips.

'The green wave of fire brings the black reproach… The retribution flame cleanses the impure… A sky swirls with delight, bringing the stench of justice…'

Carefully turning the Space Marine's head, Nestor found a wide gash carved into his helmet by a piece of shrapnel. The wound did not appear to be deep, and already the scab was thick and infection-proof. The Apothecary activated his interpersonal comm.

'Brother Hasrien? This is Brother Nestor. What do you feel?'

'The whiteness of fraternity bonds with the black wall,' came the hushed reply. Hasrien's good arm twitched, his fingers forming a fist.

Conventional brain damage seemed unlikely: the wound had barely scratched the Space Marine's hardened skull. Nestor searched through his memory, recalling all of the rites of diagnosis, but there was nothing that matched this symptom.

The only thing that was remotely familiar was a malfunction in the catalepsean node – a small organ implanted in the cortex to allow a Space Marine to rest different parts of his brain without sleeping. The dream-like whispering would be explained by damage to that organ. Perhaps the blow had involuntarily activated it or somehow displaced it. As it was, Hasrien was in no fit state to fight: the catalepsean node was only employed on extended duty as it obscured the focus required for effective combat.

At a loss concerning what else to do, Nestor helped Hasrien sit up. There was no function of the narthecium that would help. With nothing else springing to mind, the Apothecary brought his fist down sharply against the uninjured side of the Space Marine's helmet, jolting his head to the side. Hasrien slowly turned his head to the left and right and then looked up at the Apothecary, the lenses of his autosenses focussing on Nestor's face.

'Brother Nestor?' said Hasrien. 'I thought it was you.'

'What is your name? Where are you?'

'I am Brother Hasrien of Squad Scalprum, Third Company of the Dark Angels. Present location is Koth Ridge, Piscina IV, Piscina System.' Hasrien looked to his right and then back at the Apothecary. 'I appear to have lost an arm, brother, or did I just dream that?'

Nestor grabbed the Space Marine's remaining wrist and helped him to his feet.

'You have lost your arm, brother, but there is still

fighting to be done,' said the Apothecary, slapping his bolt pistol in Hasrien's remaining hand. 'The Emperor expects you to fight until you can fight no more.'

'Thank you, Brother-Apothecary,' replied Hasrien, a finger curling around the trigger of the pistol. 'I shall speak your name to the Lion when I am next in chapel.'

Nestor watched the battle-brother rejoining the three other members of his combat squad, pistol at the ready. A moment later Hasrien was firing into the approaching orks, showing no after-effects from his strange episode.

Nestor turned his attention to Anduriel.

The Apothecary assessed the damage clinically, but was forced to conclude that Anduriel's condition was best described as 'a bloody mess'. Skin, fat, muscle, bone and organs had been mashed together by the blast; the damage to the Space Marine and his armour was such that Nestor assumed he had taken a direct hit from the battlewagon shell. Nestor activated the inter-personal link again.

'Can you hear me, Brother Anduriel?'

The Space Marine's reply was barely a whisper, wheezed between laboured breaths.

'You sound far away, brother,' said Anduriel. 'I can feel nothing and everything is dark. Are my battle-brothers safe? I tried to shield them from the explosion.'

'Your brothers are still fighting,' Nestor told him. 'I cannot heal your wounds, brother.'

There was a long pause before Anduriel spoke again.

'I understand, brother,' he said. 'I have yet to pass on

my gene-seed. Please recover it for the Chapter.'

'I will, Anduriel, I will,' Nestor said, straddling the face-down Space Marine. 'There will be no pain.'

'I feel nothing at all,' said Anduriel as Nestor set to work.

The Apothecary chanted the canticles of mercy as he removed Anduriel's helmet and laid it to one side. Placing his left palm on the back of the Space Marine's head, he fired the narthecium's pneumatic spike, plunging twelve inches of reinforced alloy through the Space Marine's neck and into his brain. It was the quickest and least painful way to despatch an Astartes – a Space Marine's boosted immune system and enhanced physiology would fight against lethal injections, causing discomfort and distress.

Nestor checked that Anduriel was truly dead and set about his next task. With scalpels and saw he cut away the spine and tissue obscuring the progenoid gland located at the base of the Space Marine's neck. It was a delicate process, but Nestor's armoured fingers worked with the practiced ease of five decades' experience. He took a zero-vac containment vial from his belt and opened it, placing the jar in the dirt beside Anduriel. With two more cuts and a twist, he pulled the progenoid free. Grey and glistening, it sat in the palm of his hand. Within, the gland contained all of the DNA material of the Dark Angels, dormant and sterile, ready to be grown into fresh organs for a future recruit. Nurtured inside a battle-brother, it was the greatest gift to the Chapter a Space Marine could give.

Quickly placing the progenoid into the flask and sealing it, Nestor considered the best course of action to retrieve the twin organ in Anduriel's chest. It would be quicker to cut through and retrieve it from behind the Space Marine's thick breastplate, so Nestor set about cutting away sections of the spine and ribs, slicing away at the anterior muscles until he could see into the chest cavity. There were a few organs in the way, which Nestor efficiently cut free and placed to one side. As before, he readied a containment flask and removed the progenoid from its cluster of blood vessels, securing the precious gene-seed at his belt inside a rigid pouch. He placed the parts he had removed back inside the Space Marine's body and sealed the gaping hole with bio-foam. Anduriel would be returned to the Chapter as whole as possible. Honour and dignity demanded it.

Standing up, Nestor looked around and to his surprise realised the battle was won. He had been so engrossed in his gory work he had paid no attention to the roar of tank engines cresting the ridge or the boom of cannons ripping apart the ork lines. Looking east, he saw two battlewagons careering away down the slope, followed by a few dozen orks on foot. The black bikes of a Ravenwing squadron raced after them, gunning down more of the greenskins as they fled.

The Apothecary looked down at Anduriel and commended the fallen warrior's spirit to the Emperor and the Lion. It seemed a shame that Anduriel had not lived to see the victory he had helped to achieve. Such was the fate of all Space Marines eventually, whether young like Anduriel, or as old as the veterans of the Deathwing.

Nestor took heart from the fact that his ministrations

of the day had ensured two battle-brothers would survive to fight again. To become lost in regret and mourning would be a disservice to those who had given their lives for the Imperium across the ten thousand years of the Dark Angels' existence. Anduriel had fought well, with skill and courage, and now he knew the peace of death. Nestor hoped that when it was his time, he would pass with equal honour.

THOUGH THE ORKS had suffered terribly as a result of their assault on Koth Ridge – estimates placed enemy casualties at seventy-five per cent for a relative few Imperial fallen – the news from Kadillus Harbour was not so encouraging. Nestor listened as Master Chaplain Uriel explained the situation to Brother Sarpedon and Colonel Haynes of the Free Militia.

'The orks are stubbornly resisting any attempt to dislodge them from the docks,' said Uriel. 'Twice in the last day they have attempted to break out of our cordon, and both times they have been held back by the slimmest of margins. Ghazghkull is probably unaware that this attempt to link with the city has failed, but if there are more orks to the east we can expect them to try again. Even with the Piscina defence force, there are not enough warriors to effectively garrison both the city and Koth Ridge.'

A shout from a picket of defence troopers down the slope interrupted the Chaplain. Nestor turned with the others to see what was causing the commotion. A vague shape emerged from one of the narrow gulleys a few hundred metres away and resolved into the figure of a Scout-sergeant, cameleoline cloak tossed back over one shoulder. As the bloodied and dirty warrior strode up the slope, Nestor recognised the new arrival as Sergeant Naaman of the 10th Company. He carried his bolter in both hands and had a sniper rifle slung over one shoulder. Of his squad and the Ravenwing squadron that had accompanied him into the east, there was no sign.

Nestor hurried down to Naaman, noticing the Space Marine had a limp and that some of the blood that stained his armour and uniform was his own. The Scout-sergeant waved away any attempt at assistance.

'Thank you for your concern, brother, but I have a more urgent need,' said Naaman. His eyes were intent through the mask of dried blood that covered his face. 'I need a long-range comm. I *must* speak with Master Belial.'

Sarpedon joined the pair and escorted Naaman to Uriel's Rhino, where the Master Chaplain was already stabilising the command link. Naaman took the proffered pick-up from Uriel and slumped down onto the transport's ramp, bolter cradled in his lap. The battered-looking sergeant coughed once, took a deep breath and thumbed the activation rune.

'Brother-Captain Belial? This is Veteran Sergeant Naaman, requesting permission to make my report.'

THE TALE OF NAAMAN
Shadow Warriors

MASTER BELIAL LISTENED without interruption while Naaman delivered his lengthy account of what had happened in the east. Naaman simply laid out the facts of the mission: the times, places and sightings of the enemy. He held back his observations on what this information might mean to the Dark Angels' strategy and allowed Belial a few minutes to digest the information and consult with his advisors.

He waited close to Uriel's Rhino for the master's return signal, watching the Piscina defence troopers digging shallow graves for their fallen comrades. Several dozen more arrived along the road as dusk darkened the ridge. Some of the men were detailed to assist Apothecary Nestor as he removed Brother Anduriel's remains from the field. The eight men lifted up the dead Space Marine with as much dignity as they could muster, but the strain soon cut through their solemn expressions and they were puffing and sweating by the time they lowered Anduriel into the back of one of the Rhinos.

One young trooper caught the sergeant's eye. He leaned against the hull of the transport, mopping the sweat from his face with his sleeve, raking his fingers through his thick blond hair. There was dust and blood on his uniform, which didn't fit well: tight across his wide shoulders, baggy along his short legs.

Naaman wondered what it was like to face something like the orks as a normal man. Like his battle-brothers, the sergeant saw himself as a military asset, and the preservation of his life was a tactical objective: the preservation of force. Several times in the past day he had come close to dying, but it was the potential of failing his mission that had motivated him to survive, not an emotional attachment to his continued existence. He knew that his deeds and his memory would live on through the Chapter – and quite literally through the gene-seed he had incubated within his body – so he felt none of the sense of ending that other men might feel about death. Even his name was something that Naaman was only borrowing from the Dark Angels; he knew the stories of twenty-six Brother Naamans that had come before and also knew that the twenty-eighth Brother Naaman would learn of his actions.

The young trooper, on the other hand, went against the enemy not knowing if he would be remembered or forgotten, or even noticed. He was just one amongst many thousands – Naaman was one amongst a thousand – and there was little chance his acts, heroic or cowardly as they might be, would ever be recorded for posterity. Millions of men like him died every day to protect and expand the realm of the Emperor. Looking at the blond-haired youth, Naaman was reminded of an Imperial saying: *for every battle honour, a thousand heroes die alone, unsung and unremembered.*

Naaman strode across the ridge to the group of troopers catching their breath. They turned and stared at him as he approached. The sergeant ignored their surprise and raised his fist in salute to the blond-haired trooper.

'What is your name?' he asked.

'Trooper Tauno,' the man replied hesitantly. 'Can I help you, er, sergeant?'

'Just remember to do your duty and fight as if the Emperor Himself watches you,' said Naaman.

'I will, sergeant,' Tauno said, his gaze flickering nervously to his companions.

Naaman nodded and returned to the command Rhino, ignoring the confused whispers that erupted from the squad. Naaman could have heard them if he so decided, but it was better for the men to have their gossip to themselves.

The comm rune was blinking when he returned and he snatched up the handset.

'This is Veteran Sergeant Naaman.'

'Naaman, this is Master Belial. I cannot risk the *Unrelenting Fury* for a sensor sweep of the East Barrens geothermal plant. In your estimation, what is the strength of the remaining ork forces to the east?'

'Any figure I could tell you would be a wild guess, brother-captain,' replied Naaman. 'It seems that the majority of the force I witnessed was destroyed earlier today, but whether that accounts for all, some or only a small part of the enemy army is unknown.'

'It occurs to me that you would have seen any ship capable of holding a much larger force.'

'I am not sure that the geothermal station was the landing site, brother-captain. It may simply have been a staging area for a ship further into the Barrens. The lack of heavier vehicles, particularly large battle fortresses and war machines, suggests that as remarkable as it may seem, we may have only encountered a vanguard of a much larger force.'

'I find it hard to agree with that assessment, sergeant,' said Belial. 'We have already encountered two sizeable ork armies. It is highly unlikely that several vessels made it planetside without detection.'

'It is improbable, brother-captain, but not impossible. Without any confirmation regarding the size and location of the landing zone, any observations are pure speculation.'

There was a pause; Naaman assumed the company commander was deciding what to do. He did not envy Belial the choice ahead of him. There were no troops to spare from the fighting in Kadillus Harbour, but if there was still a significant threat from the east, the battle in the city would be rendered pointless.

The comm crackled again.

'It is my current view that the threat from the east has been neutralised. Any remaining ork forces will be scattered. It is imperative that these remnants are not allowed to regroup. I will order an eastward push towards Indola to clear any remaining resistance. This will be an advance-in-force, sergeant. I will send

Sergeant Damas and his Scouts to join with you at Koth Ridge and you will provide standard reconnaissance and support observation for the eastward push. Confirm.'

'Confirm, brother-captain. Join with Squad Damas and recon to the east alongside the main force.'

'Very well, brother-sergeant. Your action in the East Barrens is exemplary of the finest traditions of the Chapter. Though not full battle-brothers, the names of your fallen Scouts will be added to the Roll of Honour for the war, alongside Sergeant Aquila and his squadron. The Third Company owes the Tenth Company a debt for the service you have provided these last few days and your part in our victory will be lauded by your brothers.'

'I thank you for honouring the fallen, brother-captain. I will also honour them with my continued dedication to victory. Do you wish to speak to Brother Sarpedon?'

'Master Uriel is now the force commander. Please bring him to the comm, sergeant.'

Naaman hung up the handset and attracted Uriel's attention. As the Master Chaplain broke away from his discussions with the Free Militia colonel, Naaman walked away and sat down with his back to a low rock, facing east. The cloud had thinned and evening stars glimmered on the horizon, while the first curve of a moonrise crept into view. It would be some time before Damas arrived from the city.

Naaman closed his eyes and was instantly asleep.

WITH MORE FREE Militia forces arriving from across Kadillus and air-lifted from other parts of Piscina, the defence of Koth Ridge was looking more secure as Naaman and Squad Damas set out ahead of the

Imperial advance. Artillery positions were being dug, linked by a growing network of trenches and emplacements. With the Free Militia continuing to dig in, the Dark Angels pressed eastwards from the ridge.

Naaman and Sergeant Damas led their Scouts along the southern flank a few kilometres ahead of the other Dark Angels. There was little sign of the orks; what debris and trails Naaman found indicated that the new warlord had retired hurriedly eastwards again, probably to regroup or perhaps to escape. Belial's orders were straightforward: hunt down the orks and annihilate them before they could recover.

Just after mid-morning, Naaman received a comm-message on the long-range set Sergeant Damas had brought from Kadillus Harbour. It was a general transmission from the pilot on board one of the company's three Thunderhawk gunships, which had been sent on an overflight mission of the East Barrens power plant.

'This is *Zealous Guardian*, Brother Hadrazael in command. *Extremis vindicus*. Contacting Task Force Uriel. Please confirm reception of this signal.'

'Confirm, *Zealous Guardian*. This is Vet–'

'*Zealous Guardian*, Master Uriel receiving your transmission,' the force commander cut across Naaman. The Scout-sergeant motioned for the squad to halt and take cover while he listened to the exchange.

'Sustained damage from anti-air fire in vicinity of East Barrens thermal plant. Losing altitude. Please confirm reception readiness for report.'

'I can hear you, Hadrazael,' said Uriel. 'Deliver your report.'

'Approaching sensor sweeps detected growing life-form presence in the area around the East Barrens plant. Large energy spike also detected. We approached on a circling course at two kilometres distance. Visually identified numerous enemy in and around the facility, estimate one hundred or more orks. No visual identification to corroborate with energy spike signature. Engaged by multiple-missile anti-aircraft vehicle of unknown design. Exotic gravimetric field warhead as well as explosives. Stabilisation systems lost, instruments erratic. Visual estimate of altitude is at four thousand metres and falling.'

'*Zealous Guardian*, this is Uriel. Describe composition of enemy forces at power plant.'

'No war engines or sizeable armour seen. No static defences. Buggies, Dreadnoughts and bikes in low number. Mostly infantry, Brother-Chaplain. Transmission ending. Impact imminent.'

'Naaman!' Damas's shout dragged the sergeant's attention away from the comm-set.

A dozen kilometres or so to the east, a dark shape plummeted out of the clouds trailing fire and smoke. It cleared the line of ridges and seemed to settle on a stable course for a few hundred metres. Naaman could imagine Hadrazael struggling at the controls trying to wrestle the blocky aircraft with damaged mechanical systems and brute strength; the Thunderhawk's border-line aerodynamics required complex automated systems and gravity-dampeners to stay airworthy and without them Hadrazael's only option was to slow the inevitable descent as much as was possible and crash-land.

The Thunderhawk's nose dipped suddenly. Naaman could hear the whining of the *Zealous Guardian*'s engines as they were throttled into reverse. The heavily armoured gunship bobbed once, and then dived almost vertically, smashing into the ground. Stubby wings, armoured plates and tail planes spun out of the dust cloud. Naaman whipped out his monocular and through the haze and dirt could see the Thunderhawk lying on its side about four kilometres away. There was no sign of smoke or flames.

'Secure that wreck site,' Naaman snapped to the others. 'Full run. There could be orks in that area.'

As the others set off towards the rising column of dust, Naaman activated the long-range comm.

'Master Uriel, this is Naaman. We have located the crash site and are moving to secure. Any further instructions?'

'Negative, brother-sergeant. Establish condition of crew and viability of gunship retrieval. If the Thunderhawk cannot be recovered, activate the on-board charges and destroy it. If possible, retrieve sensor logs before destruction.'

'Understood, Brother-Chaplain. Will report on our arrival.'

Naaman ran after the others, bolter in one hand, comm-piece in the other. He jabbed the standard tactical frequency into the digipad.

'*Zealous Guardian*, do you receive? Brother Hadrazael?'

There was no reply.

* * *

DAMAS LED HIS Scouts in a circuitous sweep around the wreck, knowing that the crash would have attracted any orks in the area. While the Scouts patrolled, Naaman headed straight for the Thunderhawk. It was laid on the port side of the fuselage, at the end of a furrow more than a hundred metres long. The hull armour had been ripped away along with the wing and starboard portion of the tail. The starboard and fuselage engines emanated a thick haze of heat. Metal pinged and cracked as it settled. The armoured canopy of the cockpit appeared to be intact but there were shards of rock scattered in front of the Thunderhawk's path where it had struck a large boulder before being halted.

'This is Sergeant Naaman, approaching from the south-west,' he called out, cupping a hand to his mouth. It was better than relying on the comm, and he had no desire to be shot by his own battle-brothers.

The assault ramp was blocked by the awkward angle of the wreckage. Naaman used the edge of the buckled roof armour as hand and footholds, pulling himself up the six metres to the almost-horizontal starboard side of the fuselage.

'This is Damas. Area is clear of enemy.'

'Confirm, Damas. Set up perimeter on my position, brother.'

'Affirmative. Three-hundred-metre perimeter on the wreck site.'

Naaman padded along the length of the hull to the service hatch just behind the main cockpit area. Crouching, he punched the activation rune. There was a hiss of released gas, but the small door did not move.

Slinging his bolter strap over his shoulder, Naaman opened up the manual crank and grabbed the half-wheel in both hands. With a quarter-clockwise turn, he unlocked the manual bolts and heaved the hatch free, tossing it to the ground.

'Brothers?' Naaman's voice echoed tinnily from the interior of the gunship. 'This is Naaman.'

He heard a muffled reply, probably from the cockpit. A screech of twisting metal and a thump reverberated along the hull.

'Can you hear me now, brother?' came the voice again.

'Brother Hadrazael? This is Naaman, Tenth Company.'

'The fore bulkhead has sheared, blocking the entranceway. I need your help to move it.'

'Is there anybody else on board?' Naaman asked, dropping through the hatchway.

He landed on the door on the opposite side. It was strange to see the inside of the Thunderhawk at a ninety-degree angle. Naaman glanced around to orientate himself.

'Brother Mephael was in the port weapons seat when we hit,' said Hadrazael. 'I think he is dead. Check on him first.'

Naaman clambered aft along the tilted fuselage, stepping over equipment that had fallen out of the lockers, picking his way past fallen ceiling plates and dislodged cabling. He located the gunnery control position for the dorsal cannon, midway along the hull. He found the top half of a Space Marine trapped under a twisted support strut. He wore no backpack, helmet or shoulder pads, as was usual onboard a gun-ship. Not that their protection would have helped. There was no sign of Mephael's legs; Naaman assumed they had been ripped off in the crash. Without hope, the sergeant checked for signs of life, and found none.

He scrambled back to the cockpit, where the front bulkhead had buckled and torn away from the ceiling, closing off the doorway to the cockpit. Through a small triangular gap, he could see Brother Hadrazael peering through at him.

'Mephael's dead, brother,' said Naaman. 'Let us get you out of there. Is the comm unit disabled?'

'Affirmative, brother,' said Hadrazael. 'Mephael's harness release had jammed. I had released my own to assist him when the ship nose-dived. I believe it was the impact of my head that broke the comm.'

'Are you injured?'

Hadrazael laughed.

'Not significantly. The control console was hurt more than I was! Pull from your side and I will push from mine, brother-sergeant.'

Naaman grabbed the broken bulkhead, his thick gauntlets protecting his palms against the sharp edges. He braced a foot on the lip of an observation portal and pulled back. He heard a grunt from within the cockpit as Hadrazael leaned his weight against the reinforced metal. The bulkhead scraped a few cen-timetres, opening more of a gap. Using his bolter as a lever, Naaman prised the gap wider until Hadrazael could push his arm through.

'Step back, brother,' warned the pilot. 'I'll take a run-up.'

Naaman retreated a few metres from the doorway. A few rapid thuds of Hadrazael's boots rang from the ship and then he smashed into the bulkhead. With a wrenching screech, the fallen wall parted from its surviving bolts and clanged down, Hadrazael falling on top of it. Naaman helped the pilot to his feet.

'Sensor logs, brother?' Naaman asked.

The pilot pulled a datacrystal from a pouch at his belt.

'Already uploaded, brother.'

Hadrazael searched through the equipment lockers and scattered debris and located his helmet and pads. His backpack was still secure in its recharging alcove, but could not be released. Naaman climbed outside first, quickly noticing the Scouts patrolling around the downed Thunderhawk. He dropped to the ground as Hadrazael extricated himself from the wreck.

'Command, this is Sergeant Naaman,' he called over the comm. 'Brother Hadrazael is fully combat-functional. Brother Mephael is dead. Sensor logs intact. Request Rhino pick-up from the crash site.'

The comm buzzed for thirty seconds. Confused by the delay, Naaman transmitted his report again. After a few more seconds, he heard the voice of Brother Sarpedon.

'Naaman, this is Sarpedon. Negative on your request, brother. Force encountering increasing resistance. Ork numbers higher than anticipated. No Rhinos are available at this time. Escort Brother Hadrazael and the scanner data to Koth Ridge.'

'What has happened to Brother Uriel, Brother-Chaplain?' asked Naaman.

'Contact lost with force commander three minutes ago. Ravenwing Sergeant Validus reports intense fighting on the north flank. I am diverting the task force to counter the attack. Proceed to Koth Ridge on your new orders. Confirm.'

'Confirm, Brother-Chaplain. Escort to Koth Ridge.'

Naaman called Damas and the others to gather around. He related what was happening to the rest of the force with a frown.

'Just how many orks did you see at the power plant?' Damas quizzed Hadrazael.

'At least one hundred infantry,' replied the battle-brother.

'Even if they all left immediately and headed westwards, that's not enough to account for the resistance the others are encountering,' said Damas.

'No, it isn't, brothers,' said Naaman, keeping his suspicions to himself. Returning to Koth Ridge seemed like a good idea. He needed to speak with Belial.

THE WIND HAD shifted to the south and brought with it a cold edge from the sea as night fell. Naaman waited patiently for his contact request to be answered by Master Belial, and he stood watching Hadrazael having his injury treated by Apothecary Nestor. In the dying light, Naaman's eyes scoured the ridge for the trooper, Tauno. There was no sign of him. The veteran sergeant did not know why he was so interested in the youth: he was just one of hundreds randomly picked from the mass of soldiers manning the defence line. It was that randomness that held the appeal; Naaman could have picked any of the men and he was sure the story of the man's life would not be so different.

He watched the troopers with narrowed eyes. There were so many tiny differences: short or tall; fat or thin; old or young; brave or cowardly; clever or stupid. None of those differences meant anything. For the most part they were simply a finger on a lasgun trigger. In the grandest scheme of all, the great Imperium stretching across a million worlds, each of their lives was wholly pointless.

There was nothing remarkable about any of them.

Each of those men had no more impact upon the fate of the galaxy than a piece of sand would have on the orbit of a planet. But like anything else, it was quantity that mattered. Enough sand, one grain at a time, could tip a planet on its axis; enough men could decide the future of worlds or the entire destiny of mankind. One human was unimportant; a million were hard to ignore; a billion...

Tauno was just one unimpressive man, but he was one amongst countless billions. He had picked up a lasgun, for reasons Naaman could probably never understand, and decided to fight. On his own, he was nothing. With nine other men, he was a squad. With hundreds of other men, they were a company. Dozens of companies made a regiment. On and on, one man after another, becoming divisions and army groups and crusades, utterly unaware of each other, spread across thousands of star systems. Tauno was just a man picked from a crowd, but he was all of them. He was mankind, rendered down into a single body and reduplicated over and over and over.

That was what Naaman found so remarkable.

The sergeant smiled to himself and wondered if he should write his observations down. The Teachings of Naaman? It was better to leave the philosophy to other, more educated minds. The true teachings of Naaman were with bolter and blade, camo-cloak and sniper rifle. Those were useful lessons for an aspiring Space Marine to learn.

The chime of the comm interrupted his thoughts. He thumbed the reception stud on the headset.

'This is Sergeant Naaman.'

'This is Master Belial. Brother Sarpedon is leading the remnants of the task force back to Koth Ridge.'

'Remnants, brother-captain?' Naaman could not keep the shock from his voice.

'Your earlier assessment of the enemy numbers seems to be more accurate than mine, Naaman,' said Belial. It was a statement of fact, not an apology or admittance. 'Ork strength to the east has increased again. I cannot account for the appearance of these new forces. It is not only illogical, it is out of character for the orks to leave behind such a strong reserve. Why were these forces not committed to the initial attack on the city, or in the second advance on the ridge? It seems that the enemy is arriving in waves. I must know the strength of the third wave.'

'I will find the answers, brother-captain,' said Naaman. 'If I can locate the ork ship, it should be possible to make a correct gauge of their strength. Better still, it may be possible to destroy the site from orbit.'

'That is a risky proposition, brother-sergeant,' replied Belial. 'It is imperative that this new ork wave does not reach the city. To provide the troops necessary, I am suspending offensive action in Kadillus Harbour and moving to a containment strategy to keep the orks in the docks. I cannot retake the defence-laser silo at this juncture.'

The company commander hesitated. When he continued there was an odd note in his voice, a slight reluctance in his quiet words. Naaman listened without comment.

'On my instruction, Brother-Librarian Charon has sent an astropathic message to the rest of the Chapter, warning them of the worsening situation on Piscina. I expect Grand Master Azrael to divert additional resources on receipt of this message. Such help will be at least ten days away. If we can destroy the ork ship and any reinforcements, this diversion of the Chapter will not be required and Charon will cancel the call for aid.

'I need you to find out what is happening, Naaman. I do not want any more surprises. You have been further east than anybody else. You *must* bypass the orks and make a direct investigation of the East Barrens geothermal station.'

'Confirm, brother-captain. Am I to take Squad Damas with me?'

'Affirmative. Ensure that all in your patrol know how to use the long-range communicator.'

'I do not expect any of us to return, brother-captain. Survival on such a mission is typically zero-point-seven per cent. If it pleases you, I would request that the members of Squad Damas be honoured in the Chapter records as battle-brothers. Their sacrifice should be remembered.'

'I concur, Brother Naaman. *In perpetuis Leo gravitas excelsior*. Walk in the Lion's shadow without fear. Emperor speed you to victory.'

'I have no fear, brother-captain. I am Astartes. I am that which others fear.'

When the link was cut, Naaman spoke privately with Sergeant Damas, explaining the difficult mission they had been tasked with.

'You and I both know that none of us is likely to get through the orks' lines and back again, Naaman,' said Damas. 'Do you wish to inform the Scouts of this factor?'

'They are your squad, brother, it is up to you,' Naaman replied with a light shrug.

'Then I see no advantage in telling them this will be a one-way trip. Knowledge of this will cause apprehension, which will have a negative effect on combat performance and therefore decrease the chances of success.'

'I concur,' said Naaman. 'The odds of survival are exceptionally low but there is no need to make this a self-fulfilling prophecy.'

'You've been out there and back twice already; if anyone can bring us back it will be you, brother,' Damas said, slapping a hand to Naaman's arm.

THE SCOUTS REACHED the Indola Mines just before nightfall by commandeering one of the defence force's Chimera transports. There was no report of the orks west of Indola and Naaman had judged correctly that speed had been preferable to stealth. After despatching the worried Free Militia driver and his vehicle back to

Koth Ridge, Naaman and the others lay up in the mines until night shrouded the East Barrens. For two hours they waited, scanning the horizon with monoculars, alert for any ork activity.

They saw no sign of the greenskins.

Naaman called Damas and his squad together as the first of Piscina's moons rose as a sliver in the eastern sky. The wind had freshened from the south, coming off the sea, bringing a haze of cloud that did little to obscure the stars.

'There is no merit in delaying our departure,' Naaman told the others. 'It is unlikely the cloud cover will increase. Our mission is to penetrate the ork lines and reach the next series of ridges just westwards of the East Barrens geothermal station. There is no accurate intelligence on the orks' numbers or deployment. All that we know is our task force was halted and driven back, which indicates the orks have enough strength to mount a serious offensive. We are not here to kill orks – that will come later. None of you will engage the enemy without express orders from me or Sergeant Damas.'

Naaman took a deep breath, the air frosting in front of his face.

'We cannot be detected. If the orks become aware of our presence, not only will they attempt to hunt us down, we will have no opportunity to investigate the power plant. Mission success depends upon us moving like ghosts. Sergeant Damas will lead the way, I will follow you. Communication will be limited to sub-vocal comms. Our foes may be crude, but do not mistake them for being stupid. Confirm?'

There was a hushed chorus of affirmatives. Naaman nodded in satisfaction and signalled for Damas to move out. As the Scouts filed out of a gateway following a winding track to the east, Naaman stopped for a moment and checked his equipment one last time. Along with a bolt pistol, chainsword and grenades, he had a special piece of wargear that had been brought to him by Brother Hephaestus just before the Scouts had left Koth Ridge.

The cylindrical container looked unimpressive. It was about the length of his forearm, made of plain metal save for a runepad on one end and a comm-socket in the other. Inside was a different matter. Once erected, the teleport homer would send a sub-warp signal to the *Unrelenting Fury* in orbit above the planet. On board, Sergeant Adamanta waited with four of his fellow Deathwing Terminators. Within minutes of the beacon's activation, they would be able to teleport to the surface and provide support. It was a last-ditch strategy – the arrival of a teleporting squad was the antithesis of stealth – but if the mission was in serious danger of failure, the extra firepower could prove crucial.

Naaman knelt down and laid the teleport homer in the grass. Drawing a cable from the long-range comm-set, he plugged himself into its transmitter. He punched in the test-sequence on the keypad and waited.

'Teleport frequency locked-in.'

The droning voice came from one of the faceless servitors wired into the comm boards on the battle-barge. Little more than a processor embodied in a once-human shell, the servitor reeled off a stream of frequency data and coordinates. Checking his digimap, Naaman confirmed that the signal location was being accurately traced to within three metres. Confident that the beacon was operating properly, he cancelled the test signal and detached himself from the comm-link.

Using a magnetic clamp, Naaman strapped the device to his left thigh and stood up. Damas and the others had become shadows in the darkness, their cameleoline cloaks blending with the dark blues and greys of the night. If Naaman had not known where they would be – and benefited from the augmentation to his eyes that all Space Marines underwent – he would not have seen them at all.

Wrapping his cloak around him, Naaman headed after them, merging with the darkness.

PROGRESS WAS SLOW but steady. Damas and Naaman ordered the squad to halt every few hundred metres so that they could sweep the surrounding wilderness with the monoculars. The Scouts did not hurry, but kept a steady pace that gradually swallowed up the kilometres between Indola and the power plant. They had covered about half the distance when Damas attracted Naaman's attention during one of the routine observation stops. The two sergeants met atop a low hill covered with waist-high brush.

'Three kilometres east,' said Damas as the pair crouched amongst a scrub of waxy-leaved grass. 'Thermal signature. Vehicle, perhaps?'

Naaman looked for himself and saw the orange glow

of a heat haze through the monocular. The signature looked too hot and localised to be engines.

'Campfire,' Naaman said.

Damas looked again and grunted to himself.

'Of course it is. There are two more, about five hundred metres apart, to the north of the first. What is our plan?'

Naaman swept his view south and saw more campfires, a kilometre or more further away than the ones directly east, spread haphazardly across the Barrens. Some were close to each other, but he could see a path through that headed south-east and then cut to the north-east. If this was meant to be some kind of picket, it was a clumsy one.

Naaman pointed out the safe route to Damas.

'I concur,' said the other sergeant. 'No vehicle lights, but there is the possibility of roaming patrols between the camps.'

Naaman patted his bolt pistol.

'That is why we have these,' he said with a grin, which was copied by Damas, who drew his combat knife.

'I prefer this,' said Damas.

'The Lion's blessings come to us each in different ways,' replied Naaman. 'Prepare your squad to move out and I will make one last sweep.'

Damas pushed through the bushes and disappeared while Naaman scanned the rising ground for any sign of movement. He saw nothing and it seemed likely the orks had settled into their camps for the night. Naaman was unhappy that the wind had shifted direction; in the darkness the stench of the greenskins would have been just as much a warning as anything that might be seen. As it was, they would have to carry on in the same cautious manner. The slowness of their infiltration irked Naaman, as he was sure that come sunrise, the orks would move west again, and that could be very dangerous.

Padding silently through the night, the Scouts picked their way between the campsites. Concealed by the darkness and their cloaks, there was little chance the orks, night-blinded by their fires, would see the Dark Angels Scouts moving wraith-like from gulley to hill to winding river bank. Damas led them on a course that kept them as low as possible, avoiding high ground. The soil underfoot grew thinner and the rocky subsurface of Kadillus broke through in patches scattered with rocks and pebbles. The Scouts moved around these areas, keeping to the dwindling grass where possible.

Just after midnight Damas's barely audible whisper over the comm halted the squad. Naaman glided through the night, bolt pistol in hand, and joined the other sergeant at the head of the advance. He saw immediately what had caused the stop.

A little more than a hundred metres ahead, a diminutive figure sat on a rock, a flare-muzzled gun in its lap. It was a gretchin, one of the orks' small slave-companions. At first Naaman thought it was dozing, but there came a flash of red from its eyes in the growing moonlight as the wiry creature looked this way and that.

'There's another one over there,' hissed Damas, pointing a little to Naaman's right. 'And a third up on that hill.'

Over the wind, Naaman caught a brief flurry of sound: two high-pitched voices that seemed to be arguing. They were close, within fifty metres, to the left and almost behind the Scouts. Dropping to his belly, Naaman crawled through the grass in the direction of the noise, bolt pistol held out in front of him.

His course brought him to the lip of a shallow dell. In the middle of the depression two gretchin were ineffectually fighting, wrestling with each other and biting at each other's long, pointed ears. Naaman had no idea what they were saying but guessed that the source of the dispute was the thick-barrelled pistol that kept swapping between them during the scuffle.

Naaman slid closer, parting the grass with his free hand, eyes fixed on the squabbling sentries. As he rose to a crouch, cloak folded around him, Naaman aimed at the pair. They were so close he could have thrown his pistol at them, but they kept moving back and forth in their struggle, occasionally one or the other tumbling to the dirt before leaping back to its feet to resume the fight. Naaman's pistol followed them.

For a split-second, the two gretchin were locked together. One had its back to him, holding the pistol behind its back, a clawed hand in the face of the other, which had its skinny fingers tightening around its opponent's throat.

With barely a puff of decompressing gas, Naaman fired. The silenced bolt-round struck the closest gretchin in the back of the skull, blowing its head apart. The other stared wide-eyed at Naaman through the bubbling mess of blood and brains, bony hands still clasped around the throat of its companion's corpse. Naaman's second shot took the survivor in the eye and two headless bodies flopped to the ground.

Creeping up the far side of the depression, Naaman checked to the east. He could see glimmers of movement as the third of Piscina's moons slid above the horizon, casting a pale blue glow through the clouds. Despite the extra light it was hard to see the gretchin as they wandered about on their erratic patrols or stood sentry between the dozens of campfires. As the ground rose steadily into the next ridge, it undulated steeply, making it hard to see over the next lip.

'Thermis tapeta,' Naaman whispered to the squad via the comm. He pulled down his autosight goggles and thumbed through the spectral modes until he reached the far-infrared setting. The Barrens became a shifting landscape of dark blues and purples, broken by the bright yellow and white of flames. Here and there he saw the dark red blobs of the gretchin and the slightly brighter silhouettes of the orks heated by the fires.

There seemed to be no certain way through the cluster of campfires directly eastwards, but a detour to the south would add several kilometres to the journey. Naaman checked the chronometer display. Total moonfall would occur within three hours. In the utter darkness, it would be easier to slip through the ork camps. He reached a decision.

'Assemble on my position,' he told the squad.

He watched the Scouts approaching through his thermal vision. Naaman glimpsed only an occasional patch of face or exposed wrist, the cameleoline diffusing the heat signature of the Scouts' bodies. Like will o' the wisps the squad gathered on the edge of the depression.

'We have to wait until moonfall before we carry on,' Naaman said. 'We are too exposed here. Have any of you seen a suitable defensive position?'

'There is a shallow gulley a few hundred metres to the south-east, sergeant,' replied Scout Luthor. He pointed out the direction. 'It is less than two hundred metres from one of the camps, but it seems to curve southwards of them and there is not another camp within half a kilometre.'

Naaman's gaze followed the Scout's finger. He could not see much of the gulley that had been mentioned, but he could see two campfires, about fifty metres apart. Other than the dancing flames, which were growing weak, he could see little activity from the greenskins.

'That will be suitable,' he said with a nod. 'We will approach from the south, twenty metres dispersal. Follow me.'

Naaman led the way, rising out of the depression at a stoop, darting over the open ground with his bolt pistol ready. He spotted a flash of red to his left and turned his path south, ducking into the shadow of a monolithic boulder. Peering around the rock, he saw nothing between him and the gulley, which he could now see forming between two shallow, bush-strewn ridges. After another check on the position of the sentries, he set off at a comfortable run, crossing the few hundred metres to the head of the gulley without stopping. Flicking up his goggles, he drew out his monocular and examined the narrow split in the rocky hillside. Naaman could see nothing and waved the rest

GAV THORPE

of the squad to take cover inside.

While Damas split the Scouts to their observation positions, Naaman crawled out of the shallow defile and wormed his way towards the closest ork camp.

The greenskins had chosen to spend the night near some grass-filled ruins. Naaman could not tell what the buildings had once been, but they were now overgrown with thorny branches, their walls toppled to form slopes and hillocks of broken brick. A rise to his right obscured one camp, the light of its fire creating a dim aura beyond the crest. To the left, looking between the hill and one of the ruins, Naaman could see another blaze. He watched the orks around the flames for a few seconds. Some were lying down, probably sleeping. Others sat on crates and upturned barrels or simply squatted in the grass. He counted seven in total. There was no way to tell if a similar number had gathered around the other fire, but it seemed unlikely there would be many more.

A handful of gretchin mooched around the ruins and the jutting rocks, kicking at stones, sometimes calling to each other in their squeaky voices. Naaman studied them for a while, trying to discern any pattern to their movements, but concluded that there was no regular rhythm or path to their patrols. The gretchin seemed reluctant to move away from the light of the fires, but now and then one of the orks would rouse itself and shout at the closest sentries, waving them further out.

The erratic behaviour of the picket was a problem. Although Naaman could see an obvious route to the north of the camps, passing through the leftmost ruins, it would be too risky to use while there was any moonlight. By the time moonfall came, who could say where the gretchin would be? The Scouts' infiltration would have to be opportunistic and speedy.

Content that he was following the best course of action, Naaman slipped back to the others. He found them laying up at the lips of the gulley, Damas and two others keeping watch to the east, the other two Scouts watching to the south-east and north-west. Naaman stayed close to the head of the gulley and found a spot under the branches of a bush with low, twisted branches. From here he could see the left-most camp and the ruined building behind which the closest fire was burning low.

All they had to do now was wait for the moons to go down.

'SERGEANT!'

Naaman glanced along the gulley, the whispered warning instantly breaking the trance-like state that had come over him during the watch. In the darkness he saw Luthor raise a hand and point to the camp next to the closest ruined building. Three small silhouettes emerged against the low orange glow of the fire, slowly walking straight for the gulley.

'Hold fire,' Damas whispered. The squad sergeant quietly slid sideways, towards Naaman. He stopped within reaching distance. 'What do you think? Should we eliminate them, brother?'

'Not yet,' Naaman replied, his words barely more than a breath. 'Let us wait to see what they do.'

Naaman checked the chronometer. It was twenty-seven minutes to total moonfall, though only one of the three remained in the sky and it was perhaps dark enough to move out. If the sentries changed course, they would wait for complete night. If not, Naaman would have a decision to make.

His breaths coming long and shallow, Naaman kept his eyes fixed firmly on the gretchin. There was a scattering of debris between the scrawny aliens and the lip of the gulley: crates, rusted pieces of old machinery and a small slag pile. Each of the sentries carried a rifle of some sort. They probably wouldn't do much damage if they hit, but the sound of gunfire would surely alert the nearby orks, which were a far more dangerous proposition than the gretchin.

The group kept on their course, heading towards the Scouts. They were about seventy metres away when they stopped and began to pick through the junk scattered around the slagheap. Naaman didn't like them being so close even though they were currently distracted. A rattle of a stone, the clink of a weapon on rock or even a break in the cloud to let through more moonlight might attract the sentries' attention.

It was time to get moving again.

'Brother Damas,' Naaman whispered. 'Move your squad into the outskirts of the camp and eliminate those sentries. I'll swing around the north and make sure the flank is secure.'

'Confirm, brother,' said Damas. 'I'll have Luthor move in to cover the closest camp with his heavy bolter while we eliminate the gretchin.'

'Confirm,' replied Naaman. 'If the alarm is raised, concentrate your shooting on that camp. I will intercept any reinforcements coming through from the other fire.'

The two sergeants nodded to each other and parted. Naaman heard Damas's whispered commands and left the gulley, using the rise of the hill between the two ruined buildings to conceal his path northwards. Heading towards the farther of the two ruins, Naaman heard the *skritch-skritch-skritch* of footsteps on gravel. The veteran threw himself down on instinct, bolt pistol ready, eyes darting left and right, searching for the source of the noise. With his other hand, he tugged his cloak into position, covering himself from scalp to knees, peering under the rim of the hood.

Naaman saw the gretchin come around the corner of the building, a stout blunderbuss-like shotgun over its shoulder. He caught the strange, mouldy whiff of the greenskin as it sat down on a broken lump of masonry and pulled something from the pocket of its ragged jerkin. Something squirmed in its bony fingers before being popped into a fanged mouth. The sounds of loud chewing broke the stillness.

The gretchin was looking in Naaman's direction. He lay absolutely still, bolt pistol sighted on the creature's chest. Finishing its snack, the gretchin stood up and continued to wander on, passing a few metres in front of the prone Space Marine.

As soon as the gretchin had passed, Naaman surged to his feet, slipping his combat knife from his belt with his left hand. Two swift steps brought him up behind the creature. Hearing the quiet thud of Naaman's boots, the gretchin started to turn, but was far too slow. Naaman hooked his arm over the gretchin's shoulder and plunged the knife upwards into its throat, puncturing the windpipe. The sentry spasmed limply in Naaman's grasp, burbling blood as the Space Marine quickly sawed the knife out of the gretchin's throat, slicing through muscle and veins.

It fell limp in his grasp. Glancing around to assure himself he had not been seen, Naaman sheathed his knife and hefted the small creature under his arm. A few dozen strides brought him to the shelter of the ruin, where he laid the body down in a corner of the broken walls. Naaman passed through the roofless rooms until he came to the eastern side of the building. Crouched beneath the sill of a glassless window, he stopped again and watched the orks around the northern campfire.

As he waited, Naaman's attention was drawn to his right by a high-pitched wail, which suddenly fell silent. One of the gretchin had spotted the Scouts!

Suddenly the air was split by the thumping detonations of Luthor's heavy bolter. Naaman heard the shrieks of dying gretchin and the angry bellows of the orks. The greenskins in front of him roused slowly, startled by the sudden attack. There were more shouts and fire from the south where the orks ahead of Naaman grabbed their weapons and loped away from their camp.

Naaman unhooked his chainsword but did not start up the motor. His cloak flapping behind him, the sergeant vaulted through the window, heading directly for the campfire. The orks were completely unaware of his presence as they rushed to the aid of their companions. Less than twenty metres from the greenskins, Naaman opened fire. Silenced bolts ripped through the back of the rearmost ork, chewing through muscle and vertebrae. One of the other orks noticed its demise and swung around to see what had happened; by the time the creature looked in his direction Naaman was already in the shelter of a tall rock, cameleoline swathing his form. As soon as the ork's red eyes roved elsewhere, Naaman rose up and fired three bolts into the creature's face and chest, felling it instantly.

There were five more orks to deal with. Naaman broke from cover at a sprint, rushing up behind the greenskins as they lumbered towards the fighting at the other fire. Catching up with the orks, Naaman swung his chainsword at the neck of the closest, thumbing the starter mid-blow. Growling teeth sheared halfway into the ork's neck before jamming on its thick spinal column. With a grunt, Naaman wrenched the blade free and fired his bolt pistol into the back of the creature's head as it collapsed sideways.

Taken off guard by the deadly shadow charging into their midst, the orks were thrown into confusion. The pale rays of the moon shimmering from his cameleo-line, Naaman ducked beneath the hasty swing of an axe and brought the throbbing chainsword up into the ork's gut, ramming it point first through the stomach and into the chest cavity. The creature shuddered with the vibrations of the weapon, spittle flying from its thick lips.

A grunt of effort to Naaman's right warned him of imminent attack and he ducked as he pulled his chainsword free, a cleaver-like blade cutting the corner from the sergeant's swirling cloak. Naaman kicked the creature's legs from under it as he spun beneath the swinging weapon. A second ork leapt to the attack, a heavy, serrated sword aimed at Naaman. He smashed aside the blade with his chainsword; at the same time he fired a bolt into the face of the downed ork, its brains splashing out across the cracked stone underfoot.

The roar of the heavy bolter sounded closer and the ork with the serrated sword was hurled away from Naaman by multiple explosions across its chest and shoulders, ragged remains slapping into one of its companions. Naaman used the distraction to chop at the disorientated ork's arm, hacking the limb away below the shoulder. Out of instinct, the alien tried to throw a punch with the bloody stump. It stared at the ragged wound in amazement when the expected blow failed to appear. Naaman shattered its knee with a bolt and brought his sword down on its back as it fell forwards, hacking several times into the creature's green flesh until the spine finally snapped.

Having dealt with the other camp, Damas and his squad arrived, falling upon the orks with bolt pistol, chainsword and monomolecular-edged combat knives. Confused and partly blinded by the dark, the orks died swiftly, cut down in a few savage seconds.

After the clamour of battle, silence descended again, broken by the sighing of the wind and the crackle of the fires. The whole fight had taken less than twenty seconds, from the first cry of the sentry to the choking death-rattle of the last ork.

'Casualties?' Naaman demanded, glancing at the others.

MAGULANOX
❖ SECTOR ❖

KADILLUS MAP

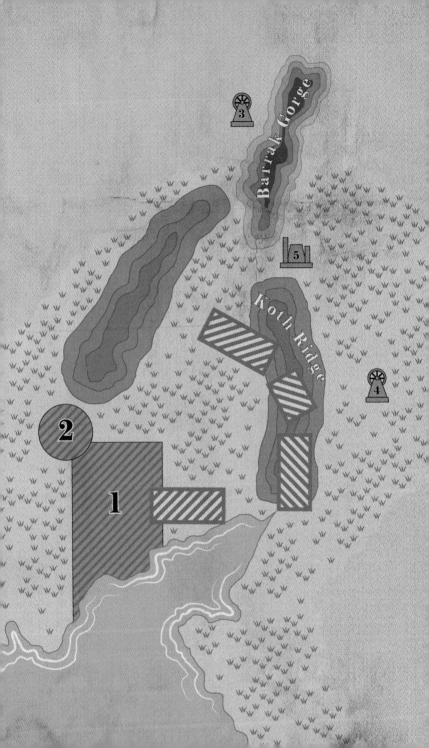

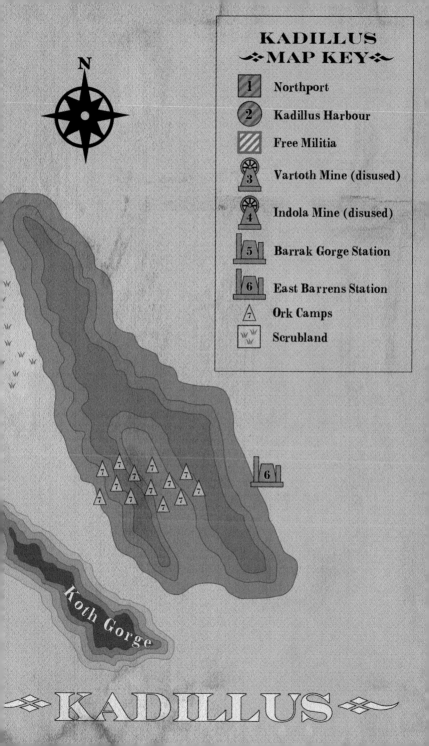

Captain Beliai

Promoted to Master of the 3rd Company for his personal bravery, skill and tactical acumen, Belial needed all three during the Battle for Kadillus. At the outset of the ork invasion he confronted Ghazghkull Thraka and was almost slain. Despite the injuries he sustained, he continued to lead the 3rd Company for the duration of the campaign.

Belial's armour and banner display the colours of the 3rd Company, his Deathwing affiliations and his personal heraldry.

'None, brother,' Damas replied. The sergeant turned to his squad with a proud smile. 'Not so much as a scratch. The advantage of surprise is the deadliest weapon in our arsenal.'

'That is good,' said Naaman.

He flicked blood from his chainsword and wiped the weapon clean on the jacket of a dead ork. He checked his chronometer. There were two and a half hours until dawn and still many kilometres to cover before they reached the ridge overlooking the geothermal station.

'Hide the bodies in the ruins, douse the fires,' Damas told his squad as Naaman pulled out his monocular and looked to the east. He could see a stretch of two or three kilometres up the slope before there were more campfires. They could cover the next leg at a comfortable run.

'Belay that,' snapped Naaman. The Scouts dropped the ork bodies they had picked up and looked at him. 'By the time the orks find them, if they ever do, we'll be far away from here. We have to keep moving.'

'As you say,' said Damas, choosing not to argue the point. 'Let's get into our observation position before dawn.'

Reloading their weapons, checking their cloaks, the Scouts ghosted into the night.

NAAMAN KEPT THE squad angling slightly to the south, avoiding the bulk of the camps ahead. Throughout the night Naaman could see mobs of greenskins and hear their vehicles, gathering north of the East Barrens station. For all their numbers, Naaman was surprised that there were not more greenskins. Certainly the forces he had seen advancing while he had retreated the day before had not been all accounted for by the assault on Koth Ridge. The orks were definitely on the move again, but it was impossible for Naaman to judge where they were heading.

The Scouts made good time, eating up the kilometres at a tireless half-run. Though the location of the ork camps had forced him further south than he had originally hoped, Naaman was pleased when they finally crested the ridge above the geothermal station. The plant itself was about a kilometre to the east.

Using the thermal setting of his monocular, Naaman examined the compound of buildings clustered around the angular bulk of the geothermal generator. He could see lots of heat, most of it coming from the plant itself, but there were also dozens if not hundreds of orks down there. He spent several minutes looking but could see nothing in range that looked remotely like a spaceship. Even further out into the Barrens, the plains stretched on without a break.

There was only one conclusion that sprang to Naaman's mind. Ork technology was unfathomable, often crudely made but highly effective. The only possible explanation for the absence of a landed ship would be that the orks had managed to hide it with some kind of camouflage field. It had to be here somewhere, Naaman reasoned: orks didn't simply pop out of thin air.

He hoped that dawn would literally shed more light on the answers and he ordered the squad to head northwards for a better view of the sprawling ork encampment at the base of the ridge. When they had found a good spot to observe the orks whilst keeping out of sight, the squad settled down to another tense time of waiting and keeping watch.

SLOWLY DAWN'S RUDDY fingers gripped the eastern skies. Naaman waited expectantly, scouring the plains for some telltale shimmer or reflection that might betray the location of a shield-screened vessel. As the minutes skipped past, his anxiety to find the ship grew. In the growing light, he returned his attention to the power plant to see if more had been revealed of the orks' numbers and the layout of their defences.

The monocular almost fell from his fingers in surprise. Naaman stared dumbfounded at the ork encampment, lost for words.

'What is it?' asked Damas from behind Naaman, sensing the veteran sergeant's shock.

'By the Lion's shade, I've never seen anything like it,' exclaimed Naaman.

Still astounded by what he had seen, Naaman fumbled for the long-range comm handset and opened up the command frequency that would put him directly in touch with Master Belial. Raising the monocular he checked again to make sure he wasn't imagining what he had thought he had seen.

'This is Master Belial. Make your report, brother-sergeant.'

Naaman wasn't quite sure what his report was. How did he explain what he was looking at?

'Naaman? What is happening?'

'Sorry, brother-captain,' Naaman managed when he

had mustered his thoughts. 'I know how the orks are getting to Piscina.'

THE TALE OF NAAMAN
Revelations

IT WAS NAAMAN'S incredulity that made it so difficult to describe what he could see to Master Belial. Never before had the Scout-sergeant doubted the evidence of his own eyes, but as he stared through the monocular it was hard for him to comprehend what he was looking at.

'The orks have taken possession of the geothermal station,' he reported, choosing to concentrate on things that did not invite speculation. 'There are several hundred of them. Composition of the force is in line with what we have already encountered: mostly infantry and a few smaller vehicles and field pieces.

'The power plant has been adapted; I can see strange machinery and energy relays of ork design. The major alteration is the addition of a large disc, like a communications transmitter, although I can see energy waves crackling over its surface. There are sporadic bursts of energy that appear to be a result of the generator systems suffering from an overload of capacity.'

'Are they using it to supplement the power of their ship, brother?' asked Belial.

'There is no ship, brother-captain,' Naaman replied.

He looked again at the ork camp. No more than two hundred metres from the geothermal station was an upright disc of pure darkness, its edges crackling with energy. The surface of the disc had a strange oily sheen, glimmering with distorted reflections of the surrounding terrain. The disc oscillated, growing and shrinking by small increments that matched the erratic pulses of lightning flaring across the geothermal relays.

'I see some kind of energy screen, no more than five metres in diameter,' Naaman said. 'Wait, something is happening.'

The rim of the disc became a solid blaze of power while the generators of the power plant erupted with fountains of sparks and electricity. The haze around the transmitter disc deepened into a greenish glow, shimmering upwards into the sky.

The disc blinked out of existence, leaving only the crackling halo of energy. Within its circumference it was if a window had been opened. Rather than the grasslands of the East Barrens, Naaman could see a dark hall, criss-crossed with metal beams receding into the distance. Colourful banners decorated with large glyphs hung from the ceiling, and what he could see of the walls were painted with more orkish designs.

He took all of this in at a glance but his attention was fixed upon the occupants of the hall. A sea of green faces leered out of the opening: thousands of orks clustered around more bikes and buggies, all swathed in the shadow of enormous war engines.

Orks poured towards the opening... and stepped through! A mob of a dozen greenskins emerged onto the Kadillus hillside, tendrils of green power lapping at them, flickering across the portal. As each alien passed through, the halo of energy flickered, dimming and then returning with less brilliance. When the thirteenth ork crossed the threshold the halo flared violently, sending blue and purple sparks cascading down onto the new arrivals. A companion detonation flared across the energy relay on the power plant. The haze from the disc also vanished. As instantly as it had disappeared, the black disc came back, closing the pathway.

'It's a teleporter!' Naaman announced. 'The orks are teleporting directly to the surface.'

'That cannot be correct,' replied Belial. 'Close orbital sweeps have revealed no ork ship in proximity to Piscina. Perhaps they are teleporting from their ship further out into the East Barrens?'

'That seems unlikely, brother-captain,' said Naaman. 'It appears the orks are siphoning off power from the geothermal plant, and it is definitely being sent star-wards, not across the plains. The connection seems to be intermittent. I saw inside the ork base, or ship, or whatever it is. They have Titan-class war engines, but they have not brought them through. It seems that the teleporter is severely restricted at present.'

'This is highly speculative, brother-sergeant,' said Belial. 'I need confirmation and solid data for the Tech-marines to analyse if we are to determine the exact nature of this device.'

'I understand, brother-captain. The orks are dispersing and moving westwards to a staging point on the other side of the ridge. It will be possible to get closer to the power station and take energy readings.'

As Naaman watched, the portal burst into life once more, existing long enough for three buggies to race through before collapsing again.

'Consider that to be your mission, brother-sergeant,' said Belial. 'Take measurements of the energy levels, timing and reinforcement rate and report directly to me.'

'Confirm, brother-captain,' said Naaman. 'We will approach as swiftly as possible.'

Naaman severed the comm-link and turned to the Scouts.

'We have to get a lot closer,' he told them. 'Follow me.'

The squad carefully picked their way down the eastern side of the ridge, keeping at least a kilometre from the ork camp. The greenskins appeared to regard their position as safe behind the encampments further west and had posted no patrols or sentries that Naaman could see. Though the Scouts said nothing of the extraordinary sight of the ork teleporter, Naaman could sense their amazement, and an undercurrent of unease at the implications it presented.

For the moment, Naaman concentrated solely on approaching the geothermal station undetected. He could leap at guesses regarding the teleporter's function, but such speculation was pointless without solid facts to inform it. As they reached the level of the East Barrens plains, the veteran sergeant was sure of only one thing: the teleporter presented an unquantifiable threat to the defenders of Kadillus. If the orks were somehow able to sustain the portal and bring through their larger war machines, there was little the Dark Angels or Free Militia had to combat them. Naaman was pleased that Belial had possessed the foresight to send a warning to the Dark Angels Chapter, even if they only arrived in time to avenge the fallen of the 3rd Company.

A steady but slow flow of reinforcements continued to emerge from the portal. These freshly arrived orks pressed westwards to join the others, so Naaman led the squad on a circuitous routing, coming at the power plant from the north-west, almost behind the ork camp. The geothermal station covered a roughly square area half a kilometre wide on each side; the central power station dominated much of this, surrounded by small clusters of maintenance buildings and dilapidated monitoring installations. There was no sign of the tech-priests and several dozen men who had worked here before the orks' arrival; Naaman presumed that they were all dead, taken by surprise by the greenskins' arrival, however that had come about.

The slope of the ridge overlooked the whole compound, which was built across three shallow hills. The portal occupied the crest of one hill, while another was crowned with a thick crop of trees, rocks and bushes, providing the perfect cover to approach. Naaman was grateful that dawn had been accompanied by a layer of thick, low cloud, increasing the early morning gloom.

Ever alert to the few orks wandering around the camp, the Scouts pressed closer, slipping into the concealing foliage of the nearby hill while Naaman took stock of the situation. Damas joined Naaman and both of them wriggled through the bushes to the southern slope of the hill, from where they could see more of the ork camp.

Naaman pulled out his auspex and set it for a wide-spectrum scan. Other than the energy spike from the power plant and the readings from the orks, the scanner provided no new information.

'We will have to close the range,' said Naaman, stowing the auspex.

'What about that outhouse just west of the plant?' suggested Damas, pointing to a half-ruined plascrete building twenty metres from the main generator complex.

Naaman considered the lay of the land. There was another building even closer to the generator, but the Scouts would have to cross a few metres of open ground in full view of the portal. The teleporter was active for only a few seconds at a time and took several minutes to recharge between each opening, but Naaman had been timing the power surges and there was no definite pattern. It was risky, but that position would allow him to scan not only the power plant but also the portal itself.

'We will close in on the plant first,' said Naaman, deciding that Damas's course of action presented the least risk of discovery, even though the Scouts would have to relocate to scan the portal. 'You will lead with the squad and I will follow you.'

Damas nodded and crawled back to the others. Naaman connected the long-range comm and hailed

Belial. When the connection was made, it was marred by bursts of static, in rhythm with the pulsing of the energy across the power plant's transformers.

'This is Master Belial, make your report.'

'Initial readings confirm that a relay is being used to project the energy as a microwave beam, brother-captain,' said Naaman. 'I will obtain a more accurate energy signature for the *Unrelenting Fury* to trace so that we can locate its destination.'

'What about the ork build-up? How soon should we expect another attack?'

'I would say that the orks will be back to their previous strength in the next two hours, perhaps a little more, brother-captain. May I make a suggestion?'

'Please do, brother-sergeant, your insight has proven very useful so far.'

'The teleporter is not directly connected to the power plant on the ground. Wherever it is coming from, the teleporter beam is being powered from the source rather than the destination. The orks' occupation of the power plant suggests that the teleporter cannot function on a sustainable basis on its own power; this is why Ghazghkull's first attack was infantry alone. If you were to bombard the power station and destroy the source of energy, the teleporter will cease to function.'

'Bombardment is an option of last resort, Naaman,' replied Belial heavily. 'The geothermal stations are located on the weakest fault lines of Kadillus, areas made more insecure by the boreholes from them driven into the island's heart. Brother Hephaestus warns me that any bombardment risks rupturing the Kadillus

GAV THORPE

magma chamber, which in turn could precipitate a chain-reaction eruption, destroying the entire island.'

'I see,' Naaman said, ashamed that he had not thought through the consequences of blasting a power station that was, in essence, an artificial volcano. He was tired and rubbed his eyes. 'Would it be possible to conduct a tactical strike, brother-captain? If we can reclaim the power plant we can cut off the source of energy in a more controlled fashion.'

'The only available resources are myself and Death-wing Squad Adamanta. We can launch an attack, but we have no means of holding any ground. If it is possible to conduct a strike, you must locate a suitable target for us.'

'I understand, brother-captain. I will report again when I can furnish you with more accurate target information.'

'You are doing well, Naaman,' said Belial, surprising the sergeant. 'I realise that you have been under a great deal of pressure the last few days and that I have placed a considerable burden upon you. I have utter faith in your abilities and judgement, sergeant. Carry on with your mission.'

'Confirm, brother-captain. I aspire to the example of the Lion. We shall not fall short in our dedication.'

Buoyed up by Belial's words of encouragement, Naaman nodded for Damas to head out. Naaman cast a last glance at the portal and then followed the Scouts, bolt pistol in hand. They moved down the slope and paused within the shadows of a stand of stunted trees. With a burst of light, the portal opened and disgorged a pair of warbikes, which raced off westwards. Certain that the portal could not open for a few more minutes, Naaman signalled for the Scouts to break cover.

One at a time they darted from the trees, crossing a few metres of ground in a stooped run until they reached a patch of rocks and boulders almost directly north of the power plant. Naaman sprinted after them, casting glances to his right until he reached the shelter of the boulders. The sergeant activated the auspex again, but still the energy signal from the power relays was too weak to get an accurate fix on their alignment. They had to get even closer.

From here it was about twenty metres to the ruined outbuilding. Most of the upper storey had collapsed and Naaman could see the walls had been torn down by the orks and the reinforcing struts within the plascrete ripped out. The greenskins had used this material to erect crude gantries around the geothermal plant, criss-crossing the pylons and transformers with a maze of struts and ladders so that they could jury-rig their own cables and generators to the main relays.

With an idea germinating at the back of his mind, Naaman took the lead. Pulling up his cameleoline hood and wrapping his cloak tight, he dashed across the rubble-strewn ground to take cover in the ruined building. The *scrunch* of footfalls sounded the arrival of the others as he ghosted through the bare rooms. It was impossible to say what purpose the building had once served. The orks had stripped out every piece of machinery and furniture, leaving only the half-destroyed shell. Even the roof had been taken away, but the sun was not yet high enough to reach into the building's interior.

A plascrete staircase still stood, jutting up from the centre of the ruin. Naaman directed the others to take up covering positions before slithering up the steps, wrapped in his cloak. At the top, he lay as still as death, auspex in hand, peering at the power plant from under the lip of his hood. Orks paced haphazardly around the station, no more than ten of them that Naaman could see. Another burst of crackling energy heralded more reinforcements through the portal, but Naaman ignored them. There was no way the Scouts would be found unless the orks were going out of their way to look for them; the truth was the orks patrolling the plant seemed bored and were spending more time arguing and joking with each other than keeping watch. It was possible that a lone Scout might be able to get into the plant itself without the alarm being raised.

Naaman counted four more portal openings while he lay at the top of the steps, the auspex beeping quietly in his hand as it absorbed and analysed the energy waves emanating from the power plant. He was no Techmarine and the intricacies of the data were as unintelligible as the grunts and roars of the orks, but he could see a pattern.

The energy from the power plant was being beamed to some other point, building in intensity roughly a minute prior to the portal opening. Once the teleporter was activated, the power link spiked at a level five times the build-up and lasted for only a few seconds. It was clear that no matter how long the pre-teleportation process, the portal could not be opened for more than a few seconds. Why this might be the case was a mystery, but it did confirm Naaman's suspicion that without the power relay of the geothermal plant the teleporter could not be opened for any significant length of time. It required all of the plant's output to generate a single pulse of teleporter energy, and all that was required to disrupt the beam was the removal of one of the bastardised relays the orks had added to the power station.

Armed with this information, Naaman contacted Belial.

'Brother-captain, this is Sergeant Naaman. I will shortly be sending my collected data via the link. It is my belief that a small disruption to the power network of the plant will disrupt the entire operation. I will append monocular images of the relays for the examination of the Techmarines.'

'Report received, brother-sergeant,' replied Belial. 'Standing by to receive data transmission.'

Naaman hooked the auspex into the long-range comm and punched in the rune sequence to uplink the information the scanner had collated. He waited impatiently until the auspex chimed three times to indicate the upload was completed. Switching connectors, Naaman attached his monocular to the comm-piece and spent several minutes sweeping the plant area with the optical device, transmitting the images to his commander. When he was done, he packed away the monocular and auspex and waited for Belial and his advisors to formulate a plan.

THE MINUTES CREPT past. Naaman retreated from the tip of the stairway and joined the others. The orks had

shown no sign that they were aware of the Scouts'
presence and Naaman felt relatively safe. He knew that
such sanctuary was only temporary. If the Deathwing
launched an attack it would stir up the orks, not only
around the power station but also those westwards on
the ridge.

There would be no way to get back to Koth Ridge, as
Naaman had known since setting out. He called the
Scouts together to make an announcement.

'The time is fast approaching when we will be called
upon to make the ultimate sacrifice for the Chapter,' he
said. He was pleased to see that none of the Scouts
showed any sign of fear or surprise. 'We have used
stealth as a weapon and it has served us well, but there
comes a time when stealth is no longer enough and pure
force must prevail. We will not live to see the success of
our mission today, for the consequences of our actions
will not be measurable in moments but in hours and
days.'

He looked at them in turn and saw nothing but determination and pride. Damas spoke next.

'We will demonstrate the most fundamental power of
the Astartes,' said the sergeant, glancing at Naaman
before continuing. 'All of your training, all of our secrecy
and circumspection is but a preliminary to one simple
purpose: the destruction of the Emperor's enemies.
Though our mission shall succeed and our part in the
greater campaign will come to an end, it still remains
our duty to slay as many of the foe as is possible. We will
fight to our last breath and even then we will fight until
death claims us. We are all Space Marines, inheritors of
the Lion's legacy, upholders of the Imperial Will.'

The comm-chime attracted Naaman's attention.

'Sergeant Naaman, this is Master Belial. We have analysed the data and discerned a weakness in the enemy structure. The orks' teleporter beam is interfering with our own lock-on signal. The orks are still in possession of the defence-laser silo and the *Unrelenting Fury* can only make a quick pass. Estimated window of operation is less than five minutes. For these reasons, you must place the teleport homer as close to the objective as you can. Is that possible?'

Naaman looked out of the window at the orks scattered around the power plant.

'Affirmative, brother-captain,' he said. 'I can have you teleported directly into the power station precinct.'

'Good,' said Belial. 'We are ready to commence the operation as soon as we receive the lock-on signal from you. Energy interference prevents teleporter lock on your squad. We will not be able to extract you.'

'We are aware of that factor, brother-captain. Squad Damas and I will provide a diversionary attack to ensure minimal resistance to your arrival. We are honoured to serve.'

'You will be remembered, Brother Naaman. You and your warriors are an inspiration to us all.'

The link went silent. Naaman unslung the comm-unit and set it to one side. He did not need it any more. He looked at the Scouts and saw that they had been listening to his part of the conversation. Standing up, they formed a circle, weapons raised in salute to each other, brothers in battle.

'Fight hard, fight long,' said Naaman. 'No surrender, no retreat. We are Astartes, the bane of the heretic, the mutant and the alien. We are the Dark Angels, the first and the greatest. Honour our battle-brothers and cherish the opportunity for sacrifice.'

'What is the plan, Naaman?' asked Damas.

'I have a teleport homer. On my signal you will open fire. In the resulting confusion I will infiltrate the power-plant complex and place the beacon. Master Belial and Squad Adamanta will insert by teleporter, disable or dismantle the energy relays and teleport back to orbit. We will remain to inflict as many casualties as possible. There will be no withdrawal.'

'Understood, brother,' said Damas. The sergeant pulled free his chainsword. 'Purge the alien.'

'Purge the alien,' the Scouts quietly chorused in reply.

'For the Lion,' whispered Naaman, heading towards the door.

The veteran sergeant broke from the building at a run, bolt pistol in one hand, teleporter beacon in the other. He moved as fast as possible, heading directly for the closest generator housing. An ork strutted across a walkway above. The greenskin stopped as it caught sight of Naaman. It started to raise its gun. A moment later, the sergeant's shot caught it in the throat, hurling it over the railing to plummet to the hard ground. Naaman heard startled grunts from the other orks around the power plant.

'*Bellicus extremis*,' he growled over the comm. 'Open fire!'

Naaman rounded the corner of the generator and came face-to-face with a startled ork coming the other way. The Scout-sergeant fired twice, putting two bolt-rounds into the creature's gnarled face. He was about twenty metres from the optimal spot for the beacon. Jumping over the fallen ork, he headed straight on while the station echoed with the snap of bolter rounds from the Scouts and the crackle of the orks' primitive guns.

The sergeant could smell ozone in the air and feel the building energy on his skin. A fork of lightning leapt across the relays above, heralding another portal opening and sending a tingle of static across the sergeant's flesh. Bare cables and bundles of wires hung like bunting between the generator blocks and the ground throbbed underfoot from the geothermal reactors hundreds of metres below.

Feeling the thrum of the power lines, Naaman realised that the place he had chosen was too close to the main transmitter: there was a chance the teleporter signal would be fractured by interference from the orks' energy relays.

He cut to his left through a crumbling archway looking for an open space and was confronted by half a dozen orks dressed in red flak jackets, with grinning suns painted on their faces. The orks were intent on reaching the Scouts and did not see him as he ducked back into the archway. He crouched in the shadow with his pistol ready and peered around the corner to see the front three orks shredded by a hail of heavy bolter rounds.

'Good aim, Luthor,' Naaman said over the comm. 'Keep up your fire!'

The orks scurried for cover as more heavy bolter fire screamed into the power plant, severing wires and ripping small craters into the generator housings.

Naaman dashed from the archway, bolt pistol blazing to cut down an ork sheltering behind an angled girder. Bullets whined in the sergeant's direction as he reached the cover of a pillar, rockcrete shards spraying around him. A glance at the portal hill revealed more orks hurrying towards the power plant, their padded vests and armour plates decorated with red and black checks. The orks wielded stubby pistols and cleavers, their fanged mouths wide as they bellowed encouragement or warnings to the other greenskins.

Naaman holstered his pistol and keyed in the activation sequence of the teleport homer. More and more bullets converged on his hiding place as the device shed its outer sheath. With a series of growls and clicks, transmitter vanes opened up, splaying from the tip of the beacon.

With a benediction to the Emperor in mind, Naaman broke cover and dashed across the dusty ground just to the south of the power plant. The black-clad orks were less than fifty metres away as Naaman speared the teleport homer into the dirt and leapt back. A bullet caught him on the arm, ripping through his sleeve to carve a furrow across his bicep. He knew he had to distract the orks from the beacon and sprinted to his left, firing his pistol as he did so. Behind him the teleport homer opened fully and sent its silent, invisible signal.

Naaman dived through the leaves of a bush as more bullets kicked up puffs of dust around him. Rolling to his left, he came up on one knee and sighted on the closest ork. Three bolt-rounds punched through the alien's jacket with spurts of dark blood, toppling the creature. The orks returned fire, howling faces bathed in the flare of their pistols.

In the storm of fire, another ork bullet found its mark, catching Naaman in the thigh. Grunting, he shot back, finger hammering the trigger of his bolt pistol to send a salvo of bolts into the orks. Two of the beasts tumbled into the dirt but the survivors were now less than twenty metres away.

Then Naaman felt something: his highly attuned senses detected a slight increase in air pressure, like the bow-wave of an aircraft. Miniature dust devils writhed across the dusty ground and the air swirled into a haze.

In a blistering ball of blue light, the Deathwing arrived with a thunderous crack. Five hulking armoured suits appeared between Naaman and the onrushing orks. The Terminators opened fire immediately, their storm bolters scything through the remaining orks in a couple of seconds.

In the glare of muzzle flare stood Captain Belial, Master of the 3rd Company. His shoulder pads displayed the heraldry of the Chapter and the skull device of a veteran, the white robe of a Deathwing warrior hanging from his shoulders. He fired a storm bolter with his right hand, a crackling power sword in the left.

Surrounded by the five heavily armoured Space Marines, Master Belial waved the squad forwards with his glittering power sword. Ahead of them the ork portal pulsed again and another stream of greenskins surged through onto Kadillus. Meanwhile, Naaman could hear shooting coming from the ridge. The orks to the west were alert to the attack and were turning back to the power plant.

Reloading his pistol, Naaman ran through the power station, heading back towards the Scouts. To his left Belial and Squad Adamanta plunged into the heart of the transformers and generators, heading for the ork power relays that were transmitting energy from the geothermal station. Pulses from weapons screamed down from the ridge above the heads of a sea of greenskins. The Deathwing moved out of sight as Naaman emerged from the power plant. Ahead of him, the Scouts kept up a constant stream of bolter and heavy bolter fire from the ruined building, gunning down the orks that had emerged from the teleporter opening.

Naaman sprinted back though the door to rejoin the squad. Looking through a window, he saw the Deathwing forming an armoured cordon around Belial as the company commander pulled himself up a ladder below one of the ramshackle ork relay discs. Broken cables hurled sparks around the Terminators as they launched a steady barrage of fire at the incoming greenskins. Belial reached a gantry above them and crossed over to one of the generator housings. Bullets skipped up from the rockcrete casing under his feet, cut ragged holes in his bone-coloured robe and scored grey welts across the dark green of his armour.

'Enemy to the south!' warned Damas, shifting his position at one of the windows.

Naaman turned his attention to the approaching orks for a moment, but they were still out of range of his pistol. He pulled free his chainsword and tested the motor. Razor-sharp teeth whirred with a satisfying growl.

Out of the corner of his eye, Naaman saw the ork portal expanding into life again, revealing the tide of waiting greenskins. After only a moment, the opening shuddered and the black disc returned, shrinking to half its size. Belial stood triumphantly atop the power plant, a piece of ork equipment in one hand, ripped from its makeshift housing. Without the relay, the generators no longer buzzed with electricity and the flare of energy along the cables had died to a trickle.

'Squad Damas, honour your commander!' Damas barked over the comm. The Scouts turned and raised their weapons in honour of Belial. The master returned the salute, lifting his glittering power sword towards the Scouts.

More blue energy swirled through the power plant, engulfing the master and his Terminators with its glow. They were swallowed up by the roiling ball of the teleporter field and faded from view. The light dimmed leaving only empty air where the Deathwing and Belial had been.

The Scouts were alone. As it always was, Naaman thought, and as it should be.

'Mission accomplished,' he quietly announced.

ENRAGED BY THE damage done to their teleporter, the orks converged on the Scouts. The walls of the ruined building exploded with bullet impacts and the detonations of rockets. Forced back from the western wall by the weight of fire, the Scouts followed Damas into the next room while Naaman once more sprinted up the crumbling stairway to gauge the enemy positions.

A swarm of gretchin were running down the ridge, driven on by the lash of their ork overseer. Behind them came several squads of infantry wielding a variety of guns, pistols, brutal clubs and jagged blades. From the direction of the portal, another mob of orks had taken up a firing position in a cluster of shallow rocks. They opened fire with their strange heavy weapons, rattling off blasts of green energy and fist-sized shells that ripped holes through the thin walls protecting the Scouts.

With a cry of pain, one of the Scouts was hurled back as a green bolt of energy screamed into a window, through the internal door and struck him in the shoulder. Bloodied and burnt, the Scout dragged himself to the doorway, fumbling with his bolter as more bullets whined into the building. He fired once in reply before a ricocheting bullet took him in the cheek and killed him.

Naaman leapt down the steps and snatched up the fallen Scout's bolter. As more blasts of energy exploded against the window frame, the veteran sergeant vaulted through another opening, determined not to be caught.

He stormed through the ork fusillade, large-calibre rounds whipping past, ignoring the ravening balls of energy flying by, and reached the cover of another ruined outhouse. Ducking inside, he found himself in what seemed to be an old store, the walls lined with broken shelves, the floor littered with crates broken open by the orks. Naaman hauled himself up a metal rack to a slit window near the ceiling. Smashing out the pane of glass with the butt of the bolter, he brought up the weapon and fired at the orks close to the portal, his salvo ripping up a hail of rock shards from the orks' cover and punching into green flesh.

The blossom of a detonation behind Naaman's right attracted his attention. Glancing over his shoulder he saw through another window an ork Dreadnought clanking towards the Scouts' defensive position. It was twice as tall as the Space Marines, a massive armoured can on stunted legs with four mechanical arms; two ended in crackling power claws, one a rocket launcher fed by a hanging belt-feed, the fourth a broad-muzzled flamethrower that dribbled burning fuel into the grass at the Dreadnought's metal feet. Naaman could see the ripple of bolt detonations across the walker's armour but it advanced into the teeth of the Scouts' fire, impervious to their weapons. Another rocket corkscrewed from its launcher and exploded inside the Scouts' position.

'Status report!' Naaman barked into the comm.

A few moments passed before Damas replied.

'Just me and Luthor, brother. Withdrawing from this position.'

The Dreadnought was almost at the building. Naaman could see nothing of the Scouts inside. Barely a heartbeat after Damas finished speaking, the Dreadnought's flamethrower roared into life, a billow of black and yellow filling the ruins where the Scouts were sheltering.

'Damas?'

The comm stayed silent, while the pop of exploding

bolt-rounds and the crackle of flames echoed around Naaman.

'Damas? Luthor?'

There was no reply. Naaman was the only Dark Angel alive on the East Barrens.

He had no time to mourn the loss of his battle-brothers or ponder the fortunes of war. The sergeant heard the crunch of a booted foot and the crash of a door falling from its hinges. Dropping to the floor, Naaman slung the bolter and drew out his chainsword and pistol again.

The first ork to enter the storeroom was met by the teeth of the sergeant's chainsword, chopping into its face to slice through eyes and brain. Naaman fired his pistol into the chest of the next, the explosive bolts throwing it back into the ork behind. Naaman hacked the arm from a third before driving the point of the chainsword into its throat. As he parried a cleaver swinging at his gut, Naaman could feel a heavy thud shaking the ground. He spared it no mind and swung his chainsword low, hacking through the knee of the next ork to appear. As the creature tumbled, the Scout-sergeant fired two rounds into the back of its head, obliterating its skull.

In a cloud of dust and bricks, the ork Dreadnought crashed through the wall to Naaman's right. In an instant the sergeant saw the flicker of the flamethrower's igniter growing brighter. He leapt towards the war machine and rolled against the remains of the wall as a sheet of fire engulfed the store room, setting fire to wooden shelves and bathing the orks with its burning fury.

Looking up, Naaman saw a fanged face had been bolted to the front of the Dreadnought, made from jagged pieces of metal. The eyes were open slits, through which he could see the red of the pilot's own eyes. Naaman raised his pistol to find a shot but the Dreadnought swung at him with a clawed arm, pneumatics hissing, pistons buzzing. The claw missed but the arm caught the sergeant on the shoulder, hurling him into the wall. By instinct he blazed with his pistol, the bolts ricocheting from the Dreadnought's armour, the small detonations leaving scorch marks across the yellow and red paintwork.

The Dreadnought lifted a claw as Naaman's bolt pistol clicked empty. Without thought, Naaman raised his chainsword to ward away the blow. The claw cleaved down, smashing the sergeant's weapon to pieces and severing his hand. Blood spurted from the ruin of Naaman's wrist. With his right hand, he snatched something from his belt and held it in his palm.

Staring at the Dreadnought, knowing what he had to do, there was no room for regret or fear in the sergeant's thoughts. He had sworn an oath to protect the Emperor and his servants, and if that meant giving his life, so be it. There were others that would continue the fight.

'Remember me, Tauno,' Naaman whispered, activating the melta-bomb's magnetic clamp.

He slammed the anti-tank grenade into the fake face of the Dreadnought and pushed himself away. Through the pilot's eye slits, Naaman saw the ork within stare in amazement at the blinking red rune of the melta-bomb. A second later the grenade detonated, punching through the armour of the Dreadnought with a focussed fusion blast. The driver's head was incinerated in an instant. A moment later, the Dreadnought's engine exploded, tearing Naaman to pieces with white-hot fire and serrated fragments of metal.

Veteran Sergeant Naaman of the Dark Angels died without fear or regret. His last thoughts were of an unremarkable man he had sworn to protect with his life.

THE TALE OF BOREAS
Battle at Barrak Gorge

THE ROAR OF the Thunderhawk's engines and the drone of the wind forced Chaplain Boreas to cut the external sound feed to his helmet as he listened to the company-wide broadcast from Master Belial.

'Through the diligence of Sergeant Naaman of the 10th Company and the industry and bravery of the Scouts and Ravenwing, we are now more aware of the threat to Piscina posed by the orks. The actions of our courageous battle-brothers have not only furnished us with this information, they have struck a blow against the greenskin menace that grants us the time to respond.

'It is my intention that Sergeant Naaman be lauded as a Hero of the Dark Angels when we rejoin with the rest of the Chapter. Even now Sergeant Naaman once more dares the ork lines to bring the bright light of truth upon the enemy's dark machinations. Until Brother Naaman reports fully, we must assume that the orks will attempt another attack on Koth Ridge with fresh forces. Be vigilant and unstinting in your destruction of the enemy.'

Boreas muttered his own praise to the heroic Naaman, head bowed. Around him the Space Marines of Squad Zaltys did likewise. A tone signalled a change of comm frequency in Boreas's ear. He adjusted the Thunderhawk's unit for the incoming transmission.

'Master Belial to Brother Boreas: stand ready to receive orders. A portion of the orks' strategy has been revealed to us. It is plain that they possess part of the Kadillus power network and we must assume it is with some as-yet-unknown reason. To what end, Sergeant Naaman is still investigating. However, if the orks desire to hold the East Barrens geothermal station we can be sure it is for some purpose that we should disrupt. It is clear to me now that it is no coincidence that Ghazghkull still controls the Kadillus Harbour power station, but there is a means by which we can neutralise its power output.

'Your pilot is being sent coordinates of a relay station linking Kadillus Harbour to the East Barrens grid. Take possession of the relay and sever the link. Intelligence at this moment suggests the enemy have a weak guard at its location. After completion of this mission, transfer to Barrak Gorge to protect the power plant at the abandoned mine head. Other forces are being despatched to provide protection at several more locations.'

'Understood, brother-captain,' replied Boreas. 'What are your assessments of the available forces and enemy threat in the area?'

'Two companies of Piscina defence troops are already en route to Barrak Gorge overland. Take command on your arrival and ensure the station does not fall into the orks' hands. A Ravenwing land speeder will be despatched to provide reconnaissance and Sergeant Zaltys will accompany you with his squad.'

There was a pause in the transmission. Boreas glanced across the command deck to the pilot, Brother Demensuis.

'Have you received the mission target coordinates, brother?'

'Affirmative, Brother-Chaplain,' said Demensuis. 'Objective is twenty-three kilometres from our current position.'

'Belial to Boreas. It is my conclusion that following the success of the first phase of your mission, the orks will again attempt a breakthrough of Koth Ridge to link up with Ghazghkull's forces in the city. Estimate of threat to Barrak Gorge is minimal.'

'Understood, brother-captain. Have you received any notification from the rest of the Chapter?'

'Affirmative. Grand Master Azrael has informed me that the fleet is redirecting back from the jump point. We have been fortunate: the rest of our battle-brothers were only six hours from warp jump. They are heading in-system again at this time. It is my intention to curtail the ork threat until their arrival and then wipe them from Kadillus with the aid of the other companies. It is imperative the ork forces remain divided and that they are denied the energy supply they seem to be seeking.'

'I understand, brother. We will cage these beasts and

exterminate them. Praise the Lion and honour the Emperor.'

'For the glory of lost Caliban,' said Belial before the link went dead.

Boreas hung the handset on the console and turned to the ten Space Marines sitting along the benches lining the Thunderhawk's main compartment.

'We have a seize-and-secure mission, brothers,' the Chaplain told them. 'Expect light resistance. Suggestions for a plan of attack, brother-sergeant?'

Zaltys pulled down a hinged digital display from overhead and studied the schematic of the objective for a moment. He smiled at Boreas.

'Gunship attack run followed by direct aerial insertion by jump pack, Brother-Chaplain.'

'Very well, sergeant,' Boreas said with a nod. 'Prepare your squad. I will provide observation and coordination from the command deck.'

'Two minutes until we are on-site at the objective, brothers,' Demensuis announced. 'Approach at fifty metres for attack run and aerial deployment. Weapon systems set to machine-spirit control. Praise the unthinking mind that brings the ruin of our enemies.'

While Boreas returned to his position on the command deck, Zaltys and his warriors readied themselves for the assault. The squad geared themselves with bolt pistols, plasma pistols, chainswords, power swords and grenades from the weapons lockers; the sergeant replaced his regular armoured gauntlet with a bulky power fist and took a hand flamer from the underfoot storage bay. Armed, they helped each other into their assault harnesses, attaching the large turbo-fan jump packs to the spinal interfaces of their armour. The hull reverberated with the whine of the fans as each Space Marine tested his pack.

'Thirty seconds until attack run commences,' warned Demensuis. 'Swift shall be our anger, deadly shall be our strike.'

The lights inside the Thunderhawk dimmed to a dull red. In front of Boreas, the armoured canopy darkened to grey. In the distance he could see the squat structure of the energy relay post. Automatic surveyors were sweeping the ground ahead of the diving Thunderhawk. Red reticules sprang up in the cockpit display, hovering over detected foes. Boreas counted twenty-eight.

Flashes of gunfire sparkled from the relay post's roof as the orks opened fire on the incoming gunship. Bullets whizzed past and bounced harmlessly from the armourplas windshield.

'Machine-spirits awakened. Targets set. Commencing attack run.'

'Faith is our shield, righteousness our sword!' declared Boreas as the Thunderhawk echoed with the whine of powering weapon systems.

The gunship shuddered as the dorsal battle cannon opened fire, sending a shell directly into the roof of the relay building. The explosion sent bodies and rockcrete shards flying a hundred metres into the air.

At another command, two hellstrike missiles roared away from the gunship's wings on burning trails. The missiles jinked and swerved, their artificial brains tracking the orks as they fled in all directions seeking cover. The first detonated a few dozen metres short of the compound, turning a buggy into flaming debris. The second banked left, following a group of orks heading for an irrigation ditch. It exploded as they reached cover, tossing their bodies across the grassland.

The battle cannon fired again as heavy bolters added their fury to the onslaught, stitching lines of detonations across the rockcrete ground of the compound. The battle cannon shell smashed into a small metal-roofed guardhouse, blowing it apart from the inside.

Heavy bolters swivelling to keep track of the dispersing orks, the Thunderhawk roared over the relay station.

'Prepare for disembarkation,' said Demensuis. 'Brace for deployment manoeuvre.'

The pilot cut the main plasma engines and hit the retro-jets. Inertia dragged Boreas sideways as the Thunderhawk rapidly slowed and banked heavily to the left, heavy bolters still firing at targets on the ground. Daylight flooded the main compartment as the prow assault ramp dropped down.

'Launch assault!' cried Zaltys. 'Show no mercy!'

The Assault Marines bounded down the ramp, jump packs flaring. In pairs they threw themselves from the gunship's open prow. Boreas tracked their descent on the external pict-feeds, watching the ten Space Marines plunge to the ground, their jump packs slowing their descent. With impacts that would have shattered the bones of lesser warriors, Zaltys's squad landed in the compound, ferrocrete cracking beneath their booted feet. The Assault Marines opened fire immediately, gunning down survivors from the gunship's attack.

'Taking up support circuit,' Demensuis said as the assault ramp whined shut and the plasma engines roared back into life.

The whole attack run and deployment had taken thirty-five seconds.

'Switch battle cannon control to my station, brother,' Boreas told the pilot.

The screens in front of the Chaplain changed, showing him the view from the Thunderhawk's main weapon system. A smaller display to the right contained a thermal scan of the area, the hot bodies of the orks showing up bright white against the fuzzy grey of the ground; to the left another screen contained a wireframe topographical display of the compound and the contours of the surrounding grassland.

'Combat squad split, brother-sergeant,' Boreas told Zaltys, analysing the data on the screens. 'Priority objectives: enemy field gun emplaced three hundred metres south of the compound gate; twenty-plus infantry using the cover of a pipeline one hundred and fifty metres south-east.'

'Confirm, Brother-Chaplain,' replied Zaltys. 'Suppression fire required to cover advance.'

'Confirm, brother-sergeant,' said Boreas.

Boreas's gauntleted fingers danced over the sturdy keys of the control panel, locking the battle cannon's aim on the long-barrelled artillery piece the orks had hidden alongside the road to the relay station. They had heaped up mounds of earth as a basic emplacement, the muzzle of their weapon poking out from a covering of branches and leaves. Had the Dark Angels approached on the ground, the gun would have taken a significant toll.

The Chaplain pressed the fire rune and the gunship shuddered from the recoil. On the display, the emplacement was engulfed with a cloud of fire and dirt. Although the explosion was ferocious, the shot had only damaged the earthworks protecting the field gun. Despite the lack of direct damage, Boreas had done what was required: Zaltys and half of his squad were already halfway down the road, bounding towards the ork position with long leaps powered by their jump packs.

Boreas switched the pict-feed as the gunship circled around the compound. The other combat squad was already fighting with the ork infantry to the south-east, exchanging pistol fire as they closed in. The Chaplain watched as the orks surged out of their cover to meet the Assault Marines head-on. Boreas knew that it was crude instinct rather than bravery that had spurred the orks to make the counter-attack, their hunger for fighting overwhelming whatever rudiments of common sense the greenskins might possess. The result was inevitable as the Space Marines fell upon their foes with pistols and blades, cutting them down in a few seconds of frenzied activity.

'Heat signal detected to the north-west, brothers,' said Demensuis. 'Incoming ork transports.'

Boreas changed the view again and saw two open-backed trucks speeding through the high grass from a rough camp half a kilometre from the relay post. The Chaplain heard the distinctive thump of melta-bombs over the comm.

'Ork gun destroyed,' Zaltys reported. 'Advancing to relay building.'

'Switch controls to anti-personnel array,' Boreas said to Demensuis. 'Bring us in over those transports.'

While the pilot turned the Thunderhawk with his right hand, his left activated the manual controls of the gunship's four twin-linked heavy bolters. The main view in front of Boreas changed again, a targeting matrix reticule dancing across the undulations of the ground below.

'Reducing speed for strafing run,' announced Demensuis.

The Thunderhawk tilted to the right for a few seconds and straightened, bringing it onto a course heading directly towards the approaching transports.

'Opening fire,' said Boreas as he locked the heavy bolter's tracking sights on the lead truck.

Flares of dozens of bolts burned through the air, the fire of eight heavy bolters converging on the ork transport. Tyres burst and the engine exploded, sending the vehicle's bonnet crashing through its low windshield, while the torrent of bolts tore along the truck's length, into the open back of the vehicle, gunning down the orks on board. The front axle snapped, turning the crashing truck's momentum into a somersault that sent it tumbling down a slope trailing burning shrapnel and oil.

'Target destroyed,' Boreas said calmly. '*Terminus excelsis.*'

The following truck veered wildly to its left, bumping over a low ridge of ground as Boreas's next salvo ripped furrows through the soil of Kadillus. The transport turned sharply again as Boreas adjusted his line of fire, the sudden change of direction sending two of the orks aboard spinning over the side. Next to the driver, the gunner angled his gun up towards the Thunderhawk, bullets spraying wildly past the gunship.

'Bring us over the transport, ten metres clearance,' Boreas told his pilot.

'Affirmative, Brother-Chaplain,' replied Demensuis.

Boreas lifted himself from his seat and headed back into the main bay as Demensuis wrestled at the controls, matching the erratic evasion moves of the driver below. Swaying to compensate for the dipping and turning of the gunship, the Chaplain strode out onto the assault ramp and hit the activation rune.

'Brother-Chaplain?' Demensuis's voice was shocked.

'Keep us level, increase speed by five per cent,' Boreas said, ignoring his battle-brother's concern. As the ramp opened the wind whistled into the Thunderhawk and set Boreas's robe madly flapping. The ground screamed past just a few metres below him, while ahead the ork truck swerved again in its attempt to outrun the Space Marines.

'Three degrees starboard, move to intercept.'

'Affirm, Brother-Chaplain.'

The view lurched again as Demensuis made the necessary adjustment.

The Thunderhawk was closing quickly on the ork vehicle. The driver had abandoned any attempt to get to the relay compound and was now simply trying to elude the massive gunship roaring down upon them. The gunner could not swivel its weapon to bear and so pulled a pistol from its armoured cabin and began to fire at the aircraft in futile defiance.

Plasma jets roaring, the Thunderhawk swooped over the truck. Snatching his crozius from his belt, Boreas leapt from the ramp. The Chaplain plummeted the few metres to the truck, arms braced across his chest. His armoured boots impacted with the truck's engine block, smashing the front of the vehicle into the ground. The transport flipped over, tossing the orks in all directions as Boreas was flung along the ground, his backpack carving a wide furrow through the soft dirt.

After twenty or thirty metres, Boreas and the truck came to a stop. Checking his suit's systems and finding them to be operating at acceptable levels, the Chaplain stood up, throwing aside the wreckage of the truck. Around him, dazed orks were pushing themselves to their feet. Choosing to conserve ammunition in case he needed it at Barrak Gorge, Boreas sprinted into the orks, smashing them from their feet with the blazing head of his crozius. Two of the stunned greenskins mustered enough sense to put up a fight, but were no match for the Chaplain. He broke their limbs and dashed in their skulls without hesitation. Others were crushed beneath his boots as they lay wounded and growling in the grass.

'Do you wish to embark, brother?' Demensuis asked as the gunship slowed and circled above the Chaplain.

Boreas guessed the distance to the relay to be less than a kilometre.

'Negative, brother,' he replied. 'Land at the compound. Help Sergeant Zaltys unload the phase-field generator from the heavy equipment store. We will need it to access the subterranean cables beneath the relay station.'

'Affirmative, brother. Enjoy the walk.'

Boreas was about to rebuke Demensuis for his facetiousness but stopped himself before he said anything. The Chaplain looked at the broken ork bodies and the smoking wreck of the truck and wondered why he had chosen such a direct approach rather than continue engaging the enemy with the heavy bolters. It seemed that Demensuis was not the only victim of unnecessary exuberance at the moment. Naaman's exploits had been a glorious example to all of the Space Marines, challenging them to match his heroic feat.

The walk back to the compound would give Boreas some time to calm down and contemplate his foolhardy action.

THE JETS OF the Thunderhawk kicked up a swirl of dust across the compound as the gunship lifted into the air. Boreas checked the chronometer display: three and a half minutes until detonation. Using the phase-field generator, Demensuis had burrowed a hole beneath the generator bunker and placed a fusion charge on the cables linking the East Barrens to Kadillus Harbour. If the Techmarine's assumptions were correct, this would simply sever the link without feedback through the whole grid.

The bewildering plethora of gauges and pipes, consoles and switchboxes had been utterly alien to Boreas, but he had faith in Demensuis's abilities. While Boreas had learned the *Calibanite Legacy* and the *Hymnals of Fortitude*, Demensuis had studied the mysteries of the

Machine and the ways to appease its spirit.

The Chaplain looked out of the canopy at the receding ground. Faith in Demensuis was one thing, but it did little to quell Boreas's unease at dealing with consequences he did not fully comprehend.

'Everything will proceed as planned, brother,' Demensuis assured him, perhaps sensing the Chaplain's slight apprehension.

'What is the worst-case result?' asked Boreas, eyes fixed on the small rockcrete block housing the relay controls.

'That depends on the criteria you use,' replied Demensuis. 'In terms of the mission's aims, the worst case would be the link is not severed and the orks are able to continue with whatever it is they need the power supply for. In a wider context, it could be that I have made the grossest miscalculation and the whole island will explode in one massive volcanic eruption, shattering tectonic plates and sending tidal waves that will scour all life from the other islands, thereby effectively destroying Piscina as an Imperial world.'

Boreas glanced sharply at Demensuis, worried by his matter-of-fact tone.

'Could that really happen, brother?' the Chaplain asked. 'Could we destroy the planet?'

Demensuis kept his gaze forwards and his voice level.

'It is a theoretical possibility, brother, but highly improbable,' replied the Techmarine.

'How improbable?'

Demensuis turned his head slowly to look at Boreas, a thin smile on his lips.

'At least one in forty-eight million, I would say.'

The Chaplain grunted in annoyance at Demensuis's levity and turned his attention back to the chronometer. Twenty seconds to detonation.

'This could be your last chance to say goodbye to the Third Company, Brother-Chaplain,' Demensuis continued. 'Any last words for them?'

'I find this attitude highly disrespectful! Your irreverence is unbecoming of a battle-brother. I feel that when this campaign is complete, it would be beneficial to all of us that you spend more time in the Reclusiam than the armoury. These consta–'

Boreas stopped as a bluish sphere of gas and fire engulfed the relay station. Electricity crackled through the expanding ball of plasma. Parts of the compound collapsed as cracks ripped through the rockcrete-covered ground. A few seconds passed before the shockwave hit the Thunderhawk, setting every surface rattling, jarring Boreas against his seat harness.

Demensuis leaned forwards and pointedly looked around through the Thunderhawk's canopy at the ground below, before his gaze settled on Boreas.

'It seems my calculations were correct, brother,' said the Techmarine. 'Sorry to interrupt. You were saying something about spending more time in the Reclusiam, I believe.'

'We *will* speak further on this when we return to the Chapter,' Boreas warned. 'Please restrain your glibness in future.'

Demensuis bowed his head in apology and steered the Thunderhawk northwards.

'Journey time to Barrak Gorge estimated at seventy-six minutes, Brother-Chaplain,' he said. 'Do you wish to apprise Master Belial of our successful mission, or shall I?'

Boreas snatched the comm handset from its cradle.

'This is Chaplain Boreas to Master Belial. Mission is complete. Power link to the East Barrens has been severed. Pass on my praises to the brothers at Koth Ridge: the fury of the orks will fall upon them soon.'

NIGHT INSECTS CHIRRUPED and buzzed around the bright lamps illuminating the mine head compound. The snores of sleeping Free Militia troopers blended with the murmurs of those on watch and the crunch of the Space Marines' boots as they walked the perimeter.

Boreas did not sleep, though he knew that there was little chance the orks would come this far north. His restlessness was born not out of concern for himself, but for his battle-brothers on Koth Ridge. There had been no word over the comm about the next ork thrust for Kadillus Harbour, but the Chaplain knew that it was likely to come soon. He stood looking down the mountainside at the distant silhouette of Koth Ridge, imagining the Space Marines staring to the east, searching for the first signs of the ork offensive.

Four thousand metres higher up the slope of Kadillus's central mount, Barrak Gorge was situated at the end of a mighty split in the rocks. Lava flows in ages past had created a nest of interweaving gulleys and valleys. The geothermal station loomed over the gorge, beneath it the gaping caverns of the exhausted mine and the jutting structures of its workings.

A muttered exchange of orders warned Boreas that the Piscina force were changing their guard. He looked at the two hundred men huddled in their field blankets beneath rubberised sheet bivouacs. They had spent most of the five hours since Boreas's arrival complaining: about the cold, about the thin air, about the rations. Those complaints had not been voiced directly to the Chaplain, but had simply hovered in the air as the squads had moved about erecting their sandbagged positions and setting up their heavy weapons.

Boreas turned back and walked through the camp, trying to ignore the quiet chatter between the men coming off watch and those about to start their patrols. The Chaplain was no keener to be here than any of the defence troopers, though his reasons were far different. It was not the inconvenience or physical discomfort that displeased Boreas: it was the sense of foreboding that he would miss out on fighting the decisive battle of the campaign. He was sure that the next ork assault on Koth Ridge would be the last chance the alien filth had to unite their forces. When the orks were thrown back, it would be a simple matter to keep them scattered until the rest of the Chapter returned to aid in the final purging.

'I only wanted to get off the mega-trawlers,' Boreas heard one of the troopers say as the Chaplain walked past a squad of men hunkered behind a low plascrete wall. 'I thought if I joined the Free Militia I'd have a chance to get off-world. Now look at me! I'll be lucky to see Kadillus Harbour again.'

Boreas could see the young trooper's face illuminated in the dull aura of a heatplate. He was surely less than twenty years old, his blond hair cropped to his shoulders. The trooper looked up with shock as Boreas stepped into the glow of the heatplate. The squad saw the Chaplain's black armour and their eyes strayed to the skull helm hanging from his belt.

'There is no luck,' said the Chaplain. He crouched so that he was closer to their level, the servos in his armour creaking. 'Warriors live and die by their skill. If there is some other force that decides our destiny, it is the hand of the Emperor, not luck.'

'Praise the Emperor,' the blond-haired trooper replied unthinkingly.

Boreas looked at the men; saw their tired, strained expressions and the tightness with which they held their lasguns to their chests.

'Skill and courage win more battles than luck,' the Chaplain told them, his gaze resting on the trooper who had spoken. 'Faith in yourselves and each other is the greatest faith you can possess. Do not dwell upon the hardships that you endure, but remember the great honour that you have been granted. Who else but you can say that they have stood upon the line, faced the foes of the Emperor and prevailed? Who else but you can say he was willing to lay down his life to protect his home? Most men pass their lives toiling in the darkness, the eye of the Emperor never seeing their labour, the ear of the Emperor never hearing their voices. The galaxy is swathed in shadows of evil and you have the opportunity to burn bright in the firmament, if only for a moment.

'We who have seen war have seen the true struggle for existence. Others rest safe tonight, on this world and others, because you are here on this cold and forbidding mountain standing guard. Perhaps our watchfulness will go untested and others will be gifted with the opportunity for glorious battle. It matters not, for you can say to lesser men that you stood ready; to watch and to fight if need be.'

Boreas realised his words were as much for himself as the Piscinans.

'My family died when the orks first entered Kadillus Harbour,' said one trooper, his face lined with age and worry. 'What do I fight for now? Everything is lost.'

Remembering that he was dealing with ordinary men, Boreas suppressed the growl that was rising in his throat. He coughed and did his best to keep his voice stern but gentle.

'You fight for their memory, trooper. Would you have the orks trample your city to dust and destroy all of those that remember your family? They exist still in your soul and your heart, and in the souls and hearts of others that knew them. A memory is far harder to protect than a person. It can be swept away by fear and doubt, far more dangerous than any bullet or shell. The sacrifice of those you love should not weaken your resolve, but harden it. They have given their lives for the Imperium, whether willingly or not. Who are you to offer anything less? The blood of martyrs is the seed of the Imperium, trooper.'

Boreas straightened and saw the glare of conviction in the old trooper's eyes. The Chaplain was about to leave when the blond trooper stopped him with a question.

'Why do you fight for Piscina, sir?'

There were so many answers to give. Boreas could explain the happenstance that had led to the 3rd

Company being on the world when the orks arrived. He could point out that Piscina IV was the Dark Angels' staging post for recruiting the savage tribesmen of Piscina V. It was tempting to explain the ancient pacts the Dark Angels held with the Imperial Commanders of Piscina. Boreas could speak about the bond of the battle-brothers that meant that where one fought, all fought.

He could even tell them that as a Chaplain it was his honour and his role to lead by example, to battle the fiercest enemies where the fighting was the most dangerous. Could he get them to understand the duty of the Space Marines, their ancient and eternal purpose as laid down by the Emperor since time immemorial?

All of these reasons and more he considered, but he settled for the simple answer that encapsulated them all.

'I am Astartes, the Emperor's finest,' he told them.

The Chaplain walked away, leaving the men to their quiet, human complaints. He found Sergeant Zaltys sitting on an outcrop of rock, gazing southwards at the cloudy sky. He cut a strange figure against the haze, the massive jump pack giving the sergeant a hunch-backed look. Zaltys looked around as Boreas crunched across the rocky ground.

'What do you look at, brother?' the Chaplain asked, stopping beside Zaltys.

'Nothing, Brother-Chaplain.' The sergeant returned to looking at the horizon. 'There is nothing to see. The orks are not coming here. Even if they are, it would take them more than a day to arrive. It is a strange role for an Assault squad, guarding a disused

GAV THORPE

mine against an enemy that is not coming.'

'Master Belial acts in accordance with the best doctrines of combat, brother,' said Boreas, resting one hand on the haft of his crozius. 'It is wise that all strategic assets are garrisoned against capture by the enemy.'

Zaltys leaned forwards and picked up a small chunk of black rock. It crumbled as he closed his fist, dark dust trickling through the sergeant's armoured fingers.

'I do not judge Master Belial to be in error, I merely lament that it was my poor fortune to be available for this duty. Surely the Piscinans are force enough to dissuade any fast ork column that might seek to take the power plant?'

Boreas glanced back at the Free Militia squads and remembered the fragments of conversation he had overheard.

'Put them in Kadillus Harbour and they will fight to the death, of that I am sure,' said the Chaplain. 'Up here, far from the eyes of their superiors, far from the homes they wish to protect? That is a different matter. It does not matter how much their commanders impress upon them the strategic importance of this place, all they hear is the empty sound of the wind. I share your misgivings, brother-sergeant, but it is because we will fight despite those misgivings that we will protect this place.'

'So you have little regard for our allies, brother?'

'They are men, brother, and nothing more,' said Boreas. 'I have no gauge by which I can measure their mettle by look alone, and everything they say is wrapped in the usual selfishness and self-pity that plague normal men. If they were left alone, I have no doubt they would fold before a concerted attack. With our presence, perhaps their backbones are stiffened, and pride if not honour will bolster their resolve.'

Zaltys pushed himself from the rock and looked back at the men clustered in the blaze of the lamps and the glow of their cooking plates.

'I think you do these men a disservice, brother,' said the sergeant. 'Was not every Space Marine once a weak and fallible man? Are we not proof that training and discipline can harden the mind and soul against the terrors of war?'

'We are not,' Boreas replied immediately. 'Even before we were welcomed into the Chapter, each of us was the best, greater than his peers, a diamond amongst the coal of humanity. We lived harsh, desperate lives and that is what makes us what we are.'

The Chaplain approached Zaltys and laid a hand on the sergeant's shoulder pad, fingers on the Dark Angels' symbol.

'The Apothecaries can shape our bodies, and the Chaplains shape our minds, but they can only build upon strong foundations. Only the perfect physiology can accept the gifts of the Lion's gene-seed; only the perfect spirit can accept the gift of the Lion's teachings. We are stronger, faster and braver than we could ever be before the Chapter accepted us, but never forget that we were never destined to grow up as *ordinary* men.'

Zaltys said nothing. The clouds scudded across the night sky as a moon rose above the shoulder of Mount Barrak, its light reflecting from the lenses of the

Assault sergeant's helm, giving him eyes that glowed a silvery red. The Free Militia camp had fallen still again after the agitation of the watch change. It was almost possible to forget that a few dozen kilometres to the south a war-hungry foe numbering in their hundreds were preparing to wreak destruction and death. Almost, but not quite.

Boreas saw Zaltys gazing skywards again.

'What is it that so concerns you about the heavens, brother?' said the Chaplain.

'I may have misled you earlier, Brother-Chaplain, and for that I offer apology,' replied Zaltys. 'I heard you speaking to those troopers about defending their homes and it reminded me of something, a memory that distracts me.'

'What is this distraction?'

'I was born on Piscina V, brother,' the sergeant said. 'Twice before I have returned to Piscina to recruit from my own people, but never before have I had to fight for their protection. It leaves me with a strange feeling of discomfort.'

'Explain it to me.'

'A Dark Angel has no home; that is what you teach us, Brother-Chaplain. The Chapter is our brother-hood and the Tower of Angels is our fortress. With blessed Caliban lost to us, the Dark Angels roam across the stars, free to pursue our foes and fulfil our duty.'

'That is true. While the future of other Chapters is beholden to the fate of a single world, never again will the Dark Angels be brought low by such dependency. It is to be expected that you feel some connection to the planet that gave you life, but it is the Dark Angels that give you purpose.'

Zaltys did not seem to hear the Chaplain as he continued.

'All I can really remember are jungles, and the huge beasts we hunted. Spears and blood, roars and the shouts of triumphant warriors. And the night the Chapter came for me, that I can still picture. For generations nobody had seen the warriors from the stars. There were those that doubted the stories, but I always believed. I listened to the tales and stared up into the starry sky and I knew that my place was elsewhere. My father and grandfather had been the finest warriors of the tribe, greater than their forefathers, but the warriors of the sky did not come from them. But I still believed they would come for me.'

'I fail to see the relevance to our current mission, brother-sergeant.'

Zaltys gently shook his head.

'Up there, millions of kilometres away, there is another youth of the tribes who can run faster than all of the others; is stronger than all of the others; who is braver than all of the others. We are supposed to be there to bring him to his destiny, but instead we are fighting here, against an enemy that does not even know about him.'

'All the more reason to see the orks destroyed,' said Boreas.

'Yes, it is,' said Zaltys. 'Understand, brother, that you fight out of your duty to the Chapter, the honour of the Lion and our oaths to the Emperor. I fight because if Piscina falls, the Dark Angels will never return here.

I am a Dark Angel now, but the people that gave birth to me would be abandoned. A hundred generations from now they will still look to the heavens and wait for the warriors of the sky, but if we fail to protect Piscina that day will never come again.'

The assault sergeant banged his fist twice against Boreas's chestplate, his armoured gauntlet ringing on the embossed design of a winged skeleton that decorated the Chaplain's plastron.

'And that, Brother-Chaplain, is why I wish that I were on Koth Ridge, fighting for Piscina, and not here waiting for an enemy that will never arrive.'

Zaltys took a step but was stopped by Boreas's hand on his arm.

'There is no reason for regret, brother,' Boreas said. 'I will speak with Master Belial tomorrow and request that you be transferred to the defence line on Koth Ridge. Your savage ancestors have provided great warriors for the Chapter, and their descendants will do so for years to come. I will make sure you have the chance to protect that legacy.'

Zaltys nodded his head.

'Thank you, brother. You have the heart of the Lion as well as his wisdom.'

The Chaplain watched Zaltys return to the encampment and then turned his gaze to the south. Zaltys's outburst worried Boreas. It was natural that the sergeant felt a greater duty to Piscina than to other worlds, but that loyalty could not be allowed to grow stronger than his connection to the Chapter. When the fighting was concluded, Boreas would have to spend some time with Zaltys, reminding the sergeant of his oaths of allegiance, leading him in the prayers of remembrance and dedication; he would help expunge these distracting memories and Zaltys would be free again to love the Chapter without regret.

Such was the nature of the Chaplains, to be ever alert to the faintest glimmer of laxity or doubt. The 10th Company trained a Space Marine; the Apothecaries created his superhuman body; the armoury provided his armour and weapons. It was the Chaplains that gave a Space Marine the most deadly tool in his arsenal: righteousness of purpose. Without it, a Space Marine was nothing.

Adherence to the Chapter's teachings, participating in the brotherhood of warriors that was the Dark Angels, was the core of discipline and fearlessness. An Apothecary could tinker with glands and hormones and proteins, but such manipulation was merely a foundation upon which the Chaplains built courage, honour and aggression.

Just thinking about his duties fired Boreas's spirit. To be a Chaplain was to demand the highest expectation, of oneself as well as one's battle-brothers. Boreas remembered the sense of justice and completeness he had felt when the last ork had died in the basilica, and felt it again as real as the first moment.

It was more than hatred of the enemy that fuelled Boreas's self-belief. Privy to the ancient secrets of the Chapter he knew the price that would be paid for a moment of hesitation or doubt. Nearly ten thousand years had passed since those days of treachery, when Lion El'jonson had been set upon by those he had trusted. Boreas had heard the lies from the lips of those traitors, extracted in the depths of the Tower of Angels. He had heard first-hand how deceit had grown in the hearts of Space Marines. If he was harsh, it was because Boreas understood the dangers of equivocation.

It was sometimes a heavy burden to bear. Boreas looked at Zaltys rejoining his squad and for a moment tried to remember what it was like to simply be a Dark Angel, before he had been inducted into the Inner Circle and learned about the Chapter's moment of weakness during the Horus Heresy. Had he been weaker or stronger for his ignorance? It was impossible to say; Boreas had been out of the 10th Company for less than a year when the Chaplains had summoned him and told him that his strength of mind marked him out to become one of their number.

He had been filled with pride that day. Not the kind of pride that leads a Space Marine to believe himself better than his brothers, but pride that he had something to offer the Chapter. Had he known then what he would learn over the next decades, he would not have been so glad that his strengths had been recognised. He had needed all of that mental fortitude, and the unending support of his brother Chaplains, to come to terms with the ignominy of the Dark Angels' failure those many centuries ago.

For a lesser man – even a lesser Space Marine – those interrogations with the Fallen would have weakened resolve. For Boreas, the opposite was true. Every different lie he heard, every false justification and self-aggrandising rationale that was spat out in the interrogation cells was a confirmation of his devotion to the Lion and his trust for the Dark Angels. No matter how persuasive the argument or reasoned the principles espoused by those that had turned on the primarch, Boreas was reminded on each occasion of the self-serving nature of those that had become traitors.

His last interrogation had been particularly fraught, his subject espousing all kinds of propaganda and venom against the Lion, challenging the primarch's loyalty to the Emperor. That treacherous viper had been amongst the worst, an instigator of the rebellion and an unashamed detractor of the Lion.

Boreas recalled the Fallen's name: Astelan. He had not repented and had clung to his self-delusional beliefs despite every effort of the Chaplain. Raving and half-mad, the Fallen had made wild claims and re-invented history for his own purposes. What truth could there be from the mouth of a self-confessed architect of genocide, who had the brazen nerve to be proud of his defiance of the Lion and the Emperor?

It was against such insanity that the Chaplains had to contend. And from the lies the truth was eked out, teased from the misinformation and posturing. Over ten thousand years the Chaplains had learnt a great deal about treachery and how to spot its earliest signs, from the evidence given by those who had succumbed.

With this knowledge Boreas could strike against the smallest seed of doubt and crush it before it took hold. Zaltys was a Space Marine of the Dark Angels and Boreas did not doubt his devotion for a moment. Yet there were those who had been trusted before, by none other than the Lion himself, who had proved the error of indulgence. Zaltys meant no harm and was no threat – yet.

His sentimental attachment to his home world was a tiny chink in the armour of his soul; one that could be exploited if it was not repaired. What today was a reason for fighting even more fiercely against the orks could tomorrow become a reason for disobedience. If, against all expectation, the Dark Angels failed to stem the ork attack and Piscina had to be sacrificed for strategic reasons, could Zaltys be trusted to obey the order, and more importantly, pass it on to those who served under him?

A thrum of anti-grav motors from the patrolling Ravenwing land speeder swept past the power plant. As the Ravenwing stood watch against the enemy without, Boreas was alert for an even deadlier foe: the enemy within.

THE NIGHT PASSED quietly. Boreas sat on a rock, cleaning his bolt pistol as the horizon to the east fringed with red. He looked around as the hum of the Ravenwing's land speeder shook the ground behind him. The black-liveried speeder settled down a few metres away, stopping just above the ground. Brother Amathael jumped out, leaving the heavy bolter to droop on its mount, its muzzle clanging against the speeder's hull. Amathael bent down and looked at something on the vehicle's underside.

'Is something wrong, brother?' Boreas asked over the comm.

'I am not sure, brother,' Amathael replied.

His black armour almost invisible, the Ravenwing

Space Marine ducked under the floating land speeder. The rocks around the mine head echoed with the sound of his armoured fist thumping against metal. The Space Marine emerged with a twisted length of branch in his hand. He held it up to the driver, Methaniel, as if in explanation.

'We must have picked this up during our last pass through that gorge to the east,' said Amathael as he tossed the offending branch aside. 'How's the sensor return now, brother?'

Hearing this exchange, Boreas stood up and walked over to the land speeder as it rose a few metres into the air, its twin-fan engine throbbing. The ground shimmered through the craft's anti-grav field, dust kicked up by the gravitic impellers keeping the land speeder aloft. The Chaplain's autosenses registered a wave of electromagnetic energy emitted by the antenna jutting from the blunt nose of the craft as the pilot activated the long-range augur.

'There is still something wrong, brother,' reported Methaniel. 'I'm getting a large, blurred return. Check the housing again.'

The land speeder settled down once more under Methaniel's direction and there followed some more thuds as Amathael effected his own form of repairs.

'The links are all in place,' said Amathael. 'Check the connections on the chin-mount.'

Pneumatics wheezed as the multi-barrelled assault cannon slung beneath the land speeder's nose swiv-elled left and right. At a command from the pilot, the assault cannon's barrel spun up to firing speed with a whine and then slowed to a low growl.

'I think your crude attentions have offended the spirit of the sensor matrix, brother,' said Methaniel. 'I told you to ask Brother Hephaestus to cast his blessing upon it before we left Kadillus Harbour.'

'Master Belial's orders were specific, brother,' Amathael said. 'There was not time to seek the Techmarines.'

Boreas cleared his throat meaningfully, interrupting the two Space Marines' bickering.

'Explain the situation, brothers,' said the Chaplain.

Amathael and Methaniel looked at each other, waiting for the other to speak. Amathael conceded first and turned to Boreas.

'We have suffered damage to the long-range augur, Brother-Chaplain,' the Ravenwing gunner admitted. 'We thought we might effect a field repair, but it seems the land speeder's spirit is more troubled than we realised.'

'You felt it necessary to abandon your patrol for this matter?' Boreas kept his tone even, masking his annoyance.

'We have been up and down the mountain all night, brother,' said Amathael. 'There's nothing more threatening than a few rock lizards.'

'How long ago did you first experience this sensor problem, brothers?' Boreas asked patiently.

'No more than twenty minutes, Brother-Chaplain,' said Methaniel.

'And you are experiencing an unexpected sensor return at the moment?'

Methaniel looked down at the console and nodded.

'Yes,' said the pilot. 'The accursed thing thinks there's a huge heat source three kilometres away. If it were caused by the orks, there would have to be hundreds of them to register like that.'

'I think we should investigate,' Amathael said hurriedly. He glanced at Boreas and then pulled himself up to the gunner's position next to Methaniel. 'Better to be sure, is that not right, Brother-Chaplain?'

Boreas allowed his deafening silence to answer for him.

'Dawn patrol protocol,' said Amathael. 'Sweep east to west. Let us not distract the Brother-Chaplain any longer.'

Boreas shook his head with disappointment as the twin glows of the land speeder's engine disappeared into the night. A certain freedom of spirit and independence was required of the Ravenwing, but poor patrol discipline was unacceptable. When the Chapter returned, Boreas would be making a report to Brother Sammael, Master of the Ravenwing, regarding Brothers Amathael and Methaniel. Such cavalier behaviour would not be tolerated by the 3rd Company.

A few minutes later, the shouts of the Piscinans' lieutenants calling for the morning watch echoed around the mine head. Troopers roused themselves wearily from their blankets, their babble adding to the noise. Walking amongst them, Boreas heard something else above the low din, echoing from the gorge to the south. It was a loud drone, like the buzzing of an immense wasp.

The Chaplain recognised the sound instantly: an assault cannon firing.

A moment after he heard the sound, the comm chimed in Boreas's ear.

'Brother Boreas!' Methaniel's voice was urgent. The comm rattled with the sound of Amathael's heavy bolter and continued sporadic bursts from the assault cannon. 'This is Ravenwing-Six. Hostile force encountered, two kilometres south of your position. We are falling back out of weapons range. Heavy enemy presence. Requesting orders, Brother-Chaplain.'

Boreas's first act was to switch the transmission to general broadcast.

'Brothers of the Lion, sons of Piscina: the enemy are upon us! Gather yourselves and prepare your weapons. Today our courage and our strength will be tested. We will not be found lacking.' The Chaplain switched back to the command channel. 'Ravenwing-Six, this is Boreas. Estimate enemy numbers.'

'Four hundred to five hundred including light vehicles and Dreadnoughts, brother,' said Methaniel, his voice calmer. 'Count five warbikes approaching, and one of those flamethrower light half-tracks. Orders, brother?'

'Engage the warbikes and slow their attack,' Boreas said, striding into the heart of his force. He looked around to gauge the readiness of the defenders. The reaction had been mixed. Zaltys and his Assault Marines were bounding off to the left, to take up positions opposite the ruins of one of the mine's administration buildings. The Piscina troopers were rushing to and fro, some of them at their posts, others caught out as they had been preparing their breakfast. 'We need at least two minutes, Ravenwing-Six.'

'Confirm, brother. Attack delayed for two minutes.'

Boreas took his place at the centre of the line, behind a crude wall of broken rock and dirt-filled rations crates. Just in front, a worried-looking Piscinan lieutenant was shrieking orders at his command squad as they set up their autocannon. The squad already inside the emplacement were reluctant to leave their cover, leaving no room for the anti-tank gun. The officer's high-pitched entreaties were only adding to the confusion. Boreas stepped up next to the frantic officer, the Space Marine's shadow falling over the men manhandling the heavy weapon onto its tripod.

'You will have more success if you site your weapon on the flatter ground over there,' Boreas cut across the troopers' chatter. He pointed to an emplacement a dozen metres to the right which was as yet unmanned. 'Do not allow haste to detract from your preparations, you have plenty of time.'

The officer bobbed his head nervously and signalled to his men to move to the empty position. Boreas grabbed the man by the arm as he set off after his squad, taking care not to hurt the officer.

'I expect you to show calmness and discipline, lieutenant,' Boreas said. 'Remember that your men will look to you for leadership. I know that you are afraid, but you must not show it. You are an officer representing the Emperor, never forget that.'

The lieutenant said nothing as he nodded again and took a deep breath. Boreas held the man back for a few seconds more until he was convinced that he was calmer. Looking across to the next emplacement, he saw that the autocannon was already set up, ready for the ork vehicles.

'Join your men and fight with courage and honour,' said Boreas, giving the lieutenant a light shove to send him on his way.

'This is Ravenwing-Six. Two warbikes destroyed, Brother-Chaplain,' Methaniel reported over the comm. 'Heavy bolter destroyed, gunner dead. Orders, brother.'

'Continue to delay the enemy,' Boreas replied. 'Sacrifice if necessary. Confirm.'

'Confirm, Brother-Chaplain,' the land speeder pilot answered without hesitation.

Boreas examined the deployment of his small force. Many of them were too far back, lingering within the protection of the power plant rather than at the front line. They had all but surrendered the outer buildings of the mine-workings with their hesitancy but it was too late to move them forwards.

The Chaplain contacted Zaltys.

'The orks are likely to gain the outer perimeter of the compound, brother-sergeant. Stay free of engagement until the moment is right to counter-attack. If the enemy force a position into those buildings you will have to drive them out; I fear our allies are incapable of such offensive action.'

'Confirm, Brother-Chaplain. We will allow the Piscinans to blunt the attack and then assault when enemy momentum is wavering.'

The comm crackled as another transmission came in from the Ravenwing land speeder.

'This is Ravenwing-Six. Revise upwards enemy force estimate. Five hundred infantry minimum. I can see heavily armoured leaders approaching up the gorge.

Must conclude that Koth Ridge is not the enemy obj–'

The comm cut and an explosion echoed up the valley. Boreas increased the magnification of his autosenses and saw a blossom of red fire about half a kilometre away. Smoke trails from the ork bikes and light half-tracks were not much further away.

The Chaplain switched his comm to universal address.

'This is your commander, Chaplain Boreas of the Dark Angels. Today will test your resolve like no other. You do not fight to protect an abandoned mine, but to halt the orks that have come to destroy your world. An enemy has come here to kill and enslave your loved ones. Our foes are many but we have a far superior position. Today each of you has the opportunity to be a hero of the Emperor. Count only the dead of the enemy and pay no heed to the fears that whisper. Every ork you kill is one less that will fall upon your homes and families. Share the rage of the Dark Angels and slay these loathsome creatures. *Sanctorius via mortis majorus*. Kill without relent and taste the sweetness of victory!'

Zaltys and his Assault Marines gave a roar of approval, though the reaction from the Piscinans was more muted. Most of the troopers were staring along their lasgun sights, worriedly awaiting the approach of the greenskins. A nervous quiet descended on the force and the rumble of the engines reverberated up the gorge towards Boreas. He could see a thick pall of smoke, presumably from the destroyed land speeder, and the paler exhaust fumes of the orks' warbikes.

As the bikes roared into view, heavy weapons teams

to the Chaplain's right opened fire with lascannons and autocannons, filling the gorge with a hail of shells and blue bursts of energy. One of the bikes exploded immediately, struck in the engine by a lascannon bolt. Two more bikers jinked their half-track vehicles between the storms of splintering rock and ravening blasts of laser energy.

The warbikes were even larger than the combat bikes of the Ravenwing, each laden with rapid-firing cannons that spewed bullets up the gorge. They both had a churning track instead of a rear wheel, which threw up huge fountains of dirt and grit in their wake.

Their ork riders wore thick-rimmed goggles to protect their eyes and their fanged mouths were hidden behind brightly patterned scarves, a crude defence against the choking dust and smoke. The orks' thick jackets were daubed with stripes of red to match the paintwork of their machines. A pennant with a flaming skull fluttered from a pole behind one rider, who wore a spiked helmet painted with a similar design. The other biker's head was protected by a black leather cap studded with small spikes. As the rider's scarf fell away, Boreas could see that the ork frothed at the mouth, driven to a delirium by the speed of his machine and the chatter of the guns.

Boreas was not the least concerned by the rapidly approaching bikes. He had studied the reports from the assault on Koth Ridge and it appeared the orks were repeating their mistakes. In their enthusiasm to get to grips with the enemy, the bikers were far ahead of the ork infantry and would be easy prey for the heavy weapons teams.

A few seconds after the bikes had emerged from behind a ruined shack half a kilometre down the ravine, a second exploded into a rising fireball of red as the autocannon gunners found their range. Debris rained down onto the rocks to either side of the valley and a thick pall of smoke wafted up around the Piscinans, the grey tinged with green fuel vapours.

The surviving biker veered wildly to the left and right, the pennant whipping back and forth, billowing dust almost filling the gorge. It was impossible for the ork to aim its weapons at such speed; torrents of heavy bullets screeched overhead and rattled around the upper storeys of the power plant. It was ludicrous behaviour and Boreas concluded that the alien had been filled by some kind of strange battle-mania.

The thudding of the heavy bolters joined the crack of lascannons and shriek of autocannons as the biker roared closer and closer. A bolt exploded against the magazine of one of the bike's cannons, igniting the shells within. Trailing fire and smoke, the warbike careened across the gorge, bouncing over rocks and cracks, until it smashed into the wall of the gorge. Fuel and oil spilled down the slope back in the direction of the orks. Ammunition continued to pop and a few seconds after impact a shower of sparks set the slick aflame, a crackling inferno engulfing the right-hand side of the gorge.

Switching his helm to terrorsight to peer through the fumes and dust filling the approach to the mine head, Boreas could see another half-tracked vehicle closing swiftly. It was a little larger than the warbikes and pulled a long trailer connected by a profusion of tubes and pipes. A diminutive gretchin clung on to the back of the trailer, holding on to a wheel-lock for dear life. Over the head of the driver extended a funnel-like spout dripping with burning fuel.

It was only when Boreas noticed that the Piscinans were not shooting that the Chaplain realised the crude cunning of the ork plan. The greenskins' commander had sent the bikes forwards knowing they would be destroyed, and in the close confines of the gorge, the dust and smoke were blocking the aim of the troopers defending the geothermal station. It was a screen to allow the orks to get closer.

'Mortars!' Boreas bellowed. 'Fill that gorge with bombs!'

The troopers responded as quickly as they could but the flamethrower half-track was already roaring out of the smog, the driver gunning his vehicle directly at the closest emplacement. Shocked Piscinans shouted warnings to each other and a few autocannon rounds zipped down the gorge without finding their mark.

The whine of descending mortar bombs joined the roar of the half-track's engine and the cries of the defence force officers. A ripple of explosions tore from left to right across the gorge, metres behind the approaching vehicle, throwing up another curtain of dust and smoke.

'Sergeant Zaltys!' Boreas turned to face the Assault squad. 'Intercept that vehicle before it reaches the defensive line!'

'Affirm, Brother-Chaplain.' The sergeant was already leading his squad forwards with long leaps as he replied.

Covering twenty metres with each jump, the Assault squad sped down the ravine, their pistols hurling bolts and blasts of plasma at the war-track. The vehicle's gunner heaved around the nozzle of the flamethrower and fired. A jet of bright orange arced across the gorge, engulfing Zaltys's squad. One of the Assault Marines was caught full by the inferno and tumbled mid-jump, crashing into the rock amidst a plume of flames and flying shards of armour. The others plunged out of the crackling wave of flame, fire licking from their blackened armour.

The gunner fired again and swung the flamethrower around as the vehicle's driver swerved away from the charging Space Marines. Burning fuel erupted across the boulders and rocky ground but fell short. Zaltys and the others burst through the sheet of flame and fell upon the vehicle with fierce war cries.

One Assault Marine landed on the front of the track housing, a booted foot smashing the driver from his saddle. The ork tumbled beneath the whirring links, the towed fuel trailer bouncing over its mangled corpse.

The mad swaying of the trailer caused Zaltys to mistime his leap; the sergeant crashed shoulder-first into the side of the trailer, dislodging the gretchin atop the cylindrical tank of fuel. Metal panels burst their rivets and thick, oily sludge seeped from the ruptured tank, spilling over the sergeant and another of the Assault Marines.

Even without a driver, the ork vehicle roared onwards up the gorge, the Assault Marines leaping after it. One of the squad landed squarely on the back of the fuel trailer. Boreas saw the Space Marine slap a melta-bomb onto the side of the leaking tank and heard the warning shout across the comm.

Less than a dozen metres from the foremost emplacement, the squad peeled away from the doomed vehicle, launching themselves high into the air with their jump packs as the melta-bomb detonated. The fuel tank exploded with a blast that sent a hot wind rushing up the valley, throwing several of the closest Piscinans from their feet. The remnants of the half-track were hurled in a burning arc across a line of dirt-filled crates, and crashed against the rough wall with another detonation.

There were a few cries of pain from wounded troopers. Sergeants and officers bellowed to their men to keep the line while two medics dashed forwards to see what could be done for those caught in the explosion. Boreas spied the gretchin who had been flung clear of the trailer crawling behind a rock. He was about to warn Zaltys but the sergeant had already seen the creeping greenskin. The sergeant's hand flamer bathed the creature's hiding place with white-hot fire.

'Live by fire, die by fire,' Zaltys grunted over the comm, no doubt with some satisfaction. The sergeant crossed the gorge to his fallen battle-brother and shook his head. 'Brother Lemaseus is dead. Remember him for his sacrifice.'

'His deeds will live for eternity,' Boreas replied.

The Assault Marines hauled up the smoking body of their fallen comrade and carried it back towards the mine head. Behind them a dark mass could be seen through the thinning smoke as the orks raced up the gorge. Boreas could hear their guttural war shouts, the jangle of wargear and the *clump* of boots on rock.

'Stand ready to engage the enemy,' the Chaplain commanded the troopers around him.

The orks rushed from the smog as a wall of green flesh, clothed in black and yellow. Boreas saw glaring red eyes and snarling fangs, repeated hundreds of times as the baying ork mob thundered between the rocky walls of the gorge. They howled and roared their challenges as they pounded up the slope.

Boreas heard answering shouts, of dismay rather than anger. Amidst the din of the orks' charge he detected the scrape of boots and the thud of dropped weapons. Turning to his right, he saw at least two dozen of the Piscinans abandoning their posts, ignoring the shouts of their sergeants.

The fleeing troopers streamed back into the geothermal station as quickly as they could run, their panicked shouts urging their fellow Piscinans to come with them.

'Hold the line!' roared Boreas, swinging around to confront the closest defence troopers. One or two that had been edging away from the barricade slunk back into position and lifted up their lasrifles. 'Open fire, damn you!'

Utterly livid at the Piscinans' retreat, Boreas wanted to snatch up the cowards and dash open their skulls on the rock. He took several steps towards the fleeing men, blazing crozius in hand, but stopped as the snap of las-fire and the crack of ork guns reminded the Chaplain that he had more immediate concerns.

'*Traitorium eternis.* May your souls rot in the darkness

of the abyss for your treachery,' Boreas snarled at the swiftly disappearing backs of the departing troopers.

He returned to his position to find the orks barely a hundred metres away. As he had feared, some of them had reached the outbuildings unscathed and were unleashing heavy if inaccurate covering fire for those greenskins still sprinting towards the troopers' line. Bullets and las-bolts criss-crossed the narrowing gap between defenders and attackers.

The mortars opened up again, ripping holes into the oncoming mass of green flesh. Swathes of orks were bloodily hurled from their feet as the autocannons added their roar to the defence.

Boreas gauged the state of the battle with one sweeping glance. The fire from around him was sporadic as the orks in the ruined administration building poured bullets into the barricades. Despite that, the orks were slowing as more and more of their numbers fell to the wall of las-fire and shells. To the right the orks were approaching more swiftly, heading for the gaps left by the troopers who had fled. The left was holding firm, pinning the orks back behind a line of rocks that jutted out from the wall of the gorge.

'Boreas to Zaltys, cross to the right flank and cover the holes left by those cowards.'

'Affirm, Brother-Chaplain.'

As the Assault Marines powered from one end of the line to the other, Boreas pulled out his pistol. The orks had slowed in their advance and stopped every few metres to snap off shots at the geothermal station's defenders. Had he been commanding a force of Astartes, Boreas would have ordered the counter-charge at this point, to drive the orks back down into the gorge. Such a tactic was not an option; Boreas knew it was a hope that the Piscinans would hold their line and there was no chance they would want to get any closer to their enemies.

'Fire discipline!' Boreas bellowed at the officers within earshot, noting the sporadic and woefully inaccurate bursts of las-fire from the troopers as they hurried their shots. 'Mark your targets and concentrate your fire.'

A small measure of order rippled along the line from the Chaplain and the rush of fire slackened for a few seconds and then intensified into proper volleys. The ork dead littered the ground and those that survived were reluctant to leave the cover of the rocks and ruined buildings. There were few enemies within range of Boreas's bolt pistol. Those that were foolish enough to show themselves were quickly picked off by the Chaplain, who fired short bursts of two and three shots with unerring accuracy.

SLOWLY THE ORKS lost interest in the firefight and slunk back down the slope, occasionally turning to unleash a hail of bullets or hurl insults.

The ferocity of the battle waned. As the odd bullet whined up the gorge from the administration building, Boreas walked the line to inspect the state of his force. About a tenth of the troopers had fled from the initial onslaught and a few more had slipped away in the confusion of battle. Casualties were surprisingly light, no more than ten troopers had been killed – along with Brother Lemaseus – and another fifteen were too badly wounded to fight on. About twice that number had suffered lesser injuries and were shepherded back to their posts by their officers, bloodied and bandaged.

All in all Boreas was pleased with the Piscinans that had held their nerve and stayed on the line. Of those that had deserted, there was no sign. They had fled along the narrow channels and gulleys that criss-crossed the slope of the mountain and were no doubt already heading back to Kadillus Harbour. There was nothing Boreas could do about them now, but he would have words with the Piscinan commanders later to ensure those that had abandoned their posts would be found and chastised.

There was a brief flurry of more intensive fire from the orks in the administration building, under the cover of which two dozen or more greenskins broke from their hiding places and occupied a low shack that had once been a workshop. The ork shooting slackened again and the two sides settled down to occasional sniping at one another as targets presented themselves. Scornful of the orks' accuracy, Boreas strode from emplacement to emplacement, reminding the officers of their duty and reassuring the troopers that the worst had passed.

Reaching the right end of the line, Boreas joined Zaltys. The sergeant was changing the fuel canister on his hand flamer.

'The enemy will come again, brother,' said the sergeant. 'Orks won't have come all this way just to give up after the first charge.'

'Our defiance has blunted their blood-lust,' replied

the Chaplain. 'They'll be more cautious next time. They'll use the administration building to gather their numbers and then come at us through those boulders on the left.'

Zaltys surveyed the lay of the land and nodded.

'That seems likely, Brother-Chaplain. We can hold this flank, and you can concentrate the Piscinans to the centre and left.'

Boreas considered this, eyes scanning the battlefield for likely routes of attack, angles of fire and blind spots.

'Very well, brother-sergeant,' he said. 'Next time the orks fall back, follow up with an attack to the administration building. I will attempt to lead a second attack along the left and come at the orks from the other side.'

The Chaplain walked back to the central emplacements, calling for the Piscinan officers to attend to him. He repositioned the heavy weapons squads to cover the administration complex and moved the bulk of the troopers further left to guard against enemies moving through the rocks and bushes that lined the eastern side of the gorge. Further down the slope the orks were also rearranging their forces, flashes of green and yellow moving between the scattered boulders and tumbled walls.

Satisfied that he was prepared for the next assault, Boreas took up his place at the centre of the reformed line and signalled Master Belial on the long-range comm.

'Chaplain Boreas to Master Belial. Have engaged enemy at Barrak Gorge station. Report to be made.'

There was no response for a minute. When Belial replied, his tone was clipped and breathless.

'This is Belial. Make your report, brother.'

'The orks have moved to Barrak Gorge during the night and attacked shortly after daybreak, brother-captain.' Boreas paced back and forth a few steps as he assessed the enemy strength. 'We have engaged a significant portion of the ork army. Several hundred infantry at a minimum. Several light vehicles destroyed. Risk to the geothermal station is negligible at present, our position is secure.'

Again there was a lengthy pause.

'It is imperative, absolutely vital, that the orks do not succeed in capturing the power station, brother. Brother Naaman succeeded in breaching the ork lines and we have located the means by which they are reaching the surface. The orks are using Piscina's power grid to power some form of high-energy teleporter to move their troops from an as-yet-unknown location. I have just returned from an attack at the East Barrens plant to disable their power link.

'Your operation to sever the link between Kadillus Harbour and the Barrens has also curtailed their reinforcements and I expect it is that which has triggered this attack on Barrak Gorge. Any advantage gained from these actions will be lost if the enemy are able to take another power station.'

'I understand, brother-captain,' said Boreas, staring at the ork army with renewed interest. 'Barrak Gorge will not fall to the enemy.'

'It must not.' Belial sharply emphasised every word. 'I expect the orks to repair the damage done at East

Barrens, but that alone will not be enough for them to resume their widespread reinforcement. If we are to contain the ork threat until the rest of the Chapter arrives we must cut off the ork forces at their source. They cannot gain access to another power plant.'

'Understood, brother-captain. The Dark Angels will not allow this world to fall to the foul xenos.'

'Their taint will be cleansed from Piscina. The orks will learn to fear the Sons of Caliban.'

THE NEXT ORK attack came just before noon.

The assault was heralded by a hail of heavy weapons fire from the administration building a few seconds before a tide of green-skinned warriors poured from the doors and broken windows and rushed to the eastern side of the gorge.

'Conserve ammunition and wait for targets,' Boreas growled to his soldiers. The orks would be desperate to claim the power station and Belial had given no word of when Boreas's force could expect relief.

The orks made use of what cover there was amongst the rocks and scrub. Rather than charge headlong into the fire of the Piscinans, the greenskins worked their way forwards with more care. For all their attempted stealth, the orks were too numerous for them to all find cover and a trail of blood and bodies marked their progress up the gorge as las-fire zipped through the bushes and heavy bolter rounds detonated across the boulders.

Boreas ejected the magazine from his bolt pistol and slipped his hand into a pouch at his belt. He brought out a fresh clip, loaded with special seeker bolts that

Techmarine Hephaestus had presented to the Chaplain after the defence of the basilica. Each handcrafted round contained a miniature cogitator capable of steering the bolt towards the heat signature of a target.

'Let the hidden hand guide thee to the doom of my foes,' Boreas whispered to the tiny spirits of each bolt as he slotted the fresh magazine in place.

He switched the tactical display of his helm to thermal view and watched for a few seconds as the orks crept along the gorge, their bodies a white glow amongst the warm yellow of the sun reflecting from stone. With a light touch against the trigger of his raised pistol, Boreas activated the weapon's targeter and zoomed in on his foes.

The Chaplain fired a burst of three rounds and watched the fiery trails of the bolts as they flashed through the air. Two of the bolts zeroed in on an ork crouched behind the twisted trunk of a tree, exploding inside the creature's back and leg. The third turned sharply, rose a few metres and dived out of sight behind a rock, detonating with a shower of blood that showed up as a spray of warm droplets.

Boreas fired twice more as the orks broke from cover with a storm of pistol fire. The blossoms of the bolt detonations were lost in the hail of las-blasts and muzzle flares that engulfed the surging orks. Boreas flicked back to normal-spectrum view and took in the change of battle at a glance.

'Mortars on the administration building,' Boreas ordered as a fresh salvo of weapons fire erupted from the complex. 'Autocannon teams, cover the centre. Left flank, prepare for close combat.'

He leapt over the rough barricade and pounded to the east to stave off the ork assault. Raging and shouting, the orks poured into the two front emplacements, hacking with their heavy blades and firing madly with their pistols. The troopers stabbed and parried with bayonets and swung the butts of their lasrifles at the greenskins while officers cut and thrust with chainswords and urged their men to hold their ground.

'With me!' Boreas bellowed to a squad of Piscinans in the next emplacement.

'You heard the commander!' roared their sergeant, grabbing one of the troopers by the scruff of his flak jacket to haul the soldier to his feet.

Boreas barely heard the padding of their boots after him, his ears filled with the thunder of his twin hearts as the surge of battle consumed him. He fired another salvo of twisting, deadly shots and plunged into the melee with his crozius blazing.

Crashing through a wall of empty ammunition boxes, the Chaplain struck out at the back of an ork's skull, smashing through bone. His backswing took another greenskin full in the throat. Pistol rounds disappeared in flares of light around Boreas as his rosarius field activated. He shouldered aside another ork, which was set upon by the squad following the Chaplain.

'Drive them back!' Boreas illustrated the order by smashing his bolt pistol into the face of an ork, splintering fangs, crushing its puggy nose. 'Let the Emperor's wrath fill your limbs!'

Boreas's pistol barked in his hand, bolts tearing

through the orks around him. His crozius carved a path of blood and shattered bone. The Piscinans were being battered to their knees and cut down by the ferocious orks, but the presence of the Chaplain bolstered the nerve of the troopers and they fought on with gritted teeth and wide eyes.

'Brother-Chaplain.' Zaltys's calm voice cut through the haze of anger that washed through Boreas. The Chaplain side-stepped a cleaver and drove his knee into the gut of the ork wielding it.

'Report, brother-sergeant,' Boreas snarled.

'Enemy are gathering for an attack against the centre, brother. Shall I move to engage?'

Boreas rammed his elbow into the jaw of a greenskin and fired a bolt into its chest as it fell back. The Chaplain was surrounded by a press of foes and could see nothing of the wider battle.

'I leave it to your discretion, brother,' he told Zaltys. 'The orks must not gain a foothold within the power plant.'

'Confirm, brother. We will engage if the enemy reach the power plant.'

A spinning, toothed blade slammed into the side of Boreas's helm, dazing him in a shower of sparks and shredded ceramite. Out of instinct, he swept up his arm to knock away the blade, its jagged edge ripping a furrow through the Chaplain's elbow pad. He kicked out and felt the ork's ribs collapsing. Blinking to restore his blurred vision, Boreas found himself face-to-face with the snarling alien, two dagger-like tusks jutting from its jaw.

Boreas let go of his crozius so that it swung on its

chain from his wrist, and grabbed the throat of the ork, fingers digging into corded muscle. The ork's eyes bulged and thick saliva drooled from its twisted lips as Boreas bent the creature backwards, twisting its spine. A hand hammered at Boreas's chest, claws leaving scratches on the embossed design. With a grunt, Boreas lurched forwards, snapping the ork's spine. The Chaplain fired a round into the greenskin's chest as it flopped in his grasp.

With a flick of his arm, Boreas snatched up his crozius just in time to ward away a crackling power claw swinging at his face. The two power fields met with a flash of blue sparks. The Chaplain matched stares with his foe; an ork even taller than Boreas wearing thick pads of armour covered with riveted plates. The bestial alien closed the claws of its glove into a fist and punched the Chaplain in the chest. Boreas's rosarius blazed, absorbing most of the impact, though the Chaplain was forced back a step by the blow.

A frown of confusion knotted the ork's brow. It glanced down at its power claw, tears streaking down its face from the light of the conversion field's activation. Boreas swept his crozius upwards, the winged angel on its top connecting squarely with the chin of the greenskin.

The ork fell to its backside, shaking its head, jaw split to the bottom lip. Boreas stamped, crushing the heel of his boot into the greenskin's face. With a spasm of reaction, the ork clamped its energy-wreathed claw around Boreas's knee. The Chaplain felt armour buckling and a warning light flashed in the corner of his right eye.

Wrenching himself free from the ork's death-grip, Boreas stumbled back a few steps, his knee flaring with pain. In a moment the acute sensation passed, to be replaced by a dull throbbing that even his armour's pain suppressants could not wholly mask.

The Chaplain was aware of shouting. He looked up and saw that the orks were falling back, limping and bleeding, dispirited by the death of the leader Boreas had slain. The Chaplain took a deep breath and looked to his right, where the fighting was still fierce.

Zaltys's squad had torn into the central attack and were pursuing the broken orks down the gorge. There was still an intense firefight between the squads at the base of the power plant and the orks in the administration buildings. The orks' position was wreathed in a cloud of dust from the mortar bombardment and Boreas could see the corpses of many greenskins piled behind the broken walls and hanging from shattered windows.

There was similar carnage close at hand. At a glance he counted at least thirty dead orks around the barricades, and more than that number of fallen troopers. He saw an officer's body draped in a tattered, blood-soaked great-coat, the Piscinan's chainsword still stuck in the chest of a dead ork. The hacked and broken bodies of squad-mates were heaped upon each other, their faces caught in their last moments of agony and horror.

Limping slightly, Boreas stepped up to the remnants of the barricade. He activated the long-range comm.

'Chaplain Boreas to Master Belial. Contact report.'

The response was far quicker than earlier.

'This is Belial. Make your report, brother.'

'Second enemy attack met, brother-captain. We still have possession of the power plant. Position secure but request further forces.'

'Negative, brother. There are no more forces available at this time. We cannot weaken our presence in the city or on Koth Ridge. Scout reports suggest that you are not facing the bulk of the enemy army. This is just a raiding force. You must continue to hold.'

'Understood, brother. We may have faced the worst of it. Casualty ratio seven-to-one, we will cleanse this unclean horde from the galaxy!'

Boreas cut the link and assessed the remaining strength of his troops. Judging by the number of bodies over half the Piscinans had fallen, while the number of those remaining showed that twenty or thirty more had broken away and fled during the fighting. His gaze following Zaltys down the gorge, the Chaplain saw that two more Space Marines had also been killed by the orks.

It was not much compared to what he had started with, but it was probably enough to see off the dregs of the ork army that had survived the last attack. The power plant's defenders still had the advantage of higher ground and a prepared position.

'Surviving officers, report to me for fresh dispositions,' Boreas announced.

Two officers picked their way wearily through the bodies and destroyed barricades. A third was pointing to the west, towards the right flank. The man turned back to Boreas with a horrified expression, his peaked cap falling from his head.

'Master Boreas! Orks!'

Boreas looked to where the lieutenant was pointing and magnified his view. A massive ork was shouldering its way through a stand of trees and bushes at the far end of the line. Encased in a solid suit of yellow armour decorated with black flames and glittering gold, the warlord was accompanied by half a dozen monstrous orks and twenty smaller greenskins.

The Chaplain quickly realised what had happened. Obscured by the rocks and foliage was another narrow defile running almost parallel to the main gorge, up to the outskirts of the power plant. Glancing down the gorge, Boreas could now see where the rocks parted at the far end. It appeared that the earlier screen of smoke and dust had not been to obscure the main ork advance, but to allow the warlord and a small entourage to slip unseen into the crevasse. The subsequent attack had drawn more and more of the defenders away from the flank and now there was nobody to stop the warlord and its bodyguard sweeping in behind the emplacements.

'Zaltys, return to the line!' Boreas snapped. 'Enemy flank attack. Engage immediately.'

'Sir, the orks are coming back,' a sergeant called from Boreas's left.

The Chaplain turned around to see the greenskins that had been hurled back gathering again in the rocks and bushes on the left flank. Boreas hissed in irritation as it dawned on him that he had been out-smarted by a greenskin.

'It's not over yet, you green-skinned filth,' the Chaplain growled. He switched his helmet vocaliser to maximum amplification, voice booming out across the gorge. 'Man your weapons! Take up your rifles! This battle is not lost. Destroy the foes of the Emperor!'

'We're trapped,' murmured one of the lieutenants beside Boreas.

The Chaplain rounded on the officer, skull helm a hair's breadth from the lieutenant's shocked face.

'Then you have nothing to lose by fighting, do you? Rally your men!'

Quivering and gulping, the officer backed away, shouting for his command squad with a broken voice. Past him, Boreas saw Zaltys's squad racing back up the gorge, bounding over the rocks and rubble.

The orks split. A mob of black-clad greenskins wielding pistols and jagged blades broke into the power plant while the heavily armoured warlord and retinue turned to confront the approaching Assault Marines. The warlord raised its right arm, which ended with a multi-barrelled cannon. Smoke plumed from the exhausts of the warlord's armour as the barrels started to spin. Around their leader, the bodyguard also lifted an assortment of outlandish energy weapons and rocket launchers.

The warlord bellowed a command and the orks opened fire. The leader's weapon spewed a hail of projectiles that glowed with a green light, the salvo rippling across the Assault Marine squad as they sprang up the slope. One of Zaltys's warriors was engulfed by the fusillade. Mid-leap, his jump pack exploded, sending the Space Marine tumbling into the rocks as pieces of his shoulder pads and chest plastron flew in all directions. Several rocket trails hissed past the leaping Space Marines to explode further down the gorge, while pulses of plasma screeched through the squad like miniature stars.

Zaltys crashed down onto the rocky ground, took three paces and jumped again, soaring high above the warlord. Behind the sergeant, the Assault Marines opened fire, flickering bolts and more plasma shots slamming into the ork bodyguards.

With a clang that resounded from one side of the gorge to the other, Zaltys descended feet-first into the chest of an armoured ork, sending it reeling. The Assault sergeant's hand flamer engulfed the greenskin from waist to shoulder. The huge bodyguard ignored the flames licking up its armour and swung a glittering axe at Zaltys, the blade crashing into the sergeant's right arm.

Boreas had to look away as a shout from the troopers reminded him of the orks surging back up the gorge. The Chaplain glanced back to Zaltys and realised there was nothing he could do to intervene as the Assault Marines and orks set upon each other with roaring chainswords and deadly power claws.

'Hold the flank!' Boreas shouted at the defence troopers. 'Fire at will.'

Las-fire and bullets raced past each other as the orks closed on the Piscinans. Autocannons and heavy bolters punched gaping holes through the attacking greenskins, but the orks were filled with a wild desperation.

Boreas realised that this was the warlord's last gambit. If the orks could be held back now, the enemy had nothing else to offer. The Chaplain sought out one of the Piscinan lieutenants, a craggy-faced man shouting orders whilst crouched behind a pile of empty cable reels. Boreas hauled the lieutenant to his feet.

'Fight to the last, victory is at hand,' the Chaplain snarled. 'Give every drop of blood for the Emperor.'

The lieutenant nodded, lifted his chainsword above his head and bellowed for his command squad to follow as he leapt over the barricade into the orks. Boreas fired a few more rounds from his pistol into the greenskins tearing up the slope and looked back to check on Zaltys.

Two of the bodyguard had been felled by the Assault Marines, but at the cost of four of their number. The sergeant was still alive, battering at the chest of an ork with his power fist. To his left one of the battle-brothers was gripped around the throat by a power claw, firing his pistol into the ork's face. The two combatants fell together, the Assault Marine's legs sticking out from under the massive bodyguard as it toppled onto him.

Zaltys grabbed a piece of torn armour and wrenched it away from his adversary, exposing the ork's chest. As the sergeant raised his glowing fist, the warlord loomed up through the melee behind him, crackling claws spread wide.

'Zaltys, behind you!' Boreas said over the comm.

The warning came too late. The claw snapped shut as Zaltys turned, razor-sharp tines slicing through the sergeant's head in a spray of shattering eye lenses, ceramite and skull.

The one surviving Assault Marine launched himself

at the warlord, hacking with his chainsword. The ork raised up a steel-clad arm to ward away the blows and fired its cannon, the hail of shot ripping through the Space Marine's abdomen. Stooping, the warlord reached into the ragged wound and lifted the Space Marine up. Spitting blood, the Assault Marine drove the point of his chainsword at the ork's face but the whirring blades missed as the warlord shook the Space Marine from side to side.

The Assault Marine flopped as his spine snapped. With a bestial roar, the warlord lifted its trophy high and then brought down its arm, smashing the Space Marine's corpse into the hard ground.

'They're falling back again,' reported the aging lieutenant. The officer clambered back over the barricade, a ragged cut across his nose and cheek, face smeared with blood. His command squad all lay dead amongst the pile of ork bodies further down the gorge.

Boreas looked down the slope and saw that it was true. The greenskins had been shot and cut down before they reached the barricades and the few that had survived were running back to the administration building with plaintive wails.

'Good work,' said Boreas. He pointed to the warlord. The greenskin was striding across the gorge flanked by two remaining bodyguards. 'Target your heavy weapons on these brutes. Detail the rest to watch the power plant. At least twenty ork infantry are inside.'

Wiping the blood from his mouth, the lieutenant nodded and yelled orders at the remaining troopers. There were less than thirty left. They manoeuvred the remaining heavy weapons to point across the gorge towards the approaching warlord: two heavy bolters, the same number of autocannons and a single lascannon could be salvaged from the remains of the Piscinans' arsenal.

'Target to the front. Open fire!' The lieutenant brought down his chainsword as he bellowed the order.

The harsh blast of the lascannon cut through the air, passing over the warlord's head. In response, the air bucked and crackled around the small group. A reddish aura surrounded the orks, wavering and indistinct. A volley of autocannon rounds slammed into the field. Boreas could see the shells slowing as they passed through the insubstantial barrier; some fell short and impacted the ground in front of the advancing orks; others skewed off-course and passed by without hitting. The few that remained on target had lost so much speed they bounced harmlessly from the orks' thick plates of armour.

The lieutenant looked over at Boreas, despair written in his features.

'Keep firing,' Boreas said, dividing his attention between the advancing warlord and the shadows of the power plant. The Chaplain relaxed his grip on the haft of his crozius and forced himself to speak calmly. 'Try to overload their shield.'

'Pour it on, men,' snarled the officer.

The force field flared and roiled around the green-skin entourage, becoming more visible with every heavy bolter round, autocannon shell and lascannon blast that hit it. Energy rippled and wreathed from each impact, sending sparks leaping into the air.

The pounding of feet drew Boreas's attention to the blocky transformers of the power plant. The black-clothed orks stormed out of the shade, firing their pistols and grunting battle cries.

'Small arms, engage enemy to the right,' Boreas told the bloodied troopers around him. 'Heavy weapons, continue to target the warlord's retinue.'

The orks' force field was fizzing madly, a dome of constantly writhing bolts of red electricity that encapsulated the warlord and his bodyguard. Smoke and steam billowed in thick clouds from the warlord's engine as the field generator struggled to hold back the Piscinans' cannonade.

'That's it, keep on them,' said the lieutenant. 'We've almost got them.'

Las-fire crackled from Boreas's right as the defence troopers engaged the orks emerging from the power-plant structure. He saw several shots hitting home, but the orks shrugged off their wounds and continued onwards, ignoring holes in their flesh and burning wounds across their skin.

'Power pack's dead, sir!' bawled the lascannon gunner. 'No more shots, sir.'

The Piscinan lieutenant cursed and waded into the mess of crates and boxes littering the emplacement, looking for fresh power cells.

'Belay that nonsense,' Boreas barked at the officer. The Chaplain turned on the Piscinans manning the lascannon and pointed towards the orks in the geothermal plant. 'Find yourselves lasguns and secure the power station.'

As the troopers snatched up rifles from the hands of

the dead, Boreas focussed his attention back to the warlord. A few seconds later, when the hulking aliens were less than fifty metres away, the warlord's field collapsed with a huge blaze of energy that spiralled rapidly around the orks before flickering into nothing. Immediately, the greenskins brought their own weapons to bear.

'Take cover,' warned the Free Militia officer.

A rocket sped into the emplacement to explode against the barricade, showering the cowering men with shards of metal and splinters from the piled crates. An autocannon loader fell back with a jag of wood jutting from his eye. His gunner turned in surprise and reached out to the screaming man. Boreas loomed over the pair of them.

'Attend to your weapon, trooper,' said the Chaplain. The Piscinan looked up at the battered skull helm of Boreas, nodded dumbly and returned to the autocannon.

A blaze of phosphorescent bullets engulfed Boreas. Each projectile had its own shimmering field and punched into his armour, cracking plates as if they were made of brittle porcelain. Something buried itself in the Chaplain's right bicep, stinging like a giant wasp. Pockmarks opened up across his chest and shoulder pad, pieces of ceramite splitting away and falling to the ground like artificial hail.

'Lion's shade,' he swore. Boreas's arm had barely healed from the injury suffered at the basilica. He was sure the bone had not suffered any further damage, but he found it hard to move the fingers of his hand. His pistol felt fat and heavy in his grasp.

The Chaplain glanced at his chest, wondering why the

rosarius hadn't protected him. He saw a small crack in the ruby power crystal.

'He has not forsaken me,' the Chaplain muttered. *'Imperator fortis exalta.* My soul is my armour.'

Another rocket screamed past the barrier, catching the lieutenant in the shoulder. An epaulette flew into the air as the officer was hurled backwards. The lieutenant sat up groggily and peered at the rocket lying next to him, a few desultory sparks popping from its propellant. The Piscinan picked up the projectile with a laugh.

'It didn't go o–'

The lieutenant's relief was cut short as the rocket exploded, ripping off his hand and sending shrapnel into his eyes. He fell back, face a bloody mask, lips and nose torn apart, burnt skin peeling away.

There were bullets whizzing at Boreas from his right. Without looking, he knew that the orks had broken out of the power plant and swept away the troopers. He pointed his bolt pistol towards the geothermal station and fired the remaining seeking bolts, letting them loose in a single burst while his eyes were fixed on the warlord stomping closer.

The towering greenskin lumbered onwards, armour pistons wheezing, heavy booted feet thudding into the packed earth. Boreas tossed his empty bolt pistol aside. With his free hand, he reached up and unsealed the clasps of his helm. He lifted the helmet away and hung it on his belt, fixing the greenskin with his stare.

The warlord met his gaze, his rubbery lips turning up at the corners in a grimacing smile. The ork said something and nodded, waving its bodyguards back with its claw. The beast lifted its right arm sideways. Mechanical clasps hissed and the multi-barrelled cannon dropped to the ground with a clang.

Boreas waited for the monster in a crouch, crozius held in both hands. He spat, though his mouth was dry. The opening verse of the Litany of Devotion sprang to mind. He began to whisper the words, his voice growing in strength as the warlord heaved itself in Boreas's direction.

'Where there is uncertainty, I shall bring light. Where there is doubt, I shall sow faith. Where there is shame, I shall point atonement. Where there is rage, I shall show its course.' Boreas broke into a run, crozius ready. 'My word in the soul shall be as my bolter in the field!'

His first blow deflected off the ork's upraised claw. The Chaplain ducked beneath the swinging fist and smashed the blazing head of the crozius arcanum into the engine block upon the warlord's back.

'Never forget!' Boreas growled, sending an exhaust pipe spinning away with a swing of his crozius. 'Never forgive!'

As the warlord stumbled around to face Boreas, the Chaplain continued to rain blow after blow against the monstrous ork's armour, buckling and ripping the metal plates.

'*Impudianta xenos, mortia et indignatia!*'

He could hear the chime of his comm from his helmet but ignored it and slammed the head of his crozius into the warlord's chest. The Chaplain raged as his relentless assault continued, every spat word punctuated by a blow from his weapon.

'Suffer... not... the... unclean... to... live!'

The ork punched out with its claw, driving into Boreas's gut. The Chaplain stumbled back, his crumpled, torn armour biting into the muscles of his abdomen. The serrated toe of the warlord's boot connected with the Chaplain's chin, slamming him to his back. The ork's face twisted in a feral snarl, heavy brows knotted deeply above its piercing red eyes. Thick blood streamed from the corner of its mouth.

Boreas's jaw was broken, his teeth shattered. He couldn't speak, could no longer give voice to his rage and hate. The warlord placed a foot on the Chaplain's chest, pinning him down. Armour creaked and bent under the ork's weight as it bowed forwards to look Boreas in the eye.

Boreas spat in the ork's face.

It was no meaningless act of defiance: the Space Marine's saliva was laced with an acidic compound from the Betcher's Gland implanted beneath his tongue. The ork recoiled, skin burning and bubbling. Boreas pushed himself to his feet and stepped forwards.

The ork warlord lashed out blindly. Boreas saw the blow coming and raised his crozius to parry but he was too weak to deflect it. The crackling claw swept aside the Chaplain's weapon and crashed into the side of his head.

Thunder roared in Boreas's ears. The world spun. The ground rushed up to meet him.

Everything went silent and dark.

THE TALE OF BELIAL
Counter-attack

THE OPERATIONS ROOM aboard the *Unrelenting Fury* was silent but for the hiss of the command comm. Master Belial looked at the speaker intently. He was dressed only in a ceremonial robe, his armour left with the Techmarines to repair the damage sustained during the retrieval of the ork power relay. Half-healed scars from his encounter with Ghazghkull marred his exposed chest and arms, bright welts against tanned skin.

Occasionally the static was broken by a background thump or muffled impact. The company captain blinked in surprise as a deafening crash resounded around the room.

'Boreas?' The captain's repeated call brought no reply. 'Brother Boreas, this is Master Belial.'

He listened for a response but there was nothing. Belial crossed to the control panel set into the wood-panelled wall and was about to cut the link when he heard a loud panting. Guttural voices could be heard in the distance.

'Brother-Chaplain Boreas? Respond. Report your situation.'

There was a scraping noise and more panting. Suddenly a bass voice echoed from the speakers.

'Dey's all dead.'

Deep laughter reverberated around the room. Then came a crash and the link died.

Belial sighed and turned the comm dial to general broadcast.

'This is Master Belial to all forces. Barrak Gorge geothermal station has fallen to the orks. It is likely the enemy will recommence teleportation reinforcements in the near future. All stations prepare your defences and stand ready for attack.' The commander adjusted the setting. 'This is Master Belial to Ravenwing Sergeant Validus. Join me aboard the *Unrelenting Fury*. I am sending a Thunderhawk to your position.' He twisted the dial again without waiting for a response. 'Brothers Uriel, Hephaestus and Charon, rendezvous at Sergeant Validus's position for transportation to orbit.'

He stepped away from the comm panel and crossed to the holo-desk that dominated the centre of the chamber. The affirmatives from his warriors sounded tinnily from the comm behind him. Punching in coordinates, Belial brought up a fuzzy display of Koth Ridge and the East Barrens. Red icons blinked here and there, showing the last recorded sightings of ork forces. He brought up the chronometer tags and sighed again. Other than those inside Kadillus

Harbour, the latest report was Boreas's. The only others were his own observations at the East Barrens station, now six hours old. He peered at the digital image as if he might see the orks on the planet below.

'Where are you?' he asked quietly, rubbing his chin. 'What are you going to do next?'

THE COMPANY COUNCIL was convened within the hour. Belial had stared constantly at the digimap while he had waited for his advisors, but was no closer to deciding a course of action. He sat now at the head of the display desk, elbow on one arm of the command throne, chin on fist.

Uriel sat on the master's left, his black armour covered by a sleeveless bone-coloured robe. His sunken eyes constantly flicked across the faces of the others in the room.

On Belial's right was the most senior Librarian in the force, Lexicanium Charon. Though of the lowest rank within the Librarium, Charon was attached to the 3rd Company as Grand Master Azrael's representative and no doubt had the ear of the Dark Angels' supreme commander. The psyker sat upright, palms together in his lap, eyes intent on Belial. The cables of Charon's psychic hood burrowed beneath the skin of his scalp and twitched with the Librarian's pulse, scratching against each other with every double heartbeat.

Beside the Librarian hunched Ravenwing Sergeant Validus, the longest-serving member of the 2nd Company present on Piscina. The black paint of his armour was heavily scratched and burnt, the ceramite underneath patched with fresh resin casts and welding. His winged helmet was on the table in front, an eye lens cracked, mouth-grille dented.

Last of those present was Techmarine Hephaestus, representative of the armoury. He looked strangely smaller than the others, having removed his servo-arm-equipped backpack and heavy shoulder pads. The Techmarine was at the display console's controls, three cables snaking from the digi-desk to sockets in Hephaestus's forearm armour.

'There is another whose advice will be invaluable,' announced Belial. He signalled to the robed serf sat at the comms unit. 'Revered Venerari, can you hear me?'

A mechanically generated voice grated from the comm speakers.

'I am here, brother. My experience is yours to share.'

'Thank you, brother. Soon we will need not just your wisdom, but your strength and determination.' Belial stood up and leaned on the edge of the large display plate, looking at each of his council in turn. 'We face a tipping point in this war, brothers. We have held the orks at bay as best we can, but it may not be enough. It is still at least seven days before the rest of the Chapter will reach orbit. The orks have control of two power stations once more and will resume their previous level of reinforcement. Though we have bloodied our foes severely these last eight days and nights, we have no such reserves to draw upon. Casualties amongst the 3rd Company and other Astartes units under my command are at thirty-two per cent. The Piscina defence force reports nearly seventy per cent casualties, mostly in Kadillus Harbour.'

Belial stepped back and folded his arms across his broad chest.

'We do not know exactly how quickly the orks can rebuild their strength for sure, or how soon they will attack, but we can be sure that the longer they wait, the greater will be the blow that lands upon us.'

'Are all forces engaged, brother?' Venerari asked through the chamber's speakers. 'Have we any other forces left to commit?'

'There are Free Militia troops and tanks en route to Kadillus Harbour from other parts of the island,' replied the company master. 'We might have airlifted them to the city earlier, but the enemy's possession of the defence laser rendered that impossible. Similarly, Ghazghkull's occupation of the docks makes any transportation by sea equally difficult. Therefore these forces are travelling overland and will be expected in two days' time.'

'It is your hope that these forces will bolster the defence before the orks attack.' Charon's words were a statement not a question. 'It is unwise to rely upon elements that are not directly under your control.'

'And I do not intend to, brother,' said Belial, sitting down again. 'If we simply wait for the orks to build up their strength, we cannot stop them. They could grow in numbers for five days and have the far greater strength, sweeping away any forces we have in a day, before the Chapter reaches us.'

'Perhaps the orks will attack early,' suggested Uriel. 'Excited by their success at Barrak Gorge they might continue their attack.'

'Possible, but unlikely,' said Venerari. 'We know that

Ghazghkull has demonstrated remarkable strategic acumen for an ork in the past, and his actions thus far have not demonstrated proof that he has lost that. This other warlord has also shown a certain amount of cunning.'

'Indeed,' said Belial. 'It is to my shame that I under-estimated the threat of the orks, and perhaps by doing so I have allowed them an advantage that we cannot now reverse.'

'From what Naaman described, none of us could have imagined how the orks were reaching the planet,' said Uriel. 'You acted in accordance with the best teachings and doctrine of the Chapter. What we have faced is quite unprecedented. Not only have two ork warlords allied themselves to attack this world – which is in itself a strangely inconsequential target – but they have also mastered an advanced technology on a scale never before encountered in the ten thousand years of the Chapter. I am sure that Grand Master Azrael will not judge your actions harshly.'

Belial turned to Sergeant Validus.

'Have the Ravenwing any fresher intelligence to offer this discussion?' asked the captain.

'No, brother, not at the moment,' Validus replied with a shake of the head. 'I have but three land speeders and a single bike squad left for reconnaissance, to cover several hundred square kilometres, and without orbital augury data. If you were to tell me where to look for the orks, we will do so, but we cannot patrol the wilderness endlessly or with any certainty.'

The company master chewed on the knuckle of his thumb as he considered this. His eyes darted to Uriel as the Chaplain sat forwards, hands on the wide table.

'You could lead another Terminator strike at the East Barrens site,' declared the Chaplain. 'It is not a permanent solution, but it would delay ork reinforcements again and generate time for us to better prepare our defences.'

'Or mount an offensive to retake Barrak Gorge,' added Validus.

Belial shook his head.

'The last attack was only possible due to Naaman's planting of the homing beacon. It has been destroyed.' He looked at Validus. 'Unless the Ravenwing are capable of planting a new homing signal transmitter?'

Validus shrugged.

'It is worth investigation, brothers,' said the 2nd Company sergeant. 'Sergeant Naaman succeeded through stealth; perhaps we will meet with similar success with speed.'

'It is a delaying tactic and nothing more, brothers,' said Venerari. 'It is not without merit but it is not a lasting solution to the situation that we face. It may succeed again, but I do not believe that the orks will be tricked a third time. We would still require a more permanent resolution if we are to resist their attacks until the rest of the Chapter arrives.'

'If it is even possible a second time,' said Hephaestus. 'It is likely the enemy have further fortified their base since the last attack. I rate the chances of a Ravenwing strike to be slim considering the likely level of opposition.'

The Space Marines sat in silence for some time,

amidst an air of frustration. It was galling to Belial that he had been wrong-footed by two savages. He wracked his brains to find some other strategy that would turn the tide back against the greenskins.

'May I make a suggestion, brother-captain?' Hephaestus broke the thoughtful silence.

'That is why I brought you here, brother,' Belial replied with some irritation. 'Speak your mind.'

'While it seems problematic to prevent the ork reinforcements from arriving, there is another alternative,' said the Techmarine. The holo-display whirled and zoomed in on the East Barrens geothermal station. 'We have a single point of entry to target. Now that we have the precise energy signature from Sergeant Naaman, we have been able to locate the teleporter beam on the long-range scanning arrays. It has not moved from its previous site. It is a logical conclusion from the evidence so far examined that the orks' arrival point on-world is fixed, for some reason we do not yet understand.'

'We don't know where the orks are that are here already, but we can be sure where any new arrivals will be coming from.' Belial smiled at the realisation.

'An orbital strike,' suggested Uriel.

'Negative,' said Hephaestus. 'Proximity to the power plant still presents a threat to the entire geothermal network.'

'Thunderhawk strike,' said Venerari. 'A gunship can deploy from orbit, attack the reinforcements and then return to the battle-barge to resupply and re-arm.'

Belial's fingers tapped an agitated beat on the desk-top.

'We have only one gunship remaining,' said the commander. 'If we lose it, we have only civilian aircraft left to us.'

'That is where the Ravenwing will help,' said Validus. 'I can have a squadron of land speeders in the area within three hours. They can report on the enemy's defences and any changes since we lost touch with Naaman.'

'Very well,' said Belial, standing up. The others stood with him. 'We will prepare for a succession of aerial strikes. Sergeant Validus will coordinate the reconnaissance and provide on-ground observation for the attack. Brother Hephaestus, prepare the remaining gunship for a heavy-bombardment role. Brother Uriel, draw up a list of surviving battle-brothers with specialist gunnery training who can crew the Thunderhawk with Hephaestus. I will organise for them to be extracted from their current duties.'

The Space Marines nodded their assent. As Validus, Hephaestus and Uriel left, Charon stayed behind.

'You have something to add, brother?' Belial asked the Librarian.

Charon sat down again and nodded.

'I detected an emanation from my brothers in the Librarium shortly before I arrived at the council.' The psyker fixed Belial with a penetrating stare. 'It is a message from Grand Master Azrael. I thought it better that I pass it to you in private.'

'Very well,' said Belial. He gestured for the Librarian to continue.

Straightening in his chair, Charon laid his hands flat

on the glassy surface of the display table. Motes of energy danced along the wires of his psychic hood. The Librarian's eyes darkened, the veins standing out in stark contrast to the whites, flickering with blue. With a shuddering gasp, the Librarian arched his neck and his eyes rolled back, showing nothing but a tracery of coruscating energy.

The psyker's face changed. The features did not alter, but the Librarian's muscles twitched and took on a different cant, approximating another's face: Azrael, Grand Master of the Dark Angels. The jaw was set firmly, lips thin, cheeks drawn in. When Charon spoke, it was with the voice of the Chapter's commander, his mouth twisting in imitation of Azrael's mannerisms.

'Master Belial. I do not have to press upon you the importance of the situation on Piscina. Know that it is my will that this world is denied to the orks, *at any cost*. I have faith in you and your company, and you should know that deliverance from these foul beasts is almost at hand. The Techmarines believe they have identified an area of space that is the source of the teleportation beam bringing reinforcements to the planet. It is my belief that at least one ork-occupied hulk is in the system, and carries forces that will test the strength of the entire Chapter. The orks must not be allowed to gain a significant hold on Piscina. If your best efforts and greatest sacrifices are not sufficient to contain the alien menace, it is imperative that the orks be denied a landing in true strength. I trust that you will take any measures to ensure this.'

Azrael-Charon's face turned away for a moment and then returned its unearthly gaze to Belial.

'You will receive confirmation of these orders by standard communication before my arrival. Praise the Lion.'

Shuddering again, Charon let out an explosive breath and slumped forwards. Opening his eyes, he looked at Belial with his normal face.

'I take it from your expression that you comprehend the intent of the Grand Master's command,' said the Librarian.

'I do, brother,' Belial replied with a nod. 'It is better that Kadillus is destroyed than fall into the hands of our enemies.'

'Very well, brother,' Charon said. He stood up and bowed his head in deference. 'I will leave you to make the necessary preparations for that event, and the means by which we might avoid it.'

Belial's eyes followed Charon's back as the psyker left through the heavy door. A blinking light on the comm panel attracted his attention.

'You heard that, Revered Venerari,' said the company master.

'I did, brother.'

'Why is it that he felt it necessary to remind me of my duty?'

'Do not take it as an admonishment. Lord Azrael wishes you to know that you have his full support for whatever actions you take.'

'We will not fail. We are Astartes.'

'The Lion is with us, brother. In his name we will triumph.'

The light winked out and Belial was left with the comms-tech. The youth, his face impassive, turned to the captain.

'Do you have any further orders, master?'

Belial thought for a moment, fingers stroking his chin.

'Send for the gunnery captains. They have preparations to make.'

HALF A DOZEN serfs bustled around the terminals of the operations chamber, moving from one console to the next as they calibrated the comms arrays and updated the scanner data for the digimap. Belial stood immobile amongst the activity; now clad in his dark green armour, power sword at his waist, an ivory-coloured robe hanging to his knees, red Deathwing icon embroidered upon the left side of its chest. Charon and Uriel were with him, sitting patiently at the display slate.

Through the murmurings of the serfs Belial could hear the reports from the ongoing fighting in Kadillus Harbour. The company commander listened subconsciously to the fragments of information being related by the Space Marines and Piscinan officers around the docks and power plant, content that nothing had significantly changed. He had issued orders for the Emperor's forces to hold their positions and continue to contain Ghazghkull's army so that he could devote his full attention to the upcoming Ravenwing mission.

Now and then he delivered a short series of orders into the comm-piece hung on the collar of his armour: directing squads to areas that were weak, or replacing fatigued troops with fresher forces. He did this without effort or reference to the digimap, his conscious thoughts contemplating the situation at the East Barrens plant.

Validus's voice cut through the others from the main speaker.

'Five kilometres from target.'

'Filter all other transmissions,' said Belial as he sat down in the command throne.

He shared a glance with Charon and Uriel. All three turned their attention to the holo-display. A flickering rune denoting the land speeder squadron moved across the representation of Kadillus east of Koth Ridge.

'Activating long-range augur. Ravenwing-Two, increase separation to one hundred metres. Sequenced upload of scan data commencing.'

The hololith strobed for a few seconds, the rendered topography of Kadillus warping as the stream of data was integrated into the display. When the image had settled Belial could see several clusters of fresh runes dotting the hillside ahead of the land speeder squadron.

Timing was the key. The Ravenwing squadron had three tasks to complete: locate the enemy forces around the landing site, provide on-ground targeting links for the Thunderhawk attack, and engage the air-defence weapons that had shot down the company's other gunship.

'Belial to Hephaestus. Launch gunship and begin atmospheric descent.'

'Confirm, brother-captain,' replied the Techmarine.

'Launching in five seconds. Attack route established. Weapons armed.'

'Scanner returns increasing in density.' Belial could sense the tension in Validus's voice. 'Identification problematic. Whatever the orks have done to the power station, it is causing havoc with the augur. Ork vehicles present, category unknown. Visual confirmation required.'

'Gunship launched, brother-captain,' said Hephaestus. 'Decreasing orbital velocity to six kilometres per second. Gravitic grip deployed. Atmospheric breach in three minutes. Time at target will be eighteen minutes.'

Two metres above the digital surface of Piscina, a small icon representing Hephaestus's Thunderhawk appeared. It hovered in the air, far too distant for its speed to be scaled down to the display. Belial touched the comm activation rune on the panel set into the tablet in front of him.

'This is Belial to Validus. Gunship is on its way. Update on scanner and comms interference from the ork modifications. Do not engage enemy.'

The commander tapped a finger on the display slate while he waited for his message to relay down to the surface and the Ravenwing sergeant's reply to return to the battle-barge.

'Was it wise to launch the gunship before target confirmation, brother?' said Uriel. 'There will be little opportunity to abort the mission if there are no–'

Validus's voice cut through before the Chaplain could finish. Belial held up his hand, silencing Uriel.

'Interference is resonating from volcanic deposits,'

said Validus. 'We will have a clearer signal once we clear the ridge. Orders, brother-captain?'

Belial checked the chronometer.

'We have fifteen minutes until last-chance abort of mission, brother. Enemy must not be alerted to your presence. Cross the ridge in six minutes and provide report. Engage enemy defences in thirteen minutes. Confirm.' The company commander looked through the translucent hololith at Uriel. 'If we wait for confirmation, the delay from launch to attack is too long and would allow the orks to respond to the presence of the Ravenwing. Pre-arranged, absolute abort signal is "Angel's fall" and every member of the squadron is authorised to issue it. Hephaestus will re-direct to Northport the moment that code is issued, without compromise.'

Excitement was growing inside Belial. Though he was not directly involved, he could feel the familiar rush of battle building up. Calling on decades of training and experience, he kept himself calm and held back the urge for action. It was Belial's patience that had first made him suitable for command, and he needed every ounce of that same patience during this critical mission.

He barely heard Validus's confirmation message as he considered the possible outcomes and options that would unfold over the next fifteen minutes. Like an actor rehearsing his lines, Belial ran through different scenarios and his responses: what he would do if the ork numbers proved too few to be worthy of attack; his orders to Hephaestus if contact with the Ravenwing was lost; targeting priorities if there was sufficient enemy presence to warrant the completion of the mission; the threat threshold of enemy defences he considered too much of a risk to the Thunderhawk if Validus deferred the abort option to his commander.

All of this and much more Belial considered and analysed and streamlined so that he would be ready whatever happened. Detached from the action, the stimulants coursing through the captain's system bombarded the neurons firing in his brain rather than flooding his limbs with physical power. Each and every consideration was crisp and precise, analysed in detail and memorised for future recall. Every thought opened up a sequence of possible consequences, which brought on further thoughts. A cascade of decisions, probable outcomes and subsequent decisions filled Belial's mind.

He looked sharply at Charon, his heightened awareness drawn by a slight movement from the Librarian. Charon returned Belial's focussed glare with a calm expression. The Librarian darted a glance at Belial's armoured hands, which were clenched into fists atop the display slab.

Belial's nostrils flared as he took a deep breath. He relaxed his hands, interlocking his fingers in front of him. He smiled at Charon and signalled his gratitude with the slightest dip of his head.

The Master of the 3rd Company looked at the chronometer. Two more minutes had passed.

'Time on target, six minutes,' reported Hephaestus. 'Undergoing atmospheric braking and energy capture. Weapons test arming complete. Awaiting targeting data from the ground.'

Belial checked the holo-display. The Thunderhawk was levelling out of its steep descent and blazing towards the East Barrens at several times the speed of sound. Validus's squadron had encountered scattered ork infantry but had swept through the patrols and were due to crest the ridge above the geothermal plant at any moment. He looked at the comms panel in anticipation.

'Validus to Master Belial. Enemy casualties at sixteen, no friendly casualties. We will achieve unimpeded augur coverage and visual sighting of the enemy in ten seconds. Energy waveform matches that of the tele-porter prior to your removal of the relay device, brother-captain. It is reasonable to assume that the enemy have restored their previous level of reinforce-ment.'

There was a crackle of static, most likely caused by an inter-squad communication.

'Collate squad comms,' Belial told the technicians. They fussed at their dials and switches for a few seconds before the voices of the Ravenwing pilots and gunners hissed over the speakers.

'...earing due east, brother-sergeant. Three enemy light transports heading directly to our position.'

'What of the air defences, brother?' This was from Validus.

'Negative at the moment. Medium-calibre weapons and... Wait! There is something behind the power plant. Moving south-east for a better view.' The silence made the seconds creep past. 'What is that?'

Another voice cut through.

'Sergeant, have visual sighting on a vehicle-mounted

rocket battery. Two of them, in that stand of trees eighteen hundred metres north-east.'

The first voice returned.

'Brother-sergeant! Sizeable missile system located south-east of the geothermal station. Looks to be anti-air capable, but who can say for sure with ork technology?'

More hissing from overlapping comm-frequencies filled the room. Everyone, Space Marine and serf, was frozen in place, awaiting the next report. Hephaestus's deep voice resounded around the chamber.

'This is Hephaestus. Weapons armed. Target sighted. Final manoeuvring for attack run. Lock-on in fifty seconds.'

Belial checked the chronometer again. It was twenty-eight seconds until Hephaestus could pull out of his attack run and avoid any defences at the East Barrens plant. He decided against signalling Validus for a decision – by the time the message reached the Ravenwing sergeant and was answered there would only be a few seconds to issue an order to the plunging Thunderhawk. He had to trust Validus's judgement.

Nothing was said for three seconds and then Validus broke the quiet.

'Ravenwing-One to Hephaestus. Angel's fall! I repeat, angel's fall! Enemy air defence too dense. Abort attack run.'

Belial could imagine the roar of retro-jets firing as the Techmarine hastily altered course. The glowing sigil in the hololith turned sharply as the gunship banked away from the power plant.

'Hephaestus to Master Belial. Abort code received,

abandoning attack run. Redirecting to Northport landing facility. Weapons deactivated. Awaiting further orders.'

A tense silence filled the operations chamber. It was broken by a broadcast from Validus.

'Ravenwing-One to Master Belial. Enemy are responding to our presence in strength. What are your orders?'

Belial activated the comm in front of him.

'Perform a recon sweep of enemy forces as best you can and withdraw. Take up preparatory position fifteen kilometres west of the East Barrens station and await further instruction. Confirm.'

The company master sighed and looked at Charon. The Librarian's expression gave away nothing of his thoughts. Uriel was gently rapping the knuckles of his gloved hand against the edge of the display desk, a sign of frustration.

'Ravenwing-One to Master Belial. Confirm orders. Withdrawing fifteen kilometres west. Avoiding contact with enemy.'

'So that is the end of that,' growled Uriel. 'What do we do now? Validus has confirmed that the orks have been able to connect the Barrak Gorge power plant to their teleporter and reinforcements have resumed. It is only a matter of time before the orks feel they have enough strength to attack again.'

Belial said nothing. He bowed his head as he thought, avoiding the inquiring gazes of Uriel and Charon.

'You have the Grand Master's orders, brother.' The Librarian's words were quiet but insistent.

Still silent, Belial adjusted the display controls to widen the scope of the hololith, until it showed the huge area encompassing Kadillus Harbour, Koth Ridge, Barrak Gorge, Indola and the East Barrens station. He looked at it for some time, staring at the runes highlighting the last reported sightings and strength of the orks.

He sighed and rubbed his chin. Only now did he meet Charon's purposeful gaze.

'I am not yet ready to concede Piscina to the orks,' said the company captain.

'Then you will prepare for bombardment, brother,' replied Charon.

'Not yet.' Belial shook his head and stood. 'There is still one path we can explore. An aerial assault has been ruled out, but we are not without other weapons.'

Belial spread a hand across the Dark Angel figure emblazoned on his chest plastron.

'Ever since the orks arrived we have been trying to keep the enemy at bay. No more. I see now what we should have done from the outset. We are Space Marines! We are the sharp tip of the Emperor's spear; the cutting blade of the Emperor's sword. We attack, surely and swiftly, and sweep all before us. Ghazghkull has made us a garrison, a defence force, and we have paid the price for allowing that. No more! We will do what we were trained to do; the purpose for which we were created. We attack!'

He pointed at the ork dispositions on the display, his gauntleted hand passing into the fuzzy hologram.

'While our forces have been stretched thin, we should not over-estimate the strength of the enemy or the concentration of their force. They have been defeated at Koth Ridge and paid a heavy price for their assault.

Though Boreas ultimately failed us at Barrak Gorge, the orks suffered there also. We cannot be disheartened by the setbacks we have endured, for the enemy have not had such success that they are guaranteed victory.

'It took the orks several days to build up the army they needed to attack Koth Ridge. If we strike now while they are divided, while fresh forces are still arriving, we can capture the East Barrens geothermal station. I saw for myself the slow progress of their reinforcements. If we cannot shut down the teleporter in its entirety, we can establish a position of strength overlooking their arrival zone and destroy them as they arrive.'

'From where will the forces of this attack come?' asked Charon.

Belial paced.

'We must take a risk. Fresh Piscina defence forces are arriving at Kadillus Harbour in the next few hours. We will give over our positions in the city to these soldiers and create a strike force.'

'What you suggest will weaken the defence of Kadillus Harbour.' As usual, Charon simply stated the facts with no hint of reproach or opinion.

'We will trust to our allies to hold Ghazghkull in place,' said Uriel. 'If done under cover of darkness, there is no reason for the enemy to suspect that our lines have been reduced.'

'Better than that, they will think them strengthened,' said Belial. 'I will contact the commander of the reinforcement column and instruct him to enter Kadillus Harbour with as much show of strength as possible. I cannot imagine that Ghazghkull has a clear picture of what is happening outside the city. The sight of newly arrived troops and a minor offensive will convince the enemy that they are isolated and that we are preparing for the final attack.'

'It is a worthy plan, brother,' said Uriel, growing more animated the more he thought about Belial's course of action. 'When we destroy the ork landing site, we will be free to return to Kadillus and purge the city of the filthy xenos, as we should have done from the outset.'

Belial directed a sharp look at the Master Chaplain.

'You believe I was overly cautious in my earlier actions, brother?'

'I do not judge your actions with the benefit of hindsight, brother,' said Uriel.

'It sounds as if you do,' replied Belial. 'If you had concerns that I was being somehow timid in my reaction to the ork attack, why did you not speak to me?'

'You misunderstand me, brother,' said Uriel. 'You acted to contain the ork menace in Kadillus Harbour and committed the greater part of the company to that effort. You could have sacrificed the city for the short term so that we might avoid getting divided and embroiled in the desperate stalemate that ensued. It was a choice of priority; neither option was better or worse than the other.'

Clearing his throat, Charon stood up and held out his hands, palms facing his two companions.

'The past is set, the future is not,' said the Librarian. He concentrated his attention on Belial. 'Do you consider this attack to be the best course of action, brother?'

Belial raised his eyebrows in surprise.

'You think that I have concocted this plan simply to avoid the alternative?' The company master sighed. 'I would avoid any cataclysmic solution to the situation by any means that present themselves, but this is not simply a fool's errand. It is our duty to protect Piscina, whatever the cost.'

Annoyed by the suggestion, Belial stalked back and forth a few paces. His eyes fell on Uriel.

'Brother-Chaplain,' said the captain. 'These are your orders. You will remain aboard the *Unrelenting Fury* and take command in my absence. I will lead the attack on the East Barrens plant. If the attack fails, you will order the *Unrelenting Fury* into low orbit to destroy the defence laser site in the city, and also Northport. You will then commence bombardment of the East Barrens facility to destroy the orks' source of power. If this proves insufficient to halt ork reinforcements, you will do the same at Barrak Gorge and, if ultimately necessary, the power plant in Kadillus Harbour. When the Chapter arrives, the orks will be stranded on this world, no matter the cost. Ghazghkull and his filth will not escape again.'

Uriel's brow creased in thought.

'Is there not a high risk attached to orbital bombardment, brother-captain?' said the Chaplain.

'There is,' replied Belial. 'Confirm your orders.'

'Confirm, brother-captain. I will assume command of the *Unrelenting Fury* and use orbital bombardment to halt all ork reinforcements to the planet.'

Belial rounded on Charon.

'Do you have any other questions, brother?'

The Librarian pursed his lips as he thought.

'No, brother. I will join you in the attack on the East Barrens, if you concur.'

'Your presence will be a great boost to our forces, brother.' Belial looked at the two of them. 'We will be victorious, brothers. The Third Company will not be remembered with shame for letting the orks take one of the Emperor's worlds from his domain.'

He nodded for the Librarian and Chaplain to leave.

'I have many preparations to make, brothers. I will reconvene the council when I have done so.'

When they had left, Belial sat down in the command throne and took a deep breath. It was a gamble: the lives of his warriors for an uncertain chance of victory. He gazed at the digimap and knew that there was no option; the alternative would simply be a stain upon his honour too dark to bear.

Dismissing his sense of foreboding, Belial focussed the hololith on Kadillus Harbour and started to analyse the disposition of the Imperial forces, looking for areas he could pull out his Dark Angels.

LUMBERING SERVITORS WITH hydraulic lifting arms thudded across the hangar deck carrying boxes of supplies to the waiting Thunderhawk. Their blank eyes stared straight ahead as Hephaestus stood on the gunship's ramp, directing the loading work with clipped commands in the language of the tech-priests. Slack-jawed, cables and pneumatics puncturing their flesh, the servitors trudged up the ramp to stow their loads while robe-clad serfs amended manifest slates.

Chapter staff from the armoury restocked the gunship's weapons caches and lockers with extra bolters and chainswords, power axes and flamers, heavy bolters and lascannons. The fighting of the previous days had demanded all of the resources of the battle-barge, but Hephaestus and his attendants had stripped the hold bare of every bolt, power pack and weapon that could be found. Even the non-Astartes crew of the *Unrelenting Fury* had given up their store of lasguns and shotguns and flak armour so that the Free Militia in Kadillus Harbour could be re-equipped.

This was the last of four runs down to the planet that Hephaestus had organised. At Northport, armoury crews were assembling two forgotten Rhino transports that had been found by the Techmarine on a delve into the deepest storage bays. Some of the long-range comm dishes had been removed from the battle-barge's on-board array to replace the primitive sets the Piscinan commanders had been using, while one of the ship's plasma reactors had been re-routed for several hours recharging fuel cells for sensors and heavy weapons.

As he watched the activity from a balcony above the flight deck, Belial knew that this was his last push for a decisive victory. He was sure of his plan; the alternative was to continue to fight a desperate war of attrition with an enemy who could constantly replace their losses. Defeat was certain if he followed that path.

There was more than simply strategy to recommend the attack to Belial. If the 3rd Company was to fail here, it would not be whimpering and bleeding from a thousand cuts, but in the furnace of battle, taking the fight to the orks. Weaker men would have called it vainglory, but Belial knew better. His Space Marines would fight even harder knowing that they faced victory or death. All of the surviving eighty-two Astartes under his command would rather decide their fate with a daring assault than be forced to fight on beneath the ignominious cloud of inevitable defeat.

The clump of boots on the mesh floor of the balcony announced the arrival of Charon. The Librarian's face was hidden in the shadow of his robe's hood, but his eyes glittered with psychic energy. From a sling across Charon's chest hung a long, double-handed blade; its pommel was a single crystal the size of a Space Marine's fist, fashioned in the likeness of a skull.

Seeing that the loading of the Thunderhawk was almost complete, Belial checked his own wargear. He unhooked the displacer field generator from his belt and inspected the power supply display. Shaped like a knight's shield embossed with the head of a lion, the displacer field contained a proximity detector and compact warp-shift engine. When activated by enemy attack, the device would snap Belial into the warp for a fraction of a second, depositing him back into the material universe unharmed, reappearing a few metres away from the threat. It was an arcane piece of equipment, and despite the constant attention of the Techmarines was temperamental and did not guarantee absolute protection.

A holster attached to Belial's right thigh with magno-clamps held the company commander's bolt pistol, loading with seeking ammunition Hephaestus had scavenged from surviving stores in the catacombs of the basilica in Kadillus Harbour. Three more magazines of the precious bolts were carried in pouches on Belial's belt. On his left hip he carried a plasma pistol, with a spare canister of fuel for the weapon. On a strap hanging across his chest, the captain carried grenades: fragmentation grenades for clearing out enemy positions, krak grenades for breaking armour and anti-tank melta-bombs.

There was not a foe that Belial could not destroy with these weapons, but he had one more: an ornate power sword. Its hilt and pommel were made in the shape of a gilded dark angel with upraised arms, a miniature copy of the sword extending along the blade, out-spread wings forming the crosspiece. Belial drew the weapon from its malachite-studded scabbard and pressed his thumb to the rune upon the angel's chest. The sword thrummed into life, forks of energy crackling along veins of obsidian smelted into the adamantium blade.

It was not simply a weapon, it was a symbol of Belial's authority and experience. Grand Master Azrael had gifted the sword to Belial, bestowing upon him the honour of bearing one of the few relics to survive from ancient – lost – Caliban. As he gazed into the white fire of the sword's power field, Belial remembered the deeds that had earned him that honour.

That had been a fierce battle also; perhaps even harder than the challenge he now faced. His foes had been renegades, traitor Space Marines who had turned their backs on their duty to the Emperor and broken their oaths of loyalty. Their commander, once a company captain like Belial, had fallen to the Dark Angels master, and his army had been torn asunder by Belial's warriors.

Belial could think of no better tribute to the sword than to plunge its blade into the heart of Ghazghkull. The promise of vengeance against the warlord who had brought Armageddon to its knees, despoiled Piscina and threatened Belial's reputation sent a thrill of excitement through the Dark Angel. He would stare into the ork's eyes as it died, just as he had stared into the eyes of Furion as the renegade's life had leaked away through the ragged cut across his throat.

'We are ready,' said Charon, snapping Belial out of his reverie.

The master looked down into the flight bay and saw Hephaestus at the Thunderhawk's controls. The serfs and servitors were clearing the launch deck. Red warning lights flashed and a low siren sounded as the inner doors of the flight deck opened with a hiss of escaping air. Air flowed into the exposed lock, sweeping up scraps of wire and tatters of cloth that had been littering the deck.

'There is another still to arrive,' said Belial.

He left the balcony with a nod to the technicians behind the armoured glass of the launch control chamber. A set of steps led down to the flight deck, their stone worn down by generations of Space Marines. Belial told Charon to board the gunship and crossed to wait by the main doors leading to the hangar's accessway.

The double doors rumbled open, hauled apart by two gigantic pistons. The decking shuddered as Revered Venerari stepped through, blocking out the light from the corridor. Swaying slightly from side to side, Venerari stomped into the flight bay, his armoured form towering over the company master.

The Dreadnought stood twice as tall as Belial and was as broad. Thick slabs of armour protected the central sarcophagus where the physical remains of Brother Venerari hung suspended in a tank of artificial amniotics. Connected to the massive suit, the Dark Angel walked and fought again, saved from death by the genius of the Apothecaries and Techmarines. Enclosed within his second body of ceramite, adamantium and hardened steel, Venerari was connected to his hydraulic limbs through a mind impulse unit that mirrored the nervous system of a normal Space Marine. The interred veteran sensed the world through augurs and scanners. So he had lived for the last eight hundred and seventeen years, following four hundred and six years as a battle-brother. Unless finally slain in battle, Venerari was to all intents immortal.

For a non-Astartes such a fate might have been terrifying, but for a Space Marine it was not only a great honour, it was an entirely natural extension to a life of battle: one that a Space Marine served enclosed in a suit of armour, connected to his vital systems through the miracle of his black carapace. A normal Space Marine saw and heard the world through his autosenses, and was just as much a machine as a man. The only difference between Belial and Venerari was that the captain could take off his armoured skin.

'Greetings, brother,' said Venerari, his voice grating from external speakers set into the ornately decorated sarcophagus; his vocal cords had been destroyed by the eldar power blade that had almost taken

Venerari's life. The artificial voice had no change in pitch or pace, but Belial could still sense the gravitas of the veteran's words.

'I thank you, brother, for joining us in this endeavour. Your might as well as your wisdom will surely bring us victory.'

Venerari lifted up a huge four-fingered hand and a shimmering blue aura surrounded it.

'It will be good to fight the orks again, brother. It is I that must thank you for allowing me the opportunity for fresh glories. The enemy will not live to regret the day they dared the wrath of the Dark Angels.'

Servos and pneumatics hissing and clanking, the metal ringing under his clawed feet, Venerari strode across the deck and up the ramp of the Thunderhawk. Following behind, Belial raised a fist to Hephaestus in the gunship's command deck and engines whined into life, the noise increasing as it reverberated from the walls of the flight bay.

Belial jogged into the Thunderhawk and slammed his palm into the control stud to bring up the ramp. The gunship shuddered as Hephaestus increased the power to the engines. Easing his way past the bulk of Venerari, Belial made his way to the cockpit and strapped himself into the harness beside Hephaestus. Through the canopy he saw the outer doors of the launch bay opening, vapour forming as the air within the flight deck streamed into vacuum.

The stars were blotted out by the dark silhouette of Piscina IV, the planet's atmosphere glowing to the right with light from the system's star. Day would not dawn over Kadillus for three hours. When it came, it would herald a day that would see bloodshed unmatched by anything the orks had yet witnessed.

The fury of the Dark Angels was about to be unleashed.

COLONEL GRAUTZ WAS waiting for Belial at the edge of Northport's main apron. Landing lights blinked in the pre-dawn dark. As the company master stepped off the Thunderhawk's ramp it closed behind him with a whine. Within a few seconds the craft was already lifting off again, heading for the defence line at Koth Ridge with its vital supplies: though Belial was set on victory in the East Barrens, he would not leave his back unguarded.

The Piscinan commander and his staff gazed in astonishment as Venerari stomped past, the Dreadnought's metallic voice subdued as he talked to Charon who was walking beside him. Belial cut straight across the landing pad and strode up to Grautz.

'Is everything ready, colonel?'

Grautz broke away from staring at the Dreadnought and focussed on Belial. The colonel was in his early fifties, most of his lined face hidden behind a thick salt-and-pepper beard, wisps of grey hair sticking out from beneath a high-peaked cap emblazoned with the Imperial aquila. Grautz held himself straight and was considered tall by normal standards, but his eyes were barely level with Belial's collar. Those dark brown eyes looked up and saw a distorted view of the colonel in the lenses of the master's helm.

'Everything is as you ordered, Master Belial.' Grautz

was softly spoken but there was a stolid timbre to his voice. It was his world that had been attacked. 'We launched an offensive through the east docks an hour ago. My troops are moving in behind a cordon of tanks while your warriors are withdrawing to the east gate. It looks like we've stirred up the orks and they're preparing to retaliate. It's going to be a long day.'

'It will be a short day for some, colonel,' said Belial. 'Let us hope that it is not for too many.'

Grautz grunted and nodded.

'We will keep the orks where you need them,' he said. 'Though we owe the Dark Angels much for what they have done to protect us, Piscina is not without its own men of valour.'

Belial looked into the colonel's eyes and saw them glistening with pride. The captain had no doubt that Grautz would make his men fight to the last if necessary. After the disappointment at Barrak Gorge, Belial was pleased to see that there was someone else on Piscina who understood how important this war had become.

'I have every confidence in your men and your ability to lead them, colonel,' Belial said quietly. 'The Dark Angels know that there is strength in Piscina, and not just on your neighbouring world. For six thousand years we have used your world; today the Dark Angels fulfil the oaths made and pay their part of the bargain.'

'I have an armoured column standing by to follow you to the East Barrens,' said Grautz. 'If you need them.'

Belial shook his head.

'The offer is appreciated, colonel, but not necessary. Your tanks are not fast enough to keep up with our advance. Keep them here in the city in case Ghazghkull makes an attempt to break out.'

'You think that your attack will be so swift?' The colonel made no attempt to hide his doubt. 'There are still orks between Koth Ridge and the East Barrens.'

'There are, colonel, but we do not intend to fight them all,' replied Belial. 'We are Space Marines: strike swift, hard and sure. Our force will cut through the ork army and descend upon the East Barrens like a bolt of the Emperor's ire. Once we have taken the ork landing zone, we will defend it against all attack until the rest of the Chapter arrives. We will have time enough to destroy the orks at our leisure.'

Belial bent forwards and laid a hand on the colonel's shoulder, his other wrapped around the hilt of his blade.

'Today, my ally, you will see why the Astartes are called the sword of the Emperor.'

EXHAUST VAPOURS AND the rumble of engines filled the air as the Space Marine column lined up on the Indola highway. The dark green livery of the Space Marines' vehicles showed much wear and damage, but on each Rhino transport, Razorback armoured carrier and Predator tank, the Chapter serfs had laboured to repaint the Dark Angels insignia. The white winged sword gleamed freshly from a dozen hulls as dawn broke over the rocks of the East Barrens. A circling vapour trail through the orange-tinted clouds over-head marked the progress of the Thunderhawk.

In the lead Rhino, Belial left his seat and climbed up through the command cupola. He pulled himself up onto the upper hull of the transport and looked back at his company. Heat haze shimmered in the morning chill; grey smoke and billowing vapours hung like a fog about the armoured vehicles, lights carving nebulae in the fume, shadows softened by the strengthening light of the rising sun. The growl of engines brought to Belial's mind the image of a hunting beast waiting to pounce, full of potential energy and terrible ferocity kept in check for the moment.

Hatches popped along the column as the vehicle crews and transported squads emerged to hear their commander's address. Belial drew his power sword and held it aloft, blade glowing in the haze, shining from his polished armour.

'This morning brings us to the day of glory we have been longing for,' he declared. 'For days we have laboured to keep back our wretched foes and have made them pay in blood for every patch of Kadillus that they seek to take from us. Now it is the turn of our filthy enemy to fight for survival.'

He swept his sword down to point eastwards.

'It is to the new day that we attack, a fitting omen for the victory that will be ours. We will strike with the speed of a flashing blade and the strength of a crushing fist. No foe will stand before us and survive; no enemy will elude the ire of our weapons. Warriors of the Third Company, your brothers from the Chapter will learn of our actions today and they will be both proud and sad. Proud, that their battle-brothers fought with such honour and ferocity; sad, that they were not here to fight beside us and share in this great battle.'

Belial sheathed his sword and stalked to the rear of the Rhino, his boots ringing on the hull. His robe flapping in the strengthening morning wind, the captain stood with one hand on his sword hilt, the other resting on the holster of his bolt pistol.

'We fight today with renewed purpose, brothers. Our mission is clear, our enemy known, our objective laid before us. We are the Lion's sons of battle, raised for war and suckled on bloodshed. Today we fight not simply to fulfil our duty, but to punish those that seek to humble our honour. Today we avenge ourselves against those who have brought discord and anarchy to a world of the Emperor. Today we will give our foes the battle they seek, and teach them the folly of daring the wrath of the Astartes.

'Above all else, remember the traditions of the Lion. We are the First. We are the Dark Angels!'

'For the Lion!' roared the answering cry from eighty throats.

Nodding with satisfaction, Belial returned to the hatch and lowered himself back into the Rhino. He sat in the command position and pulled on his harness, tightening the straps across his chest and waist. Activating the comm panel in front of him, Belial selected the channel set aside for the makeshift force he had tasked with remaining at Koth Ridge to bolster the Piscinan defence.

'Brother Sarpedon, Brother Hebron, Squad Menelauis, Squad Dominus, Squad Annihilus and Squad Erinyes. Detach from column and move to your positions.'

Affirmatives echoed around the Rhino as the nominated Space Marines broke away from the company and moved out along the ridge to mingle with the Free Militia troopers staring with awe and anxiety at the Dark Angels force.

He turned in his seat and tapped the driver, Lephrael, on the shoulder. The Space Marine gunned the engine, the vehicle shaking with unleashed power. From external pick-ups Belial could hear the roaring response from the other vehicles along the road.

Belial switched channel.

'Third Company, advance!'

The column rumbled down the ridge, following the Indola highway, picking up speed as they headed across the plains. Belial's Rhino was at the front of the spearhead, and with him rode Charon and the battle-brothers of the master's bodyguard, Apothecary Nestor amongst them. Behind followed two Predator tanks, twin lascannons in their turrets, heavy bolters mounted on armoured sponsons on each flank of their hulls. Following the heavily armoured Predators came more transports – two Razorbacks with heavy bolter gun turrets, each carrying a combat squad of five Dark Angels, and three more Rhinos with a full squad of ten Space Marines aboard each.

The Ravenwing squadrons – three land speeders and five bikes – surged ahead of the column on either side, following Sergeant Validus. Half a kilometre above, the Thunderhawk completed Belial's force, Hephaestus, Venerari and an Assault squad on board.

Each was represented by a glowing rune on the

tactical display to Belial's right. It had been a difficult task to extract his warriors from the front line in Kadillus Harbour but they had managed the withdrawal without alerting the orks to what was happening. Two hours of hectic reorganisation had followed, with Belial reassigning the survivors of reduced squads to new sergeants, and promoting two of the battle-brothers to lead the ad-hoc combat squads being carried in the Razorbacks. Weapons and ammunition had been redistributed as needed, while the Apothecaries and Techmarines had worked their way through the force, treating wounds and repairing armour.

The 3rd Company had suffered, but they remained strong.

Belial was filled with a sense of freedom he had not felt since the orks had fallen upon Kadillus with thunderbolt surprise. The responsibility to protect Kadillus Harbour and the uncertainty of what the orks were up to had weighed heavily upon every decision he had made. All of that was forgotten as the Dark Angels raced down the road towards Indola. He had a force worthy of any commander, and an enemy to destroy. The sudden simplicity of everything was a thrill almost as great as the surge of excitement brought about by fighting a foe face-to-face.

Unseen inside his helmet, Belial smiled.

THE DARK ANGELS swept down from Koth Ridge and were halfway to the Indola complex by mid-morning. The reports from the Thunderhawk and Ravenwing confirmed Belial's expectation that there were no orks directly east of Koth Ridge: the company had an open route all the way to Indola.

The abandoned mine was almost certainly occupied by the orks. Only the day before as Validus's squadron returned to Koth Ridge, the Ravenwing sergeant had detected significant enemy around the half-ruined installation.

Twenty kilometres from the mine head, Belial had to make a decision. The column could leave the highway and move cross-country through the East Barrens, ignoring the ork presence; or the Space Marines could follow the road to its terminus at Indola and clear the orks from the compound.

The first course of action would ensure the column reached the East Barrens intact and as speedily as possible. Belial weighed up whether any time lost in attacking Indola would be compensated by destroying an enemy that would otherwise be left behind his line of advance. With compelling strategic reasons for both attack and avoidance, Belial reverted to his instinct. It gnawed at him to leave an enemy with uncontested control of a position, and it seemed to the captain that he was simply leaving the orks at Indola for the rest of the Chapter to deal with. If nothing else, destroying them now would save the Dark Angels time later, when the orks might have scattered into the wilderness.

'Master Belial to Brother Hephaestus. Conduct a recon fly-past of the Indola complex and report. Confirm.'

'Confirm, brother-captain. Will commence fly-over in nine minutes. Stand by for report.'

The column sped onwards, tracks biting at the worn surface of the highway, dust trailing behind the armoured vehicles. The morning sky was cloudless and sunshine illuminated the plains as if to provide bright witness to the approaching battles.

'This is Ravenwing-One. Wreckage on the road ahead, two kilometres east of your current position. No enemy detected. Will circle to provide perimeter watch until your arrival.'

The column slowed as it neared the site. Clambering into the command cupola, Belial increased the magnification of his autosenses. Less than a kilometre ahead he saw the tangled remains of two vehicles, one a battlewagon, the other a smaller half-track. From what he could see, they had crashed headlong into each other. The bodies of several orks hung limply from the wrecks.

It looked like a typically clumsy ork accident, but Belial had been tricked by the orks before and was not going to take any chances. He signalled his force.

'Company halt. *Caliban's Wrath* and *Hammer of Judgement* provide flank protection. Transports form up into double column.'

The two Predators slewed off the road and took up positions to either side of Belial's Rhino, their weapons pointing to the north-east and south-east. Behind their guns, the Razorbacks and Rhinos drew up together, shortening the flank of the column.

'This is Belial to Ravenwing-One. Confirm lack of enemy.'

'This is Ravenwing-One. No enemy present. The only orks within a kilometre of here are rotting, brother.'

Given the unreliability of sensor reports on previous missions, Belial remained cautious.

'Advance in formation. Gunners in position, direct weapons for circuit defence.' He switched to the internal comm to speak to Lephrael. 'Advance at twenty kilometres per hour. Divert power to cupola.'

'Confirm, brother-captain.'

The Rhino slowly picked up speed, the other vehicles keeping pace with Belial's lead. To the left and right, the Predators bumped across the uneven ground, turrets swivelling in arcs from the front to either side, gunners scanning for targets. The servos of the cupola beneath Belial whined into life. Taking holding of the storm bolter mounted on the cupola ring, Belial swung the weapon to each side to check it was moving freely. Behind him, other Space Marines were doing the same, rotating their weapons to cover the convoy in all directions.

As the column neared the wrecks, Belial could see the dust cloud of the Ravenwing bikes off to the left and the blurred black shapes of the land speeders to the right, circling around the crash. Had they detected anything, they would have reported immediately.

'Stop us twenty metres short of the wrecks,' Belial told Lephrael. He kept the storm bolter trained on the twisted vehicles as the Rhino slowed to a halt. Nothing moved. Belial addressed the force. 'No threat detected. Move around the wreckage and reform in rapid-deployment formation on the other side.'

Locking the storm bolter in place, Belial dropped back inside the Rhino, slamming the hatch shut over his head. He returned to his command position as Lephrael turned the Rhino off the highway and ploughed through the dust and grass to avoid the crashed vehicles.

'If I did not know better, brother, I would think that you are showing some nervousness,' said Charon, joining Belial in the cramped front end of the transport.

The captain kept his eyes on the tactical display as the icons shifted around the blockage on the road and fell into a single line again behind the accelerating command Rhino.

'I have made too many assumptions already, brother,' Belial replied once the column was under way again. 'I committed the sin of underestimating our foes at the outset of this campaign; it is not a mistake I will repeat at its conclusion.'

'A good lesson, to be sure, brother, but do not start to second-guess yourself. Doubt leads to hesitation...'

'...hesitation leads to defeat,' Belial finished the maxim. 'Do not be concerned, brother. I am not afraid to take decisive action.'

As if on cue, the comm crackled into life.

'Primary sweep of Indola complex completed, brother-captain,' said Hephaestus. 'Confirm enemy presence. Infantry, fifty to sixty in number. Several field guns of unknown design, hidden in buildings covering the two main gates. Awaiting orders.'

Belial considered his options again in light of this intelligence. There was no way to mask the approach of the Space Marines: the column of dust being left in their wake made sure of that. He had to assume that the guns covering the entrances to the compound had anti-tank capability. That would mean disembarking and attacking on foot, which would slow down the advance even more.

'There is another option, brother,' said Charon.

Belial could not tell whether the psyker had read his thoughts or simply understood him well enough to guess them. He swivelled the chair to look at Charon.

'Make your suggestion, brother.'

'You are not restricted to ground combat,' said the Librarian, lifting a finger upwards.

'The gunship has limited ammunition,' said the commander. 'It might be a waste to expend that resource on this matter and not have it available for the main assault.'

'Brother Hephaestus has more than the guns of his Thunderhawk to commit. Consider a combat drop under covering fire of the column.'

The plan had merit. Belial could draw the ork defenders to the column with a diversionary attack, leaving the enemy vulnerable to a Thunderhawk deployment in the heart of the compound. Caught between the two forces, the orks would be quickly destroyed.

'Very well, brother, it is a bold move and today will be decided by aggression and determination.' He turned back to the comm and signalled the circling Thunderhawk. 'Master Belial to Brother Hephaestus. Have Sergeant Arbalan and Revered Venerari prepare for aerial insertion. Stand by for further orders.'

'Confirm, brother-captain. Awaiting further orders for Thunderhawk insertion.'

Belial nodded for Charon to return to the main

compartment. The commander punched in the company channel and activated the comm.

'Pre-battle checks, all squads. Column to assume standard spearhead formation two kilometres from Indola compound. Advance to within five hundred metres and engage enemy forces with all weapons. Squad Arbalan and Revered Venerari will arrive by Thunderhawk into the compound three minutes after engagement commences. Upon completing the insertion, Brother Hephaestus will provide aerial support and column will attack in force. Confirm.'

As the responses of the vehicle crews and squads buzzed back through the comm, Belial allowed his excitement to grow. After so much frustration, and a night of meticulous, focussed preparation, the 3rd Company would soon shed the first blood of this new battle. Indola would be retaken, next the East Barrens, and from then it would be inevitable that the Dark Angels would control Piscina again.

THE GUNS OF the Predators heralded the attack, lascannon beams converging on the brick and metal guardhouses flanking the compound's main gate. Behind the two tanks, the Razorbacks peeled to the left, their turret gunners laying down a curtain of fire with heavy bolters. Belial stood in the Rhino's cupola a few metres back from the Predators, finger resting on the trigger of the storm bolter.

To the right, the Devastators of Squad Vindictus took up a firing position beside the *Hammer of Judgement*, their missile launchers and autocannons directed at the compound. At a signal from their sergeant, the

Space Marines opened fire, two missiles streaking away to detonate inside one of the gatehouses while the autocannons punched holes into the brickwork of the other.

Beyond the fence Belial could see orks pouring from the central building, shouting and firing their guns to raise the alarm. Evidently the orks had not been as watchful as the commander had expected. Through the sight of the storm bolter, he followed a whip-wielding ork herding a number of gretchin into a roughly dug emplacement. A few seconds later, the muzzle of a large-bore cannon peeked out through a gap in the dirt heaped around the position.

Belial pulled the trigger, sending a stream of bolter rounds into the emplacement. The bolts sent up a cloud of grit and dirt as they exploded against the wall. The field gun fired, belching flame and smoke, hurling a shell over the *Caliban's Wrath* to explode thirty metres behind the Space Marines. Belial fired again, knowing that he was unlikely to hit anything but the torrent of bolts would interfere with the gretchin gunners' reloading and aim.

The Razorbacks were pouring their fire into the second storey of a half-ruined building halfway along the compound fence. Lethal shrapnel and ferrocrete shards cut through the greenskins sheltering behind the remnants of the wall. With a blaze, a ball of plasma erupted from the building and ripped into the ground short of the closest Razorback. At a warning from their driver, the combat squad within spilled from the main hatch and took up firing from a few metres away.

The guardhouses had been so riddled with fire that nothing could have survived. The one on the left had collapsed, its sheet metal roof trapping any orks that had been inside. Another flurry of lascannon fire from the *Hammer of Judgement* seared through the corroded steel.

'Move on to secondary targets,' Belial told the Predator crews. 'Watch that warehouse to the right.'

The tanks' turrets and sponson guns swivelled to comply with the commander's order. Belial swung the storm bolter around to aim at the orks targeting the Razorbacks, adding his fire to the torrent screaming from the transports' heavy bolters and the guns of the disembarked squad. A pall of dust was enveloping the perimeter of the compound, thrown up by dozens of bolt-round, missile, autocannon and heavy bolter impacts. Belial switched to thermal view to see through the murk and continued firing, targeting the bright glimmers of heat in the ground floor of the building.

Belial's autosenses picked up the incoming roar of jets as the Thunderhawk circled for its final approach. Screaming in from the north, the gunship came to a stop over the compound, hovering on pillars of fire. As the Thunderhawk descended the assault ramp in its prow opened, disgorging the Assault Marines of Squad Arbalan. Jump packs flaring, they bounded away from the landing aircraft, heading towards the other gate.

The cannon Belial had been targeting opened fire. With a clang that could be heard over the mass of gunfire, the shell slammed into the *Hammer of Judgement*'s turret, bouncing away from the sloped front, leaving a deep furrow in the armour. In response, the gunner turned his weapons on the emplacement, twin beams of laser energy stabbing over the mounds of earth sheltering the gun crew. Something erupted into flame and a moment later Belial saw the small greenskins clambering out of the dug-out. They were too late, as the cannon's ammunition exploded, sweeping the entire gate area with flying red-hot metal.

'Attack speed, column advance!'

Dirt spraying from their tracks, the vehicles of the Dark Angels powered towards the compound. The Thunderhawk touched down between the main mine head building and the gatehouses, bullets ricocheting from its hull. Venerari lumbered down the ramp, his power fist crackling, missiles streaking from the armoured pod on his other weapon mount. Fire engulfed the orks as the Thunderhawk lifted off, cruising low over the buildings to bathe the compound with its plasma jets.

'Go left!' Belial snapped to his driver as he saw a group of orks fleeing between the burning buildings of the mine. He jabbed the general comm button. 'Company, follow your commander!'

Lephrael slewed the Rhino towards the greenskins as Belial opened fire. Bolts ripped past the chainlink a moment before the Rhino crashed through, lurching over the raised plascrete foundation holding the fence in place. The transport rocked and skidded over the stone-strewn ground but Belial compensated for the movement, firing a burst into the retreating orks, cutting down two of them. Behind him the roar of storm bolters echoed from the ruined walls of the compound buildings as the following crews opened up at the orks loitering within.

With a whine of hydraulics, the doors covering the top hatch opened outwards behind Belial. Climbing up to the firing steps, the commander's bodyguard levelled their weapons at the buildings rushing past to either side. Bolts and balls of plasma flew in all directions, while bullets and laser blasts spat back from the orks' guns.

Throwing his weight to his left, Belial brought the storm bolter to bear on a clutch of orks heading into a gap between a rusting storage tank and a thick pipeline. Corroded metal shattered as Belial opened fire. A cloud of rust flakes engulfed the running orks a second before the bolts found their mark, thudding into green-skinned limbs and bodies.

'Purge the unclean!' snarled Belial as he ejected the storm bolter's spent magazine and reached down into the Rhino for a replacement. 'Hunt them all down!'

The snaking column of Rhinos and Razorbacks weaved between the storage sheds, hulking machinery, ore hoppers and ferrocrete hab-blocks, weapons blazing. From just outside the compound, the Predators continued to blast away with heavy bolters and lascannons, levelling any cover that might hide a foe.

Bullets pinged from the Rhino's hull and sprayed from Belial's armour as a mob of orks fired from the windows of a burnt-out tower housing the main pumping works. The angle was too steep for Belial to return fire as the Rhino rumbled past, but it did not matter. The crews of the following vehicles turned their weapons on the greenskins, the hail of fire ripping through the windows and thin walls.

'Brother-captain, this is Hephaestus. There are fifteen-plus orks leaving the compound to the north. Shall I engage?'

'Negative, brother,' Belial replied. 'Sergeant Validus is patrolling that area and will deal with any that try to escape.'

'Confirm, brother-captain. Continuing surveillance sweep.'

The column had reached the open area just west of the main compound building, where a few nights before Sergeants Naaman and Aquila had debated the nature of the ork threat. Back in the light, Belial switched off his thermal view and swung the cupola around to face the column.

'Perimeter defence. Disembark squads for building clearance.'

He slipped down into the Rhino, Lephrael taking up his commander's position at the gun a couple of seconds later. The command squad dropped down from the top hatch, the doors closing back over them as Belial opened the rear accessway. The company master was first down the lowering ramp, striding out into the bright morning sun. Around him, the Rhinos and Razorbacks formed a circle, guns directed outwards. The thudding of boots echoed around the strangely quiet compound as the squads disembarked. The Space Marines used their vehicles as cover while they aimed their weapons at the buildings around them.

'Tactical squads, clear and secure your sectors. Check for basements, storage bunkers and other hiding places. Squad Vindictus, split into combat squads, remain in reserve to provide fire support. Report strong resistance immediately.'

The Space Marines fanned out across the compound, moving building to building with grenades and bolters. The bark of a gun or crack of frag grenades broke the stillness as the Dark Angels cleared Indola room by room, shack by shack, stone by stone.

Charon joined the company commander while Nestor left the squad to attend to the few Space Marines wounded in the intense fighting. The Librarian said nothing and his silence disturbed Belial.

'You think this is a distraction?' said the captain.

Charon shook his head, his eyes scanning the surrounding buildings.

'I would not presume to think I am better acquainted with strategy. Is there any reason to doubt the wisdom of your action?'

Belial was not sure what the Librarian was implying. The master paced back and forth beside the command Rhino.

'I feel that you are the eyes of Azrael upon me, brother. You profess not to judge me, yet I feel your constant scrutiny. I am aware of the errors I have made and I do not need you to bear witness to them.'

'The interpretation is yours alone and not my intent, brother. Do not feel that you have anything to prove to me, or to Grand Master Azrael.' Charon stopped Belial's pacing with an outstretched hand. 'If there is any judgement, it is yours. If you have doubts, they are of your own fabrication. What accusation do you think I could make regarding this operation?'

Tapping his fingers against the scabbard of his sword in agitation, Belial directed a long look at Charon. The company master examined his reasoning behind the attack on Indola and could find no flaw – except for a niggling concern that crept into his mind.

'An uncharitable observer might report that I have indulged in this attack to delay the real battle in the East Barrens. This assault could be portrayed as a distraction, conceived to forestall the inevitable clash that will decide my future. Some might say it is a sign that I am fearful of confronting the resolution that awaits us to the east.'

'But that is not the case, brother.' Charon kept his words quiet and glanced away as if dismissing the comment. 'There is a more problematic and direct cause for concern.'

Belial wanted to end the conversation. The Librarian's statements probed at the master's motives and forced him to confront the possibility of failure; or worse, the possibility that Belial would be the cause of defeat. To walk away could be an admittance of guilt. He forced himself to think rationally, pulling back his thoughts from the turmoil of combat so that he could think like a commander.

'The orks are receiving steady reinforcements, and this delay will see their strength increase,' he said. Belial re-examined the strategic options that had been laid before him and continued in a firmer tone. 'While the time spent here will see enemy numbers grow, in balance it is not a factor. If we did not clear the enemy from this area, accepted doctrine says that we should leave a rearguard to protect against attack from this quarter. The growing strength of the orks is an unknowable quantity, while the loss of warriors for such a duty is defined. It is my belief that the benefits of keeping the entirety of the strike force intact out-weigh any bolstering of the enemy force.'

Belial checked the chronometer, his agitation subsiding, replaced with renewed confidence.

'I estimate it will take no more than an hour to fully secure the compound. That will leave us with just over eight hours of daylight to reach the East Barrens and prosecute the battle against the ork landing site. Though we are capable of conducting a night opera-tion, it will be better to take the East Barrens station before nightfall to reduce the chances of any orks escaping.'

Folding his arms, Charon nodded.

'You have everything under control, and nothing is amiss in your thinking,' said the Librarian. 'It is impor-tant that you recognise this.'

'I do, brother,' said Belial. He stepped up to the command Rhino's entrance hatch but stopped just as he was about to duck inside. He looked back at Charon. 'How is it, brother, that you see doubts when even I am unaware of them? Is that why Grand Master Azrael attached you to my command?'

The Librarian betrayed no emotion as he replied.

'I see into men's souls, brother, but not with any sense you do not possess. The Lion taught that we must know each other if we are to know ourselves. A moment's hesitation might go unobserved and unremarked, but can be a sign of inner debate. A

GAV THORPE

change of orders or sudden reversal of decision might be a symptom of failing clarity. These things I see, but not in you.'

Belial shook his head in wonder.

'I am sure that you see more, brother, than you tell me. Has the conflict within me been so plain?'

'No, brother,' said Charon, smiling for the first time since he had joined Belial's company. 'I saw nothing in you that would suggest doubt or indecision. It is important that you understand that. You are an excellent commander and an outstanding warrior. Believe in your instincts and trust your judgement. They will serve us all well. Grand Master Azrael sent me to you not because he thinks you are weak, but because he thinks you are strong. He believes that you are destined for greater things, Belial, and you have given me no cause to make him question that belief.'

'Why could you not simply tell me that at the outset? Why leave me thinking the worst for all this time, fearing for a verdict from my masters that was wholly imagined?'

Charon's smile faded.

'It is not our place to aggrandise each other, nor to set our sights on goals any loftier than the immediate task at hand. We must test ourselves each day; examine our loyalty, our attention to duty and our dedication to our brothers. There can be no complacency. We both know the dark road that leads from such self-interest.'

The company master glanced around out of instinct, knowing that Charon spoke of the Fallen:

the secret that had been entrusted to him as a master and a member of the Deathwing. It was not the time to think about such things. Charon was right: he had more pressing issues to address.

It TOOK A little more than the hour Belial had expected to clear Indola of the remaining orks. It was not the fighting that took up this time; the orks had been rocked by the attack and provided little concerted opposition. The delay came from disposing of the bodies. Hephaestus had insisted that the ork dead be burnt to ensure they posed no further threat to Piscina, which meant that the corpses had to be gathered up and pits dug for the cremations.

Three black pillars of smoke rose into the midday sky as the Dark Angels headed eastwards. It was unlikely that the orks would see the smoke so many kilometres away, but if they did Belial was not worried. It was his intent to draw into battle as many of the orks as possible so that they could be killed. If the greenskins were allowed to scatter into the wilds, it would make the task of hunting them down all the more difficult and would occupy the Chapter for more time. Better to eradicate them before they bolted for cover, Belial told himself.

So it was that the Dark Angels column rumbled across the undulating grasslands of the East Barrens like a dark green spear aimed at the geothermal station. Hour by hour the Space Marines advanced, no word of the foe from the Thunderhawk overhead or the Ravenwing outriders criss-crossing the plains. Having experienced the rush of battle so recently, the monotony of the journey nagged at Belial and he occupied himself with addressing some of the simple logistical issues involved in the attack.

His force had suffered only two fatalities in the battle at Indola – a Razorback gunner and one of Validus's bikers – and a further seven Space Marines had incurred serious injuries that compromised their ability to fight. Belial had removed these battle-brothers from their squads and split Squad Laetheus to replace them, sending the wounded back to Koth Ridge in the Rhino thus made available. In effect he was one transport and one squad down on his starting force, but Belial considered he would have been forced to sacrifice at least one squad and possibly two as a rearguard if he had not cleansed the orks from Indola.

The attack had used up almost a quarter of the column's ammunition, although at the end the Dark Angels had conserved their resources by using chainswords and fists to destroy the last few green-skins. Supplies had been redistributed between the squads and vehicles to ensure that they were evenly spread amongst the Space Marines.

Heavy bolter rounds were a particular issue, with nearly half of the task force's cache expended during the assault. It was not unexpected: the anti-personnel power and high rate of fire of heavy bolters made them ideal weapons for fighting orks. The two Preda-tors had sacrificed some of their supplies to ensure the squads had enough ammunition. It was a reason-able compromise, as the tanks' lascannons would be more valuable in the coming battle if the enemy had significant numbers of vehicles and Dreadnoughts; the energy weapons were powered by the Predator's reactor, a near-limitless supply of energy.

Feeling upbeat about the result of the coming attack, the commander turned his attention to events further out. As with the aborted air attack, he composed scenarios of the possible outcomes and what would be needed to deal with each of them. Defeat was not an option he considered. If that happened, Uriel's orders were unequivocal and would be carried out to the letter.

More troublesome in a way was the possibility of a partial victory. The primary objective was to seize the geothermal station from the orks, dismantle their energy relay to stop reinforcements and hold against counter-attack. If it transpired that ork strength was sufficient to stop the Dark Angels achieving this, Belial was determined to set up a point of fire on the landing site so that any arriving reinforcements could be targeted before they could get away. That mission might well last until the Chapter arrived, in at least another four days. Depending upon the scale and frequency of the incoming reinforcements, such an operation would require considerable supplies.

The other unknown was the plan of Ghazghkull in Kadillus Harbour. Belial had no idea whether the warlord had any means of contacting the orks to the east or knew what had been happening outside the city, but it would be foolish to discount the greenskins holding the docks, power plants and defence laser site.

If all went well, the Piscinans could lift their perimeter on Koth Ridge and bolster their defence in the city, freeing the Dark Angels to concentrate their efforts in the east. If only a part-victory was obtained, the defenders of Kadillus would be committed on two fronts, seriously stretching their manpower and supplies. The commander made a note in his tactical log to contact Colonel Grautz to find out what other resources could be airlifted to Kadillus from the smaller islands of Piscina.

Hour-by-hour, kilometre-by-kilometre, Belial engaged himself in this distraction, breaking only to receive the regular, negative reports from the Ravenwing and Hephaestus. It was only at these times that he paid any attention to the chronometer and noted absently the shortening time until the attack would be launched.

At the mark of one hour until engagement Belial pushed his strategic plans to the back of his mind and focussed on the coming battle. Rapid and controlled ferocity would be the key. The Space Marines were masters of shock assault, and the coming confrontation would be a test of those abilities. It was too risky to charge directly in aboard the Rhinos: the orks had rocket systems capable of shooting at aircraft and it seemed reasonable to expect they had at least some anti-tank weapons positioned around the power station. Those air defences were also a concern in themselves, preventing a Thunderhawk insertion or attack run.

A plan slowly formed in Belial's mind, the vague outlines of what would happen. Five minutes later, he called the column to a halt, thirty kilometres west of the ridge overlooking the geothermal station. He brought the squad sergeants and vehicle commanders together for a mission briefing.

'We will conduct a four-phase assault on the landing site,' Belial told the circle of Space Marines. Hephaestus and Validus listened in over the comm as they continued to circle the column to guard against attack.

Belial held up the dataslab connected to the command terminal in his Rhino and showed them a display depicting the area around the geothermal station. The geography was detailed, based on data taken by Naaman and the Ravenwing in their previous forays into the region. The runes marking out likely enemy dispositions were more approximate, based on old reports but the only information the master had available.

'First phase will be Ravenwing reconnaissance to confirm enemy force and location. Second phase will be a Razorback and Predator strike against anti-air and anti-tank weapons. Third phase will be a general assault to seize key firing positions around the landing site, supported by Thunderhawk attack. Fourth phase will be a narrow-front assault against the station itself, coordinated with an aerial insertion.'

He paused, offering the assembled Dark Angels an opportunity to voice any comment or question regarding the overall plan. Nothing was said. When he continued, his fingers worked the keypad of the dataslab, bringing up lines of attack, arcs of covering fire and other tactical details.

'Most of you fought beside me at Aggreon, and will recall our assault on Forgewell.' There were a few nods from the sergeants. 'The same principles apply here.

The key element is establishing a base of fire as soon as possible. Once the Predators, Razorbacks and Devastators are in position, the rest of us can move on to take the main facility.'

Again he allowed any questions to be raised, and again there were none.

'Initial attack formation will be *cohortis rapida* and individual squad deployments will be sent to your tactical displays. After that, it is a matter of how many enemy there are to kill and where we will find them. All non-intra-squad communication will take place on the prime command channel. Facing an uncertain foe, we must be alert and flexible to every opportunity and threat.'

'Withdrawal rally points, brother-captain?' It was Sergeant Livenius that asked the question.

'There will be no general withdrawal or extraction,' Belial said. 'If we are unable to capture the geothermal station, we will hold any ground captured. We are not leaving the East Barrens until the orks are destroyed, one way or the other.'

'Understood, brother,' said Livenius. 'No retreat!'

The call was echoed by the others.

'Victory or death!' Validus added over the comm.

Belial laughed.

'Indeed, brothers,' he said. 'Today it truly is victory or death.'

THE BLAST FROM the exploding ork missile carrier shook the ground. Mangled debris cascaded down onto the greenskins in a shower of metal and flame. With one target destroyed, the *Hammer of Judgement* plunged onwards to the ork landing site, lascannons cutting brilliant traces down the ridge. The *Caliban's Wrath* followed close behind, heavy bolters thundering, slashing a swathe through the enemy camp. To the left – the north – the two Razorbacks of the column laid down covering fire whilst the combat squads disembarked into a defile running down the ridgeline towards the geothermal station.

Belial monitored the destruction on the tactical screen, the interior of the Rhino bathed with soft yellow light. The data from the Ravenwing reconnaissance had been ideal, pinpointing the concentrations of the ork forces and confirming that the anti-aircraft rockets had not been moved. It was a tactical nuance – the redeployment of defensive elements after an enemy encounter – that had been lost on the greenskins, and the Dark Angels made them pay with blood.

'Master Belial to Brother Hephaestus. Elimination of air defences proceeding quickly. Take position to begin your attack run. Confirm.'

While the Techmarine's confirmation sounded from the comm, Belial adjusted the display settings and zoomed out for a wider view. Collating sensor sweeps from the Ravenwing to the north and south, the tactical metriculators presented the commander with a view of the battlefield only a few seconds old. If he was attacking over a narrower front, Belial would have witnessed the action by eye, and been able to respond even more quickly, but the undulating ground and mile-wide attack made that impossible. Instead he saw his forces from the signatures of their identity transponders and looked at enemies that were nothing more than augur returns and thermal responses.

The main comm feed was a chatter of information as vehicle commanders and squad sergeants exchanged information and coordinated their attacks. The constant battle commentary was like a background hum, attracting his attention only when something out of the ordinary was reported. He would then spend a few seconds dealing with the issue before leaving his leaders at the front to carry out their orders as they saw fit.

It was not Belial's place to interfere with the close-range squad actions, but to provide an omniscient guiding hand: steering the entire assault in the desired direction, keeping an eye on the wide picture for emerging threats and opportunities.

One such threat was growing in the outbuildings between the power station and the left flank of the attack. A battery of ork howitzers and mortars were tossing their shells up the ridge. The bombs were not strong enough to pose any genuine threat to the armoured hulls of the Rhinos, but as the transport rocked from another close blast, Belial did not want to take any chances. A lucky hit on a hatch or the breaking of a tread link would be enough to remove a whole squad from the fight.

'Razorbacks, close and engage enemy artillery in grid omega-five. Keep them pinned down. Combat Squad Bellaphon, follow in and take up a position at grid omega-six. Confirm.'

Belial waited for the responses before turning his attention to the other flank, where the *Hammer of Judgement* was fast approaching the teleporter opening.

Since the Space Marines had arrived, a steady stream of orks had continued to arrive through the portal and were massing in a copse of trees to the south.

The Predator's rune flashed red in warning a moment before the commander, Brother Meledon, cut through the other comm traffic.

'Engaged with anti-tank rockets from the south-east. Right sponson damaged, gunner unharmed. Request orders, brother-captain. Shall I push on to the last anti-air missile or pull back?'

Belial made the decision in a moment; the advantage of clearing the airspace over the plant for the Thunderhawk outweighed the possible loss of a Predator.

'Advance and engage your target, Meledon. *Caliban's Wrath*, divert to provide flank support.'

'Confirm, brother-captain. *Hammer of Judgement* moving in on last air-defence missiles.'

'Confirm, brother-captain. *Caliban's Wrath* engaging enemy in the woods with all weapons. *Hammer of Judgement* clear to advance.'

Panning the display back to the left, Belial saw that the Razorbacks and combat squad he had sent forwards were doing a good job of suppressing the enemy artillery. It had been several seconds since the last shell had exploded around the Rhinos.

'Hephaestus to Master Belial. On-station for attack run. Weapons armed. Targeting systems linked to Ravenwing spotters. Awaiting attack order.'

'Confirm, Hephaestus. Validus, can you get a clear target signal on those transports to the north-east?'

While he waited for the reply, the commander

touched the screen and focussed on the two Predators. The *Hammer of Judgement* was rounding a ruined building and would have a clear view of the last anti-aircraft missile in a few seconds. The other tank was engaged in a furious firefight with the orks hiding amongst the short trees; Belial could picture the screaming heavy bolter rounds shredding orks and foliage, lascannon blasts splitting twisted trunks while wild rockets flew out of the depths.

Belial reached a decision.

'Master Belial to Hephaestus. Begin attack run. Primary targets designated by Ravenwing squadrons. Validus, can you confirm you have the ork transports in view?'

'Apologies, brother-captain. There are two columns of ork vehicles to the north-east. Closest is less than one kilometre away, light vehicles only. Second is three kilometres away, two heavier transports and a battlewagon. Which do you wish to engage?'

'Send the bike squadron to target the heavier vehicles for the gunship. Engage lighter vehicles with your land speeders. Confirm.'

'Confirm, brother-captain. Bike squad despatched to target for gunship. Forming land speeder strike on approaching ork light vehicles.'

With a detonation that Belial could hear through the thick hull of the Rhino, the ork missile carrier was destroyed. The elimination of the orks' last air defence was confirmed over the comm channel by the Predator's commander.

'Withdrawing to primary fire position with *Caliban's Wrath* to provide long-range support. Confirm, brother-captain.'

Belial checked the display once more. The orks in the woods would have to wait to receive retribution until the Tactical squads could move in to clear them out: there was no point risking the Predators in the narrow confine of hills and buildings any longer.

'Confirm, *Caliban's Wrath* and *Hammer of Judgement.* Withdraw to provide fire support.'

The momentum of the attack was building as Belial had foreseen. With all of his force now capable of playing its part, the time was swiftly arriving to push home the attack. The commander gave the display one last scan to ensure there was nothing amiss, and signalled the Thunderhawk.

'Master Belial to Hephaestus. What is your time on target?'

'Hephaestus to Belial. One hundred and five seconds until optimal firing range. Still awaiting target confirmation.'

'Belial to Validus. Report status of bike squadron.'

There was a pause while the Ravenwing leader consulted with the squad sergeant.

'Validus to Brother Belial. Target acquisition in thirty seconds. Enemy vehicles now two-point-five kilometres away.'

'Confirm, Brother Validus.' As with the destruction of the air defences, it was time to pre-empt the probable result of the Thunderhawk attack. To delay further would risk losing the shock and impetus of the first assault. 'Master Belial to all units. Commence phase three, general assault. Proceed to your designated attack points with all speed.'

He stood up and slapped his driver on the shoulder.

'Let's get going, brother. It is time to push forwards.'

'Confirm, brother-captain.'

Belial pulled himself up to the cupola and threw open the hatch. His autosenses darkened as the commander emerged into the bright afternoon light from the artificial twilight of the Rhino's interior. Taking a hold of the storm bolter's grip, he checked the magazine and sighted on a cluster of rocks a few hundred metres away.

With a lurch, the Rhino set off, rumbling down the ridgeside, tracks grating through the thin soil, engine throbbing. The transport hurtled over a rise of rock and crashed down on the far side, but Belial's armour and innate balance allowed him to ride the violent movement without problem. Across narrow gorges and around boulders, the Rhino sped towards the orks, other transports flanking it two hundred metres away to the left and right.

Belial looked up as Hephaestus's Thunderhawk roared overhead, swooping onto the enemy reinforcements north-east of the attack. Fire rippled along the gunship's wings a moment before four missiles streaked away to the north, leaving dark contrails cutting across the sky. The distant crack of the detonations echoed along the ridge a few seconds later.

Fire from the right attracted Belial's attention. The outermost Rhino had run into a mob of orks trying to sneak up a gulley to retake their earlier position. Storm bolter rounds split the air as the gunner unleashed a series of short salvoes. The Rhino slewed to a stop, access ramp slamming down even before it had finished moving. The squad within burst down the ramp, Brother Cademon at the front, flamer in hand. Fire licked through the scrub while the bark of bolters added to the crackle of flames and the pained bellows of the orks.

'Keep moving forwards,' Belial warned his warriors. 'I want every squad in position within two minutes.'

Just as the commander finished speaking he caught sight of a dark blur in the air. An instant later, something slammed into the front of the Rhino, showering Belial with paint and splinters of ceramite. The transport shuddered under the impact and bounced wildly over a rock as Brother Lephrael lost control for a moment. The vehicle skidded sideways down the slope, tracks churning up grass and mud.

Belial looked back along the estimated trajectory of the shell. He saw what at first might be mistaken for a rubbish heap: piles of rags, discarded metal, bones and broken bits of machinery. From under one pile protruded the long barrel of a gun, smoke drifting from the muzzle.

'Belial to company. Anti-tank weapon three hundred metres to the east. Suppressive fire.'

The commander opened fire with the mounted storm bolter, loosing off single rounds in the direction of the anti-tank gun. Other bolts whirred against the field piece from the left and right.

'Keep going,' Belial told Lephrael. 'Close the range.'

A puff of smoke, a sharp crack and the scream of the shell speeding overhead were the only results of the orks' next shot. Belial slapped his palm against the fire selector of the storm bolter, shifting the weapon into rapid-fire mode. In three-second bursts, he walked the salvo of bolts across the opening into the pit dug beneath the rubbish piles. He could see nothing of the results, save for the flashes of the bolt detonations.

A distinctive thud broke the air from above: the battle cannon of the Thunderhawk circling high above. Belial detected the screech of the descending round just before the whole rubbish tip disappeared in a flash of fire and smoke.

'Target destroyed,' Hephaestus announced over the comm. 'Hephaestus to company. Commencing first attack run on landing site. Do not proceed ahead of ascribed positions. Repeat, commencing aerial fire support on the landing site.'

The Rhino sped forwards again under Lephrael's guidance, cutting between two massive boulders. The ground was rapidly levelling. The first buildings of the geothermal complex were only two hundred metres away.

The comm buzzed with squads reporting that they were in position. Firefights erupted to Belial's left amongst a row of empty fuel tanks. From even further north, the distinctive blaze of plasma and the white trails of missiles cut the air: the Devastators were in position overlooking the power plant itself and providing cover fire.

A hundred metres from his objective, Belial dropped back inside the Rhino. He glanced at the tac-display to confirm what he had seen from the cupola: phase three of the attack was well under way and progressing well. He turned to Charon and the other Space Marines in the main compartment.

'Disembarking in thirty seconds. Ready weapons.'

The Rhino rang with the sound of magazines being slapped into place and chainswords whirring as the bodyguard tested their weapons. Amongst the noises from within, Belial heard something rattling against the hull from without.

'Small-arms fire, brother-captain,' Lephrael assured him. 'Stupid orks don't know that bullets won't do a thing to us.'

'Where from?' asked Belial. In a crouch, he moved up beside the driver and peered through the vision slit.

'Two-storey building thirty degrees to the left, brother-captain.'

There were at least a dozen orks at the windows of the building, muzzle flares flashing from their long tusks and red eyes. Belial turned back to the others.

'Prepare for building breach. Ready grenades.'

The commander had taken a step back towards the main compartment when Lephrael gave a shout. A red light winked on the console in front of the driver.

'Projectile detected!'

Something heavy slammed into the right flank of the Rhino, the explosion tilting the transport off one track for a moment. Lephrael wrestled at the controls, hissing curses.

'By the Lion, what was that?' Belial demanded, hunching over the tactical display.

All he could see was a thermal register seventy metres away, between two low buildings. He hauled himself back up to the command cupola and looked for himself. In the shadow of the alleyway was an ork Dreadnought-class walker, a rack of missiles mounted on one shoulder, a power claw hanging from the other. It advanced into the light as another rocket slid down a feed rail into the launcher.

Boots clanging loudly, Belial dropped into the Rhino. He punched the activation rune of the transport's hunter-killer missile system. Above him, next to the cupola, the firing case of the launcher extended itself from the hull. Belial flipped the switch that opened the launcher, while his other hand turned on the artificial eye mounted into the missile.

The feed fuzzed into life on a small screen above the controls just in time to show the smoke trail of another rocket passing a few metres in front of the Rhino, which was still speeding towards the ork-held building.

Belial swivelled the launcher until he caught a glimpse of the ork walker stomping forwards. He thumbed the fire switch and the Rhino rattled as the hunter-killer missile streaked away. With deft movements, Belial guided the hunter-killer towards the Dreadnought, eyes fixed to the small circle of the pict-feed. The missile curved around and straightened under Belial's command; with his final touch the view dipped towards the hip joint of the machine.

Pipes, cables and pistons came closer and closer on the screen, and then the display went dark. The detonation of the missile sounded through the open hatch above. Belial pulled himself up to check the results of the hit. Bullets from the orks in the building pattered around him as he watched the Dreadnought topple to one side, leaking thick smoke and oil, one leg sheared away, the rocket launcher driving point-first into the dirt.

Seizing hold of the storm bolter, Belial turned the weapon on the orks holding the upper storey of the building, sending steady bursts through the broken windows. The Rhino ground to a stop a few metres from the remnants of the main doors, one of the pair hanging haphazardly from a single hinge, the other nowhere to be seen, probably stolen.

Charon and the command squad needed no order from Belial to deploy. The rear hatch slammed down and the Rhino rocked from side to side as the six Space Marines charged out. Belial fired off another burst and then pulled himself fully out of the cupola. Unholstering his plasma pistol and drawing his sword, he ran to the side of the Rhino and jumped down, landing in a puff of dry dirt, feet sinking into the ground.

'Sons of Caliban, with me!' he called to the others, plunging into the shadowy interior of the building.

Tactical acumen swept aside by natural ferocity, the orks abandoned their superior position in the upper floor and raced down the stairs to confront the Space Marines. Belial fired a ball of plasma into the mass of green-skinned beasts pouring down the steps, while the commander's honour guard fanned out around him, bolters and plasma gun thundering.

There were more foes than Belial had realised as the green mass continued to crash down on him: at least two dozen orks, three of them huge specimens that towered over the others.

Charon dashed past the Dark Angels master, force sword in both hands, his whole body swathed in a mist of blue and black. The orks' bullets melted into mist as they touched the Librarian, leaving a trailing glitter of metal particles in his wake. He swept his sword effortlessly through the first alien, parting it from waist to shoulder in one blow. Charon caught a jagged axe-head on the guard and twisted his wrists, sending the point of the gleaming blade through the ork's face.

Not to be outdone, Belial sprinted into the mass of greenskins, pistol spitting another blue blast. He opened the throat of an ork with a short cut, barged aside its falling body and rammed his sword through the chest of a second. He smashed the pommel into the face of a third, sending it reeling back into its companions.

One of the ork leaders shouldered its way through the throng, a bloodstained cleaver-like blade in both hands. As it swung the cumbersome weapon back, Belial pounced, slashing his power sword into the beast's ribs, the shining blade parting muscle and bone and internal organs in one cut. Though grievously wounded, the ork was not down. Its cleaver swung at Belial's head with deadly momentum.

An instant before the blow struck, the captain's displacer field activated. Belial's stomach lurched as he was shunted into warp space; for a fraction of a second he was surrounded by a cacophony of wailing, screaming and shouting while his limbs shuddered with unnatural energy and his eyes danced with swirling light of every colour.

Reality reasserted itself with a popping of air pressure. Belial found himself a few metres back towards the doors. His senses took half a second to adjust, by which time he was already pounding across the bare stone floor, sword raised for the next attack.

Charon was surrounded by a pile of gently smoking body parts. An ork ducked beneath the Librarian's sword and lunged at his groin with a serrated dagger. The blade scraped harmlessly from Charon's armour. He let go of his sword with one hand and grabbed the ork's out-stretched wrist in his fist. Psychic energy snarled across the ork, skin charring, fat bubbling as the psychic power fizzed along tendons and blood vessels. The greenskin collapsed, convulsing wildly, steam rising from melted eyes, frothing blood pouring from its nose and ears.

Charon kicked the corpse aside and took up his sword in both hands, ready for the next foe.

The fighting was brutal and swift, but not entirely to the favour of the Space Marines. By the time the last ork was dead, Apothecary Nestor was already tending to Brother Mandiel, whose right hand had been sheared off by an ork blade. The armour of the others showed numerous cracks, scarred paint and bullet holes as testament to the fury of their foes.

'Secure the rest of the building,' said Belial, leaping up the stairs.

There were bodies on the upper floor, and two orks wounded by Belial's storm bolter fire. They looked up at the Space Marine with beady red eyes, one clutching a ragged hole in its gut, the other trying to heave itself up on its remaining leg.

Belial's power sword made short work of the crip-pled greenskins.

Surrounded by calm for a moment, Belial linked in his autosenses to the tactical cogitator in the Rhino outside. The view through his right lens was replaced by a miniature version of the battle map. Minute eye movements scrolled the display, allowing Belial to see what had happened while he had been fighting. With his left eye, he looked through a cracked window pane, confirming what the map was showing.

The other squads were in position, forming a semi-circle around the geothermal station and the portal. Battle-cannon craters broke the open ground around the teleporter site, while fires burned in several of the other buildings, smoke drifting lazily on the breeze. The portal was still active though; as Belial watched, it bloomed into life and disgorged a pair of trikes, their heavy weapons opening up on the Space Marines almost immediately. The Predators on the ridge over-looking the landing site returned fire, lascannon shots lancing down to blow up one of the trikes; the other swerved wildly and disappeared into the rocks and gulleys further south.

Belial could not see the whole of the power plant from where he was standing. He moved into the adjoining room. The roof was low and sloping, but a ragged hole gave him a better view. He could see orks moving around the transformer blocks, and on the maze of gantries and ladders above the station, now protected by crudely welded metal sheets and piles of rocks and junk: from his earlier foray when he had stolen the power relay, the orks had learnt the impor-tance of keeping the Space Marines away from their precious energy transmitter.

Charon joined him, stooping beneath the rafters.

'The battle goes well, brother,' said the Librarian.

'Well enough,' said Belial.

He switched off the tac-display and hailed the other squads.

'Belial to company. Tactical report by unit. Casualty and supply details.'

In turn, the sergeants reeled off the statistics. As he heard the reports, Belial realised that the swiftness of the assault had been a great success, but not without a price. There was not a squad that was at full strength, and two of the Tactical squads had lost half their number securing the buildings at the centre of the landing site.

He looked again at the power plant, trying to guess the number of orks within. Several hundred, he reckoned, and they seemed more than happy to keep themselves hidden away. The Techmarines' analysis of whether a Thunderhawk attack was as risky to the geothermal network as orbital bombardment had been inconclusive. Without that support, taking the station would be bloody work indeed. If the Dark Angels tried and failed, they might lack the strength to contain the reinforcements still arriving.

Belial looked at Charon. The snap of bolter fire and crack of lascannons could be heard across the landing site, answered by the rattle of ork guns. The roar of Hephaestus's Thunderhawk passed overhead accompanied by the sound of heavy bolters.

'Would it be weakness to change the conditions by which we judge victory?' the commander asked.

'It is the nature of war that we must continually revise our expectations and objectives,' said the Librarian. 'It would be weakness to affirm victory simply for quiet contentment, but it would be folly to strive for the unachievable and risk what has been gained. What are you considering?'

'I think that it is a greater duty to contain the orks until Grand Master Azrael arrives with the rest of the Chapter,' said Belial. 'It would be hubris to try to destroy them in a vain demonstration of commitment. While we must have the strength to fight alone, we must not forget that we are a brotherhood. We can be proud of what we achieve but cannot allow pride to master us and drive us to act for the sake of reputation alone.'

Belial took a deep breath, looked at the power plant again and opened up the command channel.

'This is Belial to company. Mission accomplished. Abort phase four. We will not be assaulting the power plant. Maintain positions, fortify defences and destroy any enemy that opportunity presents.'

The landing site belonged to Belial. That was victory enough. All that remained was to keep the orks occupied until the Chapter arrived to sweep them away. If the orks wanted Kadillus, they would have to come and take the landing site back.

The Dark Angels would be waiting.

THE TALE OF TAUNO
Death by Moonlight

THE CRACKLE OF campfires and the aroma of rehydrated protein stew wafted along the defensive line on Koth Ridge. The grass and dirt had been trampled into a hard mat by hundreds of feet, here and there scarred by the tracks of vehicles. The barricades had been rebuilt following the last ork attack, several of them strengthened by plascrete blocks hauled up from ruined buildings in Kadillus Harbour. Nightfowl screeched and squawked to each other beyond the glow of the fires.

Dumping his pack behind the ration-box barricade, Tauno slumped down beside the fire with a yawn.

'Don't get comfy, trooper,' said Sergeant Kaize. He scribbled something on a scrap of paper and passed it to Tauno as he clambered to his feet. 'Take this to Lieutenant Laursor.'

'Yes, sergeant,' said Tauno before setting off.

'You'll need this, moron,' said Kaize, picking up Tauno's lasgun and tossing it to him.

GAV THORPE

He ambled off into the darkness, heading for the
tent housing the command squad. The wind was picking up, bringing a chill with it from further up Kadillus
Island. Tauno squinted at the notes on the paper, but
could make little sense of them. There were some let-
ters and numbers he recognised, and the odd word,
but most of it was a meaningless jumble of symbols. It
was probably nothing important, he thought, as he
crumpled the paper into the pocket of his jacket.

Turning up his collars against the cold, he slung his
lasgun over his shoulder by its strap and thrust his
hands into his trouser pockets to keep them warm. He
heard laughter and chatter from the other squads,
arguing over bets, complaining about the poor food or
swapping friendly insults. One sergeant with drooping
moustaches berated his men for sloppy dress and
other acts of slovenliness. Behind the front line, heavy
weapon crews dozed next to their guns.

Blinking in the bright light, Tauno ducked under the
awning covering the comms equipment given to the
company by the Dark Angels. Behind the trestle tables
laden with consoles and dials, cables snaked into the
darkness to the dish array that the Techmarines had set
up for the company commander. The officer, Lieutenant Laursor, sat on a small canvas-seated stool with
a comm pick-up in hand. His staff milled around him,
as bored as Tauno.

'...pecting the orks to launch an attack to retake the
landing site.' Tauno recognised Colonel Grautz's voice
coming through the comm speaker. 'That said, it is
possible that the orks will make a last, desperate bid
for Kadillus Harbour in an attempt to link up with

their forces in the city. If they do, it's unlikely that they will assault your part of the line, lieutenant, but your company must be ready to provide reinforcements to the officers further to the north.'

'I understand, colonel,' said Laursor.

'Make sure that you do, lieutenant,' said Grautz. 'Also be aware that the Astartes can cope with the level of ork reinforcements at their current level, but the enemy cannot be allowed to increase the power to their teleporter. That means ensuring the relay station between Kadillus Harbour and the East Barrens remains out of their hands. That relay station is your responsibility, Laursor.'

'Yes, colonel,' replied the lieutenant, his voice mustering more enthusiasm than his expression.

'Let me spell it out for you, lieutenant, in case I have not made my point.' Laursor rolled his eyes at his command squad, but his expression grew serious at the colonel's next words. 'If the orks can establish a power link between three geothermal stations, the Astartes commander has told me that there will be an orbital bombardment of those stations. Even if that does not cause a catastrophic eruption to destroy the island, damage will be extreme.'

Hesitating just underneath the awning, Tauno caught the eye of the staff sergeant and pulled the paper from his pocket. The stocky Piscinan nodded and beckoned Tauno further inside.

'Patrol report, Sergeant Maikon,' said Tauno, keeping his voice quiet while Grautz continued to labour his point over the comm. He dropped the scrap of paper into the staff sergeant's proffered hand. 'Short version is that we didn't see nothing, sergeant.'

Tauno rubbed his hands together and blew on his fingertips, darting a glance at a pile of gently steaming meat steaks left on a plate.

'Sit yourself down for a moment, lad, and grab yourself a bite to eat,' the sergeant said with a sympathetic smile.

'Thanks, sergeant,' said Tauno. He pulled his bayonet from his belt and skewered a lump of half-charred meat and sat down on an empty stool next to the staff sergeant. 'What is it?'

'Whitehoof, son,' said Maikon. 'The lieutenant shot it himself earlier today. Found a herd of them by the stream just south of here, having a drink just before dusk.'

'Sergeant Kaize wouldn't let us shoot nothing on patrol,' huffed Tauno. He sank his teeth into the steak, juices dribbling down his chin and onto the front of his jerkin.

'That's 'cause officers make the rules, son, and last I checked you ain't an officer,' said Maikon. His lip curled in distaste. 'You best clean that off your jacket before you get back, or Sergeant Kaize will have you up on watch duty all night too.'

Tauno looked down at the greasy stain and grimaced.

'You got a cloth or something, sergeant?'

Maikon puffed out his cheeks and sighed.

'What's a useless soldier like you doing in the defence force, son?'

'Better'n working the omnitrawlers like me pa and grandpa,' Tauno replied between chews. 'The recruiting sergeant told me I might even get off-world, see other planets, if the Munitterum come for a tithe.'

'Mew-nee-tor-umm, son. Departmento Munitorum. They'd take one look at you and ship you off to the Mechanicus to be made into a servitor. That recruiting sergeant must have known you was hauled in on the last net...'

'It was you, sergeant,' Tauno said. He gulped down the last of the venison and licked his fingers clean. 'You were the one that recruited me.'

Maikon laughed and slapped Tauno on the knee.

'Well, I'm sure I must have seen something in you.' The staff sergeant glanced across the tent as Lieutenant Laursor ended his conversation with Grautz and tossed the pick-up onto the table. 'Best get back to your squad, son.'

'Appreciate it, sergeant,' Tauno said with a wink.

He slipped out from under the canvas roof and sidled back to his squad's rough billet. A few of them were already sound asleep, their deep breaths and gentle snores another part of the background noise. Remembering Maikon's warning, Tauno kept to the shadows until he could pull his guncloth from his pack and wipe away most of the mess on the front of his grey tunic. Approximating something like the appearance of a proper defence trooper, he joined the others, tin mug in hand. He poured himself some nu-char from the pot boiling over the fire and settled down, propping himself up on his pack.

'So, the Space Marines want to blow up Kadillus if the orks break through,' he said.

There was a chorus of surprise and dissent from the others.

'True enough; heard the colonel himself say as much,' Tauno continued.

'They would never do it,' said Lundvir.

'Sure they would,' said Sergeant Kaize. 'What do they really care about us, eh? Letting the orks run wild would be a bad mark against them, don't matter if a few ordinary folks get killed along the way.'

'I think I'd rather get blowed up by the Astartes than taken by the orks,' said Tauno. 'Least if the island goes, it'll be quick.'

'I don't want to be stuck out here if that's going to happen,' said Jurlberg, standing up. 'I've got family in Kadillus Harbour. If this is the end, I'm going back to the city to be with them I love.'

'You are not going anywhere, trooper,' said Kaize. 'You'll bloody well stay here and guard this bloody ridge. Those are our orders.'

Kauninnen stood up next to Lundvir.

'Karl's right, we should be protecting our homes, not stuck out here where nothing's going to happen.'

'Sit down, the pair of you,' growled Kaize. 'If the lieutenant spots you, it'll go badly for you.'

'I'm sure there's others would come with us,' said Lundvir. 'If we get enough of us together, nobody's going to stop us. We got to warn our families, get them off Kadillus!'

Tauno's gaze moved back and forth between the two men and the sergeant. Looking past Kaize, he saw pinpricks of red and yellow in the darkness, about a hundred metres away: the glowing eyes of the Space Marines.

'I think the lieutenant would be the least of your problems if you tries to get away,' said Tauno, sipping his nu-char. He nodded at the Astartes.

'It went all right last time,' said Lundvir. 'We got away from Barrak Gorge, didn't we? We told them we managed to retreat at the last moment and nothing was said.'

'Only because they need us here. And I shouldn't have listened to you then,' said Kaize. 'We're staying put this time.'

Tauno shared his sergeant's feelings; abandoning the power plant had probably been a bad idea. It hadn't seemed such a big deal at the time – there had been plenty of Space Marines to protect the station – but on reflection it left a bitter taste in Tauno's mouth and an uneasy feeling in the pit of his stomach. This time he was determined that if the orks did come he would stay and fight.

Regardless, they had all agreed not to mention it again.

'Keep your voice down,' said Tauno, looking at the Dark Angels. If they discovered the truth of what had happened at Barrak Gorge, there was no telling what they might do. 'You never know who's listening.'

Kauninnen followed Tauno's gaze and laughed harshly.

'Them? Nah, they can't hear us.' With a wordless growl, Kauninnen sat down again. 'You're probably right we'll never get away with it twice.'

'Just shut up about it,' said Kaize. 'There's nothing to worry about. There's been patrols all day and night and not an ork's been seen within ten kilometres. We sit tight here for a couple of days, the rest of the Dark Angels turn up and we can all go home.'

'It's all right for them,' said Kauninnen, voice growing louder with annoyance, still looking at the distant silhouettes of the giant Astartes. 'Tell you what: give me armour like that and I'd be just as brave.'

'I know what you mean,' added Daurin, rolling over on his blanket to look at the men gathered around the fire. He plucked disparagingly at the padded tunic covering his torso. 'They call this armour? My brothers have hauled in raspwhales with thicker skins than this.'

'And what about those bolters, eh?' said Kauninnen. 'Put a hole the size of your gob in an ork.' He stabbed a finger at his lasgun leaning against the wall of boxes. 'These things are junk. Never mind shooting orks, I wouldn't use one of these to find something in a dark room.'

Tauno laughed, but didn't really agree with the others. He'd lingered behind for a few minutes at Barrak Gorge and had seen the Space Marines fighting the greenskins. It had been terrifying, even just watching from a distance; the way they got stuck into those monsters without a moment's hesitation. Even with armour and a bolter, Tauno was pretty sure he wouldn't want to go head-to-head with an ork unless he had a two-hundred-metre head start.

'Yeah, yeah,' Daurin was saying. 'I blame the Imperial Commander. If she wants a defence force that can fight orks, we have to have the proper equipment.'

Tauno could see a large figure approaching through the darkness.

'Shut up,' Tauno hissed.

'I mean, it's all well and good being brave when the enemy can't hurt you, isn't it? I bet them Astartes wouldn't be half as eager to get stuck in if they had this garbage to fight with. What do they care, anyway? They can just leave if they wanted to, while we ain't got no choice. I mean, if things were starting to get really dangerous, they could just up and go, and leave us to do the dying.'

'*Shut up*, Daurin,' Tauno said between gritted teeth.

'What's your problem?' Daurin asked. 'They might have magic eyes and ears, and all them sensors and whatnot, but they can't really hear us all the way over th…'

Daurin trailed off and his eyes widened as he saw the gigantic figure looming through the firelight. Tauno didn't know much about Space Marines, but he had been around them long enough these last few days to recognise the markings of a sergeant.

The Space Marine's dark green armour was polished, edged with reflection from the fire. Yellow eye lenses swept over the squad as Sergeant Kaize scrambled to his feet.

'Can we help you, sir?' said Kaize.

The Astartes stepped into the emplacement and sat back against the wall, boxes crumpling and settling under his weight.

'Constant vigilance is the price of survival,' said the Space Marine. His voice was quiet, edged with the buzz of his helm's vox system. 'In thousands of years, an ork had never set foot upon Piscina before ten days ago. Though you cannot see the enemy at this moment, it does not mean they have gone. My commander has reported no significant counter-attack against his forces holding the landing site; that means that the orks are somewhere else.'

The sergeant's helm hid all expression, but the way his eye lenses lingered on the squad made Tauno uneasy.

'The orks that were allowed to capture Barrak Gorge are unaccounted for,' said the Space Marine. Though he detected no accusation in the statement, Tauno cringed with guilt. 'Our patrols sweep the wilderness for them, but they have not been found. Do not think that you are safe from attack.'

'So you think that orks will attack here?' said Daurin, sitting up. His rebelliousness seemed to have evaporated as he flicked a nervous glance towards his squad-mates.

'It is a possibility,' said the sergeant. 'It is your duty to stand ready in case they do.'

Kauninnen crossed his arms defiantly, though there was a quiver in his voice when he spoke.

'Why are the Dark Angels waiting here with us? Why don't you hunt down the rest of the orks?'

The sergeant slowly turned his head to stare at Kauninnen.

'We all have our orders, trooper,' said the Space Marine. 'A better question would be to ask why you are not hunting the orks. As you have agreed, it is your homes that need defending. Perhaps the Piscinans would prefer that my brothers and I left them to fight this war by themselves?'

'I wasn't being ungrateful,' stammered Kauninnen. 'I mean…'

The Space Marine's gaze did not move as the soldier trailed into quiet.

'You said, "They can just leave if they wanted to, while we ain't got no choice. I mean, if things were starting to get really dangerous, they could just up and go, and leave us to do the dying," just a minute ago.'

Kauninnen gulped as the Space Marine threw his words back at him. 'That you would make such an accusation betrays your lack of understanding of what it is to be an Astartes.'

The sergeant stood. Tauno craned his neck to follow the Space Marine as he leaned forwards and plucked Kauninnen's lasgun from his weak grip. The Space Marine looked at it and handed it back a moment later.

'Your weapons are inferior because better would be wasted on you,' said the sergeant. 'It takes as much effort to create one round for my bolt pistol as it does a whole lasgun. Would you entrust that one shot to such a poor marksman?'

He bent forwards, armour creaking, mouth-grille a short distance from Kauninnen's face.

'My armour is many thousands of years old, from before the Dark Angels came to Piscina.' The Space Marine's voice was harsher, a tone of anger in his words. 'Would you have it dishonoured by a wearer that flees from battle? Would you entrust the days of labour that go into its maintenance to a warrior that thinks only of protecting himself?'

Straightening, the sergeant looked at the others, who flinched as his gaze passed over them. Only Tauno managed to meet that glowing stare, and with much effort.

'There is a selfishness in men to protect what is theirs alone,' the sergeant continued. 'It is a short-sighted belief; for all a man is, he owes to the Emperor. The Astartes swear oaths to be the protectors of the Emperor's realm and His servants, beyond any personal desire or ambition. We have the armour and the weapons you desire because we are the few who are worthy of them. Such riches would be squandered on lesser men; frail, frightened men like you.'

'That's a bit harsh,' mumbled Kaize. 'We're doing the best we can.'

'Are you?' the Space Marine snarled, his words cutting into Tauno's conscience. 'Which of you would leave this world, travel across the galaxy and lay down his life for the home of a family he had never met?'

The squad exchanged glances; nobody said a word.

'Which of you would place yourself directly in danger, to save the lives of others? And do this not just once, on a spur of heroism, unthinking, but for a whole life, time after time, in full knowledge that one day you *will* die, and it will be a painful, bloody death. Which of you would not only do this thing, but embrace the sacrifice of the self it entails, not just dedicating one's death to the Emperor, but one's whole existence?' The Space Marine's voice softened. 'You cannot answer these questions, and thus you cannot know what it is to be Astartes.'

The troopers were speechless: Kaize hung his head in shame while Daurin stared out into the darkness, eyes glistening. The Space Marine turned away. Tauno jumped up and called after him as he left the emplacement.

'Excuse me, sir? There was a Scout-sergeant. He spoke to me a few days ago, asked my name. I haven't seen him since, and I never learnt his name. Come to that, what are you called?'

The Astartes sergeant swung back to the squad.

'I am Sergeant Ophrael of the Third Company. The sergeant you speak of was called Naaman; he proved many of us wrong and you owe your continued survival to his bravery and dedication.'

'Was called? So, he's dead?'

Ophrael nodded slowly.

'Like many of my battle-brothers, he gave his life for the protection of your world. He will be remembered and honoured. He died alone, amidst a sea of enemies. Master Belial recovered his body a few hours ago. What did he say to you?'

'He told me to do my duty, and to remember that the Emperor watches us.'

The sergeant stepped up, towering over Tauno, but his voice was gentle – as gentle as it could be with its metallic, clipped tone.

'Wise words. Do not forget them again, nor the warrior that spoke them to you.'

'I won't, sergeant.'

'You can never be Astartes, but you can still be a good soldier. Remember what you...'

Ophrael stopped and straightened, head cocked to one side. Tauno felt a buzzing across his skin: the Space Marine's comm activating. The sergeant turned towards the east, his pale yellow eyes shifting to a bright red. Tauno felt nervous at the sudden change. The Space Marine's size had been intimidating from the moment he had walked over, but now there was something else about his demeanour that caused Tauno to shrink away; Ophrael's posture, the tilt of his head, the balling of his fists, all pointed towards a sudden unleashing of energy, like the rev of an engine or the whine of a power cell being slipped into a lasgun.

'Return to your squad, trooper,' said Ophrael. His tone was businesslike, abrupt. *'Bellum instantium.* Ready your weapons. The orks are coming.'

THE DEFENCE LINE was in tumult; sergeants shouted, troopers ran back and forth, ammunition boxes were broken open and weapons given final checks. All through the Free Militia one question was being asked: where were the orks?

The Dark Angels had seen something with their infra-sight and were convinced an ork force was moving up the ridge. Tauno and the others peered into the dark but could see nothing.

'Hush up!' Kaize told them. 'Perhaps we can hear something. Orks aren't the quietest, are they?'

The squad fell into silence and Tauno strained to hear anything; the only sound was the wind across the rocks.

A rocket screamed out from the Devastators to the left. It exploded about four hundred metres down the ridge. In the flash of light, Tauno saw bodies being flung into the air and a mob of bestial faces.

'There!' he shouted. He levelled his lasgun in the direction of the blast and opened fire, sending a hail of blue las-bolts into the night.

The others joined him, shooting at shadows, until Kaize bellowed at them to cease fire.

'Save your power packs,' said the sergeant. 'Wait until you see something before you shoot.'

The Devastators were unleashing the full fury of their

weapons: missiles streaked into the gloom while the squad's two heavy bolters split the air with thudding bursts, rounds cutting the night with flickering propellant trails.

'To the right!' said Hanaumman.

Tauno switched his view and laid his lasgun on the top of the barricade. The light of two moons broke through open patches in the cloud and a little way down the ridge he saw hunched bodies picking their way through the rocks. He sighted on one of the dark shapes and pulled the trigger. He saw the bolt of laser energy flash down the slope and hit, but the ork did not fall.

The sparkle of muzzle flare split the night. An instant later, bullets were rattling against the crate wall. Tauno flinched, ducking back into cover. He felt a hand grab the scruff of his jerkin. Sergeant Kaize hauled him back to the firing position.

'Hiding ain't going to make them go away, is it?' said the sergeant. 'You want to stay safe? Shoot the bastards!'

All along the line squads were firing. A couple of brave souls ventured down the ridge line and hurled illumination flares. The patches of guttering red light revealed even more orks; the two troopers who had made the foray were cut down in a hail of fire as they sprinted back towards the defences.

'Come on, come on,' Tauno whispered to himself. The orks were using the undulating ground to work around to the squad's right.

'Sergeant, they're getting too close,' said Kauninnen. 'We should pull back.'

'No chance, trooper,' replied Kaize. 'Vinnaman! Get that flamer over to the right. Torch that stand of bushes. Give covering fire!'

Trooper Vinnaman was propelled out of the emplacement by Kaize's shove. Tauno added his lasfire to the rest of the squad's, firing past the slowly advancing flamer-man. When he was just about in range, Vinnaman opened fire, emptying the tank of his weapon. The dried branches of the bushes erupted as yellow fire bathed the slope. Orks thrashed in the inferno; some fell, many retreated, patting frantically at burning clothes and patches of lighted fuel sticking to their bodies.

The burning bushes gave the squad more light to see by and Tauno was able to pick his targets more clearly. He shot an ork in the arm as it lumbered from behind one boulder to the next. The hit caused it to drop its pistol. Stumbling back into the open to retrieve the weapon, the alien was met by another blast from Tauno's lasgun. The shot hit the ork square in the chest. Glaring back at the troopers, the ork snatched up its pistol and fired back, oblivious to the smoking hole in its padded armour.

Tauno gritted his teeth as more bullets whirred past, missed his next shot, but scored another hit with the following one. Finally the ork went down, its leg wounded. Tauno shook his head in disbelief as he saw the ork dragging itself away through the long grass. He fired twice more, a growl in his throat, until the ork stopped moving.

Lausso shouted in pain and stumbled back from the barricade, blood streaming from his left shoulder.

Tauno turned to help him but was pushed back to the wall by Kaize.

'Keep shooting, I'll sort him out,' said the sergeant.

The next few minutes blurred into a harrowing experience of feral faces lit by las-bolts and dancing flames, the crack and whistle of bullets flying around answered by the zip of the lasguns. At one point the orks came close enough to throw stick grenades into the emplacement to the squad's right. Tauno watched in horror as troopers were flung across the barricade by the detonations.

'Direct your fire to the south!'

Lieutenant Laursor strode along behind the defence line, waving his chainsword at the orks, his command squad tailing him. The bark of autocannons added to the cacophony and tracer shells tore through the blackness from higher up the slope.

'Look at that!' said Kauninnen.

The trooper pointed north. The Dark Angels Assault squad that had been left to guard the ridge leapt forwards, jump pack jets burning with bright blue flame. Plasma flickered from a couple of pistols as they descended on a group of orks a few dozen metres from the line. Tauno watched the ensuing fight as he ejected the spent power pack from his lasgun and fumbled home a fresh charge.

The trooper winced as he saw pistols blazing, blades and chainblades swinging. It looked a complete mess, but the Assault Marines carved into the larger body of orks with purpose, seeking out their towering leader. The mob of greenskins swirled around them, hacking and firing.

'Don't worry about them, lad.' Tauno looked over his shoulder and found Staff Sergeant Maikon crouched in the emplacement. The command squad veteran pointed south. 'Worry about them.'

Following up their grenade attack, the orks had swarmed from cover and were trying to get into the emplacement. The few survivors of the squad within desperately swung their lasguns like clubs, battering at the orks as they clambered over the barricade. Two of them fell to the surging greenskins; the other two turned and ran, dropping their lasguns in their haste to get away.

No sooner had the orks poured over the wall of boxes and dirt-filled sacks, then they were engulfed in a wall of fire from both sides. Tauno added his own shots to the volleys; cramped by the emplacement's walls, the orks were a hard target to miss, even if only a few of Tauno's shots did any serious damage.

Tauno ducked involuntarily as a missile streaked over his head. It exploded in the heart of the onrushing orks, scything down half a dozen with shrapnel. Heavy bolt-rounds whickered through the air a few metres from the Piscinans, cutting down the surviving greenskins. Another missile streaked along the ridge from the Space Marine Devastators, passing almost within reach of Tauno before it detonated twenty metres further on, blowing apart even more orks.

'Emperor's fury, I thought they were going to hit us,' gasped Kaize, slumping back against the barricade, eyes fearful.

'Show a little faith, sergeant,' said Maikon. The staff

sergeant stood up and looked south. 'Looks like that attack has been dealt with.'

Tauno scanned the ridgeside to the right. There were a few orks still alive, skulking back down the slope, some limping along. He fired a few more shots at them to hurry the orks on their way.

'And don't come back!' Lisskarin shouted after the retreating greenskins. 'We got more where that came from!'

Tauno laughed with relief. His first proper battle with orks, and he had survived. His mood swiftly changed, though.

'Sergeant Maikon, redress the squads,' said Lieutenant Laursor. 'Astartes report more infantry coming, this time with vehicle support. Rasmussen! Run with these coordinates to the mortar crews and tell them to lay on a heavy bomb.'

The lieutenant showed none of his earlier indifference. His eyes gleamed in the glow of the fires. Tauno thought Laursor looked like he was enjoying himself; truly officers were a different species.

It wasn't long before the troopers could hear the deep growl of ork engines. The smoke from the guttering fires was tainted with the oily stench of exhaust fumes. Motors revved in the darkness, a mechanical war-cry every bit as unnerving as the howls of the orks that had come before.

Tauno looked at his lasgun and pictured the little damage it had done to the orks. Against anything tougher, it was useless.

'Sergeant, should we move a bit closer to the heavy weapons squads?' he suggested. 'You know, to give them some protection.'

'Nice try, Tavallinen,' laughed Kaize. 'We're staying right here. My advice is to shoot at the green bits.'

There was a ripple of flashes several hundred metres down the ridge. Half a second later, Tauno heard the deep retorts of big guns. Above, shells whined as they plunged downwards.

'Incoming!' Tauno bellowed, hurling himself to the base of the barricade.

The troopers hit the ground a moment after, as the two shells exploded some way behind the defensive line. From his prone position, Tauno found himself looking into the dead eyes of Lausso. The shadows from the dying light of the fire made the trooper's face appear to move, grimacing at his fate. Tauno shuddered and looked away.

'Get up,' said Sergeant Kaize, kicking the men back to their feet.

As he set his lasgun back on the barricade, Tauno saw more flashes of field guns in the distance, perhaps a kilometre northwards up the line. The orks weren't holding back, that was for sure.

This time the shells fell around the Devastators. The Space Marines ignored the dirt and flame exploding around them and continued to fire, picking out targets only they could see.

'Look lively!' The call came from Staff Sergeant Maikon. 'Maintain fire discipline. Hold the line.'

Maikon gestured for Kaize to join him. Tauno kept one eye down the ridge as he listened in on what was said.

'The lieutenant's just received word from Colonel Grautz,' Maikon said. 'The orks are trying to push out of Kadillus Harbour to link up. Although the whole line has been attacked, it looks like the greatest numbers are here. The colonel thinks the orks are making a bid for the relay station. Grautz is sending an armoured column, it'll be here just after dawn. We have to hold, no matter the cost.'

'Why don't we fall back and protect the relay station?' asked Kaize.

'Better defensive position here, Saul,' said Maikon. 'We fight and die on Koth Ridge.'

Kaize nodded and rejoined the squad as Maikon walked on to talk to the other sergeants.

'Looks like the worst of it will be coming our way,' he told them. 'This is it, boys. This is where you get to defend your homes.'

Tauno remembered what the colonel had told Laursor: if the orks linked up, the Space Marines would bombard Kadillus rather than let it fall into enemy hands. He looked at the Space Marines along the ridge – now firing their bolters as well as their heavy weapons – and wondered if they would be withdrawn before that happened.

He dismissed the question. If what Sergeant Ophrael had said was true, the orks would only break through when the last Space Marine on the ridge was dead. It gave cold comfort to Tauno; he realised that he was far more likely to die before the last of the Astartes.

'Pay attention,' snarled Kaize, cuffing Tauno round the back of his head. 'Targets to the front!'

Snapping back to the immediate threat to his continued survival, Tauno sighted down his lasgun. The roar of engines was everywhere, to the left and right. He saw orks on massive bikes hurtling up the ridge straight at him. He fired vainly along with the others, most of their las-bolts missing the fast-moving bikers or harmlessly striking the heavy machines. A few lucky shots hit one rider, sending him crashing from his ride, the half-tracked bike careening on for a few metres before toppling into a crack in the volcanic rock.

Slightly ahead of them, the Assault Marines were bounding back up the ridge. The bikers opened fire, unleashing a storm of bullets, tracer rounds and shells from their mishmash of cannons and guns. Tauno had difficulty seeing what happened; he saw one of the Space Marines land badly, his leg wounded mid-jump. The Astartes toppled to one side, overbalanced by his jump pack. More rounds crashed into the squad as the Space Marines formed up around their fallen battle-brother.

Tauno opened fire at the bikes closing in on the Assault Marines, his finger tapping the trigger over and over, sending a hail of las-bolts into the orks. The flashes of energy zipping down the hillside lit the entire ridge, searing blurred lines across Tauno's vision.

Mortar bombs erupted, lascannon blasts burned through the dark to ignite fuel tanks, autocannon shells screamed and heavy bolters thundered. Tauno could barely hear the words of those around him as they shouted in fright or hurled abuse at the onrushing greenskins. He realised he was shouting too, a meaningless torrent of insults and curses.

Two remaining bikers slammed their machines

directly into the Assault Marines; the orks' guns were still blazing as they hacked wildly with fearsome blades. One Space Marine was hurled from his feet by the impact, but the bike fared little better, flipping and tumbling across the rock from the crash. The Space Marine slowly rose to his feet; the ork biker did not.

For all the fury of the troopers' fire, the orks were still advancing, no more than a hundred metres away. More shells exploded around the Piscinans and bullets thudded into the barricades. Ork walkers – four-armed Dreadnoughts that made even the largest greenskins look small – stomped alongside the infantry, hurling rockets and flares of explosive energy.

A Space Marine land speeder darted out of the night, skimming just above the ground. The rip of its assault cannon cut through the other noises of war, the speeder illuminated by several seconds of fire. A swathe of orks fell to the attack run, gunned down by hundreds of rounds. The gunner strafed left and right with his heavy bolter, firing short bursts, every salvo ripping apart an ork warrior.

It was a chaos of flashing light and deafening sound. Tauno tried to block it all out. He exchanged his charge pack again and kept firing, pouring shot after shot into the greenskins. Maybe one in three found his intended target; of those, few stopped the ork they hit.

Slowed by the biker attack, the Assault Marines were in danger of being swamped by the tide of green aliens pouring up the ridge. Tauno did what little he could: firing endlessly into the mass of orks closing with the Space Marines.

'By the Holy Throne!' Kauninnen gasped next to Tauno.

The other trooper was looking further north. Tauno dragged his eyes away from the enemy to see what had prompted such a reaction.

A lone figure clad in power armour and blue robes strode purposefully towards the orks. In one hand he fired a bolt pistol with metronomic repetition; in the other he carried an ornately carved staff tipped with a winged skull decoration. A nimbus of power surrounded the Space Marine, a swirling aura of black and red.

White spears of energy danced from the staff as the Librarian pointed it at an ork buggy racing in his direction. Lightning leapt, arcing across the gap to engulf the vehicle, crawling over the machine and its crew. Something caught fire and a moment later the buggy was a ball of flame rolling back down the ridge. The Librarian advanced further, bolts of energy shrieking from his staff, scouring the orks from moss-covered ruins.

Tauno had little time to wonder at the terrifying powers he was witnessing. The orks had reached the Devastators and a vicious melee was unfolding. With his power fist glowing, Sergeant Ophrael was leading the defence, smashing down any greenskin that tried to clamber over the barricade; others in the squad gunned down the orks with their bolters and slashed at them with combat knives.

For all that the ork dead were piling up by the Dark Angels' barricade, there were too many to be held back. One or two greenskins managed to get inside the emplacement while others were swamping the Space Marines to either side.

The sight of the beset Space Marines filled Tauno with panic. If the Astartes fell, what chance did the rest of them have? He glanced around. There was a lull in the fighting close at hand – the heavy weapons not far behind him had taken a heavy toll and the orks were funnelling northwards, away from their deadly fire.

If ever there was a time to get out alive, this was it.

A tap on Tauno's shoulder attracted his attention: it was Daurin. He flicked a glance behind Tauno. The trooper turned and saw Sergeant Kaize face-down sprawled in the dirt, half his head missing.

'Come on, we've done the best we can,' said Daurin.

Tauno quickly looked around: Lieutenant Laursor was back in his command tent, talking on the vox-caster. There was no sign of Maikon. The defence trooper took in the other squads around him, many of them numbering only a handful of survivors. He looked back at the Devastators, punching and hacking at the middle of a growing number of orks. When they fell, the greenskins would be able to sweep along the line and break out westwards; any line of retreat would be cut off.

He saw Sergeant Ophrael punching his power fist through the skull of an ork. Desperation filled Tauno. He wanted to run so badly, to get back to Kadillus Harbour and see his father again. He had been an idiot to join up.

But he had joined up. He had sworn oaths on big

books full of words he did not understand, but that promise he understood well enough. It was a promise to keep his father and grandfather safe. A promise just the same as the Space Marines had made: to lay down his life in defence of the Imperium.

'We have to do our duty,' he said, his voice flat, as if spoken by someone else.

'What?' said Daurin. 'Are you touched?'

Something inside Tauno snapped.

'The Emperor is watching us!' he screamed. 'He is judging us right now!'

Tauno snatched the bayonet from his belt and broke into a run, vaulting over the barricade. His fingers fumbled with the blade as he sprinted, but he slotted the bayonet onto its lug at the fourth attempt.

He heard panting and realised it was him. But there was someone else with him. He glanced over his shoulder and saw Laisko and Kauninnen. A few metres behind them, the others followed, Daurin included.

'No running away this time, eh?' gasped Laisko.

Tauno gritted his teeth and pumped his arms and legs, charging headlong at the orks fighting the Space Marines. He focussed his attention on the aliens, picturing what would happen to his family in Kadillus Harbour if the orks won this battle.

'For Kadillus! For Piscina!' The words bellowed from his mouth unbidden, but his next shout he knew was his, boiling up from the guilt and the horror and the fear that swirled in the pit of his stomach. It was the only thing he could say that made any sense of what he was doing. 'For the Emperor!'

Some of the orks turned to face the onrushing troopers, startled by the sudden attack. Terror gripped Tauno as he looked at their horrid fanged faces, corded muscles and beady, fury-filled red eyes. Some of them looked like they were laughing. Tauno's dread fuelled his rage further and he sprinted harder, screeching a wordless cry.

He speared his bayonet into the chest of the closest ork, his momentum sending the creature crashing backwards. Ripping out the blade, he plunged it again, and again, and again, screaming all the while. Something smashed into the back of his head and he slashed out wildly, the tip of his bayonet cutting across an ork's face.

Dazed, Tauno staggered back a step and the others rushed past him, each crying out their own anger and fear. He felt blood trickling down the back of his neck, and wondered idly for a moment if he would be in trouble for getting another stain on his uniform. Shaking off his dizziness, he threw himself back into the melee, stabbing and lashing out at anything with green skin, not caring whether his blows landed or not.

Daurin collapsed in front of him, a cleaver wedged into his forehead. As the ork struggled to free its weapon from the skull of Tauno's friend, the trooper rammed his bayonet into its face, punching through its eye into its brain. He remembered his training and gave his lasgun a twist before wrenching the bayonet free.

'What am I doing?' he muttered to himself, the surge of energy that had propelled him to the fight evaporating as the ork's body fell onto Daurin. 'Emperor protect me!'

Lundvir fell next, his head blown apart by a pistol shot under his chin. Tauno acted on reflex, bringing up his rifle to stop a blade that would have lopped off his arm. The lasgun buckled under the force of the blow and almost fell from Tauno's hands. To his left, Kauninnen screamed in pain and slumped sideways, his leg flopping away with a life of its own. Tauno fended away another attack but in doing so tripped over Lundvir's corpse.

Winded by the fall, Tauno stared up numbly as a greenskin battered its way past Laurssen and loomed over him. He pointed his lasgun at the alien's leering face and pulled the trigger.

Nothing happened.

Grunting, the ork kicked away Tauno's weapon and pointed a pistol at the trooper's chest. In a moment, Tauno could see everything with startling clarity: the drool dripping from the ork's fangs, the strange glyph carved into the metal casing of the bulky pistol, the dirty claw of the finger tightening on the trigger.

Something towering and dark blocked Tauno's view. He saw a blaze of blue energy and heard crackling noises. Blood splashed onto his boots. The headless body of an ork slumped into the dirt.

Sergeant Ophrael stepped away, tossing aside the remnants of the ork's head with his power fist. Tauno saw blood spitting and steaming from the energy-wreathed glove. The red eyes glowing in the faceless mask of the Space Marine sergeant's helmet were more frightening than anything Tauno had seen in the orks. He lay rigid with fear, paralysed by his close call with death.

'On your feet,' said the Space Marine.

Ophrael turned and caught a whirring chainblade on the side of his power fist. His bolt pistol barked once and the ork's chest disappeared in a bloody explosion.

'I have no weapon, sir,' Tauno said, his voice hoarse and weak.

Tauno winced as an ork blade crashed against Ophrael's shoulder pad. The Space Marine turned with the blow and smashed his helmet into the alien's face as it stumbled forwards. Fingers stretched, the sergeant plunged his power glove into the creature's gut. Fat and blood steamed as Ophrael ripped out the ork's innards.

'Take this,' said the sergeant, holding out his bolt pistol. 'Five rounds left. Make every bolt count.'

Tauno pushed himself to his feet and grabbed the weapon. He had to snatch it with both hands, the weight too much for one arm.

'Thank you, sir,' he said, but Ophrael had already turned to other matters and was wading into the orks outside the emplacement, his power fist crushing and smashing with relentless ferocity.

Tauno tentatively raised the bolt pistol, arms quivering. He saw an ork stepping in behind one of the Space Marines, a jagged blade ready to strike, and pulled the trigger with a wince. There was a kick from the weapon as the bolt's firing charge sent the projectile out of the barrel, but nothing more than the autoguns he had fired in training. A split-second later, the bolt no more than two or three metres away, the internal propellant kicked in with a crack that set Tauno's teeth on edge, its brief flare making him squint.

Straight and true, the accelerating bolt hit the ork just below the left shoulder blade. Skin and flesh buckled as the projectile punched in; a moment later the mass-reactive warhead detonated, ripping a hole the size of Tauno's head in the ork's back, splitting the shoulder blade from one end to the other.

The ork dropped sideways and smashed face-first into the dirt.

Tauno laughed.

'Take that, you green bastard!'

Four shots left, he reminded himself. Be an Astartes; make every shot count.

The brutal hack-and-slash moved a few metres further down the slope as the Space Marines countered the ork charge and pushed back. Still holding the pistol in both hands, he swung to his right, catching movement in the corner of his eye. A couple of orks had broken away from the press of fighting and were heading straight for him. Aim wobbling with fear and the weight of the bolt pistol, Tauno fired again.

The bolt hit the ork in the gut with another spray of blood and tissue, but the alien kept advancing. It returned fire, spraying bullets just past Tauno, one of the rounds ripping a burning wound across his shoulder. The trooper fired again, ignoring the sudden pain, holding his breath, every muscle in his body clenched with fear.

The bolt took the ork clean between the eyes, blowing its head apart. Its companion lumbered into a run, ripping a stick grenade from its belt. Even as it hooked the grenade's ring over a tusk to pull it free, a salvo of three bolts screamed in from Tauno's left, forming a neat triangle of detonations in the ork's chest.

Tauno glanced across and saw one of the Devastator Marines, one foot up on the remnants of the barricade, smoke drifting from the muzzle of his bolter. The Space Marine raised his weapon in salute and turned back to the others fighting down the slope.

Someone else staggered out of the darkness. Tauno did not recognise him at first, half his face swathed with blood from a cut across his forehead. The moustaches gave it away as the man limped into the light of the guttering fires.

'Sergeant Maikon!'

The staff sergeant almost fell against Tauno, one arm draping across the trooper's shoulders.

'Got yourself a pretty little pistol there, lad,' said Maikon. 'Saw what you did just now. You should be proud. I think you've done enough for now.'

'I still have two rounds left, sergeant,' protested Tauno.

'Save 'em for later,' said Maikon. 'Let's get you looked at.'

Now that the sergeant mentioned Tauno's injuries, he became aware of the throbbing pain in his head and the harsh cut across his arm. Letting one arm drop with the weight of the bolt pistol, he reached up to the back of his head with the other. He took a sharp intake of breath at his own touch. He could feel pieces of bone moving around in the wetness of the blood.

He felt faint and Maikon shifted his weight, helping the trooper to stay on his feet.

'How bad is it sergeant?' Tauno asked. 'Am I going to die?'

'I reckon you will need to wear a hat to catch the ladies' eyes, because you're going to have the Emperor's own bald spot to cover up; but I reckon you'll be all right.'

Tauno was feeling quite nauseated now. He swallowed hard to stop himself from throwing up.

'I'd like to sit down, sergeant, but we should get back to the fighting.'

'You need to pay more attention, lad.'

Maikon helped Tauno over to a rock and lowered him down gently to rest against it. From here, Tauno could see the glow of dawn in the far distance. The ground was trembling under his backside and he wondered if he was imagining it. But the smell of fumes and the rumbling of engines were unmistakable.

Lolling his head to the north, he saw grey-painted tanks cresting the ridge, their main guns booming. Shells ripped through the advancing orks while lascannons and heavy bolters spat death in the pre-dawn twilight. Transports were disgorging dozens of Free Militia onto Koth Ridge. Everywhere Tauno looked the orks were falling back from the fury of the Piscinan counter-attack.

He wondered why he hadn't noticed them before; he had been quite busy, he realised.

'Have we won, sergeant?' he asked.

'Yes, trooper, we've won the battle.'

The staff sergeant looked down the ridge and Tauno followed his gaze. All along the ridgeline, the surviving defence troopers were slumping to the ground in exhaustion, patting each other on the back, drinking

from canteens or tending to the many corpses that littered the slope.

A transport slewed to a halt not far from Tauno and
the upper hatch popped open. Colonel Grautz
emerged and surveyed the scene with a pair of magnoculars. Satisfied with what he saw, he hung the
magnoculars around his neck and looked down at the
troopers gathering around.

'A glorious fight, men!' the colonel said. 'You have
the greatest thanks from Imperial Commander Sou-
san. I am sure that each of you will be praised and
rewarded highly for your efforts here and over the last
few days. Though we cannot be complacent, it is fair
to say that the ork threat to Piscina has been defeated.
The Dark Angels will be here soon to help us clear out
the rest. Time for a couple of days' recuperation for
you all. Well done for winning the war!'

The transport moved on, heading after the line of
tanks. Ahead of them the Space Marines were pushing
forwards, harrying the orks as they fled from the
armoured vehicles.

'You know who really won this war?' Tauno said.
Maikon nodded, and pulled his canteen from his belt.
He raised it in toast to the dark-green-armoured
figures continuing their relentless fight.

'Emperor bless the Astartes,' murmured Tauno.

THE SWISH OF the fan overhead was the only sound
Tauno could hear. He lay with his eyes closed, tucked
up tight in the blanket, the infirmary bed solid and
supportive beneath him. After the nightmare of Koth
Ridge, the quiet and solitude were a blessing from the

Emperor Himself; almost literally, as he was being
tended to by sisters of the Order Hospitaller.

Footsteps slapped on the tiled floor, their pace mea-
sured, the gap too long for a normal man's tread: the
footsteps of a Space Marine.

Tauno opened his eyes and sat up. Sergeant Ophrael
ducked his bulky frame through the doorway. He was
dressed in a heavy, sleeveless robe of dark green, but
out of his armour he was no less impressive, a mass of
tanned flesh, muscle and cord-like veins. He had a
surprisingly young-looking face, square-jawed with
close-cropped blond hair and penetrating green eyes.
The Space Marine strode up the ward, the curious buzz
of the other patients surrounding him.

Tauno sighed.

'I knew it was too good to be true,' he said to
Ophrael, pushing back the blanket to sit up. 'I have to
go back to the fighting, don't I?'

'One day,' replied the Space Marine, pulling the
blanket back into place. 'Orks are notorious for being
difficult to eradicate. The defence force will have more
to do than ceremonial parades for years to come, I am
sure. That is not why I am here.'

'Oh?'

The Space Marine looked a little awkward as he
reached out and opened his fist. In his palm lay a
small chunk of something; it was a few centimetres
across, of a light grey material, blackened on one side.

'This is for you,' said Ophrael. He passed the object
to Tauno, who took it gingerly.

'What is it?' asked the trooper.

'I told Master Belial of what happened during the

392

second defence of Koth Ridge. He was moved by your actions and felt it was important that the Dark Angels recognise your bravery and your dedication. We have no military title or medal suitable for non-Astartes, but there is a term we have for men who have served the Chapter well. You may call yourself a Son of Caliban.'

'Thank you,' said Tauno, taken aback but still confused. 'And this is?'

Ophrael smiled, but it was a sad smile.

'A Son of Caliban gets no physical reward, but I thought that you might like this.' The Astartes closed Tauno's hand around the object, the action surprisingly delicate for his massive fingers. 'It is a piece of Sergeant Naaman's armour. I see that in you, his example to us all lived on. Mount it in gold, put it on a shelf, lock it in a vault; it is yours to do with as you wish. Simply remember what it is and the cost it carries.'

Tauno had to blink back tears and his voice was almost a sob as he thought of the Space Marine who had spoken to him once to ask his name; and, amongst many others, given his life for every person on Piscina.

'Do your duty and fight as if the Emperor Himself watches you...'

THE TALE OF BELIAL
Aftermath

STORM CLOUDS SWATHED the heights of Kadillus, fierce rain lashing down upon the rocks, a gale bending the stunted trees. Rivulets of water gushed between the rocks of Barrak Gorge, sending broken branches and small rocks tumbling down the defile. The downpour was a steady drum on the hull of the Rhino as it slewed to a stop in the mud.

Belial took his storm bolter from the weapons rack as the ramp lowered. He followed his command squad out into the gorge, booted feet sinking into the mire, his robe spattered with splashing mud as the other Dark Angels squads formed up around their commander.

'Enemy signals confined to the power station, brother-captain,' Hephaestus reported from the gunship overhead. A flash of lightning broke the gloom, followed quickly by a crack of thunder. 'Unable to determine number, interference from the geothermal station blocking surveyor sweeps. Impossible to engage at the current time. Atmospheric conditions worsening.'

'Confirm, brother,' replied Belial. 'Return to North-port. There is no advantage in risking our last Thunderhawk here.'

'Acknowledge. Returning to Northport.'

The Space Marine squads fanned out across the gorge, taking up positions amongst the rocks and ruins, weapons trained on the power station ahead. A Predator trundled between the boulders, turret playing left and right as the gunner searched for the enemy. Belial magnified his autosenses and scanned the mine head and station, looking for the orks. Here and there a thermal signature registered, but there were no clear targets.

'*Bellum vigilus et decorus operandi.*' Belial advanced slowly, waving the three Tactical squads forwards, cov-ered by the guns of the Devastators and Predator.

The water sluicing down the gulley had piled bodies against the rocks: human and alien, heaped together without distinction. Belial spared the mangled corpses the slightest glance as he strode carefully amongst the debris of battle.

The Dark Angels had advanced to within two hun-dred metres of the geothermal station when the orks opened fire.

Energy blasts from looted lascannons speared down the gorge while a hail of bullets rattled from stone and plascrete. One lascannon shot scored a welt across the hull of the Predator, which returned fire immediately, lancing the station with its own lascannons, its heavy bolters erupting with a furious salvo. The Devastators added their own fusillade to the fire, bolts and plasma blasts streaking through the rain.

'Secure the perimeter, full charge!' roared Belial, breaking into a run.

The commander and his squad pounded up the slope, sparing no time to fire. He hurdled the remnants of a barricade that had been built by the Free Militia, crushing a body as he landed. Cowed by the ferocious supporting fire, the orks were driven into cover, rattling off sporadic and ineffectual bursts as the Dark Angels swiftly closed across the open ground.

Slowing as he neared the sprawling mass of generators and transformers, Belial spied a group of orks on a gantry above him. He stopped and brought up his storm bolter, its targeter linking to his autosenses as he placed his finger on the trigger. Seven target reticules sprang into view a moment before he opened fire. The bolts ripped through the thin wall of corrugated metal protecting the greenskins, as fire from the rest of his squad rattled between the steel beams and punched through rockcrete bricks.

Ruined ork bodies toppled from the walkway onto the ferrocrete apron. To the left and right, the sound of more bolter fire echoed from the blocky substations. The comm crackled with reports from the squad leaders.

An explosion just ahead drew Belial's attention. By its pitch, he identified it as the detonation of an ork grenade. He broke into a loping run, drawing his power sword.

'Be alert for mines and traps, brothers,' came a

warning from Sergeant Lemael. 'Danger minimal.'

Belial ran straight into a mob of orks attempting to outflank the squads to his left by cutting between two arcing generator coils. He fell upon them with a roar, storm bolter spewing rounds. Startled, the orks turned to face the company commander, their weapons spraying bullets wildly around him. A plasma blast incinerated one of the greenskins in a flash of pale blue energy a moment before Belial was amongst them, power sword hacking and slashing. He dashed in the skull of a greenskin with the butt of his storm bolter and chopped the leg from another with his glowing blade. Something crashed against his back-pack and he turned to confront an ork raising a double-handed cleaver for another blow. Charon's force staff smashed into the greenskin's chest with an eruption of psychic energy. The ork flew backwards into an energy relay, sparks exploding from its juddering body.

With the perimeter breached, the Dark Angels pressed on to the central buildings, but met little resistance. The few orks they encountered were poorly armed and easily overcome. Within five minutes of the assault beginning, the Barrak Gorge geothermal station was in the hands of the Dark Angels.

While the other squads conducted a secondary sweep to ensure all enemies had been located, Belial led his command squad out of the power plant. With the fighting over, he had time to analyse what had happened here. Amongst the many dead Free Militia he saw knots of dark green armour.

'Check on our fallen brothers, Nestor,' he said. 'It has

been three days, but there may still be survivors.'

The Apothecary headed off as Belial continued to appraise the bloody evidence of the first battle.

'A token garrison, nothing more,' said Charon. He pointed to a group of ork bodies, far more heavily armoured than the others. 'These have the look of a warlord's bodyguard. No such corpses were found at Koth Ridge.'

'The second warlord has escaped,' said Belial. 'For the moment. The teleporter site is still watched by our forces. Even if one has escaped, the Beast is still trapped in Kadillus Harbour.'

Charon seemed distracted. He gazed along the line of defences, eyes narrow, a glow emanating from the cables of his psychic hood. Without word, he set off at a run, heading to the western side of the gorge. Belial headed after him.

'What is it, brother?' Belial asked as the Librarian came to a stop amongst a pile of dead Free Militia.

'Here,' he said, pointing at a black-armoured corpse.

It was Boreas.

'He shall be remembered,' said Belial, kneeling beside the Chaplain.

'You misunderstand me, brother,' said Charon. 'Brother Nestor! We have a survivor!'

Belial looked more closely. Boreas's skin was deathly white, a ragged gash across the side of his head, his armour torn and crumpled in many places. Switching on his thermal sight, the commander saw the tiniest vestiges of warmth moving along the Space Marine's blood vessels.

He stood up as Nestor approached.

'He is in the grip of his sus-an membrane, brother,' said Nestor, crouching over the fallen Chaplain. 'Life signs are minimal but steady. Cryptobiosis must have happened automatically in response to his injuries. The Orks probably thought he was dead, and thank the Emperor that they did not deal any further damage.'

The Apothecary spent some time examining Boreas before straightening.

'It is best that we leave Brother Boreas in his suspended metabolic state while we return him to the *Unrelenting Fury*, where we can better resuscitate him. He has extensive external and internal injuries, brother-captain, but some augmetics and surgery should suffice to return him to full duty in the fullness of time.'

'Praise the Emperor,' said Charon. 'We have lost many battle-brothers and it is a blessing to have even one of them returned to us.'

'Praise the Emperor indeed, brothers,' said Nestor, humour in his tone. 'The bodies He created for us are proof almost against death itself.'

Leaving Nestor to detail a squad to remove Boreas, Belial walked back to his Rhino. His own injuries ached, perhaps a psychosomatic response to Nestor's words. Alone for the first time in many days, Belial sat in his command chair and removed his helmet. He whispered the verses of a dedication to the Master of Mankind, and a few words of thanks to the primarch of the Dark Angels. It would be three more days before the rest of the Chapter returned; three days to keep Ghazghkull contained in the harbour and a tight watch on the ork teleporter.

They would perhaps be the hardest three days of the

whole campaign for Belial. Militarily, they would be straightforward, but with the orks all but defeated, there would soon come the time when his conduct would be examined by Grand Master Azrael.

Charon had spoken words of encouragement, but Belial knew that he had made some bad decisions. The best he hoped for was an acknowledgement of the unique difficulties the Dark Angels had faced on Kadillus. He should have listened to Sergeant Naaman's concerns earlier. Had the teleporter been located before the first attack on Koth Ridge, the orks would not have posed such a threat. Belial did not naturally indulge in hindsight or second-guessing, but he was keenly aware that he had allowed confidence to become arrogance; he had underestimated the ork threat and, in refusing to acknowledge the potential dangers, he had cost the lives of Astartes and thousands of Piscinans. It was likely that he would lose command of the 3rd Company and return to being a brother of the Deathwing.

Belial pushed aside these morose thoughts. The judgement of Azrael would wait. For the moment, there were still orks on Piscina and the campaign was not yet done.

He activated the comm.

'Master Belial to all units. Free Militia forces are en route to secure the geothermal station. Embark on transports for immediate return to Kadillus Harbour. *Diem victorum non.* The battle continues, brothers.'

A STRONG SEA breeze wafted smoke over the city, bringing with it the crack of artillery, the snap of las-fire and the rattle of bolters. The blackened ruin of the basilica stood proud, its spire hidden by the smog.

Much of the city was nothing more than rubble, dust-coated corpses of men and orks buried beneath piles of bricks and shattered girders. The rumble of tank engines reverberated along the streets as a column of Free Militia edged their way through the destruction, flamers scouring the ruins, shells pounding possible enemy hiding places.

As Belial had expected, the orks were not content to sit and wait for the inevitable. Fighting had been fierce, but the combined might of the 3rd Company and Free Militia was keeping the greenskins penned in the area around the docks.

And now the time was fast approaching to crush them.

From the lip of the main apron at Northport, he looked up at the vapour trails of Thunderhawks cutting through the cloudy skies. Far above, the Tower of Angels floated in orbit, the whole Dark Angels fleet in attendance. Transporters and gunships were landing around the city, while others headed to Koth Ridge to reinforce the Free Militia. In the evening twilight, what looked to be shooting stars glittered over the East Barrens: the drop-pods of the 6th Company descending on the East Barrens.

A Thunderhawk bearing the livery of Grand Master Azrael dropped through the cloud, diving sharply for the starport. Belial felt some trepidation as it landed on pillars of plasma fire. The wheeze of servos sounded in his autosenses as Revered Venerari stepped up next to him.

'Your judgement on yourself will be harsher than that of others,' said the Dreadnought.

Belial said nothing as the Thunderhawk touched down. His armour picked up the wash of heat from the gunship's engines and he could hear creaks of cooling metal. With a hiss of hydraulics, the ramp lowered. Beyond the gunship transporters were dropping down onto the other parts of the docks, carrying Land Raider heavy tanks, Vindicator assault guns and other treasures of the Dark Angels arsenal. The full force of the Chapter was being brought to bear.

Grand Master Azrael, Keeper of the Truth, was the first to disembark. The supreme commander of the Dark Angels wore ornate armour, the insignia of the Chapter and his personal heraldry inlaid with precious gems and rare metals. A small entourage accompanied him down the ramp: Brother Bethor carrying the sacred Standard of Retribution; Space Marines in the livery of Librarians and Interrogator-Chaplains and Techmarines; half-machine servitors; and numerous other functionaries garbed in the robes of Chapter serfs. A cowled figure no more than a metre tall followed close on Azrael's heels, carrying the ornately winged Lion Helm of the Grand Master; a Watcher in the Dark, one of the strange creatures that shared the Tower of Angels with the Chapter.

Azrael's expression was stern, his dark hair close-cropped, deep-set eyes shadowed in the evening sun. Belial detected the buzz of the interpersonal comm and a moment later Charon strode out across the plascrete to welcome the Grand Master.

Belial watched patiently as the two held a long conversation. He noticed Azrael's eyes flicking in his direction on occasion, but could tell nothing of the

Grand Master's thoughts. Eventually the two of them parted and Azrael headed in Belial's direction. The company master stepped forwards to meet his superior.

'The blessing of the Lion upon you, Grand Master,' said Belial, sinking to one knee before Azrael. 'I am grateful for your presence.'

'*Non desperat countenanti, exemplar est bellis fortis extremis, mon frater*' replied Azrael, gesturing for Belial to stand. 'I know that you have misgivings about calling to me for aid, brother. Put them from your mind, for there is no shame in what you have done. It takes strength to stand alone against the dark forces of the galaxy; it takes greater strength to admit the need for help.'

Azrael laid a hand upon Belial's shoulder and smiled, a simple gesture that did more to alleviate Belial's concerns than any amount of spoken praise.

'You have done your duty,' Azrael continued. 'To me, to your Chapter, to the Lion and to the Emperor. By your actions, Piscina IV remains safe from the orks, and through that action the world of Piscina V stays free of taint. Future generations of Dark Angels will give thanks to you and your warriors for what their sacrifice has preserved here.'

'I am grateful for your words, Grand Master,' said Belial. 'There are many that deserve praise more than I, none more so than Sergeant Naaman of the Tenth Company.'

Azrael nodded.

'Many will be the names recorded in honour for this campaign,' said the supreme commander. He looked towards the war-torn city. 'Others may be added to that list before we are finished. You have brought the Beast of Armageddon to battle, now we must finish the task.'

'Yes, it is time to unleash a storm of vengeance against these foul aliens,' said Belial. His fist crashed against his chest in salute. 'What are your orders, Grand Master?'

EPILOGUE

THE SOUND OF shells was growing louder and louder. An explosion ripped the roof from a storage shed at the end of the street, burying a mob of orks under a heap of tiles and bricks.

Ghazghkull shook his head in disappointment; he guessed the humies had retaken the big laser cannon by now. It would only be a matter of time before their ships started blowing up his army from space. After that, they'd start looking for Nazdreg's hulk. Humies would figure that out quick enough, he was sure of it.

'Oi, Makari, grab me banna!' The gretchin appeared as if by magic and plucked the huge flag free from the mound of rubble it had been driven into. 'We's goin' fer a bit of a walk.'

Ghazghkull headed back into the shell of an empty warehouse, the clanking of his armour echoing from the walls. Makari scurried behind, hauling the giant banner with him.

'We's gonna give the humies some more boot levver, boss?' asked the gretchin.

Ghazghkull nodded.

'We'll give the humies plenty of boot levver, but dere's no need ta rush fings.'

The warlord unhooked an unlikely-looking device from his armour. The core of it seemed to be a battered wheel hub, coiled about with lots of coloured wires, with a red button in the middle.

'What'cha got dere, boss?' asked Makari.

'Grab 'old,' said Ghazghkull, holding out the device. 'It's a tellyporta fingy. When I push dis button, we's gonna go back to Nazdreg's 'ulk.'

'What about da rest of da boyz? We ain't runnin' away, is we?'

'Nah, dis ain't runnin' away. Dis is strat-er-jee. Runnin' away's only fer humies and pointy-ears. We's just leavin' for a bit. Da rest of da boyz is 'avin' fun. We'll let 'em keep da humies bizzy while we do sumfink strat-ee-jik.'

Ghazghkull bashed his fist against the button on the tellyporta device. Green lights glowed into life around the central hub and the thing began to shake in the warlord's grip. Sparks sputtered along the wires and the warlord smelt burning plastic.

'Is it meant to do dat, boss? Is it me–'

The warehouse disappeared and Ghazghkull found himself back in the warp for a moment. Like last time, there were all sorts of strange noises and faces leering at the warlord out of the soupy green miasma. He thought he could hear the guffaws and shouts of Gork (or possibly Mork).

Then they were back in the big room of Nazdreg's hulk. With a puff of smoke, the tellyporta device stopped its shaking; bits of molten metal dropped onto the floor. The hall was almost empty, but the litter of the teeming horde that had been waiting a couple of days before covered the metal floor.

Still in his ornate mega-armour, Nazdreg was standing at one end of the hall, talking to his nobz. He looked up as Ghazghkull appeared in a flash of green light.

'I wundered if dat fing would work,' Nazdreg called out. 'Good ta see ya again.'

Ghazghkull strode up the hall and pushed his way through the Bad Moon leaders.

'Dis tellyporta stuff is all right, Nazdreg,' said Ghazghkull, handing the fried piece of equipment to his fellow warlord.

'I dunno,' replied Nazdreg. 'It's a pain to get da power fer it.'

'Just sum little problems, dat can be worked out,' said Ghazghkull. 'Makes me teef feel funny.'

'Speakin' of teef, dis little trip 'as been most good in da loot stakes,' said Nazdreg. 'Picked up all kinds of great gear from da humies. Plenty of dakka and teef.'

'I didn't too bad meself,' said Ghazghkull. 'Listen, if yoo don't want ta keep da tellyporta, I will take it off yer 'ands.'

'Fer sum extra teef...'

'Course, fer sum extra teef. We 'ad a deal, din't we?'

'If da price is right, da tellyporta is yours. What do ya want wiv it?'

Ghazghkull's mind went back many years, to a world

of towering cities and choking wastes. A world that had almost been his, but for one stupid, brave, remarkable humie. This time he wouldn't go easy on them.

'I never did want dis place anywayz. Dis woz just practice fur da big wun. I've got a score ta settle…'

ORDER OF BATTLE

The Dark Angels 3rd Company at the start of the Kadillus Campaign

THE 3RD COMPANY was at full strength at the outset of the campaign. Due to its duties overseeing the final stage of recruitment from Piscina V, the 3rd Company had more than the usual number of Chaplains and Librarians attached from the Chapter Headquarters. In addition, the 3rd Company had been reinforced with many squads from the 1st, 2nd and 10th Companies.

Note on reorganisation: All forces underwent ad-hoc reorganisation throughout the campaign to account for losses and the splintering of Dark Angels across the two main fronts. This involved the battlefield promotion of several battle-brothers to the rank of sergeant and the allocation of temporary squad nomenclature (such as Exacta, Vindictus, Annihilus).

Headquarters

Master Belial, Company Commander

Interrogator-Chaplain Boreas, Company Chaplain

Brother Nestor, Company Apothecary

Brother Arael, Company Standard Bearer

Revered Venerari, Dreadnought

Additional Headquarters

Master Chaplain Uriel

Interrogator-Chaplain Sarpedon

Lexicanium Acutus, Librarian

Lexicanium Charon, Librarian

Lexicanium Hebron, Librarian

Armoury

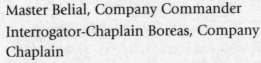 *Unrelenting Fury*, Battle-barge

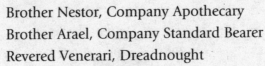 *Zealous Guardian*, *Divine Judgement*, Thunderhawk Gunships

Brother Hadrazael, Techmarine

Brother Hephaestus, Techmarine

4 Predator Battle Tanks

12 Rhino Transports

4 Razorback Transports

3rd Company Squads

Squad Andrael, Tactical Squad

Squad Azraeth, Tactical Squad

Squad Dominus, Tactical Squad

Squad Lemael, Tactical Squad

Squad Nemeaus, Tactical Squad
Squad Peliel, Tactical Squad
Squad Menelauis, Assault Squad
Squad Zaltys, Assault Squad
Squad Heman, Devastator Squad
Squad Scalprum, Devastator Squad

1st Company (Deathwing)

Squad Adamanta, Tactical Dreadnought Armour Squad

Squad Malignus, Tactical Dreadnought Armour Squad

Squad Vigilus, Tactical Dreadnought Armour Squad

2nd Company (Ravenwing)

Squad Aquila, Bike Squadron
Squad Laertius, Bike Squadron
Squad Orphaeus, Bike Squadron
Squad Validus, Bike Squadron
5 Land Speeders
2 Attack Bikes

10th Company (Scouts)

Squad Arcanus, Scouts Squad
Squad Astarael, Scouts Squad
Squad Damas, Scouts Squad
Squad Naaman, Scouts Squad
Squad Volcus, Scouts Squad

ABOUT THE AUTHOR

Gav Thorpe has been rampaging across the worlds of Warhammer and Warhammer 40,000 for many years as both an author and games developer. He hails from the den of scurvy outlaws called Nottingham and makes regular sorties to unleash bloodshed and mayhem. He shares his hideout with Dennis, a mechanical hamster sworn to enslave mankind. Dennis is currently trying to develop an iPhone app that will hypnotise his victims.

Gav's previous novels include fan-favourite *Angels of Darkness* and the epic *Malekith*, first instalment in the Sundering trilogy, amongst many others.

You can find his website at:
mechanicalhamster.wordpress.com

MORE
DARK ANGELS
ACTION